VIRGIN CAY

Gus Robinson has lost his boat—sunk beneath the waves thirty fathoms down—and nearly lost his life as well. But he manages to swim to land at Spanish Cay, and that's how he meets Clare. She offers him her bed, her body, and later offers him the one thing he needs most of all— $20,000 which he can use to buy a new boat. Robinson is lost without his ketch, stripped of his freedom to set sail whenever the mood strikes him, to live life on his own terms. All he has to do to earn enough for a new boat is to commit murder, to kill the one person who stands between Clare and the inheritance she needs to continue to live her extravagant lifestyle. But it's not until he meets Gwen that Robinson is forced to make the roughest choice of all.

A NIGHT OUT

Johnny Flake is trying to outrun his past, which is how he finds himself captaining the Vixen on a run down to Cuba with Cutter and Cruze. Cutter would just as soon kill you as look at you, and Cruze is so far into the bottle he's beginning to smell like death itself. Flake has a bad feeling about this trip, and isn't surprised to find that instead of smuggling booze off the island, he finds they're carrying heroin instead. But he soon discovers new problems when mutiny sends him into the waters and onto the yacht being manned by playboy Allan Chambers and his oversexed wife, Jessica. All Chambers wants to do is feel the salt air in his hair. All Jessica wants to do is feel the next man. With the storm raging, and the two ships both heading for a little island off Key West, it's going to be a long and turbulent night.

BASIL HEATTER BIBLIOGRAPHY
(1918-2009)

Fiction

The Dim View (1946)

The Captain's Lady (1950)

Sailor's Luck (1953)

Act of Violence (1954)

A Night Out (1956; expanded from "The Empty Fort," 1954)

The Trouble With Love (1960)

Any Man's Girl (1961)

The Mutilators (1962)

Virgin Cay (1963)

The Better Part of Valor (1964)

The Naked Island (1968)

Harry and the Bikini Bandits (1971)

The Scarred Man (1973)

Devlin's Triangle (1976)*

The Golden Stag (1976)*

Bitch (1979)

The Einstein Plot (1982)

The London Gun (1984)

*Tim Devlin series character

Young Adult Fiction

Wreck Ashore! (1969)

Non-Fiction

The Black Coast: The Story of the PT Boat (1967)

The Sea Dreamers (1968)

Eighty Days to Hong Kong: The Story of the Clipper Ship (1969)

Against Odds (1970)

A King in Haiti: The Story of Henri Christophe (1972)

Short Stories

The Dim View (*Liberty*, Dec 14 1946; published as novel)

The Last Raid (*Cosmopolitan*, Nov 1946)

Island Happy (*The Saturday Evening Post*, Sep 23 1950)

Strike at Madang (*Argosy*, Nov 1950; *Trap of Gold and Other Great Adventure Stories from Argosy* 1952)

Hunter's Moon (*The Saturday Evening Post*, Nov 4 1950)

The Empty Fort (*Manhunt*, Sept 1954, expanded as *A Night Out*)

The Ghost of Old 21 (*Adventure*, March 1957)

The Big One (*Argosy*, Oct 1957)

Ladies of the Night (*Argosy*, Feb 1958)

Night Fight (*Redbook*, April 1958)

The Lady's Choice (*The Saturday Evening Post*, Jan 1959)

The Pirate of Prospect Park (*Argosy*, Jan 1959)

VIRGIN CAY
A NIGHT OUT

Basil Heatter

Introduction by Steve Lewis

STARK HOUSE

Stark House Press • Eureka California

VIRGIN CAY / A NIGHT OUT

Published by Stark House Press
1315 H Street
Eureka, CA 95501, USA
griffinskye3@sbcglobal.net
www.starkhousepress.com

VIRGIN CAY
Originally published by Gold Medal Books, Greenwich, and
copyright © 1963 by Basil Heatter.

A NIGHT OUT
Originally published by Popular Library, New York, and
copyright © 1956 by Basil Heatter. An earlier, shorter version appeared
in Manhunt as "The Empty Fort," copyright © 1954 by Basil Heatter.

"A Night Out on Virgin Cay" copyright © 2017 by Steve Lewis.

ISBN-13: 978-1-944520-27-4

Cover art by Greg Shepard
Book design by Mark Shepard, SHEPGRAPHICS.COM

First Stark House Press Edition: July 2017

FIRST EDITION

A NIGHT OUT ON VIRGIN CAY
By Steve Lewis

For an author with a double dozen books to his credit, over a period of over three decades, there is not much known about Basil Heatter (1918-2009), except for one fact that is invariably mentioned whenever his name comes up.

Here, for example, is the biographical blurb about him found on the first page of *A Night Out*, a paperback original published by Popular Library in 1956:

> "Born on Long Island in 1918, Basil Heatter attended schools in Connecticut, then went abroad when he was 16 for a two year travel stint in Europe. "Returning to America, he went to work for a New York advertising agency. During the war he served as skipper of a P.T. boat in the southwest Pacific. "He is the son of Gabriel Heatter, the radio commentator, and at present he, Basil, is a news commentator for the Mutual Broadcasting System."

That was in 1956. From *Crime Fiction IV: A Comprehensive Bibliography, 1749-2000*, by Allen J. Hubin (2015), we learn just a little more:

> "Born on Long Island, the son of radio commentator Gabriel Heatter; was advertising copywriter in 1970s living on a boat off Florida, and racing and chartering; died in Miami, FL."

Heatter has thirteen books included in *CFIV*, one marginally, but at the moment *A Night Out* is not one of them, and it should be. The crime involved is not a major one, I grant you, not at the beginning, at least — that of smuggling some booze out of Cuba to shrimp boat skipper Johnny Flake's home port of Key West — but small capers like this often run into trouble, matters escalate, and some people end up wounded or dead, and that's exactly what happens here.

While this is criminous enough to suit most readers of this new reprint from Stark House, I'd have to admit that most of the book consists of character studies of the players in it. All of them have a past, and events in the past have a way of making people who they are today. It takes a while for their paths to converge, however, ending in a midnight shootout in an abandoned fort off the islands of Dry Torgugas, but the getting there is well worth it.

There are two women involved, Molly being the one that Flake let get away, and the other Jessica, the promiscuous live-in lady friend of yachtsman Allan Chambers, who can't live without her, but neither can he live with her. Another player is an old rummy named Cruze, who was at one time a terrific ship's engineer, and it's only because Flake needs someone in a hurry does he hire on the old man now with the shakes and an unquenchable thirst.

More than a crime novel, what this book is is pure noir. Most — not all — of the participants in the drama that takes place in this book are doomed, in one way or another. Most have no future, save what chance and pure luck give them. There's little they can do to help themselves.

Although far from being in their league, Heatter channels F. Scott Fitzgerald and maybe Ernest Hemingway in this novel, more so than he does either of the two old standbys of Hammett and Chandler. While all but forgotten today, Heatter is more than adequate as a writer — he certainly knew his way around boats and the Gulf of Mexico — and he brings his characters enough to life that I know I'll remember them all for a while yet to come.

If only they had filmed this back in the 1950s. John Payne could play Johnny, and Walter Brennan would be perfect as Cruze. Gail Russell could easily be Molly, but to tell you the truth, no matter what movie taking place in the 50s that I happen to be casting, there'd always be a part for Gail Russell.

□ □ □

The primary protagonist in *Virgin Cay*, just as it was in *A Night Out*, is once again a dedicated boatsman plying his trade in the Gulf of Mexico off the Florida shore, and if anything, even more so.

But "plying his trade" is not entirely accurate. When asked what he does for a living, Gus Robinson's reply is:

> "A man alone on a boat doesn't have to make much of what you call a living. To me living and sailing are the same thing and when you're out at sea there's no place to spend money even if you have it, which I don't."

Asking the question is a fine-looking woman whose home on Virgin Cay is where Gus washes ashore after his boat goes down about ten miles out to sea. They hit it off so well that before he leaves the next morning, the delectable Clare Loomis has a business proposition for him, one that if accepted will net Gus a cool $20,000.

The proposition? Murder. Ordinarily Gus wouldn't think twice before refusing, but without a boat, he'd be lost trying to survive on land. The next question: who would he have to kill? And there, as it turns out, is where the rub comes in.

The first twist in the story is an obvious one, or it was to me and I suspect it will be to you as well. After that, though, the beauty of this story is that you, the reader, have no idea of what happens from there.

But what does happen will have you reading the last 40 pages about as fast as you can turn them. Is the ending a happy one? I won't tell you. Why spoil your fun?

Heatter is a more polished writer than he was in *A Night Out*, written some seven years earlier, but this time around, while the sense of doomed futility is there, it is not nearly as strong. This is a suspense novel more than it is a crime thriller, and even then, the emphasis is on being a novel.

In that regard, there are some not-so-subtle hints of John D. Mac-Donald in this later book, most evident when Gus reflects with dismay upon what the Florida landscape is starting to become. He's a boat person, through and through, which from all we know about the author, is as statement that was as true about him as it is about Gus Robinson.

—April 2017
Newington, CT

....

This introduction first appeared in two parts in Steve Lewis's *Mystery*File* blog, with a few slight changes. Steve, now a retired professor of mathematics, has produced *M*F* for over 40 years, first as a printed zine, then as a website, and for the past 10 years as a blog.

VIRGIN CAY

Basil Heatter

CHAPTER ONE

The big sea twisted under him, turned and tossed him like a ball. The light on the beach vanished. Black water rolled over him and he went under but the life jacket pulled him up again. He tried to keep his head up long enough to let a little air seep down the raw passage of his throat but another great crest came hissing down on him in clouds of ghostly phosphorescence, thrusting something felt but unseen, some spiny sea creature against his side, so that he jerked away in instinctive revulsion. But when he surfaced again the light was closer and he thought that by God he might yet make it. He was being carried into the beach now and all around him was the booming of the surf and the drag of the undertow. He was in among breakers crashing on coral. Any one of these great seas could bash his head in or leave him skinned alive.

When he first saw the light he had hoped that by aiming for it he might find a clear spot of sand. On an island like Spanish Cay people didn't usually build their houses on the coral bluffs. So, despite the apparent hopelessness of it all, he had struggled on toward the light. It was solely his body that struggled now, not his mind. His mind seemed half dead. For with *Charee* gone what was there left to struggle for? The ketch was lying in thirty fathoms with the sea surging through her and it seemed that all his future lay there with her. His body fought to survive but the reason for the struggle escaped him.

Something dug painfully at his foot. He was into the coral now and a great wave coming up behind rolled him over and under, sucking him down and then spewing him out onto the beach. He staggered forward in water that was only up to his waist now, water that still gripped him and tried to suck him back and at last reluctantly let him go.

He sprawled on the sand, ribs heaving, lungs pumping. A string of purple rockets seemed to soar before his eyes and then to explode and die. Ten or fifteen minutes went by before he could begin to breathe comfortably and push himself upright.

He raised his arm and tried to read the dial of his wristwatch by the light of the moon. The waterproof watch was still running. It was the one thing of value he had salvaged from the wreck. The watch read five minutes before midnight, which meant that he had been in the water for a full five hours. He wondered why he was subject to this slavish devotion to time. What difference did it make? Why is it that in moments of crisis—when, for instance, the hotel is burning down and we are summoned from sleep by what perhaps will be the last alarm bell we will ever hear—do we glance instinctively at the time?

The wind nipped at his sea-wrinkled flesh. Force Five, his sailor's mind registered automatically, but swinging a point easterly. By tomorrow she will probably have slacked off. Tomorrow the seas will be down and there will be only the long purple swells heaving in toward Spanish Cay. If the damned hose clamp had held a few hours longer he might have saved the ketch.

He unsnapped the buckles of the life jacket and shrugged out of it and held it loosely in one hand as he walked toward the light. Approaching the house, he was aware of a great deal of glass and a flat modern roof and walls white as bone in the moonlight. The light that had saved his life was still shining behind a great expanse of glass that was one wall of a bedroom. A filmy curtain was drawn across the glass but it concealed nothing. People lived like goldfish in these modern beach houses, but then they hardly expected waterlogged sailors to come strolling up out of the sea at midnight.

As he stood there, the dripping life jacket still clutched in his hand, a small blonde woman came into his range of vision. She was wearing a tightly belted yellow silk dressing gown. She removed the gown and tossed it carelessly across a chaise. Beneath the gown she wore a nightdress that was made of some material as diaphanous as that of the window curtains. Weak as Robinson was from his long battle with the sea, he was not too far gone to admire the curves of her rather full breasts and the rosy hint of nipples.

She pulled back the pink sheet and got into bed and took a cigarette from a pack on the table. Robinson, exhaustion still numbing his brain, stood there watching her. It seemed probable that a man would enter the room. It was a big bed and she did not look like the kind of woman who slept alone.

She had picked up a woman's fashion magazine with a shiny cover showing a model in a full-length evening gown and was leafing slowly through it. Robinson, weary of his role as a peeping Tom, moved away from the window toward a terrace and a clump of white furniture and a door with a brass knocker. He let the knocker fall twice and heard it echo throughout the stone-floored house. In his mind he could picture the woman sitting up in bed and wondering who would be knocking at this hour. He waited for what seemed like several minutes and was about to knock again when he heard the click of heels on the floor and then a floodlight was switched on suddenly, bathing him in its white glare. A curtain in a window beside the door was drawn back and the woman peered out at him.

Her hesitation was obvious and he could hardly blame her. I must be some sight, he thought. If I were in her place I'd be damned if I'd open. Well to hell with it; I'll just go and flake out on the beach somewhere. But to his surprise the door swung back on a short length of chain and she said, "Yes? What is it?"

He was so bone-weary now that he could hardly speak. The wind drowned his voice when he answered, "I've been in an accident. I could use some help."

His bedraggled appearance, sodden life jacket, face gaunt under the light, must have been somehow reassuring because he heard the chain released and the door swung back and she said, "All right. Come in."

"I don't want to mess up your floor."

She looked down at his bare feet and the blood still welling out of the deep cut and said, "Then perhaps you'd better come around to the back. I'll bring a towel."

He nodded and stumbled across the sand past an open carport housing a small English car and stood waiting at the back door. When it clicked open and a shaft of yellow light sprang out at him, he saw that she had put on the yellow silk dressing gown and high-heeled mules with white puffs. Despite his exhaustion he was able to note also, with a sort of thin amusement, that she had taken the time and trouble to touch up her lipstick. She thrust an oversize bath towel at him and he mopped his face and hair and then his feet.

"Come in," she said.

He followed her in, a big-boned, sun-browned man with a wild shock of black hair. He stood awkwardly on squares of black and white kitchen linoleum, the blood still welling from his coral-gashed foot.

"We'd better do something about that cut," she said.

"I'm sorry about your floor."

"Don't be silly. Sit down over there and I'll be right back."

He sat numbly in the shining kitchen world of chrome and aluminum until she came back with gauze and iodine and tape. "I'll do it," he said holding out his hand. "I'm used to doctoring myself."

He poured the iodine over the wound, mildly grateful for the fact that his flesh was still too waterlogged to feel pain, and then wrapped the gauze bandage several times around his instep and covered it all with a wide strip of tape.

She waited until he had finished with the bandage before asking in a businesslike voice, "What happened to you?"

"My boat sank." It was the first time he had spoken the words aloud and they left a bitter taste in his mouth.

"Were you alone?"

"Yes."

"Where were you?"

"About ten miles off shore."

"Well you certainly picked a fine night to go sailing. It's blowing a gale out there."

"I've sailed in worse," he answered, his vanity still capable of being piqued.

"How long were you in the water?"

"I'm not sure but it must have been at least five or six hours."

Her voice was a little softer when she said, "Oh my, you really have been in trouble, haven't you?"

He nodded.

"I'm sure you could do with some food and hot coffee," she said.

"I could, but if you have a little rum or whiskey first I'd be grateful."

"I'll get it." At the door she turned back and said, "You'd better get out of those wet pants while I see if I can find you something to wear."

He stripped off the sodden khaki and wrapped the towel around his waist. When she returned she was carrying some clothes over her arm and a bottle of dark Barbados rum in her hand. She took a glass out of the kitchen cabinet and poured it half full of rum and handed it to him. He tossed the liquor down his throat. The rum made a pool of warmth in his belly. He stopped shivering and said, "That helped."

She held up a rather loud man's sport shirt and a pair of flannel trousers and said, "You can try these on but I don't think we have any shoes that will fit over that bandage."

He looked down at his strong, tanned feet and said, "I'm used to going barefoot."

"Would you like a shower while I fix something to eat?"

"I would indeed."

"How do you feel about scrambled eggs?"

"Anything at all will be fine."

"Well you'll find a bedroom through there and the shower is just beyond."

Carrying the clothes she had given him, he went through a small guest room and found a bathroom with a stall shower. He dropped the towel and stepped inside and let scalding water wash away the salt and the weariness. When he came out he toweled himself briskly and put on the clothes which, as he had suspected, were too small across the shoulders and too big in the waist. With the lifelong habit of tidiness acquired in small boats he folded the towel carefully and placed it on the rack. His strength was returning and with it a surge of hunger that clawed at him like a wild animal. He pushed open the swinging door to the kitchen and said, "By the way, my name is Gus Robinson."

"I'm Clare Loomis," she said putting a frying pan on the stove and turning a low flame under it. When she turned back to look at him she smiled for the first time since he had entered the house and said, "Who's your tailor, Mr. Robinson?"

"Not the Duke of Windsor's," he acknowledged, "but I'm certainly not complaining. Regardless of the way the pants look they feel damned good. Whose are they? Your husband's?"

"I have no husband," she said, "nor is this really my house. The owner lent me the place while he went off to Vermont to try to break his pudgy neck skiing. Those are his pants you're wearing."

"Then you're all alone?"

"The maid has the night out. She'll be back in the morning."

She mixed the eggs and poured them into the frying pan and set out bread and butter and a cup and saucer for the coffee. He watched her as she moved around the room. She moved well. She was not young—perhaps thirty-five or thirty-eight—but she walked gracefully with the carefully controlled sexy motion of the hips that is often found in rather small women. Her figure, if perhaps a shade too lush, was still exceptionally good. In a few years she might begin to have a serious weight problem but at the moment she was certainly a fine-looking woman. The yellow silk gown was open low in front and did little to conceal her full bosom. He remembered the rosy hint of nipples he had seen when she had taken off the robe in the bedroom and the thought brought a slow stirring of desire.

"I suppose you could do with another drink," she said.

"It may knock me flat."

"I doubt it. You look rugged enough."

She handed him the bottle and the glass. He took a smaller drink this time and let it go down slowly. By the time he had finished it she had the food on the table.

"Don't stand on ceremony," she said. "Go to it."

He wolfed down the food and then went through a second cup of coffee.

"Feeling better?" she asked.

"You're looking at a new man."

"Does the foot hurt much?"

"Nothing hurts now."

She lit a cigarette and puffed the smoke out reflectively and said, "Why were you sailing alone?"

"I like it that way."

"Where were you bound for?"

"Miami."

"From where?"

"Aruba."

"You mean that island in the Dutch West Indies?"

"Yes."

"But that's a thousand miles or more from here."

"That's right."

"Mr. Robinson, you must be quite a man. Do you often do this sort of thing?"

"I've been living that way for the past ten years."

"But this time you apparently guessed wrong. What happened?"

"Unless you're familiar with boats it's a little hard to believe. Now that I look back on it I can hardly believe it myself. Anyway, there's a piece of rubber tubing eight inches long and two inches wide that is the water inlet for the toilet. The water comes up through there and is held by a check valve. The tubing is clamped to the toilet pipe by a stainless steel clamp. As a rule I make it my business to check the clamp every so often but this time I apparently got a little careless. The best way I can reconstruct it is that sometime during the evening the clamp worked loose and the tubing slipped off the pipe. After that she just quietly filled with water. I was dozing in the cockpit and by the time I realized that she was answering sluggishly to the helm she already had two feet of water in the bilges. Even then I still could have pumped her out easily enough but it was beginning to blow fairly hard. While I was down below trying to plug the pipe a big following sea caught us and because she was so heavy and low in the water she broached on top of the wave and took the next one straight over the side and filled and went down like a stone. I just barely had time to grab a life jacket and fight my way through the hatch. When I was in the water I saw your light and started swimming for it."

"Then you hadn't intended to put in to Spanish Cay at all?"

"No."

"So no one knows you're here."

"No one but you."

She had fitted her cigarette into a long ivory holder and the smoke curled before her eyes like a fine blue veil. She said, "Tell me, Mr. Robinson, what do you do for a living?"

"A man alone on a boat doesn't have to make much of what you call a living. To me living and sailing are the same thing and when you're out at sea there's no place to spend money even if you have it, which I don't."

"But when you come ashore you must have certain expenses. You need money for food, gas, whiskey, paint, canvas, all that sort of thing, don't you?"

"Now and then, but not much."

"Well what do you do for the now and then? Do you have some kind of an income?"

"Not a sou. Occasionally I make a little money lecturing but when there's no chance of that I take a temporary job of some sort in a boat-yard."

"And what will you do now without your boat?"

Her eyes, he saw, were rather strange. Cat's eyes. Longer and more pointed at the corners than most and with small dark pupils. "I don't know," he answered bleakly. "Take a job somewhere and try to save up for another boat."

"Poor Mr. Robinson." Her voice was soft. She was beginning to flirt with him. The gown had opened even further and as she leaned forward to refill his coffee cup the soft white cleavage between her breasts was fully exposed. "How much would a good boat cost?" she asked.

"That would depend on the size of the boat and the state of the market at the time. But a good boat, capable of transoceanic passages, would certainly run around ten or fifteen thousand."

"It will take you a long time to save up that kind of money."

"Just the rest of my life."

"I'm sorry," she said leaning forward and touching his cheek with the tips of her fingers. Her hands were tiny and soft and smelled faintly of some expensive cream. "Do you know something, Mr. Robinson? You look like a real pirate. You ought to be wearing a sash around your waist and a gold ring through one ear."

"I usually do."

"What would you do for twenty thousand dollars in a lump sum, Mr. Robinson?"

"Anything short of murder," he said, and then added lightly, "and I'm not so sure I'd stop at that."

She smiled and said, "You must be terribly tired."

"The mention of twenty thousand dollars brought me wide awake."

"Why don't you rest for a while?"

She had gotten up from her chair and moved around behind him. She put her arms around his neck and drew his head back again her bosom. Robinson remained that way for a moment and then turned to face her. She took his hand and led him toward the bedroom. As they passed through the doorway she switched off the bedroom light. He heard the rustle of silk and saw the dressing gown slip to the floor. The nightgown followed it. Her nude body looked white as snow in the moonlight.

"I ought to shave," he said thickly.

"Why?"

"I'll scratch you."

"Please scratch me, Mr. Robinson."

In his nightmare he was back on *Charee*, struggling to save her as she went down. The moment of the full broach, relived in the dream, was fearfully real. He felt the little ship sway, stumble, fall off the crest and swing sideways. In all his years of sailing on many oceans he had never lost a ship but he had known instantly, when she had failed to bring her head up, that *Charee* was gone. She hesitated, hung painfully on to life, and then surrendered to the vast weight of the sea and went over. Black water poured over him. He cried out...

The hand shook him into wakefulness. He lay quietly readjusting to reality. Moonlight on ceiling. Perfume. Soft bedding. Faint, musky odor of the woman's body. Twenty thousand dollars. There was an Alden-designed yawl in Miami, *Senegal*. Thirty-eight feet. Built along the lines of *Malabar*. He had seen her once under sail and had studied pictures of her in various yachting magazines. A lovely ship. Mahogany and teak and lines as crisp and functional as those of a gull. She was built to last a lifetime, to reach out for a thousand and one horizons. Very likely she could be picked up for seventeen thousand. A wire to his old friend Caldwell at Florida Yacht Sales would confirm it....

He pulled himself sharply out of it and sat up. To hell with this adolescent daydreaming. The facts were that he was in a lady's bed and that very shortly he would have to leave it and that he had no place in particular to go and was virtually penniless. What a strange woman she was. Her attitude had been so cold at first and then she had left teeth-marks in his shoulder but he had sensed no real abandon. It had all been rather premeditated, as though she were sitting on the other side of the room watching two strangers on the bed. Well, no matter, one could-n't be greedy. The whole thing had been a totally unexpected windfall. He would really have to get shipwrecked more often.

She flicked on the light. The clock on the night table read three A.M.

"Gus," she said, "I want to talk to you."

There was certainly nothing flirtatious about her voice now. It was all business, leaving-the-money-on-the-dresser-as-you-go-out sort of voice. Even her appearance had changed. She looked her age. Aware of his glance she drew the robe up over her breast and held it against her throat.

His voice mocked her when he said, "Do you want to talk about the twenty thousand dollars, Clare?"

"Yes."

"It's a nice little joke but I think we've carried it far enough."

"I've never been more serious."

He let that sink in. She apparently *was* serious. It was wild, but no wilder than everything else that had happened to him this night. "I gather that what you have in mind is not exactly legal," he said.

"Let's face it, Gus. Would anybody pay you twenty thousand dollars to do something legal?"

"I guess not."

"Do you want me to stop now?"

"As far as I'm concerned, listening doesn't commit me to anything. Go on."

"The way you wandered in here tonight was a heaven-sent oppor-tunity. Apparently you're alone in the world and don't really give a damn for anything but boats. No one knows you're on this island and when you leave this house—as you will before daybreak—no one can connect you with me or prove that you were ever here."

He reached across her to the night table for the cigarettes.

She said, "Still interested?"

"So far it's just a fairy tale. I'll have to know a hell of a lot more."

"Of course. But not yet. That part will come later. Now here's what I want you to do. While you were asleep I figured the whole thing out. To begin with you've got to go out and get shipwrecked all over again."

"Thanks very much."

"Not really shipwrecked, of course, but what I want you to do when you leave here is to go on down the beach a mile or so and take that bandage off your foot and have another good dip and then come ashore all over again just as though it were the first time. But instead of coming back to this house you'll go to another house that belongs to a friend of mine."

"I'm game," Robinson said lightly. "I like the hospitality on Spanish Cay."

She ignored the minor thrust and went on in the same businesslike voice. "The house belongs to a man named Stanley Walker. He has more money than brains and he stays half drunk most of the time, but he's a mad yachtsman. For that matter he may even know your name. In any event I'm sure there is nothing in the world that would give him a bigger kick than to have a real sailor washed up on the beach in front of his house. It will make him a local nine-day wonder and give him something to talk about besides taxes and baseball, and he's almost certain to invite you to stay on."

"And after that?"

"After that we'll have another chat. I'll get word to you somehow about the time and place. How does that sound to you?"

"Stanley sounds like a dope but not a bad sort. Does this involve him in any way?"

"Not at all. And if you have scruples about lying to him you can take my word for it that you'll be doing him a favor to break the monotony."

"All right," Robinson said. "I don't guess I have much to lose at this point."

"Then you'd better get dressed and be on your way. My girl comes in before seven and it would spoil everything if she saw you here."

"How do I find Stanley's house?"

"Go straight south on the beach until you come to the wreck of an old schooner. You can't miss it. It's the only wreck on the beach. Just above it is Stanley's house."

"Was it his boat?"

"No. It came ashore years ago and Stanley built his house there because he thought the wreck was romantic. Now remember, if we meet at Stanley's house or in town we never saw each other before."

"I understand."

He swung his long legs out of the bed and walked naked into the kitchen and pulled on the clammy khaki trousers.

"Don't worry about puddles," she called. "I'll clean up after you."

There was no intimacy at all in her voice. It was as if he had delivered fifty pounds of ice. A tired old joke about the iceman came into his mind and then vanished into the dusty limbo where old dirty jokes are filed.

She came into the kitchen, holding the robe tightly around her body, and followed him to the door. "Come here, you lug," she said.

She reached up and pulled his head down and kissed him on the lips. There was no warmth in the kiss. It was like the scrambled eggs, part of the routine for shipwrecked sailors.

"Good-bye, Gus."

"Good-bye, Clare."

"Don't forget your life jacket."

He nodded without speaking and went out closing the door behind him. Down on the beach with the wind cold against his wet shirt and the moon now obscured by clouds, he felt curiously lonely and somehow even sadder than when he had first come ashore.

The wreck was precisely where she had told him it would be. She was obviously a very efficient woman. He removed the bandage from his foot.

CHAPTER TWO

Stanley Walker hovered over him like a mother hen while he tried to cram down a second breakfast. "More eggs? More toast?" Walker asked.

"No, thanks," Robinson answered.

"Well, then what about some more coffee?"

"Another cup of coffee would be fine."

Robinson's host appeared to be in his early forties. He was a small wiry man with a totally bald head that was somewhat oval on top and resembled an ostrich egg. He had faded blue eyes, a very red face and a guardsman's mustache. A network of veins made his nose look like a road map. He reminded Robinson of that small foppish playboy who used to appear on the cover of *Esquire* magazine. He could see Walker in a blue blazer and yachting cap and surrounded by chorines. The man was pathetic but appealing.

Walker kept shaking his head and saying, "I just can't get over it. Gus Robinson. And the funny part about it is I was reading a piece about

you in *Yachting* just a couple of weeks ago. I think it was that time you
sailed singlehanded from the Galapagos to Tahiti. Listen, Gus, is it really true what they say about Tahiti? I mean about the girls. Are they
really so...?"

"Yes, Stanley. They are and they do."

"Fantastic. What are we wasting our time here for?" He reached a
terry-cloth-clad arm into the kitchen cabinet, drew out a bottle of Scotch
and said, "You sure you won't have one?"

"Not after all this food."

"I should think after what you've been through you'd need one. I
know I do. You can believe me when I tell you we're not accustomed
to this much excitement around here. Usually it's a pretty dull place."
His hand shook noticeably as he poured the drink.

Robinson shoved his chair back and stood up. "You've been damned
kind, Stanley, but I think it's time I moved on and let you get back to
bed." If Clare's script was accurate this was the point at which Walker
ought to insist that he stay.

The little man did not disappoint him. He shot the whiskey down his
throat like an injection and sputtered, "Move on? Move on where?
You're staying here, old boy."

"I don't want to put you out."

"Good God, will you listen to the man. One of the most famous
sailors in the world is washed up right on my doorstep and talks about
putting me out. I can't tell you what a pleasure it will be for me to have
you here. I consider it an honor. A very real honor. How often do I have
a chance to talk to a real deep-water singlehander. I mean it's like old
Joshua Slocum himself rolling up out of the deep in *Spray*. No sir, Gus,
I won't hear of it. You're staying right here. I want to tell you about
the time I sailed with Alan Carlisle on the *Big Ti* in a race from Mar-
blehead to Halifax. Head seas all the way, Gus, and the jib sheeted
home and that damned fog and booting around all night among the
rocks looking for that bloody lightship, and when we finally gave it up
as a bad job and went on in the whole city stank of codfish and they
had the gall to tell us they had taken the lightship in the day before for
an overhaul. Taken it in, mind you, without even notifying the race
committee. It's that sort of thing that drives a sailor to drink," he said,
pouring himself another healthy shot. "Of course I'm not saying I'm
a sailor in your class, but I do mean honestly that it would give me real
pleasure to have you stay on with me until you've made your plans."

Although Walker's voice was unsteady and his blue eyes rolled like marbles in his red face, he was obviously sincere and Robinson could not help but like him for it.

"All right, Stanley."

Walker smashed his fist down happily on the table. "Done then! And now you've heard enough of my blather for a while. You must be dead for sleep, old boy."

"I could do with a bed at that."

"And you shall have it, sir. Tom! Oh Tom! Where are you, you lazy devil?"

The Negro servant who had admitted Robinson to the house came in looking fresh as a new golf ball in his sparkling white jacket.

"Tom, I want you to show Mr. Robinson to the spare room. Is the bed made up?"

"Yes, sir."

"And we've got to do something about clothes for him until he can get his own. Who do we know that's as big as Mr. Robinson?"

"There's Mr. Lacey."

"Of course. Good old Jocko. I'll run over there later and steal his pants. Now you show Mr. Robinson the way and put him to bed."

Robinson began to express his thanks again but Walker interrupted him with a raised hand. "Not a word, old boy. Not a word."

Robinson followed Thomas and found that the ultra-efficient servant had already turned back the sheet for him. He shucked off his clothes and fell gratefully into bed. It had been a long twelve hours since the ketch had gone down and a lot had happened. Thomas drew the blinds and switched on the air conditioner. Robinson said, "Thank you, Thomas."

Thomas had the monumental dignity that is sometimes found among people of his race, particularly among old-time Pullman porters. "Not at all, sir," he answered gravely.

Just before Robinson fell asleep he thought again that it was really too bad about the hoax he had played on Walker, who was so obviously a crashing bore without a really mean bone in his body.

He awoke to the sound of music and loud voices. The sky, faintly visible through the drawn blinds, was dark. He looked at his watch and saw with surprise that it was after eight o'clock. He had slept through the day.

He swung out of bed and groped his way into the bathroom, took a quick shower and used the razor he found in the medicine chest.

When he returned to the bedroom he saw that someone had already been in there and turned on the lights, opened the windows, made the bed and laid out well-polished loafers, crisp white linen shorts and a blue oxford-cloth short-sleeved shirt which, he was glad to see, bore no swaying palms, fading sunsets or leaping sailfish. The clothing fit him reasonably well and he dressed quickly and then ran a comb through his mop of hair.

When he had dressed he followed the babble of music and laughter to the main part of the house. The living room was jammed with a couple of dozen people all applauding loudly while the host, glass in hand, was attempting, with indifferent success, to walk a straight line. When he had somehow wavered to the end of it he was greeted with another burst of applause. Wild with overconfidence he placed the half full glass on top of his oddly-shaped head and balanced it there for a brief moment before the glass came crashing down. Walker stood there grinning foolishly until the grave-faced Thomas appeared from the kitchen with dustpan and broom to sweep up the broken glass.

Walker looked up and saw Robinson in the doorway and darted over to seize him by the arm. With an accomplished bellow that finally brought quiet to the room he introduced Robinson all around. Walker was enjoying the stir created by Robinson's arrival. He stood there holding the big man's arm as proudly as though Robinson were some world's record fish landed on light tackle. Robinson felt increasingly foolish and was relieved to see that their interest was short-lived. He would not even be a nine-day wonder. Nine minutes was more like it. After a few polite questions they drifted away. He had never known how to handle drunks anyway.

A slender, dark-haired girl with a smoothly tanned oval face and wearing a lime-colored linen dress came up to him and said, "You look as though you could do with a drink, Mr. Robinson."

"I guess I could."

"Let me get it for you."

"I'll go with you," he said, glad of the chance to escape the crush.

When they had their glasses she took him by the arm and led him to a wicker couch at the side of the room. "My name is Gwen Leacock," she said.

"You're a right purty gal," Robinson said.

"Thank you, sir."

"But you seem out of place here."

"In what way?"

"You're just not the type for this sort of shindig."

"What type do you have to be?"

"A little harder around the jaw, with maybe a few divorces, a couple of crackups and perhaps a short tour of duty in an expensive laughing academy."

When she threw back her head to laugh the lovely clear line of her young throat was exposed. She said, "It sounds like fun. I might try it. But I'm afraid that in those long lonely days at sea you've been letting your imagination run away with you. There *are* some reasonably normal people here, you know. Why I..."

She was interrupted by the arrival of a tall young man who bent down and kissed her hand and said in a voice much like that of a certain well-known Italian movie actor, "I've missed you, darling. You really shouldn't go off and leave me like that."

The girl smiled and looked up at the tall young man with soft eyes and said, "Hello, Dino. Have you met Mr. Robinson?"

"Ah, the famous castaway. How do you do, Mr. Robinson." His slimness was deceptive. There was plenty of strength in that hard broad fist.

"This is Dino di Buonaventura," the girl said. Her tone indicated that Robinson ought to know the name.

Dino sat down on the arm of the couch beside the girl and crossed one elegant yellow trouser leg over the other. He had a small aristocratic head, something like a greyhound's, and yellow hair and dark blue eyes. The combination of colors went superbly with his tanned skin and brilliantly white teeth. His teeth showed beautifully when he smiled. And he smiled, Robinson thought, just a bit too much. Making a quick judgment, he decided that Dino was not especially his cup of tea.

But certainly he and the girl made a pretty picture together. By contrast to their elegance Robinson felt oversized, outlandish. Preoccupied with his thoughts he had lost track of the conversation and he brought himself back to reality now when he heard the girl say, "... it seems as though I ought to be able to get her closer to the wind. But every time I try it that darned jib begins to rattle and shake. Obviously I'm doing something wrong but I don't know just what it is."

"I'm sorry," Robinson said. "What kind of a boat did you say it was?"

"A Lightning."

"I don't know much about day-sailers; I've always been more interested in cruising than racing but I'll take a look at her sometime if you like." To annoy the young man hovering over her so jealously he added,

"Perhaps the best thing would be if we went out for a sail together."
The girl's eyes lit up. She said, "That would be wonderful."

Dino rose smoothly to his feet and took the girl's two hands in his and said, "Have you forgotten that we have a date to meet Chuck and Lila for dinner? I think we had better go now."

"All right, but I'm going to hold you to your promise, Mr. Robinson."

"I suppose Stanley knows where to reach you."

"Yes, of course."

"Then I'll be in touch," Robinson said.

He watched them going off together, lime-green dress and yellow slacks. He had seen them before, or others very much like them, in all the best watering places. Montego Bay and Palm Beach and Portofino and Monte Carlo. The golden people spending their inheritance of money and charm and health and vast good looks. He had mingled with them briefly and as a rule they had been kind enough, but he had never really belonged. Hardly anyone did. You had to be born to it.

The party was slowly breaking up. Walker had managed to torpedo himself with a final double Scotch and had been dragged off to bed. Jocko Lacey—a large, foolish man with a face somewhat like General de Gaulle's—had arrived dragging a small foul-smelling goat on a leash. The goat made a mess on the rug and they all stood around watching while Thomas attacked the spot with soap and water. Two couples were necking furiously in the garden. They were married, but not to each other.

This confused, half-witted, forced gaiety always made Robinson uneasy. It was the sort of thing he went to sea to get away from. Lacking a ship there was still the beach. He strolled down across the sand to the old wreck. She had once been a fine big-breasted schooner, and although the hull was still reasonably intact, she had been gutted from the inside. How she must have looked spanking along on a broad reach, brightwork and white topsides gleaming.

Robinson was not an especially sentimental man but he could not help but feel saddened by this old hull on the beach. It brought back with almost unbearable immediacy the memory of *Charee*. For five years he had known and loved the little ship with her gleaming black hull and green bottom and white cabin and oiled fir deck. They had been through so much together and had saved each other's lives a dozen times or more. It was hard now to remember which had been the best of it—the landfall after weeks at sea, lights going on along the shore, creeping into a strange new harbor, the adventures of a city, new faces and new women—or the sudden knowledge one morning that he had had enough, and hoisting anchor and making ready for sea and *Charee* responding to the first long swells like a colt fresh out of stable and pretty much sailing herself under that beautifully balanced rig. The stout little ship had never failed him; in the end it was he who had let her down.

Well it was still the only life for him and he would do anything to get it back.

CHAPTER THREE

Clare Loomis held the narrow golden head of Dino di Buonaventura in both hands and kissed him passionately on the lips. Dino permitted himself to be kissed but displayed no particular ardor in return. When she had released him he got up and mixed himself a drink of Clare's whiskey and took one of her cigarettes out of a walnut box on the coffee table.

Her face hardened as she watched him and she said; "I have mixed emotions about you, Dino. I'm not sure if I love you or despise you. Right now I think it's the latter."

"That too is a part of love, my sweet," he answered complacently.

She controlled her anger long enough to ask, "How was Stanley's party?"

"Like all of Stanley's parties. Everyone drinks too much and since none of them are too bright in the first place they become even stupider as the evening progresses."

"If you feel that way why do you go?"

"It is my profession. When one wishes to paint portraits of the idle rich one must go where the idle rich are." He sighed and said, "On a night like this I sometimes think the only solution for me is to marry a very rich woman."

"Was there anyone interesting at the party?"

"A fellow named Robinson. A sailor. It appears his ship sank in a storm and he was forced to swim ashore."

"Really. How exciting. What's he like?"

"About what you might expect. A big rugged outdoor type."

"He sounds attractive."

"I suppose he might be, if you like the type. But I think you once told me you hate boats."

"I do. That is, anything smaller than the 'Queen Mary.'"

"Well there you are, my love. What would you talk about?"

"You never know," Clare replied airily. "We might have something in common."

He smiled at her above the rim of his glass and asked, "Are you trying to make me jealous?"

"Of course. Am I succeeding?"

"Not yet."

"Not one little pang?"

He shook his head.

"Then tell me who else was at the party."

"I told you, the usual crowd. I left early."

"And what did you do then?"

"I went back to the hotel and napped for a while. I slept a bit too long, which is why I was late getting here."

Her mouth was compressed with anger and her eyes had drawn up into slits. She looked almost ugly. "You are a damned filthy lying pig," she grated. "You know very well you took Gwen to Stanley's party and that afterwards you went on to the Masons' together."

"Where do you get so much information, Clare? Are you perhaps an undercover agent for the CIA?"

"This is a small island, you fool. There are no secrets here. Ten minutes after you showed up with Gwen, my best friends were calling with the latest bulletin. They couldn't wait to twist the knife."

"Well, what of it? Suppose I did go with Gwen. After all, she is your cousin, isn't she? It's all in the family."

"She's hardly more than a child, Dino."

"I'm not so old myself."

Her motion was like a cobra's strike as she launched herself forward and slapped his cheek. His face went pale. The angry red imprint of her hand showed clearly on his skin. His look was so venomous that for a moment she felt a genuine thrill of fear.

"*Puttana sporca*," Dino said in a low voice. "And just in case you don't understand I will translate for you. It means filthy old whore. And that's what you are, Clare. The mother of all whores."

Tears had formed in her eyes. "Forgive me, Dino," she begged.

"Forgive you nothing. We are through."

Anger swept her face again. "What do you mean, through? Do you think you can get along without me? Who were you before I picked you up in New York and introduced you to the right people?"

"That may have been true at one time but now that the introductions have been accomplished I think I can manage very nicely."

"You're talking like a conceited fool. They'll toss you back into the gutter in no time. Once you've run through this little group here how many commissions do you think you'll get? You need me, Dino. You need my contacts."

The color had returned to his face. He smiled and said, "Not any more."

"So that's it. It's Gwen now, is it? You want something a little younger and fresher. All the time we've been lovers and the plans we made together go down the drain now, and just because some little milk-faced sop comes along. If nothing else I gave you credit for good taste, Dino, but perhaps I was wrong. Do you think that child can give you the same thing you get from a real woman? Or have you found that out already? Maybe that's why you're here tonight, eh?"

"I appreciate your concern, Clare, but you don't have to worry about me on that score. I will be well taken care of. Your little cousin is all woman. No, the reason why I came tonight was to tell you that I am going to marry Gwen. We thought you ought to be the first to know."

"Marry! And live on what? Love? Don't make me laugh, Dino. You're not the type. Any more than you're the type to go back to living in that Third Avenue dump. Without me you couldn't make even half a living. Why even the clothes you have on were bought by me."

"I grant you all that, my dear, but you have overlooked something. Gwen's father is a very wealthy man. He is sixty-eight years old and has already suffered a severe coronary. I don't wish him any harm but I doubt very much that he can last more than a year at the outside. Gwen is an only child and when he dies she will come into something like ten or twelve million dollars carefully invested in the very best blue-chip stocks. I think that will be some compensation for her inexperience. And even that inexperience, I might add, I find refreshing."

If he had expected another explosion from her, he was disappointed. She passed in front of the mirror and touched her hair lightly. When she looked back at him all the ugliness of her rage was gone. She was very beautiful again. Despite himself he felt a renewal of desire. She was an extremely accomplished woman in bed and almost completely his type. He had always had an interest in somewhat older women. His first affair, as a schoolboy, had been with the mother of his best friend. She had been very grateful and had lavished gifts on him and he had learned to enjoy the adulation that older women provided.

That yearning for him that gave him such a pleasant sense of self-importance was clearly evident in Clare now. Her rage had passed and she wanted to go to bed with him. She was ready to accept him on his own terms. Well, why not? One more time. She had, after all, been good to him. And it was true that without Clare he would never have met Gwen.

"So you would really marry a woman for money, Dino," she said, smiling at him.

"Of course."

"Any woman?"

"Well, almost any woman. Of course she would have to be reasonably chic and presentable. Otherwise it would be too embarrassing."

"What about me?"

"Clare, my darling, if you had ten million dollars I would marry you like a shot."

"Sooner than Gwen?"

"Of course," he lied. "But what is the use of talking? Unhappily..."

"Unhappily I am only the older and poorer cousin of a very rich young girl," she said, completing the sentence for him. "But do you know something, Dino? It would be better if the money were left to me. I would know what to do with it."

"I believe that, Clare."

"What a shame that I'm so poor. We could be so right for each other."

She had moved closer. Her perfume enveloped them both. He saw the beginnings of tiny lines around her eyes and mouth. Despite all the fiendishly expensive lotions she indulged in, her youth was slipping away. When he left her she would grow old rapidly. He enjoyed the thought of it. The gap between them would increase with the years. When he was still a comparatively young man Clare would be in her forties. And she hated age more than anything else. Age and poverty. He could almost feel sorry for her except that he did not, after all, really owe her anything. He had paid all his debts in bed and he would pay the last one now.

She put her head against his cheek and said, "You're such a bad boy. A really terrible boy. I ought to spank you. You'd like that, wouldn't you, darling?"

He let his hands slide down over her hips and squeeze her buttocks. "In moderation," he said, smiling at his own image in the mirror.

He balanced the champagne glass on his naked brown chest. Clare leaned over him so that one of her breasts just touched the glass. She was justifiably proud of her bosom. She might be getting a little thick in the waist but her legs and breasts were still exceptionally fine. She let the point of her nipple touch the icy liquid and then she moved it quickly to Dino's lips.

"A vintage year," he said.

"Ah, Dino."

It required some effort to hide his annoyance and faint disgust. Now that it was over he really wanted to be up and showered and on his way. This sort of love play after the act was all right only if the girl was exceptionally inviting. Then there would be the slow, delicious reawakening of desire. But with Clare there was nothing new about it. He found that going to bed with Clare now required a little effort on his part. What he really wanted was to be alone. He was in need of sleep and he knew that Clare would not let him sleep. She wanted him again a second time but he could not force himself to it. Yet if he tried to leave immediately she might go into another rage and he did not think he could stand another scene just now.

She was choking him. He pushed her away and reached for a cigarette.

"What are you thinking?" she asked coyly.

The eternal feminine question. It wasn't enough that they possessed your body; they had to get inside your mind. "Of you," he answered dutifully.

"I love you so terribly, Dino, I think I would kill you if you ever really tried to leave me. But first I would torture you so that you would never be any good for anyone else. I would take a small sharp knife and cut off this... and this. Or perhaps I would use my teeth instead. I have very sharp teeth."

"Ouch! Stop that."

"Poor little boy. I will kiss it to make it better."

"You're really a witch, Clare. A regular Borgia."

"I would like to have been a Borgia. How simple it would be to slip a little poison into a glass of wine for my dear little cousin." She nibbled at Dino's ear and whispered, "You *have* given her up, haven't you?"

He was tired of the game. It would have been nice if he and Clare could have parted as friends but with a bitch like this that was impossible. She refused to accept reality and she would continue to chase after him until Gwen learned the truth about their relationship. Gwen was still young enough, still provincial enough to be shocked by the knowledge that he had been Clare's lover and that Clare had supported him. Once they were married it would not matter, but what if Clare went to Gwen now and told her the whole story? Gwen might not believe it, but on the other hand, if she did, it might destroy all his plans. And it was just the sort of thing Clare was capable of. Well, if it happened he would have to convince Gwen that Clare was insane, mad with frustration. And perhaps she was. There were times when he was aware of a furious intensity in her that was really frightening. But he had no patience with her any more and he would have to end it. "No," he said in answer to her question. "I have not given her up."

He was relieved to see that he was not in for another outburst. Instead she drew away slightly and leaned on her elbow and asked casually, "Tell me, Dino, are you superstitious?"

"A little," he admitted. His parents had come from Sicily and the dark roots of old Sicilian blood feuds were still twisted in his mind.

"Then I will tell you something. Something that is as true as the fact that you are here now. I can see your future clearly and I tell you you will never marry her."

He got out of bed and began pulling on his clothes. She did not say good-bye and she did not see him to the door.

When he stepped out of the house the ocean wind was fresh on his face. He was glad to be away from her. She really was, he told himself, quite impossible and perhaps more than a little insane.

CHAPTER FOUR

Clare's voice was half lost in the rumble of the surf. Robinson waited for it to come again. "Gus," she called in her small husky voice.

"Where are you?"

"Over here."

She was on the seaward side of the wreck, her back against one of the smashed ribs. As he sat down beside her she said, "You're late."

"I couldn't break away. Walker kept insisting on one more drink."

"Were you surprised when I walked in on you like that?"

"I've been sort of expecting you to show up."

Actually he had been startled when he saw her. Three days had gone by without a word and he had decided that the whole business of the twenty thousand, like her quick, avid lovemaking, had been little more than a dream. Then she had come strolling into Walker's house in her immaculate pink linen and kissed dear old Stanley on the top of his skull and said, "It's Mr. Robinson, isn't it? I've heard about you. What a shame about your boat."

They had chatted about nothing special until Walker left the room and then she had said, "How are you, Gus?"

"I'm all right. And you?"

Ignoring his reply she whispered, "Can you meet me tonight?"

"I guess so. Where?"

"Ten o'clock at the wreck."

When Walker came back she rambled on about people they both knew and then said, "I must run now, Stanley darling. It's been so nice meeting you, Mr. Robinson. I do hope we'll see each other again.

"I'll look forward to it."

"Perhaps Stanley will bring you over to my house sometime."

"If I do he'll just fall hopelessly in love with you like all the rest of us," Walker said gallantly. "And by the way, what do you hear from Binky?"

"Not a blessed word."

"Is he still off skiing?"

"I suppose so. The last I heard he was in Vermont and I wrote him a letter there encouraging him to go on to Kitzbuhl. I know the most divine little Viennese countess there that Binky would go absolutely out of his head for. Anyway, I hope the snow is wonderful and he stays away a long time. If he comes back here I'll either have to move out of his house or start living in sin."

"I thought you were already," Walker said.

Clare laughed and as she passed through the door she said, "You know I'm saving myself for you, darling."

Walker saw her out to the car. When he came back he looked tired. He slumped down in his chair like an old man. The tremendous daily intake of liquor was beginning to catch up with him. The network of veins in his nose seemed more prominent than ever.

"She's something, isn't she?" Walker said.

"What's her story?"

"The usual thing. Married. Divorced. Married again. Widowed. Left with a modest income. Runs with a younger crowd. About par for the course. When you sum it up that way it sounds pretty empty, doesn't it?"

"Everybody's story does. Take mine, for instance. Cornell. Crewed. Loved boats. Never settled down. Lost boat. Kaput."

Walker stared at him bleakly and said, "Mine is even shorter. Had money. Boozed. Lost money. Died."

There was an unspoken bond between them. In a way that would never be apparent to either one they were much alike. They had both run away from the world, and although the sea Walker had elected to sail on was compounded of Scotch instead of salt water, the end results were much the same. They were both lost and lonely and turning aimlessly in the same remote eddy.

"I'll tell you something, old boy," Walker said. "I envy you."

"For God's sake, why?"

"I guess it's just that you've got more of everything. More height. More hair. More youth. More strength. More guts."

"Well there's one thing I certainly haven't got more of and that's money."

"Money is crap."

"Unquestionably, but the only people who can afford to believe it are those with either no money or too much."

"I'll tell you about money, Gus. My old man was Walker of Walker Tool & Die. He started off pouring pig iron in a mill and worked his way up to be boss of his own outfit. Somewhere along the way he paused just long enough to marry and spawn a kid named Stanley. Like most self-made men he wanted the best of everything for his son. He hired the most expensive nursemaids to turn him into a mollycoddle and every time the young snotnose sneezed there was a rush call for two specialists. Finally young Stanley went off to a good eastern prep school and while he was there the old man died of hypertension and a few other assorted ailments.

"When they straightened out the estate they found that young Stanley had been left the income from a very sizeable trust fund. An irrevocable and untouchable trust. It seems the old boy never really had much confidence in young Stanley after all. Still, it was a nice income. Just enough so that he would never have to work for a living. I guess he was still protecting me all the way, even after his death. And that was the biggest mistake he made. If he had left me a few million bucks where I could get my hands on it I probably would have thrown it away in one big binge and then been forced to go out and earn a living. In that case I might have been an insurance salesman somewhere and married the kind of nice little girl that marries small, bald-headed insurance salesmen.

"Or if I didn't throw away the dough I might have reinvested it and made a pot more and been able to call myself my own man. Either way I would have been better off. As it was, he crippled me. I didn't have enough to play around with and at the same time I had too much of an assured income to ever really be forced to take a job. Right now, for instance, I'm waiting for next month's check which won't be here for another three weeks, and until I get it I'm absolutely flat. So it's all been wasted. Everything. And when I let myself think about it it's like a knife in my guts. Maybe that's why I booze so much."

"You could have refused to take the income," Robinson said.

"Maybe once but not any more. It's too late now. I'm too old and too scared. And anyway, I like the dough. It may be crap but I like it."

"What you need is a wife, Stanley."

"They're all too young or too old. Too soft or too hard. If I marry some child bride who doesn't know the score she'll let me drift along the way I'm going and in the end I'll just wind up dragging somebody else down with me. On the other hand, if I ever got involved with a woman like Clare Loomis she'd chew me up and then spit me out like a used piece of gum. No, if I have one saving grace, old boy, it's that I know my limitations. I've got the house and Tom to look after me and my old pal Johnny Walker to kill the pain and that's all there is and that's all there will ever be. I guess it's enough; still, I like to dream. I like to dream that I still might do something positive...."

The clownish expression that Walker habitually wore had gone. For one brief moment there was a touch of strength in the weak jaw and the faded blue eyes. That, Robinson thought, is how the old man must have looked.

"You won't laugh at me?" Walker said.

"No, of course not."

"What I'd really like is to be another Gus Robinson. I'd like to sell the house and put the money into a boat and take off."

"Why don't you?"

"I told you; I know my limitations. How far do you think I'd get? I'd wind up drunk and scared and lonely. And besides, I'd get sick as a wet cat on a boat. I like to talk about sailing but I'm really just a fraud." The foolish, self-deprecating grin had returned. "No, I'll stay here where I belong, waiting for the checks that will always keep coming as long as the market doesn't go to hell. In a way it's right for me but it's no good for you, Gus."

"I know that."

"I wouldn't want to infect you with the same disease."

"No fear, Stanley. My old man left me nothing but his best wishes. Anyway, I'll be leaving in a few days."

"I'll be sorry to see you go but I guess it would be best."

"Maybe someday when I get another boat I'll come back and you'll take a cruise with me."

"Yes," Walker said, knowing they never would, "maybe someday we will."

From that point on Walker began to drink steadily. He had lost another in the series of sharp little skirmishes he had fought with himself over the years and now he turned to the Scotch for relief. Eventually Thomas led him away to bed.

Robinson was glad to see his host go. The maudlin self-pity of a drunk always made him uncomfortable. Walker was likable enough and there were times when you could feel sorry for him but he was still a fearsome bore. When the house was quiet he slipped out through the sliding glass door and walked rapidly down the path through the dunes to his meeting with Clare.

"Have you thought any more about my proposition?" she asked.

"I still don't know what your proposition is," Robinson said.

"What do you think it is?"

"You really want me to guess?"

"Why not?"

"Well it might be almost anything, but since you specified that you needed a sailor and since you're probably too smart to go in for anything as foolish as smuggling or gun running, I'd have to guess that it's some sort of insurance fraud."

"And if you were right would you be willing to go through with it?"

"If I thought I could get away with it."

"Well, it has nothing to do with insurance. Do you remember you told me that first night when I mentioned the twenty thousand dollars to you that you would do anything short of murder?"

"I remember."

"Well, murder is what I want done."

She had spoken in the calm, slightly overbearing voice that she might use instructing a bartender in the proper preparation of a dry martini. Robinson waited for her to go on and when she didn't he said, "I hope this is your idea of a joke."

"I've never been more serious."

"All right," he said. "Good-bye. It's been nice knowing you."

"Don't you want to hear the rest?"

"No. You've got the wrong boy."

"I think I've got the right boy. Don't you want to know why?"

"That much might be interesting," he said, sitting down again. "Go on."

"I'm surprised to find such an initial feeling of righteousness in you. You just don't seem like the sort of man who would be bound by the usual phony crap of accepted convictions. Tell me, Gus, were you in the war?"

"They called it a police action."

"You mean Korea?"

"Yes."

"Well, whatever they called it it was a war."

"That was the way it seemed to me."

"Were you actually in combat? I mean did you kill anybody?"

"Yes."

"Why?"

"They were shooting at me."

"No, before that."

"Because I was told to."

"No other reason? No strong convictions about saving the world for something or other?"

"No."

"Well at least you're honest about it. What did you feel about the men you killed?"

"Not much."

"They gave you a reason to go out and kill and you went and did it. And as far as I can tell from looking at you it doesn't keep you awake nights. The only trouble was it was not a very good reason. Now I can give you much better reasons. Twenty thousand of them." Her voice had grown warmer and she had moved a little closer to him as she talked so that her arm was pressing softly against his. "Your fellow creatures can't be so terribly sacred to you, Gus, or you wouldn't have gone to war and you wouldn't be sailing around the world alone. What it boils down to is a question of your life against somebody else's. You told me yourself that without a boat life for you wasn't worth living. So if you want to spend the rest of your life puttering around some miserable boatyard painting other people's yachts, all you have to do is get up from here and walk away right now. But I know you won't because we're two of a kind, Gus. We both take what we want out of life and to hell with everybody else."

Isn't it great, he thought, how they keep seeing themselves in me? Walker thought he saw something of himself in me and now this bitch does the same thing. And the funny part is they may both be right.

She was going on about morality. Her point was that it is all a question of degree instead of any fundamental sense of right or wrong. We never hesitate to break the law in dozens of small ways all the time. We sleep with other men's wives and we cheat the customs inspectors and we lie to the tax collectors and we fix parking tickets and we use influence to obtain government contracts and we duck the draft and we pad expense accounts and we rig insurance claims and we even let the damned dog mess on the damned sidewalk when he should be in the damned gutter. So, according to her, if you follow that reasoning to its inescapable conclusion, why the hell should anyone shy away from murder?

"I'll tell you why," she went on. "For only one reason. We're afraid of getting caught. Isn't that so?"

"You're doing the talking. Go ahead."

"Suppose I were to present you with an absolutely foolproof scheme for murder. What would you say then?"

"I'd say there is no such animal."

"Well you're wrong. It happens all the time. A very dear friend of mine got away with murder and she's currently a member in good standing of international cafe society, and you'd know her name if I told it to you because it's in all the gossip columns."

"I don't read the gossip columns," Robinson said, "but who did she murder and how did she do it?"

"She murdered her husband with a box of pills."

"And you mean to say they couldn't trace the pills?"

"There was nothing to trace. She didn't give him the pills; she just kept him from getting at them. He was an invalid with a bad heart. The doctor had prescribed certain pills to get him through his attacks. My friend, who was about thirty years younger than her husband, just waited until he was in a bad way and then tucked the pills into her bag and went for a good long walk. When she came back he was dead. She put the pills back where they belonged and then began screaming for help. No matter what anybody may say there's no way they can prove anything. It was an absolutely foolproof murder."

"Since you've got it all so well figured out, what do you need me for? Why don't you do it yourself? Or haven't you the guts?"

"I have the guts all right, sonny boy, but as I told you it needs a sailor."

She stood up suddenly, then bent down and kissed his cheek and said, "Good night, Gus. Think it over."

Gwen Leacock rattled up to the Walker house the next morning in a flame-red Hillman and said, "I have every intention of holding you to your promise, Mr. Robinson."

"About the sailing lesson? Fine. Let's go."

She looked exceptionally lovely. Her smoothly tanned skin was without makeup and needed none. Her hair was drawn back simply and tied with a ribbon. She wore a blue and white striped shirt and tiny faded denim shorts. Her limbs, as revealed by the skimpy outfit, were slender but beautifully rounded. She opened the door for him and he got in and they drove around the point and toward the lagoon. A brisk easterly sent a flock of whitecaps racing across the usually calm water.

"It may be a little windy out there for a Lightning," Robinson said.

She raised one eyebrow and asked in a mocking tone, "Frightened?"

"Maybe. Aren't you?"

"Not with you."

"Well that's where you're wrong. I'm far from infallible. I lost my own boat and I wouldn't want to lose yours."

"But that's the nice thing about a day-sailer. About the worst that can happen to you is a good ducking."

"You can get clobbered by the boom of a Lightning just as well as in a forty footer."

"I'll keep my head down and do as I'm told. Okay?"

"All right," he said. "We'll give it a whirl anyway. Where do you keep the boat?"

"At a dock on the far shore."

They turned off onto a narrow track and went over a rise to a landing where two sport-cruisers lay gleaming in the sun. Between them was moored a handsome day-sailer with all loose lines coiled and sails neatly furled.

"You keep her shipshape," Robinson said approvingly, "Or is that the work of the hired help?"

"The hired help don't have a thing to do with it. Captain Leacock is responsible for everything you see here."

"Before we start out you'd better tell me just what you have in mind.

Do you plan to race her or just to knock around the lagoon?"

"There's a one-design race scheduled for next week and I thought it might be great fun to enter it if I knew a little more about the technique of racing."

"Then I think the best way to start would be for you to do everything just as though you were alone. While you're at it I'll sit back and watch you with a lecherous eye."

She got the sails up, let go lines and moved smartly away from the dock. It was very neatly done. They went out fast on a broad reach and although she was a little afraid of so much wind she handled the boat nicely enough on port and starboard tacks.

"Don't you want to take it?" she asked.

"Not just yet. Let's just drop the sails for a few minutes and sit and talk. You sail very well but you have something to learn because racing is not only technique but psychology as well. I'll try to be very learned and professional with you, and I'm betting that by the time I finish you'll be ready to give the boat away to the first taker."

She nodded happily. Her cheeks were rouged by the wind and her eyes were shining with excitement. If there is such an animal as a born sailor, Robinson thought, she is certainly one. You could see it in the way she handled the tiller, as lightly as a good horseman handles his reins, and in the way she responded to the heel of the boat, not getting nervous or panicky but just instinctively easing the sheet or coming a touch closer to the wind. But most of all it was in her eyes as she followed the sweep of canvas and in the pulse of excitement that showed in her throat as she prepared to come about.

He helped her drop the sails and when the boat was comparatively still they sat side by side in the cockpit. He offered her a cigarette and cupped a match in his fist.

"Let's talk generalities first," he said. "To begin with you're not paying enough attention to the jib. Did you know that for its size the jib develops about twice the pulling power of the mains'le?"

She shook her head. "I just assumed they threw it in for something a little extra."

"Well if you want to win a race don't ever neglect that jib. Try to see that it's set up as smoothly as possible. I don't want to sound too pontifical about it but you have to think of it as a kind of aerofoil, something like the wing of a bird or an airplane. The surface should be smoothly arched and at the same time as stiff as possible. It isn't just a question of the wind flowing onto the sail; it's got to flow off it as well.

Every little wrinkle or hard spot sets up eddies on both sides of the sail. These eddies break up the flow of the wind and cut down on the sail's efficiency. Are you properly confused now?"

"No, not too much."

"Then let's talk about racing. A good many people have written volumes on the subject, many of which are largely over-technical nonsense. The main thing to remember is that the start is most important. More sailing races are won at the start than at any other point. It's not like a horse race or a foot race or even an automobile race where the animal or the man or the machine is in danger of breaking down from too fast a start. All other factors being equal the first boat across the starting line should win the race. For one thing it's always easier to keep a competing boat behind you than it is to catch up with the one ahead. If you're ahead you can use such nasty little tricks as blanketing his sails or leaving broken water in your wake, both of which will slow him down. And then too, the boat in the lead seems to sail better. She's lighter in the water and easier on the helm. A lot of that is probably due to the fact that the skipper of the trailing boat is trying too hard to catch up and it forces him to press. But if you just remember to get across that line first it's my bet that you won't have any trouble staying in front."

"Couldn't I just tuck you away somewhere in the bilge?" she asked. "That way when I need advice you could flash signals at me."

"I weigh two hundred and five pounds and I don't think that kind of ballast would do you any good. The main thing you have to remember is that if we have the same kind of wind on the day of the race that we're having today—which is pretty likely for this time of year—it will make for a windward start. In that case you make darned sure you get off on a starboard tack. And the reason for that is very simple—you have the right of way and you don't have to worry about fouling the other fellow. This gives you a very clear advantage over the boat on the port tack. Savvy?"

"I savvy, Gus."

"Good. Then get those sails up again and take her off on the starboard tack just as you would for a race. And while you're at it I'll see if I can't tune up the stays and the rest of the rigging."

The time had slipped magically away. In the joy of sailing and in the pleasure of Gwen's company Robinson had been able to forget himself and most of his troubles. The little boat swept back and forth across the lagoon. Robinson drove her down almost to her beam ends. White water nipped at the weather boards as the Lightning beat to windward. If Robinson was showing off to some degree it was hard to blame him.

When they finally brought the boat in she said, "How can I thank you, Gus?"

"No thanks are needed, Gwen. It was just as much fun for me. I really came alive out there today for the first time since losing *Charee*."

"It's none of my business, of course, but I'm wondering what your plans are now. Surely you'll get another boat."

"I suppose I will someday if I can ever put that many dollars together."

"But wasn't the *Charee* insured?"

"Singlehanded sailors crossing oceans are not generally considered a good risk. Even if you could find a company willing to carry the policy the premiums would be way out of line. But, I'll make out. Something usually turns up. But what about you, Gwen? Where do you go from here?"

"You mean from Spanish Cay?"

"Yes."

"I've got to go back to New York. I'll be leaving next week, right after I win that race."

"It's too bad you can't stay on. The really fine sailing weather will be coming along in a few weeks."

"My dad is seriously ill and since I'm an only child and my mother died several years ago I don't like to stay away from him too long. Oh I don't suppose a few weeks either way really matters too much but my plans are made and I think I might as well stay with them."

"Perhaps it's just as well that you're leaving Spanish Cay."

"Why is that?"

"I'm not sure but somehow you just don't seem to be the type."

"What type do you have to be?"

They were standing close together and the atmosphere between them was suddenly charged with tension. He found himself very much aware of the smoothness of her skin and of the rise and fall of her firm young breasts. Gwen's smile had faded. She looked long and seriously into his eyes. She started to say, "Gus, dear... " but then broke it off to add, "it's getting late. I'll drive you back."

Robinson shook his head. "I think I'll walk."

"It's an awfully long walk."

"It will do me good. I've been sitting around on boats for too many years."

"Are you angry about something, Gus?"

"Of course not. What made you ask that?"

"Well, I don't know you very well but I have the impression that you've suddenly gotten very reserved."

"Because I want to walk? Forget it. I assure you it's nothing like that."

A car on the road hooted at them. They looked up to see Clare Loomis at the wheel. Her beautifully done blonde hair was piled high on her head and she wore pink gloves and a frilly pink dress. She sat very straight in the little car and she waved at them as she went by and called out, "Hello, you two."

They both waved back.

"Do you know her?" Gwen asked.

Robinson nodded. "I met her yesterday when she was visiting Stanley."

"Don't you think she's extraordinarily beautiful?"

Robinson answered with a slight shrug.

"That's not a very convincing answer," Gwen said.

"It wasn't meant to be."

"I'm glad."

"Why?"

"Most men who meet Clare for the first time fall violently in love with her. It makes me jealous. I guess when you come right down to it I've been a little jealous of Clare all my life. She's my cousin and, of course, she's always been older and more beautiful and more exciting. We never saw too much of her but we used to hear all about the way she moved in the most glamorous circles in Rome and London and Cannes. Lately we've been spending more time with Clare though, and it was at her insistence that I came down here this winter. I suppose I really shouldn't sound so ungrateful. She's introduced me to some very exciting people."

"Like Dino di Whatsisname?"

"Di Buonaventura. Yes, Clare introduced me to Dino. He's more or less her protégé. Don't you like him?"

"He's hardly my dish of tea but what does it matter? The thing is, *you* like him."

She nodded, smiling.

"Well he's a pretty boy, all right."

"He's more than that, Gus. He's a very aware and very sensitive person."

"Stanley told me he was an artist. Is he any good?"

"I'm not sure. Right now he makes his living doing portraits and that's pretty much a job of making the subject look impossibly beautiful."

"And he gives them what they want."

"Well, he tries."

They had run out of words. The charge of sexual excitement was rising between them again. She looked uneasily at her watch and said, "I'd better go. Are you sure you want to walk, Gus?"

"Yes, but thanks anyway. And maybe we'll sail again before the race."

"That would be wonderful."

When he left her he felt curiously let down. She had gotten under skin, managed somehow, even those few hours on the water, to crack the carefully constructed armor that had served him so well during all the years of loneliness. He was, he knew, in a vulnerable position right now. When *Charee* went down his sense of independence went with her. No matter what had ever happened to him ashore there was always the ketch waiting at her mooring to take him out of it. His attachments were as transient as a raised anchor and an outgoing tide could make them. The singlehander … the one-night-stander. Leave 'em laughing or weeping, but always leave 'em.

It was daydreaming, of course, but what a combination Gwen and *Charee* would have made. Walking along the crushed coral path he let his mind play with it. Out through the canal to the Galapagos and then on to Papeete. The island of Mangareva mouldering under the weight of the past, almost all its people gone now, sacrificed to the mad ambitions of the French priest Laval who had built the great stone convents with slave labor. What crazy dreams had ravaged the Frenchman's mind? The immense stone privies overgrown by the jungle …

They would be heading out to sea in the cool dawn and she would be clinging to the jibstay with her dark hair loose in the wind.

Knock it off, Robinson. The party is over. The music has stopped and they've turned off the lights and you change back into a pumpkin on the stroke of midnight. And it's nobody's bloody fault but your own. If you had only taken the trouble to check that filthy clamp. Who was the bastard who first put a toilet on a boat anyway? In the old days they used a cedar bucket and the damned boats didn't sink. On his next one...

What next one? You haven't got a pot and you know it and you probably never will have. Well, there's always the gorgeous Mrs. Loomis. Twenty thousand bucks per murder. C.O.D. Not a bad price for a beginner. And there's plenty of room for advancement. With a little push you could work your way to the top. Give it some thought, Augustus.

It's beginning to sound a little more palatable all the time, eh? And that's what she's counting on. When you didn't get up and walk away the first time she mentioned it she figured you were half hooked right there. And maybe she's right. Maybe she saw something in you you never saw in yourself, old dear. She had put it so neatly too, flashing that fine pair at him and sizing him up with those lovely ice-blue eyes and asking softly, "Who would pay you twenty thousand dollars for something legal?"

It's all a matter of degree, she had said. Degrees of illegality. Maybe she was right. Why be so squeamish? Maybe it was just a question of how badly you needed something. When the bombardier looks through his bomb sight what does he see? The faces of ten thousand poor devils who will be incinerated? Hell no. If he is a good workman all he sees is a table of calculations and a set of cross hairs. Look at it that way, Gus. You just drop the bomb, is all.

He kicked savagely at a bit of rock in his path and then stood hesitating. He was in no mood to go back to the house. Instead he turned off onto the side path that led to town.

The town of Spanish Cay sits on the southeast tip of the island. There is not much to it. A tailor, a barber, the commissioner's office, the straw market, the big game fishing club and half a dozen bars. There are always plenty of bars, a hangover probably from the old days when they ran booze from the Bahamas across the Florida Straits.

He became aware of the mutter of calypso drums and a shaft of yellow light streaming through an open doorway. From inside came the sound of laughter and a ripple of applause. The sign outside, hand-lettered on cardboard, told him that the name of the place was the Flame Club. In his present mood it was probably as good a place as any. He turned in through the open doorway and entered a world of smoke and chatter, of drums and sweat and the musky odor of sex. Some of the men wore soiled captain's hats and long-billed mate's caps. White teeth gleamed in dark faces, bodies pressed together on the tiny dance floor. "That line came out of the outrigger like the stroke of doom and when he jumped he looked as big as a house. Two hundred and fifty pounds if he was an ounce"... "She says to me, 'Why don't you take me fishing tomorrow? My husband is leaving for New York and I won't have a thing to do.' I told her the port engine was overheating and I didn't think we ought to run her. She gives me that long look and asks me what the hell do we need an engine for...."

At about ten o'clock the better element began arriving. Among them were several people Robinson knew—Gwen, Dino, Clare, Jocko Lacey and half a dozen others who had been at Stanley's party. They sat apart, the arrogant rich. He kept his back to them. If they recognized him they might invite him for a drink. He could not afford to return the courtesy.

Suddenly, except for a single spotlight on the dance floor, the lights went out. There was a rattle of drums and a fanfare. Faces glinting with sweat turned in anticipation. The black figure, her muscles beautifully outlined as if carved of ebony, came leaping soundless as a panther toward the center of the floor. She wore only an orange-colored bud over each nipple and a paper flower clutched between muscular thighs. She came with naked buttocks gleaming and breasts swinging and head thrown back in silent orgasm. She swept full circle around the floor, her belly muscles seeming to writhe with a life of their own like a nest of snakes. A drunk at a ringside table reached a flabby paw toward her breast. She snatched him out of his seat and danced wildly with him for a moment, holding him helpless and slack-jawed, before flexing her hips and hitting him square in the belly with her pelvis and sending him crashing backward among the tables.

There was a great burst of applause and laughter as the drunk lay under a table with spilled whiskey dripping onto his red, insensible face. The drums rolled on. The dancer's hands roamed lovingly over her own body, kneading and titillating. Masturbation as an art form. The girl was good in her primitive fashion but Robinson had seen better in Cairo and Port Said. He let his eyes swing away from the dancer toward the audience. Clare looked faintly bored. Gwen's cheeks were paler than usual. Dino had the elegant, disinterested air of a thoroughbred stud watching the clumsy coupling of plowhorses.

The black girl coiled her steely legs one last time and swung her orange-tipped breasts in a defiant gesture and went leaping back out of the light. For a moment there was no sound but the exhalation of many breaths. They had seen the naked face of the jungle and their blood had been stirred by something they did not quite understand.

CHAPTER FIVE

Dino looked down at the tips of his beautifully polished loafers and said, "I will tell you something, Mr. Robinson. We are really very much alike, we two."

Here it comes again, Gus thought. Walker said that and Clare said it and now Dino. Why do they use me as a mirror for their faults? Augustus Robinson, the flexible man. Step up. Step up. Are you long, short, fat or thin? See yourself in that new marvel of the mechanical age—the flexible man. He adjusts to each and every situation. Put one in your pocket and take it home with you, ladies and gentlemen. Take two for the price of one.

"You say we're alike," Robinson said. "Just how do you figure that?"

"We are both adventurers. In different fields perhaps—I happen to hate the sea—but we both have the same attitude toward life."

"What attitude is that?"

"We understand how unpredictable it all is. We wait for a fair wind and then we sail before it and we never quite know where we will wind up. Isn't that so?"

I wonder what he wants, Gus thought. You can see that he hates my guts and that he somehow senses that I'm a threat to him, but why did he come all the way out here to have breakfast with me?

Robinson had been sitting on the terrace in the cool of the morning when Dino drove up and got out of the car and strode jauntily up the path.

"Good morning, Mr. Robinson," Dino had said. "Is Stanley still asleep?"

"I guess so; he tied on a beauty last night."

"It is just as well; it will give me an opportunity to have a chat with you."

"Care for some breakfast?"

"Splendid."

During the meal Dino said, "I try to understand how a man like yourself can sail alone in a little boat for days or even weeks at a time but it confuses me. I wish you would explain it."

"What is it that you don't understand?"

"You must get some pleasure from it or you wouldn't do it, but I should think the boredom would kill you."

"There's always a job to be done on a boat and there are still a couple of thousand good books I haven't read."

"But how do you go so long without a woman? At our age this is the only thing in life that really matters."

"I manage. The same way I manage without television, ice cream and the morning paper."

"To me it would be unthinkable. I would kill myself." Dino had finished his coffee and now he leaned back and lit a cigarette and said, "By the way, what do you think of our little Gwen?"

"I like her."

"Of course. We all like her. She is a wonderfully charming child. It was kind of you to be so helpful about her little boat. Perhaps now she will win the race, eh?"

"She has a natural talent for sailing. The only thing I could contribute was a little technical advice."

Dino leaned back and put his long legs up on a chair and said, "She has a natural talent for many things. It is amazing with these shy little American girls. So carefully brought up. So proper. So unexposed. And then when you turn them loose—bang! It is like when you take an underprivileged child to the candy store. They can't seem to get enough."

Well blast his pretty eyes anyway, Robinson thought. The sonofabitch has a sure knack for getting under my skin. We're like a pair of dogs around a bitch in heat. So the bitch is his. Well, then let him keep her at home where she belongs and out of sailboats.

Dino smiled and said, "Perhaps I have shocked you a little or destroyed some of your illusions. I hope not. You are, after all, a man of the world and why should not such men discuss women as freely as they discuss golf scores or fish they have caught or animals they have shot? If we mount the head of a deer so that our friends can admire our prowess why should we not—in spirit that is—mount the virgins we have deflowered. It is perhaps more of an accomplishment than bagging a defenseless deer, eh? If a man is honest he will admit that he takes pride in bedding a virgin. Some men have a talent for sailing boats or making money, others for painting pictures or making love. Why should we be so hypocritical as to pretend that this is something we don't talk about?"

"I can give you one reason for keeping your mouth shut."

"And what is that?"

"If you open it someone is liable to knock your teeth down your throat."

"But my dear Robinson, forgive me. Have I touched a nerve? Are you perhaps in love with little Gwen? In that case, I am so sorry."

Steady on, old boy, Robinson told himself. A swat in the nose seldom accomplished much. And if she wants to be a blasted international whore for this type of Via Sistina gigolo, what business is it of yours? "Somehow I would have thought Mrs. Loomis was more your style," he said.

"Forgive me if I have offended you," Dino went on. "It is all lies and foolish boasting anyway. Like the golf score or the size of the fish. No one really tells the truth in these matters. I just came to have a visit, a chat as you say, about unimportant things. As I have said, we are much alike. Adventurers. Men not bound by all the accepted and over-worked conventions. And I was right; we are attracted by the same girl. Our tastes are similar. But Mrs. Loomis, that is something else again. There is a real woman for you, a regular man-eater. That woman could write an encyclopedia of the bed. If you will forgive a little friendly ad-vice, you should cultivate her. You would find it, even for a man so widely traveled as yourself, quite a remarkable experience. Ah, but I forget. It will be difficult. She does not like you."

"No?"

"We saw you last night at the bar in the Flame Club. And by the way, that savage was something, eh? Anyway, Clare seemed to take a poor view of you. She said you were a bit of a phony. Are you a phony, old boy?"

"Who isn't?"

"You see, we understand each other. Of course we are all phonies."

Dino looked at his wafer-thin gold watch on its black suede band and said, "Damn! Eight o'clock already. I must run for I have promised to breakfast with our little Gwen. Now I will have to conceal the fact that I have already breakfasted with you. You see how we all have to lead double lives. But then I am lucky; I have a big appetite. Well so long, Gus."

"Good-bye," Robinson said.

Dino climbed into the car and shot off with a spurt of gravel. Robin-son lingered over his second cup of coffee. If Dino had come there solely for the purpose of bedeviling him, he had succeeded. Despite a strong effort to control his imagination, visions of Dino and Gwen together, naked on a bed, the painter's hands caressing her small firm breasts, swam through his mind. He was not usually susceptible to jealousy— it was a passion that a sailor away at sea for months at a time could ill afford—but now he found that he was certainly jealous of the handsome Italian.

And it was doubly foolish because he had no claim of any kind on her. If he had permitted himself to indulge in daydreams about the voyages they might someday make together he should be realistic enough now to accept the fact that she was Dino's girl and that there would never be any voyages. At least not for the two of them. He was to be, it appeared, forever the singlehander. And unless he found the money for a ship he would not even be that any more.

Well, he would find the money, he told himself. The only things hamstringing him at the moment were some tired old scruples. Dino had no scruples and was getting along just fine. God knows, Clare Loomis had few enough scruples and she would almost certainly have her way in the end too. Artificially bright and deadly cruel they were, like barracudas let loose in shoals of school fish. He knew them from way back and he had been bruised by them often enough so that by rights he should no longer be vulnerable. It was time he learned to cheat them at their own nasty games. Dino and Clare cheated mostly with their bodies, but for an enterprising, thirty-two-year-old, six-foot two-inch, shipwrecked sailor of poor but honest family, there must be other ways to cheat. You could cheat, for example, with a simple statement of intentions. A sort of moral I.O.U. Dear Devil: I, Gus Robinson, being reasonably sound in mind and limb, do herewith commit my soul to you in exchange for one thirty-eight-foot Alden-designed yawl. Pending survey, of course. Well, it was an idea all right and chances were a lot of good men had sold their immortal souls for less. Why had it always been assumed throughout the ages that the Devil was male? The Devil in this case was blonde and blue-eyed and the purveyor of a fine bag of tricks in bed. But there was a way to skin every cat and if you could cheat the Devil at her own game, why so much the better for you.

"I wasn't sure you'd come," Clare said. "Are you sure Stanley didn't see you?"

"Stanley has just belted himself out of this world and I doubt he'll wake up until tomorrow afternoon. Anyway, it wouldn't make much difference if he had seen me leave the house. As far as he knows I just went for my evening stroll on the beach."

"Still, I'm a little worried that someone may spot us from the house."

"Not with the lights behind us. The only way we could be seen would be from the seaward side and I don't imagine there's anyone out there.

By the way, I had a visit from your boyfriend this morning."

"What boyfriend?"

"Dino."

Her silence seemed an affirmation of what Dino had said. So it was
true that he had been making the best of both worlds. Quite a lad.

"What did he want?" she asked at last.

"I'm not absolutely sure but I think what he really came for was to
tell me to keep hands off your cousin."

"Gwen?"

"Isn't she your cousin?"

"Yes. Are you interested in her?"

"No. I'm not interested in anybody."

"That's good."

"Why is it good?"

"Because she's the one I want to get rid of."

"If you called me out here to make jokes I think we can both find
something better to do with our time," Robinson said.

"If you think I'm joking why don't you leave?"

She must be serious at that, he decided. Whatever else she might be
she was no practical joker. Her voice could cut like a knife when she
wanted it to and it was honed to an extra fine edge tonight.

"What have you got against her?" he asked.

"That's my business."

"The hell it is. If you're going to get me involved in this then I intend
to be involved all the way. Or did you think I was going to stick my
neck out without any idea of what was going on?"

"I really don't see how the motives concern you."

"Don't you? We are under British law here, lady, and murder is pun-
ishable on the gallows. My neck happens to concern me quite a bit. Unless you're willing to let me in on the whole deal we can forget it right
now." Listen to the boy, he thought admiringly. A regular Humphrey
Bogart. Where is your belted raincoat tonight, Augustus, it may come
on to shower.

"Gwen's father is a rich man. He is also a sick man. When he dies,
which may be soon, he will leave her quite a lot of money."

"So?"

"I want that money."

"And how does disposing of Gwen get you the money?"

"There's no one else. As long as Gwen doesn't marry I am her clos-
est surviving relative. I went to the trouble of becoming a rather dear

friend of the attorney who drew up the will—so dear, in fact, that he was willing to do something unethical. He told me the terms of the will. As it now stands I am next in line of inheritance after Gwen."

"No trust funds in between?"

"A few bequests to charity but the major portion goes to me. Henry Leacock has a strong sense of family."

"So do you."

"You can spare me your feeble moralizing, Gus. When I need that I'll go to a priest or an analyst. Let's stick to the point. Are you still with me?"

"I'm still listening."

"Then this is what I have in mind. It all ties in beautifully because you've already taken her out sailing. You'll take her out again in that silly boat and when you come back you'll be alone."

"Just like that, eh?"

"Why not? Accidents do happen. Couldn't she be hit on the head by the what-do-you-call-it?"

"The boom."

"Yes, the boom. She is hit on the head and falls overboard. You dive in after her but she has disappeared. You swim around until you're exhausted but apparently she has gone straight to the bottom. At last you give up the search and come in. How can anything ever be proved against you? You had no motive, in fact you hardly knew her. It's all very sad, of course, but still it's a perfectly feasible accident. As long as there are no witnesses you are safe. We're the only two people in the world who will ever know anything about it and for obvious reasons neither of us will ever do any talking."

In a way you had to admire her, he thought. The Ilse Koch of Spanish Cay. I wonder if her lampshades are tattooed. For sheer cold-blooded murderous efficiency he had never seen anything like her. For that matter he wasn't doing so badly himself. He was sitting here taking it all in as calmly as though he knocked off beautiful young girls every day of the week. She had sized him up pretty well at that. Yes, she was the Devil all right and he would sell her his soul for twenty thousand dollars, but before she collected he would give her a run for her money. A plan had already began to take shape in his mind.

"The only way it would be safe would be to do it out of sight of land," he said. "Do you expect me to take her offshore in that damned little day-sailer?"

"Why not? That's your business, isn't it?"

He sat there looking out to sea and saying nothing. Finally she said, "Well?"

"I'm thinking."

A full five minutes of silence lay between them before he said, "How do I get paid?"

"C.O.D."

"No, that won't do. I'll take half in advance."

Clare laughed and said, "Why should I trust you with ten thousand dollars? What's to keep you from taking the money and getting on the next plane out of here?"

"That would be just too bad. And you could hardly complain to the commissioner, could you? Of course, I can always sign a contract specifying that for twenty thousand dollars I agree to murder your cousin. That way the law will be on your side."

"You're a scream, Gus."

"I know. That's one of the nice things about doing business with me. I keep it light. You'd be surprised how many paid killers have no sense of humor at all. Look, Clare, you have to trust me and I have to trust you. It cuts both ways. Suppose after I do the job you refuse to pay up and tell me to go fly a kite? What do I do then? Do I go crying to the FBI? No, the only way is like I say. Half and half. Half in advance and half when it's over. You can figure I won't run out because I want that other ten, and that's the truth of it. So let's leave it that way. Half in advance and the rest when it's over. And you had better pick up a plane ticket for me too."

"Plane ticket to where?"

"Miami. After it's done I want to get off this island *muy rapido*."

"But won't that make them suspicious?"

"Maybe. But what of it? What can they prove? It's like you say, I had no motive. I hardly knew her. And if they do come looking for me they'll have a hell of a time finding me in twenty thousand square miles of the Caribbean. I'll stay at sea for a long time after this."

"I still think it would be better to wait here until the investigation is completed."

"Honey, when this is over you go your way and I'll go mine. And my way is out."

"But don't you see, you fool? If you run away they'll know there was something wrong."

"I don't agree. The worst they can say is that I was bowled over by the tragedy and that I panicked and lost my head. They may want to ask me some questions but by the time they find me I'll have all the answers under control."

"No, Gus, it doesn't make any sense."

"Well it does to me and that's the way it will have to be. I'm not so damned cold-blooded that I can sit around here and go through an investigation without batting an eye. We agreed that this thing had to be foolproof. Well it won't be foolproof until I'm out of the picture."

She hesitated and then said, "When will you do it?"

Look how we edge around it, he thought. Even now we don't want to use the word murder. We refer to it only as "it." "It" is a nice clean word. What a lovely pair of cutthroats we are.

"The sooner the better," he said. "Let's get it over with. I'll get in touch with her tomorrow and make a date to take her sailing. It will either be tomorrow or the next day."

"How will I know?"

"I'll run an ad in the local paper."

"Goddamn you, Gus," she flared, "save your filthy humor for some other time! Do you think this is a joke?"

"No," he said. "Whatever else it is, it's certainly no joke. All right then, I'll call you."

"Calls can be traced."

"How? Do you think I'm stupid enough to blab the whole thing over the phone? I won't use my name. I'll just say something like 'Tomorrow is a good day for sailing.'"

"There's still one big trouble."

"I can see a lot of big troubles but which one did you have in mind?"

"How will I know that you've really done the job? I won't pay you the balance until you prove it."

"Why don't you come along and watch?"

"Are you being funny again?"

"I told you that as killers go I'm a card. I'll tell you what. I can lop off one of her ears and bring it back. Will that satisfy you?"

"Oh shut up; I'm thinking." After a moment she said, "Where will you take her?"

"There's only one place. Out there," he said pointing to seaward. "Out of sight of land."

"Then you'll have to come through the channel and sail past the beach, won't you?"

"That's right."

"If I'm on my terrace watching you through binoculars I'll be able to see you going out and coming back."

"Will that answer your question?"

"Of course. All right, Gus. How do you want to be paid?"

"In cash, and like we said. No, wait a minute. I'll take the half in advance in cash and you can wire the rest to a yacht broker in Miami. Naturally I'll want to check with him first before I leave the island. The name of the outfit is Florida Yacht Sales in Miami."

"All right." She shivered and crossed her arms over her breast and said, "I'm cold."

He did not answer. To hell with her, he thought. Let her sit there and think about the old man's will. That ought to keep her warm.

The breakers made a long mournful drumming on the beach. "I hate the sea," she said.

"I know. You told me."

"Why are you so hostile, Gus?"

"What am I supposed to be? It's a business proposition, isn't it?"

"Is there anything else we have to discuss then?"

"Just the money. When do I get it?"

"Surely you don't think I keep that kind of money in the house."

"Well, is it someplace you can get it in a hurry and where it can't be traced?"

"It's in a private vault in the local bank. I can get it tomorrow after the bank opens. There is no way it can be traced because no one knows how much I have in there."

"Then we'll do it this way. I'll make the date with Gwen for the day after tomorrow. You meet me here tomorrow night at this same time with the money."

She rose to her feet and hesitated a moment before asking lightly, "Do you want to walk back with me?"

"No."

"The house is empty and the girl won't be back until morning. No one will see us."

"Let's stick to business," he said.

When she was gone he sat there in the dark. In his mind he went over and over again the details of the plan, trying to think where it might go wrong. There were any number of places where it could fail. The plan itself was all right but it was dependent on weather and timing and, most of all, on an intangible human element. Still, with any luck he could pull it off. Twenty thousand. A lot of money. Would she really pay up? He didn't trust her any farther than he could throw her but he thought she would pay up all right. When he came back without the girl she would be happy to pay up just to get rid of him. Even an icicle like Clare Loomis wouldn't try to pull a fast one in the face of murder.

CHAPTER SIX

Robinson had his breakfast early and left the house while Walker was still asleep. He went first to the airline office and made a reservation on the flight to Miami for the following day. Then he went to the small combination hardware and grocery store and bought a tarp, a flashlight, a blanket, several yards of mosquito netting, a five-gallon jeep can for gasoline and a dozen cans of various kinds of food. He instructed the clerk to hold the purchases until they were picked up and then he walked down to the dock and borrowed a Bahamas chart from one of the charter boat skippers and spent twenty minutes studying the various shoal depths around Spanish Cay.

When he had completed these preparations he called Gwen and arranged to take her sailing the following day.

After his call to Gwen he returned to the house and spent much of the afternoon walking on the beach. Walker had gone out to dinner with friends, which made it easier for Robinson to leave the house after dark in time for his appointment with Clare.

He waited for her at the wreck. She was late. When she finally did come there were no greetings exchanged between them.

"Well?" she asked. "Is it tomorrow?"

"Yes."

"What time?"

"She's picking me up at around ten. I'll sail close to the beach so that you can see us clearly from your terrace. I'll probably even wave at you just to prove how sociable I am."

"And when will you come back?"

He shrugged. "Who knows? It may be late in the afternoon or even after dark. You'll just have to keep your eyes peeled for the boat."

"Why do you think it will take so long?"

"I don't know how long it will take. I'll pick my own time and place and I don't want to be bound by any schedule."

"All right, Gus. All right. You don't have to be so tough about it."

"Don't I? Do you think you hire boy scouts for this kind of work?"

"So you're no boy scout," she said with a conciliatory gesture. "What will you do with her boat?"

"I'll leave it on the beach. Have you got the money?"

She thrust a bulky envelope at him. He took it and put it into his pocket.

"Don't you want to count it, Gus?"

"I trust you."

She laughed and said, "You're a poor fool if you do. You won't find any ten thousand dollars there. Did you think I'd be idiotic enough to hand over that kind of money in advance? No, I'm willing to risk a thousand but no more. Take it or leave it."

To her surprise he did not argue. All he said was, "Okay. We'll play it your way. I'll take the thousand."

"And that brings up something else. You wanted me to send the rest of it on to Florida but that's absolutely out. There's no way that can be done without a record of the transaction showing up somewhere and I won't go for that. I don't want my name connected with yours in any way. There's got to be no way in the world anybody can ever prove I gave you a dime."

"What do you want to do then?"

"I'll give you the nineteen thousand in cash right here on the beach when you're finished."

"I just hope you don't get any bright ideas like having me arrested at the airport for stealing your money."

"Do you really think I want to get mixed up in a murder investigation for a miserable twenty thousand dollars? You underestimate me, Mr. Robinson. I assure you that when this is over the last thing in the world I would want would be to detain you at Spanish Cay. But that brings up another point. You can't just ditch the boat and take off. They'll be after you like a shot. No one can get away with a thing like that. They'll have the FBI waiting for you at the Miami airport. No, there's got to be some other way."

"There is another way," he said. "I've been thinking about it and you're right. That would be too messy. But how does it sound if no one knows I was ever in the boat with her. That way when she fails to come back they'll simply assume she had an accident at sea, which can happen anytime to somebody sailing alone. And they won't have a reason in the world to connect me with her disappearance. How does that sound?"

"It's a neat trick if you can do it but I'm damned if I see how you can get her out in the boat with you without anybody else knowing."

"She'll go out alone. I'll meet her later where no one can see us. And the way I'll manage that is to rent a skiff and tell them I'm going out to hunt for the wreck of the *Charee*."

"I can shoot holes in that one easily enough," she said. "All she has to do is to mention to someone that she's meeting you out there and your goose will be cooked when she doesn't come back."

"She won't mention it to anyone. That's where your pretty boy Dino comes in handy."

"What has Dino got to do with it?"

"He's having an affair with her and if he thinks she's out sailing alone with me he'll raise the devil of a row. He has already paid me a visit to tell me in an indirect way to keep hands off her. All I have to do is to point out to her that it will be much better for her love life if nobody knows she was out with me. It's a little secret we'll keep between the two of us."

"Do you really think she'll swallow that?"

"Why not? She's a sensible girl. I'm sure she hates scenes."

"And how will you get back?"

"I'll bring both boats back here after dark. I'll leave her sailboat right here on the beach. That will make the whole thing even more convincing. She fell overboard and the boat got away from her and drifted in here to shore. In the morning I'll take the skiff back to the boat livery and tell them it was late when I got back and that I tied it up for the night at the fishing pier. That way nobody can ever find a connection between us."

"It's too risky. It depends too much on luck."

"Have you got a better idea?" he asked flatly. "And just remember that we don't have much time to fool around. She's leaving next week. After that it's all over. But if you want to forget the whole thing it's all right with me. It's not exactly my idea of a honeymoon, you know."

"It's just that you're rushing me. You've gotten so damned bloodthirsty all of a sudden."

He stood up and said, "Let's get this straight, Clare. The whole thing was your idea, not mine. I have nothing against the girl." He tossed the envelope down on the sand beside her and said, "There's your thousand bucks. Now let's just forget we met."

He had taken half a dozen steps before he heard her voice calling after him, "Gus. Wait."

"What is it?"

She handed him the envelope.

"What does that mean?" Robinson asked. "That you want to go ahead with it?"

"Yes."

"Then I'll see you here tomorrow night at the same time."

His voice was like stone. She could barely make him out in the darkness but he looked enormous. Somehow their roles had been reversed. It was he, now, who was dominating the situation. For the first time she felt a nip of fear. Given a good enough reason he would not mind killing her too.

CHAPTER SEVEN

The skiff was twelve feet long and painted blue and white. Hung on the transom was an eighteen-horse Evinrude. The bugger should move, Robinson thought.

Up forward, covered by the tarp, were the supplies he had bought the day before. Beside him was an extra five-gallon can of gas. As he crossed the lagoon under half throttle he gazed up at the sky. Cloudless. As close to a dead calm as you ever got in these waters. There would be a little wind when the sun was well up but not much. A perfect day for piracy, kidnapping, murder, and playing games with an ageing nymphomaniac. Augustus, I salute you. The gods of crime seem to be looking for you with favor this day.

He stayed on the range going down the channel and when he had crossed the sandbar the open sea was before him. Except for a big sports fisherman trolling for marlin some miles to the westward, he was alone on the ocean. He kept his eye on the boat until he saw that it was heading south toward Gun Cay. That was fine. In twenty minutes it would be out of sight.

Robinson ran out until he was well offshore, then cut the motor and got out his rented tackle and pretended to fish. That was part of the act too; there was no use in having anybody wonder just what the hell he was doing out there. Two hours passed slowly and by that time the breeze had freshened to a gentle three or four knots. At nine o'clock, coming steadily on the outgoing tide, he made out the tip of a sail moving above the fringe of vegetation that outlined the southern tip of the island. When it had cleared the point it swung north and he had a clear view of it and he could see that it was Gwen's Lightning. Although it was still a long way off he could see her sitting alone in the stern sheets. A nice child. Comes to her assignations alone and on time as ordered. If Clare is watching she must be very happy.

Gwen tacked across the channel into deeper water and when she was past the bar she came neatly about and headed north on a broad reach. It was a good point of sailing and would take her parallel to the beach and not much more than a quarter of a mile to seaward. In an hour or so she would be approaching the northern tip of the island which was low and swampy and hidden by a fringe of pine. Because of the low ground and the mosquitoes there was no habitation on the northern tip and he had already decided to meet her there.

From where he sat in the slowly drifting boat he had a good view of Clare's house. He watched it carefully. At first there was no sign of life, but then he saw a splinter of light from the terrace. When it came again he grinned wolfishly. The sun was being reflected from a lens. Some-body at the house was using binoculars. Clare was right on the ball.

He let Gwen get well up to the north before he cranked up his mo-tor and moved off on a course that would intercept her. He tried to make it look casual, moving slowly, leaving a trolling line over the stern. Gwen saw him coming when he was still some distance off and waved happily at him. Since he was now hidden by the fringe of trees from anybody watching on shore he could afford to wave back. Ten min-utes later he was alongside, eyes sparkling with excitement.

As she took the line from the skiff she said, "This is all darned mys-terious, Gus."

"Don't you like mysteries?"

"I love them, but where are we going?"

"Wait and see."

He took the helm and let the sails fill away. Even with the skiff trail-ing behind the Lightning moved smoothly. "You might trim that jib sheet a bit," he said.

"Aye, aye, sir."

His course was straight out to sea. Spanish Cay dropped away behind them until only the tip of the radio tower was visible.

Gwen's face wore a puzzled frown when she turned to him at last and said, "Gus. Where are we going?"

"Honey, I have bad news for you. It seems you're not going to win that race after all. In fact, you won't even be in it."

The day seemed endless to Clare. When the girl brought her tray out to the terrace Clare did not even bother to lower the binoculars. "Just leave it there," she snapped.

The girl put the tray on the table and stuck out her tongue at Clare. She did not like Mrs. Loomis and now the day was starting badly. Mrs. Loomis was obviously in a foul mood. When her boss, Mr. Carpenter, had gone off skiing and told her he was lending the house to his friend Mrs. Loomis, Lisa had welcomed the change. Mr. Carpenter was a bachelor and threw a lot of wild parties and usually had the place in an awful mess. It would be nice to work for a lady for a change.

At first Mrs. Loomis had seemed very kind and charming but that had soon changed. Now she was nervous as a wet cat. It probably had something to do with that boy Dino. They said he was a painter but Lisa had seen his type before and they didn't make their living painting. A couple of times she had seen Mrs. Loomis giving him money. And the way that bedroom looked in the morning you could tell they hadn't been holding any art classes in there. And it wasn't only the bedroom. Like when she had come in a few days ago and found sand and water all over the kitchen floor. And that floor had been neat as a pin when she left it the night before. You could see that somebody had tried to clean up the mess but they hadn't done much of a job. Running around the beach at night. Probably without any clothes on. Something funny going on all right.

There had probably been a lot of funny things in Mrs. Loomis' life. Like the story that her husband had killed himself. Shot himself through the head. Man doesn't shoot himself unless his wife gives him good reason.

Mrs. Loomis was still looking through the binoculars. Without lowering them she snapped, "Well what are you hanging around for? Don't you have work to do?"

"Yes'm."

"Then get on with it."

Before leaving the terrace she tried to see what it was out there that had Mrs. Loomis so interested. Standing in the doorway and looking past Mrs. Loomis' shoulder she searched carefully over the broad expanse of ocean but all she could see was the far-off white rectangle of a little sailboat.

When the boat was out of sight Clare put down the glasses and had her coffee. The coffee had gone cold and bitter. She lit a cigarette and smoked half, then threw the rest away and immediately lit another. Despite the brilliant sun light on the terrace she felt cold. Freezing. Her hands were damp with nervous perspiration. She wanted to scream. To throw something. To strike out. She would like to go in right now and smack that silly Lisa in the face. Or she would like to be in bed with Dino. Damn Dino anyway. Why wasn't he here when she needed him? Didn't he know she was doing all this for him? No, how could he? And it was better that he was not here. She had to get a grip on herself. It wouldn't do, if questions were asked, for people to remember that she had been close to the screaming meemies this day.

She left the terrace and went through the bedroom to the bath and got out the plastic bottle of little pink pills and popped one into her mouth. It would take twenty minutes to half an hour for the pill to take effect. In the meantime she must keep calm. Stop pacing. That black slut is watching. She hates you and she would like nothing better than to get you into trouble. Lie down on the bed. Put a damp towel over your forehead. Close your eyes.

For no good reason at all she began to think about Harry Loomis. She had not really thought much about Harry in a long time. Not really since his death. And certainly she had never grieved over him, although she had managed to work up a few tears at the funeral. What a filthy, gray, rainy day that had been. It had been raining all that week in London with Harry unshaven and sitting in his dressing gown hunched over a gas fire in that wretched hotel. For a solid week he had refused to leave the room. He wouldn't go any where or see anyone. He had just sat there, a damp, flabby little man come to the end of his rope.

How quickly he went downhill. With the loss of the Wilhelm property Harry's world just fell apart. Money was the key to Harry's personality and when he lost his money be lost all his guts at the same time.

But she could still remember how he had looked that first time she saw him on board the liner. A square-shouldered cocky little fellow full of confidence and all decked out in a double-breasted blue yachting blazer and cream-colored pants, and white shoes. She could remember watching him and thinking how after she married him she would have to teach him about clothes. The only people who still wore white shoes and yachting blazers on board a transatlantic liner were hardware merchants from Massillon, Ohio, who had been reading the whiskey ads in the *New Yorker*.

Harry Loomis was her target and she proceeded to hunt him down with all the skill acquired by long practice at the game. It had been pitifully easy. She had tipped the dining-room steward twenty-five dollars to seat her next to Mr. Loomis and that night she had worn one of her lowest cut gowns. Poor Harry never had a chance. When he thought no one was looking his eyes remained fastened on her bosom. She had let him soak all that in before she said, "I'll tell you a little secret, Mr. Loomis. I bribed the steward to put me at your table. In fact, the only reason I'm on this ship at all is because of you."

"I'm afraid I don't understand."

"It's very simple. There was an article about you last month in *Fortune*. I read it and liked what I read. It described you as one of the most imaginative, daring and successful of our younger businessmen. I made up my mind then to meet you and when I heard that you were sailing for Europe I booked passage on the same ship. So there it is. Do I shock you?" She had decided that a direct approach with Loomis would be the best bet. He would be overwhelmingly flattered.

"But I still don't understand. Why were you so anxious to meet me?"

"Because I intend to marry you." She drew a deep breath and let his eyes linger on her half revealed breasts. She was not wearing a brassiere and she knew that if she leaned over a little more he could see almost to her nipples. His face was flushed and he seemed to be having a little difficulty with his breathing. That was perhaps the last time she ever told him the whole truth about anything.

The second night out she slept with him and it was a revelation to the pudgy little man, who had certainly never known anything like that in Massillon or even at the conventions in Pittsburgh or Los Angeles. He was enchanted by her intimate knowledge of international society. He counted himself the luckiest man on the ship, and for those few days he may well have been. By the time they reached Southampton he was mad to marry her. But she cleverly put him off for a week with a carefully calculated program designed to make him sweat. And sweat he did while he showered her with gifts from the best shops in London. At the end of the week she gave in and married him.

Two weeks later, at the Negresco in Cannes, with Harry still floating on a sea of sex and champagne, she introduced him to her old and good friend Max Wilhelm.

What Harry Loomis was to Massillon, Ohio, Wilhelm was to the world. International finance. Cartels. Holdings in the Congo and West Germany and the Argentine. Nickel. Cattle. Copper. Oil. Land. Nothing was too big for Wilhelm. What was he interested in just now? Why he was playing around with a little project in the British West Indies. He had bought an island in the Bahamas. That was certainly the coming area for people in the know. Florida was dead now. The Bahamas had everything. In the age of jet planes you were only a few hours from New York, and look at the advantages. No taxes. Cheap help. Free port. It was one of the last places left for a gentleman, where the mobs traveling on the installment plan had not yet taken over. The hotel would be the center of it, but there would be a big development of private homes as well. And a marina for yachtsmen with a deep-water channel all the way. The secret was exclusivity. You had to keep it restricted to the very best people—the Vanderbilts, the Woolworths, Lord and Lady Docket. How could it miss?

No, we don't need your money, old man. Money is no consideration at all. Our corporate structure is quite complete. Sir William Braden is chairman of the board. You don't know Sir William? Pity. Well perhaps as a favor to me and because your charming lady seems so anxious about it we might let you in for a small amount. Say a million or so. In the meantime I'll leave the prospectus with you. By all means take your time. I'll try to prevail upon Sir William to hold off for a week while you think it over.

Two very big things happened to Harry that week. The first was that he gave Max Wilhelm a check for one million dollars entitling him to shares in the Wilhelmville development. The second big thing happened when he came back unexpectedly from a round of golf and found his beautiful new wife in bed with a man.

It had occurred to him, while he was on the course, there were certain very valuable contributions he could make regarding the installation of plumbing in the new hotel. So enthused had he become that he could not wait to finish the round. Instead he had hurried up to Wilhelm's room to discuss his ideas. He bad knocked but there was no answer. Acting on one of those small inexplicable impulses that alter the courses of all our lives, he had tried the door. It had swung open and, thinking Wilhelm might be in the shower, he was had stepped into the suite. The bedroom door was open and he could see straight through, and what he saw struck him like an explosion. A woman, fair-haired and nude, was sitting upright in the middle of the bed with her back to him and beneath her he could see the long hairy legs and broad chest of Max Wilhelm. There was a mirror behind the headboard and in it he could clearly see his wife's face. At that moment Clare raised her head and her eyes met his. She screamed....

The pink pill was taking effect now. She was no longer so nervous. Strange that she should remember all this about Harry now when she hadn't thought about it for so long....

After she had screamed Harry had rushed out of the room. She had tried to find him but he had left the hotel. And an hour later Max Wilhelm had checked out without a word to her.

Three days later Harry came back. He was red-eyed and unshaven and his clothes were stained with vomit and spilled liquor. She had half expected him to beat her but instead he had wept. She had felt nothing for him then but hatred and contempt.

When Harry had sobered up he tried desperately to stop the check he had given Wilhelm but it had already cleared the bank. A month later the Wilhelmville bubble had burst. Several prominent people were caught in the scandal, among them Sir William Braden who had apparently been used as a front by Wilhelm. Wilhelm himself was said to be somewhere in British Columbia. Others said he had fled to Rio to escape extradition.

Four months later, in that small room in London with the never-ending rain streaking the window, Harry Loomis—erstwhile king of a small plumbing empire and a man whose profile had once appeared in *Fortune* magazine—blew his brains out. Investigation showed that there was not much left of his once tidy fortune. His widow was able to recover only thirty or forty thousand dollars from the wreckage of his affairs.

Clare slept fitfully. When she awoke and looked at her watch she saw that two hours had passed. Was it over? Was Gwen dead, sinking down through the green water? Clare felt no pity for her, any more than she had ever felt pity for Harry Loomis. What she preferred to think of was Dino. Dino would never leave her now. Money was the chain with which she would hold him. She would buy him what he wanted but never too much at one time. And never enough cash so that he felt independent. Oh, she knew how to handle him all right. And with Dino by her side she could preserve the illusion of youth. In a year or two she would go to the best plastic surgeon, that man in London who hid the scars behind the hair line. And later, when her breast began to sag too much, she would have an operation to restore their shape. With massage and watching her diet and not drinking too much and the proper amount of sex she could keep going for a long time.

The day dragged on. The house was very still. Lisa stayed in the kitchen, out of Clare's way. Every few minutes Clare would pick up the binoculars and sweep the horizon, but no sail showed. At last, when it was too dark to see anything any more, she put the binoculars away.

Her impatience was now almost uncontrollable. An hour before the time she had arranged to meet Robinson she was waiting at the old wreck. She kept staring out to seaward until her eyes and head ached, but in the blackness sea and sky seemed to merge together. It was past the time he had said now and there was still no sign of him. Twice she thought she heard the sound of a motor and she waited feverishly, but no boat appeared. The sense of panic mounted. What had gone wrong? Well, if he talked no one would believe him and there was no way anything could be traced back to her. She had covered all her tracks.

She took a firmer grip on herself. There might be some simple explanation; everything might yet come out all right Perhaps his motor had failed on the way back. She understood that outboard motors were chancy little devils. In that case he would have to sail back in Gwen's boat. That could account for everything.

Twenty agonizing minutes later she distinctly heard the sound of a motor. A moment later the sound stopped, to be followed almost immediately by the grinding of a prow on sand. She ran down to the water's edge. It was the skiff all right and behind it, roped astern, was the sailboat.

Robinson stepped out into the shallow water and pulled the bow of the skiff higher onto the beach. "Hello, Clare," he said.

She made an effort to control her impatience but even so her voice was shrill when she asked, "Did it go all right?"

"Sure it did. Were you worried?" His voice mocked her.

"Did she... struggle?"

"You don't really want all the pretty details, do you? As you can see, I got rid of her. Let's just let it go at that. The less you know about it the better. Did you bring the money?"

She handed him the envelope.

"This time I'll count it," he said.

She waited while he bent down behind the skiff and flicked a cigarette lighter and counted the bills.

"It's all there," she said.

"So I see."

He tucked the envelope into his shirt pocket and then waded out to the stern of the skiff and untied the sailboat and drew it in toward shore.

"Are you leaving it here?" she asked.

"It's as good a place as any. The way the wind is this is just about where she might have drifted to with the sheet loose and the boom swinging free."

"What about our footprints? They'll see that people have been around the boat."

"So what? Anybody might have stopped to take a look. Besides, it's low tide now. When the tide rises it will wipe out most of the prints."

They stood there for a moment in silence and then she said, "Are you taking the morning plane?"

"Yes."

"Then I guess we won't be seeing each other again."

"I guess not." The conversation of two murderers on a beach at midnight, he thought. As prosaic as buying a pound of salami. Well, what had he expected, some slight show of remorse on Clare's part? You might as well look for pity from a black widow spider. The bitch was like ice. Curiously enough, what bothered him most of all now was the knowledge that he had once made love to this woman.

"Good-bye," he said.

"Good-bye."

He pushed the skiff out and turned it around and drew it out into the deeper water. A moment later she heard the sound of the motor. She listened to it until it faded out and was gone.

She turned and began the long walk back to the house. She was cold and to keep herself from shivering she hugged herself with both arms as she walked.

CHAPTER EIGHT

The plane from Nassau was late. Robinson sat in the tin-roofed shack and looked out at the concrete landing strip alive with heat devils. "How much longer?" he asked the girl clerk behind the counter.

The pretty girl in the sky-blue airlines uniform shook her head and said, "I'm sorry, sir, but we can't be sure. The last word we had was that they were having a little trouble with the port engine but that they expected to take off any time now. But once they're in the air it won't take them more than half an hour to get here. Have you checked your luggage, sir?"

He shook his head. "I have no luggage."

"Oh? Traveling light."

"You could call it that," he said, thinking of the twenty thousand in the envelope buttoned inside his shirt pocket.

The girl stared at him curiously. He got up and went outside and stood in the blaze of morning sun, smoking a cigarette. Two men wearing short-sleeved shirts and straw hats passed him and went into the shack. One of them had the flat cold eyes of a policeman. He gave Robinson a passing glance. Robinson felt his muscles tense. But the man was carrying an attaché case, and in the other hand was a wicker basket of rum. Policemen did not carry attaché cases and baskets of rum. And anyway, no one could have found out yet what he had done with the girl. He forced himself to relax.

There had been a bad moment with Stanley Walker earlier in the day when they had said good-bye. Stanley had looked at him out of his poached-egg eyes and asked, "Where are you going from here, Gus?"

"I don't know yet, Stanley. I'll make up my mind after I get to Miami," he had answered cautiously.

"Gus..."

"Yes?"

"Take me with you."

"What do you mean?"

Tears formed in Walker's eyes and dribbled slowly down his cheeks into his untouched plate of bacon and eggs. "I feel so alone, Gus. When you're gone there won't be anybody. Not a friend in the world."

"That's nonsense, Stanley. You've got dozens of friends here. Your house is crowded with them all the time."

Walker shook his head sadly. "Do you think these people are my friends? They're not. They come here to drink my whiskey and to laugh at me. Stanley, the clown. Good old Stanley. Give him one more and he'll stand on his head or fall into the swimming pool or pass out under a table. Old Stanley is always good for a laugh. Don't you think I know how they really feel about me?"

"Why don't you stop drinking then?"

"For what? What else is there in my life? You've got to help me, Gus."

"How can I help you? What would you do if you came with me?"

"I don't know. I thought... well I thought we could buy a boat together. I mean I'd put up the money for it and you'd run it. We could go anywhere you'd like. Anywhere you'd go if you were alone. Oh hell, Gus, I don't care where we go just so it's someplace warm and where the seas aren't too big and where we can get ashore now and then for a drink. I've got to give up this way of life and I haven't got the guts to do it myself. But with your help I could. With your help I could make it. You've got to do this for me, Gus. If I go on this way I'm just waiting to be shoveled into the grave."

"But why do you want to go off on a boat? You're not in shape for it. You told me yourself you get seasick. If you want to get away why not just go to a hotel somewhere?"

"Because that won't accomplish anything. If I sit alone in a hotel room I'll either jump out the window or wind up downstairs at the bar." Walker's hands were trembling. His eyes were like those of a sick dog. "I thought maybe if I got off on a boat where I was really up against it and where there wasn't any booze around I could make it. You could force me to make it. Please, Gus."

Robinson shook his head. "It wouldn't work, Stanley. Going to sea in a small boat in bad weather can be the most rugged experience a man can endure. You're in no shape for it. It would kill you. And anyway," he added brutally, wanting to end it, "I wouldn't have the time or the inclination to nurse you. I hate to say it, but I suspect that what you need is a doctor, Stanley, not a sea voyage in a small boat."

Walker's eyes filled with tears again. Suddenly he got up from the table and left the room. Robinson waited until Thomas came back and asked, "Is he all right?"

"He'll be all right after a while," Thomas said.

"Then I'll leave now."

"He'll be out soon."

"No, it's better this way. You say good-bye for me."

When he left the house he had felt like a thief. He had not taken anything from Walker except the last of his pride, and God knew there was little enough of that....

He re-entered the shack and heard the girl say, "... it's just awful. And they haven't even found the body yet."

"When did it happen?" the man with the attaché case asked.

"Sometime yesterday. She went out early in the morning and she was gone all day and then someone found her boat washed up on the beach this morning. There's nothing wrong with the boat so they figure she just fell overboard and wasn't able to get back."

"That's awful. That's an awful way to die. But she was really asking for it going out alone like that. Me, I'll stick to Chris-Crafts. To hell with sailboats. How old was she?"

"About my age, I think."

"But not as pretty I'll bet," the other man said.

"I don't know. They tell me she was really beautiful."

"Listen, honey, don't you ever get over to Miami?"

"Sometimes I do. Sometimes I get a free ride over."

"Next time you get over to Miami you give me a ring. I'm at the Dupont Plaza. You give me a ring and we'll go out on the town. I'll show you the best time you ever had. We've got a lot in common, kid."

"Do we?"

"Yes, sir," he repeated, staring at her with heavy significance. "A lot in common."

"I wonder what it is."

"That's what we'll find out, honey."

At last the plane, a rather small twin-engined British job, something like the old DC3s, dropped down onto the runway and taxied to a stop in front of the shack. The passengers, led by the pretty girl in blue, trooped out toward the plane. Several of them looked curiously at Robinson—a big, gaunt man in faded khaki and battered sneakers and without any hand luggage.

He took a seat in the rear, fastened his seat belt and concealed his face behind a newspaper left behind by one of the passengers who had come in from Nassau. He felt reasonably secure now, but still one never knew. Despite all his careful planning something might have gone wrong. Yet the conversation of the airlines clerk seemed to indicate that everything was in order. They had found the boat and they believed she had fallen overboard. The pressure of the heavy envelope in his pocket was reassuring. There were times when he was inclined to believe that the whole Spanish Cay experience—beginning with the loss of the ketch and the long swim ashore and ending with the last voyage with Gwen—was nothing more than a strange dream. But the money was tangible. It had all happened.

Through his small round window he could see the pilot smoking a cigarette and chatting with the airlines girl in the doorway of the shack. The minutes dragged on. It was stifling in the plane. The passengers sat in a brooding aura of mounting anger. Finally the engines turned over, crackled once or twice and then caught. The plane turned around and taxied down the runway and turned into the wind and came roaring back and lifted easily over the channel, and after that they were climbing over the southern tip of the island and there was only the blue sea beyond.

They were flying parallel to the beach now and he could see Stanley Walker's house and the wreck on the beach and beyond it Clare's place. He examined the house carefully as they flew by but there was no sign of life on the terrace. Somehow he had imagined that she might be out there with her binoculars trained on the plane.

Then the tip of the island was behind them and the white houses and the fringe of pines and the curling line of surf. Far off to port, looking like a chalk line scribbled on the vast blue cardboard of the sea, was a tiny spit of sand. He craned his neck to watch it as they swung by but at that height it was impossible for him to see if there was any living thing on it.

The sand spit Robinson had observed from the plane window was not more than seventy-five yards long and fifteen yards wide. At no point did it rise more than three or four feet above the level of the sea. In August and September when the great storms come boiling up out of the overheated air above the Caribbean it was often entirely awash. Now it lay dead as a stranded whale. Not a single blade of grass punctuated its bone-white length.

There was, however, one living thing on this rib of sand. Gwen Leacock sat in the shade of the green tarp Robinson had rigged for her. She was reading a paperback novel and eating out of a cold can of so-called Chinese chop suey. Beside her, half buried in the sand to keep it cool, was a five-gallon jeep can filled with drinking water.

She looked up to see a flock of birds milling over bait in the water. Suddenly the water boiled; something was driving a school of small fish to the surface and the birds were attacking them from above. A big fin slashed like a sabre across the living carpet that agitated the water. The birds swooped screaming to the attack. At that moment, without warning, a hole seemed to open in the sea and out of its depths shot a great black and silver shape with spread dorsal and armored forehead. It hung for a moment in the foreign element, spear gleaming, and then dropped down with a mighty crash. She stared at it in astonishment, heart pounding. She had seen marlin before but never this close and never so unexpectedly. She waited for the fish to burst into the air again but it was gone.

Then she heard the plane. She ducked out from under the tarp and shaded her eyes against the sun. The silver bug in the sky was far off but she recognized it as the Miami-bound plane and knew that Gus was aboard. Could he see her? She stood waving until the plane was gone and then went back to her book.

But it was hard to concentrate. The glimpse of the plane and the knowledge that Gus might have seen her waving at him were too exciting. It brought back the sound of his voice, the odor of his sun-warmed flesh and the great strength of his arm as he had carried her back to the blanket. She was able to relive again that revelatory moment on the beach when the delicious warmth of fulfillment had coursed all through her veins like wine. She was still a little sore from it. Her thighs ached. But even the soreness was sweet to her now. She felt so marvelously alive. All her nerve ends seemed to be playing tag with each other beneath her skin.

Had it all really happened as she remembered it? It seemed so impossible now. And yet here she was, marooned on this strip of sand in the middle of the ocean. That part was certainly real. And the lovemaking had been real enough too, as vouched for by all the delicious sensations that still seemed to wing through her body. She put down the book and began to go over the whole thing again from the beginning....

She had taken the Lightning out to sea as he had directed her until she had seen him coming in the blue and white skiff. She headed the Lightning up into the wind and let it lie that way until he was alongside.

"Hello Gus," she called out. "Any luck?"

"Just a couple of mackerel."

"I despise fish."

"That's too bad. I thought we might have them for lunch."

"Raw? I don't think even Gus Robinson is that rugged."

"Well, we'll see. We might go ashore somewhere to build a fire. "

He tied the skiff behind and took the helm and headed the Lightning seaward. As she looked back at the skiff she saw that he had a tarp in the bow and what appeared to be several packages under it.

"This is all pretty mysterious, Gus," she said.

"Don't you like mysteries?"

"Up to a point, but I still like to know where I'm going."

"Wait and see, Gwen."

The land fell away behind them. She closed her eyes, relaxing to the motion of the boat. When she looked back again she could barely make out the tip of the radio tower. The muted alarm bell that had been ringing in her mind for the past hour let out a shrill clang.

She sat up straight and said, "Gus. I want to know where we're going."

He was clearly not joking when be answered, "Honey, I have bad news for you. You're not going to win that race after all. In fact you won't even be in it."

"What are you talking about?"

He sighed and said, "It's a pretty involved story, Gwen, and you may have a little trouble believing it at first but the plain fact is I took you out here to kill you."

"I like you, Gus, but I don't think much of your sense of humor. I've always hated practical jokers."

"I can assure you, Gwen, that I've never been more serious in my life."

It was beginning to get through to her now. He *was* serious. That explained all the mysterious preparations, the secrecy, his insistence that she not tell Dino anything about it.

Her voice was very small when she said, "Why would you want to kill me?"

He smiled at her and leaned forward to pat her arm. She shrank away. He said, "Don't worry. I have no intention of killing you or anybody else."

"Then why are you acting so crazy? Why are you telling me all this?"

"Because I'm going to ask you to help me, but before I do I want you to understand how serious the whole thing is. When I tell you I was hired to kill you I mean just that. Do you believe me?"

"I suppose so, but who would want to see me dead?"

"Clare."

"Oh, that's ridiculous."

"Is it?" He reached into his pocket and took out the envelope. "There's the thousand dollars she gave me as a down payment. I'm supposed to get another nineteen thousand after I finish the job."

"But you don't even know Clare. You only met her that one time at Stanley's house."

"We've been meeting secretly. It began that first night when I was washed ashore."

She sat very still while he told her the whole story. The only thing he left out was the fact that he and Clare had gone to bed together. That part of it seemed to have no bearing on anything that had followed.

"But I still don't understand why Clare would want me dead," she said at last. "Is she crazy?"

"She may be a little crazy. But on top of that she's a coldhearted conniving bitch who will stop at nothing to get what she wants."

"What is it she wants?"

He told her about the will and about Dino.

"But any relationship between Clare and Dino was over long ago," she said.

"Clare doesn't seem to think so."

"And how could she know about my father's will?"

"I gather she had a brief affair with one of the attorneys who drew it up."

"Oh that's fantastic."

"Is it? Don't underestimate her. When she turns on the heat your cousin Clare could seduce an angel. Delilah wasn't in the same league with our dear Mrs. Loomis."

She looked around her at the limitless expanse of sea and said, "All right. I believe you. What happens now?"

"I have a proposition for you."

Her courage had returned. She said contemptuously, "I suppose you want me to beat Clare's price, is that it? All right, Mr. Robinson. How much is my life worth? I don't know what the going price is on kidnapping."

"You're not kidnapped and I don't want a dime from you."

"Isn't my money as good as Clare's?"

"Look, I'm working a con game with Clare. I'm planning to cheat her and I haven't a scruple in the world about it because I don't mind cheating a psychopathic bitch who cold-bloodedly planned a murder for profit. And apart from that, if she gets her comeuppance this time she'll be finished. She'll never have the guts or the money to try it again. Particularly after she knows that you know. So just climb down off your high horse and listen to me carefully and then when I'm finished if you want me to take you back I will. All right?"

"Do I have a choice?"

"Of course you have a choice. I'll head straight back now you say so."

She smiled for the first time since he had begun to talk and said, "I believe you would."

"Then you're willing to listen?"

"I'm willing to listen."

"To begin with I'm sorry I frightened you. But I had to do it that way in order to let you know that I'm absolutely serious. If I'd just sort of mentioned casually that your cousin Clare had hired me to drown you but that I'd figured out a way to outsmart her, you know how far we'd have gotten, Clare is a pretty shrewd cookie but in her hurry to get the job done she made two mistakes. First, she picked the wrong guy. And second, because she has no interest in the water, she never bothered to study a chart of the area surrounding Spanish Cay. Anyway, as the situation now stands I can't collect the rest of the money until I've satisfied Clare that you're dead. And short of her being there to see it with her own eyes there's no way I can do that except to take you out to sea and dump you. Clare knows I'm with you now. She had a pair of binoculars trained on us from her terrace this morning."

"I saw her," Gwen said. "I wondered what could possibly have gotten her up so early."

"That's what got her up all right, her hurry to see you dead. She'll be looking for me again tonight when I come back without you."

Gwen gazed around her at the open sea and said, "I don't understand. Do you really mean to go through with it after all, after everything you said?"

"Of course not." He pointed ahead of the boat and said, "Look. Look out there. Do you see anything?"

"Just an awful lot of water."

"Well look again. Over there to the northeast. Do you see something white?"

"It looks like surf."

"It is, and it's rolling up onto a spit of sand, a reef that just barely projects above the surface of the water. It's so small that the average person would never know anything about it unless he'd had occasion to study the charts very carefully. For that matter some of the older charts don't even show it. I happen to know about it because I knew I would be coming through here at night in *Charee* and I wanted to make damn sure of what was ahead of me. As soon as she made this proposition to me—that I take you sailing and knock you on the head and dump you overboard—I remembered this reef and realized how I could use it."

"You're planning to put me ashore there?"

"Yes."

"For how long?"

"Long enough to collect the money, fly to Miami, buy a boat and come back for you."

"But that might take days."

"Only four. A day for me to get to Miami and buy the boat. Another day to put her in shape for sea and two more days to get back to you. What do you say?"

"Just how badly do you need that money?"

"In the worst way, or I wouldn't be messing around with this lunacy at all. I've got to buy another boat and so far as I can see this is the only chance I'll ever have to put that many dollars together in the same place at the same time."

"And you won't consider taking the money from me?"

"Absolutely not."

"We could call it a loan."

"Call it what you like we'd both still know what it was for. You'd be buying your life back from me. I'm not in the business of selling lives."

"So you'd rather steal it from Clare."

"Yes."

"Good for you," she said laughing. "I think I like you, Mr. Robinson."

"Does that mean you'll go along with the idea?"

"I don't know yet. Don't rush me. Look, why do you have to maroon me in the middle of the ocean? Why can't you just take me back to Spanish Cay and I'll promise to stay out of sight until you get away?"

He shook his head. "I thought of that but it wouldn't work. Spanish Cay is too small and there are too many people on it. Somebody would be sure to spot you."

"But if she's waiting to give you the money as soon as you come back what difference would it make if she found out the truth after you were gone?"

"She'd never let me get away with it. The chances are she'd claim I held her up and stole the money. I'd be stopped here or in Miami."

"She could still do that even after you have your boat."

"It's not very likely. That would mean a wait of at least four days before reporting the theft and it wouldn't take a J. Edgar Hoover to know something was fishy with that. Once I have the boat it will be too late for her to do anything about it. What do you say, Gwen? Will you give it a whirl?"

"I'm not promising anything but I'll at least take a look at your desert island." He was, she realized, a disarmingly honest sort of pirate. He could just as easily have dumped her there by force if he had been so minded.

Thirty minutes later they were able to make out the thin white line of sand above the surf. When she saw how tiny it was her resolution began to fail.

Robinson looked at her and said, "Getting cold feet?"

"A little."

"I warned you it wasn't much."

"Maybe it looks bigger when you're ashore," she said hopefully.

Robinson let the Lightning slide up on the beach on the leeward side of the reef and drew the skiff up after it. He dropped the sail and dug the Lightning's anchor deep into the sand to hold her. Gwen stepped out and began to walk curiously along the thin strip of fine sand. When she returned he was unloading the skiff.

"This is a five-gallon can of water," he said. "As long as you don't decide to take a shower in it it will last a long time. And here's mosquito repellent, a flashlight, reading matter and an assortment of the finest imported foods recommended by *Gourmet* magazine for well stocked castaways."

"Chop suey. Ugh!"

"We also have beans and Spam. You couldn't do better at the Waldorf."

"What's this?" she asked holding up a package sealed in heavy Pliofilm.

"Those are flares."

"What are they for?"

"Just in case you get too unhappy about the whole thing. There are always yachts working down through Hog Island Channel, about five miles to the north. You can watch for their running lights at night and then shoot off a distress flare."

"I guess that would mean answering an awful lot of questions, wouldn't it?"

"I guess it would."

"And then, of course, the whole business about Clare having hired you would come out. I wouldn't want that. I wouldn't want my dad to know about it."

"Your dad will know about it anyway."

"Why?"

"You've got to tell him about it in order to make him change that will. As long as Clare stands to profit in any way by your death you won't be safe."

"I guess you're right. What about Dino?"

"What about him?"

"He'll be terribly worried."

"I'm sorry but I don't know that there's anything I can do about it," Robinson said.

"Couldn't you tell him the truth?"

"Absolutely not. He's entirely too chummy with Clare. It would only take one word to blow the whole thing out into the open and make the biggest scandal that ever hit Spanish Cay."

"But I can't have him thinking I'm dead."

"Don't you realize how close you *came* to being dead. This isn't kid stuff, Gwen. Your cousin Clare means business."

"But there's got to be some other way."

"There is no other way."

"Poor Dino."

Robinson did not say anything. He suspected that poor Dino would be well taken care of.

"How do you know you'll be back in four days, Gus?"

"Because I've told you I would be."

"But you know yourself that anything can happen on the water."

"Then you use the flares or hoist your undies upside down. Someone will pick you up. There's plenty of traffic in the general area; it's just that no one comes over here to the reef unless there's a special reason. But I tell you what I will do. If for any reason I'm more than twenty-four hours late I'll radio ahead to Spanish Cay and tell them to pick you up. However, there's still one serious loophole in the whole thing, one that I haven't been able to lick."

"What is it, Gus?"

"When you're reported missing they'll notify your father. I don't want to be responsible for throwing that kind of a scare into him."

"Poor Gus. Have you been racking your brain over that?"

"Yes."

"You're sweet."

"I've been called everything but that. And it wasn't so long ago that you were convinced I was a murderer."

"A sweet murderer. But you don't have to worry about Dad. He's out of the country. He's staying at a sanatorium in Switzerland. If they contact anyone it would be his attorney in New York."

"Is that the one who was involved with Clare?"

"No, this is Jess Holland, a very respectable married man. But he knows Clare and I know he doesn't like her. I think if you told him the whole story he'd believe you."

"All right. I'll call him from Miami."

"What happens if I get a burst appendix?"

"Are you apt to?"

"I never have."

"Then I suggest you forget it. But if you do get sick, use the flares. Look, you can even see Spanish Cay from here although they can't see you."

She could barely make out a dim bulge on the horizon and above it the fretwork of pine tops and the tip of the radio tower. It was faintly reassuring.

Robinson began setting up her camp. He found a few scraggly lengths of driftwood and rigged the tarp over them as a shelter. He then attached stakes to four short lengths of line and drove them deep into the sand to hold the tarp in place. All her supplies were placed on a blanket under the tarp. When he had finished, rivulets of sweat were running down his neck. He wiped his brow and said, "What about a swim?"

"No, I think I'd rather go to an air-conditioned movie."

"Wait four days and I'll buy you a lifetime pass to the neighborhood drive-in."

He stripped down to his trunks and dove into the clear green water. He swam out with slow powerful strokes and then rested on his back. "You don't know what you're missing," he called back to her.

She had been watching him thoughtfully. Her dark eyes seemed larger than ever in her small heart-shaped face. Slowly she unbuttoned her shirt and drew off her slacks. She stood there looking very small but beautifully formed in her lacy bra and panties. Her limbs were almost perfectly round and smoothly tanned. Robinson turned over and looked at her and his heart seemed to stand still. He thought he had never seen a human body quite so magnificently shaped. She reminded him of a dark-haired Javanese dancing girl he had once loved. The Javanese girl had possessed the same intriguing combination of childlike innocence and adult sensuality.

If Gwen was embarrassed by her near nudity she did not show it. She walked down to the water's edge and put one toe in. September Morn, thought Robinson sourly. That damned pimp Dino has taught her well. He turned over and dove beneath the surface and held his breath until he began to hear bells. When he finally came up he found her floating nearby.

"It's wonderful, Gus."

"That's right," he said trying not to look too hard at her firm young breasts which were clearly revealed by the wet bra.

She laughed at him and said, "This isn't doing much good, is it?" and reached behind her and unsnapped the hook and tossed the useless bit of silk up onto the sand. Her creamy breasts with their delicate pink nipples hardened by contact with the water jutted above the surface as she floated. Robinson did not think he could take much more. He turned over and dove again. He was close to her and he could clearly see her tanned thighs and white panties, her tiny waist and the darker triangle beneath the wet silk.

She was teasing him. It must run in the family. Damn all high-priced international whores anyway. Dino's words came back to him. "It is amazing with these shy little American girls. So carefully brought up. So proper. And when you turn them loose—bang! They can't seem to get enough." Well to hell with her. She was Dino's and he could have her. He swam to the beach and lay down on his belly with his eyes closed. When she came out of the water he did not turn to look at her.

Gwen went back to the tarp and shucked off her wet panties and pulled on her slacks and shirt. When she was dressed she walked back to the Lightning and got out a wicker basket that had been lying under the stern thwart. She walked back to Robinson with it and asked softly, "Asleep?"

"No," he answered in a surly voice.

"Care for some champagne?"

"Why not? And a shrimp cocktail and filet mignon while you're at it. Not too well done please."

The cork made an unmistakable pop. He opened his eyes and sat up. She was holding a beautifully iced bottle of champagne. Putting the bottle down beside him she reached into the insulated ice compartment in the basket and drew out two chilled, narrow stemmed glasses.

"Well I'll be damned," Robinson said. "Do you always travel this way?"

"I didn't know I was going to be murdered today but I did think I was going on a sailing party, so I came prepared."

She filled a glass and gave it to him, then filled her own and raised the rim to the level of her eyes and said, "To my assassin."

"To the victim."

The wine was superb. It was impossible to remain angry with her. To hell with Dino. Her hair was still wet and a drop of water glistened on her brown cheek. If she was a tart she was the most charming one he had ever imagined.

"I don't think the noonday sun is the best thing for champagne," she said. "Won't you step into my parlor?"

They walked back and sat on the blanket in the shade of the tarp. "I might even have some more goodies in this magic basket," she said. "We have a fair selection of hors d' oeuvres. Also ham and cheese sandwiches. What would you like?"

"And ruin the effect of good champagne? Let's worry about the food later."

The world had settled into a golden glow of light and shade and cool breeze and the murmur of surf on the beach. When he had imagined roaming the islands with Gwen it had been much like this. He reached across and kissed her softly on the cheek. She turned and put her mouth against his. Her lips tasted faintly of sun and salt.

"Gus," she said.

"Yes?"

"I think I love you."

"That's some champagne."

"I mean it."

"Are you sure you're not just thanking me for having refrained from clouting you on the head and kicking you overboard?"

"Do you want to know what I love about you?"

"Yes."

"I love the way you look and the way you taste and the way you talk and the way you don't really give a damn for the rest of the world. And I think I'm still a little afraid of you and maybe I love that too."

"We could have a lot of fun together."

"I know, darling."

She lay in his arms with her back against his shoulder and her head resting beneath his chin. Looking down he could not see her eyes but only her long delicate lashes. There are so many places I would like to show you, he wanted to say. Islands and sunsets and great purple seas without end. Mangareva and the Tuamotus and Papeete and God knows what else. Come with me, he wanted to say, it can be a better life than either of us have ever known.

He bent down and kissed her still damp hair.

"Touch me," she whispered up at him.

He put his big brown hand under her shirt on her warm belly. A shiver of excitement rippled her flesh. His hand moved up and cupped her naked breast and he felt the small nipple rigid against his palm. There seemed to be a roaring in his ears. Was it the wind or the champagne or the intoxication of so much beauty? He was aware that she had reached down and unzipped the slacks and rolled them down over her softly rounded hips.

She buried her face against his chest and murmured, "Gus, darling."

Her little brown fingers were everywhere. She was endlessly curious and provocative. With unspoken consent she arranged her body for him.

He bent over her. She cried out in pain. Astonished, he drew back. "Why didn't you tell me?" he asked.

"Does it matter?"

"Of course it matters. I thought that you and Dino..."

"Oh don't talk about Dino, darling. Please. Please."

When she moaned again he knew that this time she was not in pain.

While they slept, the sun had inched across the sky. Gwen stirred and kissed him lightly on the cheek and nibbled at his ear and said, "The champagne is all gone, my love."

"I'll run down to the corner grocery."

"And bring up the morning paper while you're at it."

"What about a swim?"

She leaped up and ran down to the edge. "Don't look at me that way, you lecherous old man," she called back at him. "Just because you've taken my virginity is no reason to get any funny ideas."

"I've got all kinds of funny ideas."

"So have I, darling."

He dove in after her and they floated together in the sun-warmed shallows. She lay lightly on his arm and when she turned to kiss him he rested one knee on the bottom and supported her with the other.

"Have you ever made love in the water?" she asked.

"No," he lied.

"You've never really made love to any other girl, isn't that so?"

"That's right."

"Oh you're such a liar."

"Yes."

"I hate the idea of your being with someone else."

"There is no one else," he said. "And if we don't think about it there never has been. We're all alone on the edge of the world and if we're not careful we'll fall off."

"I want to fall off. I want to..."

"Hey. What do you think you're doing down there?"

"Searching for underwater sea life."

"Find anything?"

"Why yes. There are all sorts of interesting things. For instance there's an enormous... Ah, Gus. Darling, darling."

Toward evening he collected driftwood and built a small fire and cooked dinner for her. She had been going over the canned goods he had brought her and she said, "You must think I have a passion for spaghetti and meatballs. Was that all they had?"

"There are beans. Don't overlook the beans."

She made a wry face and said, "Four days of this and I'll have as much shape as a tube of toothpaste. I think I'll change my mind and go back with you."

"There's some canned hamburger too. That ought to make a difference. Anyway, I'll make it up to you on the new boat. Fresh oysters and champagne all the way to Panama and through the canal and across the Pacific. And when we get to Papeete I'll hire one of those coffee-colored French chefs for you."

She did not return his smile. Instead she got up and walked away and stood for a moment on the tip of the sandbar, looking out at the darkening sea and the first faint star. When she returned her face was serious.

"What is it?" he asked.

"Nothing."

"It's something all right. You'd better tell me. Do you want to go back?"

She shook her head. "I told you I'd stay and I won't go on my word."

"Then what is it?"

"Can we have our dinner first?"

"Sure. I always talk better on a full stomach."

When they had eaten he said, "Okay, honey, what's on your mind?"

"Do you want me to be honest with you, Gus?"

"I wouldn't want you to kid me about a thing."

"I know you think I'm going to Papeete with you but I don't want to."

"Then we'll make it Turia or Vanavana," he said lightly. "Take your choice."

"It won't be either one, Gus. I'm going to marry Dino."

She was obviously not joking. He felt as though she had taken her small brown fist and hit him between the eyes.

"Say that again."

"I'm going to marry Dino."

His voice was very cold and formal when he said, "Then will you kindly tell me what all this business on the blanket and in the water was about?"

"Is that what it was to you, 'business'?"

"What was it to you?"

"It was because I love you."

"Fine. Very good. Now we're getting somewhere. You love me and you're marrying Dino."

She nodded.

"I must be losing my grip," he said. "Or it's all this running around in the sun that has finally got to me. You'll have to spell it out."

"Why do you think I wanted you to make love to me?"

"I'm damned if I know, now."

"I know you thought I was having an affair with Dino but certainly it should be clear to you now that I never had anything to do with him that way."

"So?"

"I don't love Dino the way I love you. I wanted you to be the first. The first and best and truest love. I wanted to have this afternoon with you to carry with me for the rest of my life. And don't think for a moment that I don't want to go off with you in a boat. I know what heaven it would be. But I have to ask myself how long it would last. I don't love boats that much, Gus. I've cruised on small boats for two or three days at a time along the New England coast and I know how uncomfortable they can be. I just can't picture myself spending the rest of my life that way."

"We could stay ashore part of the time," he said without any real conviction.

"And do what? Lock you down to a desk selling insurance? We both know what that would lead to. You'd be itching to get to sea and I'd be determined to stay ashore. In the end we'd wind up resenting each other and spending more and more time apart. Let's face it, Gus. I like having interesting people around me. And I like big cities and night clubs and theatres and restaurants and fine apartments and good clothes. All the things you probably despise. You see, I'm just a very ordinary sort of girl."

"You're beginning to sound a little like your cousin Clare," Robinson said grimly.

"Maybe in some ways I am. I want all the glamour and excitement that she had. But don't you see, my darling, that I can't live your life and that it would be a fatal error for me to ask you to live mine? If I asked you to give up the sea you'd never forgive me. You told me yourself that without a boat you might as well be dead. Isn't that so?"

"Yes," Gus said, knowing that what he was really saying was, goodbye. God Bless. You're the beginning and the end of everything and there will never again be anybody quite like you and not time nor distance nor anything else will ever really fill the void.

"And I understand Dino better than you think," she went on. "I know he's an opportunist and only a second-rate painter and maybe even a bit of a gigolo. And I know too that I'll never have the same feeling making love with him that I had here with you today. That's why I wanted the first time and the best time to be with you. But Dino can give me the kind of life that is right for me. He can give me Paris and New York and Rome and St. Tropez. He's handsome and charming and gets along well with people. We'll make a very presentable couple. All these things are important to me, Gus."

"I understand," he said, understanding only that there was a calculating wisdom in this tiny girl that he could not cope with.

"I hope you do."

He looked up at the darkening sky. "I'd better get going. I wouldn't want to keep my business partner waiting. She might get nervous."

Gwen said nothing. His coldness and reserve left her numb. Robinson walked down to the water and pushed the two boats off the beach.

"You can still change your mind," he said.

She shook her head. "You won't forget to call Mr. Holland, will you?"

"I won't forget." His voice was icy.

She looked very small and childlike when she asked softly, "Won't you even kiss me good-bye, Gus?"

"No, I don't think I will." As soon as he said it he was sorry but the wall between them now was impossible to breach.

He waded out to the skiff and climbed aboard and rigged a towing line to the sailboat. Using one of the oars he poled out into deeper water and then started the engine. He was keenly aware of the solitary figure on the beach but he avoided looking at her. Instead he pushed the throttle up and steered toward the first stars that were lying to the westward over Spanish Cay. Gwen waved at him but he ignored it.

CHAPTER NINE

Dino was one-third of the way through a bottle of Scotch. He was not an habitually heavy drinker and he knew that in a little while he would be very drunk. The thought contributed to his unhappiness; he despised people who lost control of themselves. But, he told himself, he would never have a better reason.

The phone rang but he paid no attention. It had been ringing every few minutes for the past hour and he knew who it was. Clare was trying to get him. Well he did not want to talk to Clare just now. Eventually he would have to make a decision about her but he wanted to put it off.

He stood up and moved close to his easel and stared moodily at the half-finished portrait. It was of Gwen, one that he had been working on from memory. It was one of the best things he had ever done—less stylized and more impassioned than most of his other work—and now it would never be finished.

Unlike most artists Dino was able to regard his own work objectively. As a draftsman he was not too bad but his paintings lacked vitality and inspiration. His portraits were cynical. They had brought him a certain amount of commercial success but never any artistic satisfaction. But this picture of Gwen was different. In it he had captured an elfin sparkle and joy of living that had brought the canvas to life. It seemed to reflect his hope that from now on things might be different. Now that he had Gwen his whole life would change. He might even attempt some serious work, enough for a one-man show. Di Buonaventura's Sketches of the Caribbean. Sunstruck. Harsh. Primitive. Totally unexpected from the hitherto strictly society painter, the reviews would say. Some bright new influence has entered the painter's life and reached sources of previously untapped power....

He had come so close to snatching the merry-go-round ring. He had held it in his fingers only to drop it at the last second. She was the kind of golden girl a man meets once in a lifetime—gay, young, beautiful and rich. Now there was nothing ahead but a succession of women like Clare—each a little older, a little more corroded by time and bitterness, a little more demanding.

He took another drink. Tears rolled down his tanned cheeks. Was he crying for Gwen or for himself? It did not really matter because in a way it was the same thing. At least it was something to know he could still weep. It had been years since he had felt any genuine emotion. Or was it the whiskey?

When he heard the knock on the door he ignored it. It came again, more demanding this time. "Yes?" he said. "Who is it?"

"It's Clare, darling."

"What do you want?"

"I want to speak to you. Please open the door."

"Go away."

"Dino, open the door right now."

The instinct for survival was still too strong. He was alone now and he might need her again. He got up and unlocked the door.

"Where have you been, darling? I've been calling you for hours." She was crisply beautiful, her fair hair and pale skin set off by the pink linen gown. Her eyes were sparkling and the room was filled with the expensive scent of her perfume. She looked, he thought, as if she had just been notified that she held a winning ticket in the Irish Sweepstakes.

"I see you're all broken up by grief, Clare."

"Should I be? I may be many things, darling, but at least I'm no hypocrite. Do you want me to say I'm sorry about it? Well, I'm not."

"My God, Clare. She was your cousin. Don't you feel anything at all?"

"Only an honest sense of relief that she's gone."

"How can you talk that way? Is there nothing human in you at all?"

She came closer and caressed his cheek. "Don't you know that you're the most important thing in the world to me? Gwen wanted to steal you from me. How can I pretend that I'm not glad she's dead? Anyway it's over now, darling. Let's forget it."

The whiskey surged through his brain. He tried to focus his bright blue eyes on her face but she seemed to swim in an alcoholic haze. What was it she had said? 'Gwen wanted to steal you from me.' Was there a threat of some kind in that?

"You sound as if you had something to do with her death," he said thickly.

"Do I? Well, if she had been poisoned you might be right. I'm afraid, however, that I could hardly push her overboard when she was alone in a sailboat. We'll just have to put it down to wishful thinking. I do plead guilty to that."

"What an incredible bitch you are."

"Of course, my sweet. And so are you. That's what makes us so right for each other."

"No! We are *not* right for each other. I have sold almost all of myself but there is still a little something left. I can still love and I can still weep for the one I love. But not you. If you cried, the tears would be made of stainless steel."

"And what are your tears made of, my love? Of whiskey and self-pity for the fortune that has slipped away from you. You'll soon get over your grief and then everything will be as it was before, only better."

"God, how I hate you, Clare."

"You'll get over that too."

"Never."

"After you've had time to consider the prospect of supporting yourself you'll be surprised how your attitude toward me will change."

"Behold the superb American female in all her glory. Fresh from the hairdresser and the couturier. The chromium heart and the iron gut. You are the bitch of all bitches, Clare, and you will not be happy until you have emasculated me."

"You'd be very little use to me that way, dear. It's really the last thing in the world I'd like to see happen."

"Go away."

"Are you ill, dear? You look terribly pale. Shall I get you some coffee? You never did have a head for liquor."

"Go away."

"Why don't you lie down for a while, darling, and I'll fix you a cold compress and hold your hand."

"Go away, damn you," he said weakly.

"Just think of the wonderful life we're going to have, darling. All the best places and the best people. Oh, we'll have a lovely time, Dino."

"I'll tell you something, Clare," he said sadly.

"What is it, dear?"

"With her I might have had a chance."

"Now what does that mean?"

"I might have done some serious work."

"Is that what's worrying you, Dino? Well there's nothing Gwen could have done for you that I can't do. Perhaps we ought to go to Florence. I think Florence would be lovely. We'll find you a nice little studio somewhere near the Piazza Della Signoria—a little *pied-à-terre* all your own. And of course I know some very important people in the Uffizi and the other galleries and I'll arrange for you to meet them and we'll give marvelous parties for the sort of people who can afford to commission you. Oh we'll be a great success, you'll see."

"Not with you," Dino said. "You will suck out my insides and leave nothing but the husk. With you I will be nothing but a lap dog, a damned manicured French poodle on a gold leash."

"I'm really beginning to lose patience with you, my love. I do wish you'd stop talking such utter, bloody, filthy nonsense."

He stared up at her somberly and said, "And I'll tell you something else. I never slept with her."

"More fool you. What do you want? A gold star?"

"No, I don't want any stars. I tried hard enough but she would never let me."

"You don't have to feel defeated, darling. She was one those awful professional virgins."

"Better a professional virgin than a professional whore."

"There was a time when you enjoyed it well enough," she answered coldly.

"Yes, I enjoyed it. I have also enjoyed it with other whores. Many of them. They are full of tricks. Some are even more competent than you. Would you like to know? For instance there was your friend—"

"I'll forgive you for this, Dino," she said interrupting him, "because you're drunk."

"Don't forgive me, Clare. Please don't forgive me. I think can stand anything but your goddamned forgiveness."

"I would watch myself if I were you. I think you're going too far."

"How does one go too far with you, Clare? Do you mean to tell me there is some insult you will not accept so long as it suits your purpose?"

"Stop it, you fool."

"You are as smart and cold and dangerous as a snake. Someday I will do your portrait and when it is finished it will be that of a female cobra. No one has ever beaten you at anything but one thing is beating you now—age. Each day another little line, a little wrinkle to mark the place where you have lost a battle. All your forces are in retreat, Clare. The battle is going against you and," he added venomously, "there is not a single bloody thing you can do."

She raised her hand to strike at his face but he caught her by the wrist and bent her arm down. Her face went white with pain.

"Don't ever try that with me again, you murderous bitch," he said.

Their eyes were not more than six inches apart. Suddenly she spat directly into his face. He released her with an expression of disgust and said, "All right. Very good. Thank you. Now we are quits. I was going to tell you how many times I was ready to vomit when I saw your face on the pillow beside me but now it is no longer necessary. Now we understand each other."

She was speechless with rage. At that moment she could have killed him. But she managed to bring herself under control. Now, when she had won, was she to toss it all away because he had succeeded in driving her blind with anger? She would only be defeating her own purpose and in a way it would be a victory for Gwen. Without Dino she would be alone, and she could not stand to be alone. When you were alone you remembered the way Harry looked with the top of his head blown off and the spatter of brains on the English carpet. And when you were alone you remembered Gwen as a child and taking her to the Bois in Paris to ride in a donkey cart and eat a strawberry ice. To be alone and growing old was the most terrible thing that could happen.

Dino sat motionless, his head turned away from her.

"Dino," she said in a softer voice. "Please look at me, Dino."

He continued to ignore her.

"Won't you even talk to me?"

"Get out."

"I must talk to you. You've got to give me a chance to explain."

He leaped to his feet so suddenly that she backed away. "All right then," he said. "If you won't get out, I will. And to hell with you!"

The door slammed behind him. She sat down on the bed telling herself it would be all right. He would come back. He had, after all, nowhere else to go.

Dino walked along the white shell road to the village. He entered the Flame Club and sat down at the bar. It was early in the day and the place was empty but it was cool and dark and suited his mood.

He stared at his face in the mirror behind the bar. How would he size up that face if it belonged to a stranger? It would not be hard. He was a type. The Portofino, Nice, Cannes type. A stock model. You saw them at all the resorts lying in wait for very young girls or ageing widows. The hair was always a bit too long and the shirt was usually open halfway down the chest to expose the bronzed skin. Often there was a medallion on a thin gold chain around the neck. Or if it was not the exposed chest bit then it was the open collar and blue blazer and silk square-knotted at the throat. And always there were silk slacks fitting at the hips as though they had been sewed onto the wearer. And, of course, suede shoes pointed in the Italian style. And the eyes—vacant, opaque eyes that automatically translated everything they saw into terms of money. The eyes were like one of those American Express cards that immediately converted dollars into francs and lire at the current rate of exchange. And the mind was like that of a concierge or a headwaiter or a whore—trained to distinguish at a glance between those who possessed genuine wealth and the others who were simply off on a weekend toot.

Oh yes, he decided, I am a stock model indentifiable at once by anyone who has had a little experience with the type. And, like all of them, selling one commodity. Sex. In all its fascinating and endless ramifications. I am the male equivalent of the rich man's mistress—flirtatious, elegant, vacant and always a little dangerous for the unwary or the inexperienced. A man with only one thing to sell—myself. And the product must always be available for women like Clare....

He had deluded himself that with Gwen he could break the mold and look at himself in the mirror and see not a goddamned half-assed fairy, but a man. Well that final illusion was destroyed now and he was back where he had started. Even this last scene with Clare was play-acting, and they both knew it. She had let him off the leash for a bit of a run, but by God when she blew that whistle he had better scamper right back to momma.

In this bitter moment of self-revelation he wanted to pick up his glass and hurl it at the handsome face in the mirror. What kept him from it was the knowledge that it would be at once overly theatrical and expensive. Money would soon be a problem again. By the end of the week he would have to make a decision—whether to leave Spanish Cay or go back to Clare. But how—even for a trained whore like himself—would it be possible to conceal the hatred and contempt he now felt for her?

CHAPTER TEN

Caldwell, head of Florida Yacht Sales, came charging out of the office with outstretched hand when he heard that Robinson was in the waiting room. "Gus, old man. Where the devil did you spring from?"

"It's kind of a long story, Ed, and I'm in a hurry. I'll tell you some other time."

"I don't know what all the rush is but I hope you're not in too much of a hurry to have a drink," Caldwell said leading the way into his office.

"Hell, no."

The yacht broker pushed back a section of paneling in the knotty pine wall and revealed a built-in bar and refrigerator.

"Very impressive, Ed," Robinson said. "What's in the other wall? A swimming pool or half a dozen blondes or both?"

"Nothing so exciting. I'm afraid it's just a wall. But I must say you've given me an idea."

Robinson took the glass Caldwell offered him and looked around the room and said, "Well anyway it's pretty posh. The brokerage business must be good."

"It's terrific."

"I'm glad to hear it. Aren't you drinking?"

Caldwell shook his head. "Not in the middle of the day and not when I'm working. If I started drinking now I'd be dopey all afternoon."

"So all this elaborate layout is just for customers."

"And friends."

"I might be both, Ed."

"Don't tell me you're tired of old *Charee*."

"She's sunk," Robinson answered flatly.

As briefly as possible he told him how the ketch had gone down.

"I'm sure sorry to hear that, Gus," Caldwell said. "*Charee* was a sweet little boat. Anyway, you were damned lucky to get ashore."

"I want another boat, Ed, and I want it in a hurry."

"It's tough to find a real bargain right now. Everybody and his mother seem to have been bitten by the boat bug. I've never seen anything like it. We've done more business in the past year than we did in five years previously. But I'll show you our listings and then if you give me a few days to look around I'll see what else is available."

"What about *Senegal*?"

"She was sold two months ago to some hot shot in Palm Beach."

"Will he sell?"

"You can buy anything for a price, Gus, but the price will be steep."

"How much?"

"Well he paid twelve five and I guess it's a little too soon for him to have gotten tired of her. And he's put a little money into her—stainless standing rigging and a new genoa. I doubt if he'd listen to anything much under fifteen thousand."

"Make him an offer."

"Of what?"

"Fifteen thousand."

Caldwell pursed his lips in a soundless whistle and said, "*Charee* must have gone down right over one of those old Spanish bullion wrecks."

"That's part of the long story. Anyway, I have the money and I want *Senegal*."

"You don't even want to see the boat before making an offer?"

"That won't be necessary. I know what she's like."

"Why the big blitz, Gus? Can't you take a few days on it? That's a powerful lot of money."

"I want to get back to sea. I'd like you to make him the offer today."

"Okay, chum. It's your dough. I'll call him right now." Caldwell dialed a number and Robinson heard him say, "Mr. Marple, this is Caldwell at Florida Yacht Sales. An old friend of mine is in town and he wants to make you an offer on *Senegal*. That's right, I told him you hadn't listed it for sale but he wanted me to call you anyway. Yes, I know you've put some money into her. He's offering fifteen thousand." Caldwell turned to Robinson and said, "He wants to know if that's cash, Gus."

Robinson nodded.

"Fifteen thousand cash, Mr. Marple." Caldwell listened to the answer and then said, "No, I don't think he'd be interested in anything like that but I'll pass it on to him and if he has a counterproposal I'll call you back." He hung up and turned to Robinson and said, "What a crook!"

"What does he want?"

"Eighteen thousand. A measly profit of five and a half thousand just for holding the boat for two months. Of course he knows he'll never get it but he's just gutty enough and rich enough to think he might pull it off. Forget it I can do a lot better than that for you with some other boat. How about a nice little Rhodes Weekender? There's a sweetheart up at St. Pete and on that one I can guarantee you the price is right. Take a few days to look around, Gus. This is no way to buy a boat."

Robinson shook his head. "Call Marple back and tell him I'll take the boat at his price."

Caldwell shrugged and said, "You always were a stubborn cuss. Okay, it's your dough."

"There's only one thing. Tell him I want the whole deal completed today. Tell him to get a bill of sale ready and I'll take the afternoon train up there to Palm Beach."

"What did you do, Gus? Stick up a bank somewhere?"

"Sure. Get on the phone, Ed."

Caldwell completed the transaction and when he had hung up he said, "Now I'll have that drink. After all, you don't buy a boat every day. Or do you? Hell, Gus, you know I'm busting with curiosity. Can't you tell me what this is all about?"

"Sorry, Ed."

"Well, if you won't discuss your shady past at least tell me about the future. Where are you going after you have the boat?"

"I'm putting to sea the day after tomorrow but I won't know where

I'm going till I get there."

"How long are you going to go on this way, old boy?"

"What way?"

"Knocking around the globe. Don't you ever feel the urge for a wife and kids?"

"Occasionally, but I do my best to fight it down. I don't want to spend the rest of my life watching some broad making love to herself with a cake of soap on teevee and then go out to wash the car on Sunday afternoon and eat non-fattening ice cream and wear plastic pants and live in a goddamned stainless steel, air-conditioned kennel."

"All the same, you can't live on a boat forever, Gus."

"I don't see why not, but even if you're right the house I want won't be here. It will be made of natural wood and it will be open on all four sides to let the breeze blow through and there won't be any windowpanes or screens because it never gets cold and there aren't any bugs."

"I'll have to admit it sounds good. Where is this paradise?"

"In the valley of Paea in Tahiti. And if I do get stuck with kids I won't need any diaper service because they can run bare-ass through the woods and wash in a waterfall. And from my front porch I'll be able to see the mountains of Moorea and there is nothing in this world more worth while for a man to look at than a sunset over Moorea. But if I ever do get tired of looking at it then I can look at *Senegal* moored in the lagoon and maybe get on board and go away for six months and see how the sunsets look on the other side of the world. You can take 'Gunsmoke' and 'Rawhide' and 'What's My Line?' and all the other juvenile crap you call civilization. I'll take Moorea any day."

"I know money is no object to you these days but I've been wondering what you plan to live on while the sun is going up and down over Moorea."

"I might marry a rich woman," Robinson said. "I'll require that she own at least five pigs and a couple of goats. If you go barefoot and shirtless and there are no movies and the food grows on trees, what the hell do you need money for?"

"I guess you're right but it's kind of a shame," Caldwell said.

"Why?"

"It's a funny coincidence that you should come walking in here today. I was just thinking this morning of some way to get in touch with you. As a matter of fact, I wrote to you a couple of times in the past few months but I guess your mail never caught up with you. Or did it?"

"No," Robinson said. "What was on your mind?"

"I wanted you to go into business with me."

"Hell, Ed, you know I'm no businessman."

"I know you're not but I am. The thing is, you probably know as much about sailing auxiliaries as any man in the world. As I told you, the boat business is terrific. With the roads as crowded as they are there's damned little fun left in automobiles any more and so more and more people are turning to the water. Most of them start out with those damned little Fiberglass outboards with fins sticking up all over them, but eventually they learn what it's all about and they want to move on to cruising and real sailing. It's my guess that in another year or two, barring some major financial calamity, there will be a tremendous market for a really good, sound auxiliary in the 28- to 35-foot class. And that's where you come in. With your experience you know exactly what ought to go into a boat of that sort. I figured you could design the boats and Charlie Edwards over at Miami Shipbuilding could build them and I know damn well I can sell them. It would make a great combination, Gus."

"I don't see what you need me for, Ed. There are plenty of damn fine naval architects around who could do the job for you."

"Of course there are but I have something more in mind than just a design. I want to exploit your name as well. There's a lot of romance attached to a man who has sailed singlehanded across most of the world's oceans. To the average weekend sailor that sort of accomplishment is on a par with climbing Mt. Everest. He'll never do it himself and he probably wouldn't want to if he could, but he's willing to pay handsomely to share in the experience of the man who did. In addition to which he'll get a little vicarious thrill out of picturing himself at the helm of a boat designed by such a man. I see no reason why we shouldn't cash in on your background just as I intend to cash in on my own selling experience and on Charlie Edwards' experience in building boats. I still say it would be a great combination."

"I'm surprised at you, Ed. I always thought you had me figured for nothing more than a seagoing bum."

"That's all you are," Caldwell said, "but I plan to make a solid citizen out of you yet. Since I'm caught up in this rat race of earning a living and keeping up with the status symbols I don't see why the devil you should be allowed to go and sit on a porch with some big-bosomed wahine and do nothing but enjoy the view of Moorea. And if money isn't the right bait for you then I have a few other tricks up my sleeve. You're coming to us for dinner tonight and I have a date for you. My sister-in-law. Twenty-seven, a knockout and freshly divorced. Let me work on you for a couple of days, Gus, and you'll never know yourself. What do you say?"

"I'm sorry, Ed, but it's no deal. I'll be in Palm Beach tonight on board *Senegal*. My regrets to your sister-in-law."

"You're the most stubborn cuss I've ever met and you're passing up a hell of an opportunity. Will you do me a favor then?"

"Just so long as it doesn't keep me from getting to that boat tonight."

"This won't hold you up. I just want you to keep an open mind on it. Think about it. Let me know where you're headed for and when you get good and lonesome I'll send you a picture of the sister-in-law in a bikini. That ought to bring you racing back with your tongue hanging out."

"I thought you were running a yacht brokerage here, Ed, but I guess I'm wrong. It's a goddamned marriage bureau."

"We'll talk about it some more on the way up to Palm Beach."

"Are you going with me?"

"I'm personally driving you up. You happen to be a very important customer. I don't turn over an eighteen thousand dollar deal every day in the week, you know, and if I let you go off by yourself you might change your mind and decide to sock it away in a motel in Ft. Lauderdale."

"Suit yourself, but if you're going let's go."

"I never saw a man in such a hurry to get rid of his money. That dough must be hotter than hell, Gus."

Caldwell had the top down on the Buick. As they drove north on One they passed orange juice stands, monkey jungles, parrot jungles, snake farms, seaquariums, glass blowers, wax museums and a seemingly endless parade of hideous gingerbread motels—jerry-built horrors laid out back to back with every sound from fornication to defecation seeping through their cardboard-thin walls. And beyond the motels, mile after mile of concrete-block housing developments thrown up on government mortgage money with the full knowledge that they would have long since crumbled apart before the final payment was made. And dominating the whole scene—triumphant in the tepid air—a forest of television antennas sucking in mass culture through their hollow steel fingers.

Caldwell, accustomed to this nightmare landscape, drove through without giving it a thought, but to Robinson it was a scene straight out of hell. Any brief temptation he might have felt in regard to Caldwell's offer vanished in a miasma of pink stucco and melting tar and nylon-girt buttocks.

Senegal was lying at the far end of a pier that fronted on Lake Worth and the towers of West Palm Beach. The yawl rode the blue water as lightly as a gull. With her dazzling white topsides and gleaming mahogany deckhouse she was perhaps more of a yacht than Robinson fancied but he did not hold these affectations against her fundamental soundness and beauty of line.

Thirty-four feet long and generous of beam, she still had a racy look that promised a good turn of speed. Her deckhouse, while ample and offering full headroom, was not high enough to spoil her appearance, and though she had a bit more glass in her than he liked in a heavy sea he knew from long experience in the tropics how welcome that extra ventilation would be when he was anchored in some harbor.

All in all he was more than pleased with what he saw. To a sailor it is the first impression that matters. Unless he falls in love with a ship at first sight his heart will never really go out to her. And best of all she had been well kept up and was obviously ready for sea. Her lifelines were rigged in heavy, through-bolted stanchions and her rigging was stainless steel and dacron. Her sails were neatly furled under green canvas covers and lashed amidships was a small Fiberglas dinghy.

Caldwell looked at Robinson's face and saw the admiration in his eyes and, with the experienced broker's sure instinct in these matters, remained silent. No one could *sell* Gus Robinson a boat. If he wanted to buy it he would, but certainly no one could sell him on it.

"It's hot work in this sun," Caldwell said. "How about a cold beer?"

"Have you got some?"

"I picked up a carton at that grocery when I called Marple. Let's sit in the cockpit while we drink it."

Robinson shook his head. "She's not mine yet. We'll drink on the dock."

"What a scrupulous devil you are."

In his mind Robinson made a mocking bow in his own direction. Scrupulous is the word, he thought. He thinks nothing of milking twenty thousand bucks from a poor old widow (what's a slight case of murder between friends?) but he won't drink a can of beer on board a boat until he is the legal owner.

They sat on the pier with their feet over the edge drinking the beer. An hour later the owner, a heavy-chested man in shorts and a flaming sport shirt, arrived in a monstrous projectile of shining steel and flamboyant fins. He unlocked the hatch cover and Robinson stepped down the companionway ladder into the cabin. Apart from a slight mustiness from being closed up the yawl was as fresh below decks as above.

"You keep her shipshape enough," Robinson said approvingly.

"I can't claim much credit for it," Marple said. "I have a paid hand who does the work. If I couldn't afford to maintain her properly I wouldn't keep her. You want me to show you around or would you rather go by yourself?"

"How would it be if you and Caldwell have a beer together while I look her over?"

"Fair enough."

The yacht was ready for sea, even to all the small items such as dishes, towels and fuel for the alcohol stove. He pressed the starter and listened to a satisfactory rumble from the small diesel. The bunks were carefully made up with fresh linens and he was pleased to see that instead of the four rather skimpy bunks that were usually found on a yacht of *Senegal's* dimensions, there were only a pair of vee bunks up forward and a large double berth in the main cabin. He was a big man and he would enjoy the luxury of a big bed. Then, too, one never knew what the sea or the land would turn up and it was nice to be prepared.

Gwen would have looked marvelous in that big bed. Like a child. Dark hair spread out on the pillow, sparkling eyes watching him as he fussed over the galley stove. Was she all right on that sandbar? He supposed so. A little lonely and scared perhaps. Well, she had plenty of courage. How many girls would have gone so blithely into such an adventure? He wasn't angry at her any more. We each have to do what we feel is necessary. No matter how phony her reasons were for wanting Dino she was still entitled to the free choice.

He went back up to the cockpit and said to Marple, "Did you bring that bill of sale?"

"It's right here."

Robinson took out the envelope Clare had given him and counted out eighteen thousand dollars. Marple took the money and held up each bill individually and examined them all very carefully. "I hope you don't mind," he said to Robinson, "but, after all, this is a damned funny way to do business. I mean all of it in cash and you being in such a tearing hurry."

"I don't mind. Take your time."

When Marple had finished examining the money he said, "Okay, you've bought yourself a boat. She's a sweetheart all right but personally I think you're nuts to have paid that much. However..."

"Is there anything you want to take off the boat?"

"I don't think so. How much of a hog can I be? At that price she goes as is, right down to toothpaste and binoculars. Here are the keys."

"Where do we get the bill of sale notarized?"

"There's a place a couple of blocks from here. Let's drive over."

When they came back to the boat Caldwell said, "I've been in this business for fifteen years but I've never seen anything go as fast as that. Now seriously, Gus, isn't there some place where I can write to you? You must have a general idea of where you're going."

"I don't know. I was thinking about going back to the Pacific but now I'm not so sure. Anyway, I'll be going south and I'll call in for mail when I get to the Canal Zone. General Delivery in Panama ought to reach me all right."

"I know I threw all that stuff at you too fast today and I guess I scared you off with all that talk of marriage and kids. Hell, that's no business of mine. Forget it. But if I write to you concerning our broad thinking on the type of boat we want to build will you look it over and drop me a line?"

"Of course."

"Then happy sailing and for God's sake check those toilet connections this time."

"I'll do that. So long, Ed."

When he was alone he checked over the galley and found a can of sardines and a tin of salted crackers. There was still one can of beer left. He sat on a blue cushion in the cockpit and looked at the beautifully joined teak deck under his feet and at the bronze winches shining as softly and expensively as gold and let the slow realization that all this was really his now soak in. He had achieved his life's ambition, to own a supremely beautiful yacht capable of going anywhere in the world. But, strangely, he felt no real excitement. The flavor seemed to have gone out of it. What was wrong was that he was no longer a true singlehander. He wanted to share it all with someone else, and the girl he wanted to share it with was sitting on a sandbar on the other side of the Stream and thinking of another man.

He pulled himself out of it by casting a practiced eye at the sky. The sun was setting behind a heavy bank of clouds that had a peculiar purple sheen. Red sky at night, sailor's delight. The clouds looked swollen, as if they carried a belly full of wind and rain. If they were in for a change of weather he would have a mean crossing.

CHAPTER ELEVEN

He awoke early and at six-fifteen he tuned in the first marine weather report of the day. The forecast called for southerly winds of ten to twenty knots. Not good. A strong southerly at this time of year meant that they were on the advance edge of a northwesterly front. The Stream flowed north at roughly five knots and when it bucked head winds of twenty to thirty knots the result was a very formidable chop. He would much rather be out in the open sea in a gale than have to cross the Stream against even a moderate northwester.

And apart from his own troubles there was the question of Gwen on her tiny spit of sand. At no point did the reef rise more than three or four feet above sea level, and in a really good blow the entire bar might be awash. Sitting there alone at night and listening to the wind and watching the water rise would be no joke.

There was a strong temptation to head out right then and beat across while the weather still held. He could make it across the Hump in ten or twelve hours and pick up Gwen the following morning, a full day ahead of schedule and probably well in advance of the storm. But it would not do to rush. *Senegal* must have a shakedown first. If a turnbuckle or stay let go he could find himself dismasted in the Stream in the face of a northwester and in serious trouble.

He ate a big breakfast of ham and eggs and when he had done the dishes and squared away the galley he started the engine and let it run for ten minutes to check any tendency toward overheating. At the end of the test run the gauge held steady at 140 degrees. He shut off the engine and checked the oil and found it full up. Then he opened up the floorboards and checked the stuffing box and found it leaking slightly. Using a hammer he took up a turn on the gland nut and stopped the leak. Then he took off the sail covers and raised the main and mizzen and let the sails flap in the wind for a few minutes while he checked the various blocks and sheets. Satisfied that everything was in order he lowered the sails again and let go his mooring line and edged the yawl away from the pier. He worked carefully down the channel and twenty minutes later he was approaching the inlet, where the rising wind was already kicking foam over the jetties.

Senegal pitched madly in the wicked chop inside the inlet. Spray poured over him, soaking his clothing and matting his hair. He might have put on foul weather gear but he disliked the restricted feeling it gave him and he never minded being wet. He let the spray pour over him and sucked the damp sea air into his nostrils. The feeling of toughness and independence that he had enjoyed for so long on *Charee* began to come back to him. He flicked the ignition switch off and went forward to hoist the jib. He had already made up his mind that someday when he had the time he would set fair-leads in the deck and lead all his sheets straight back to the cockpit so that in really severe weather he would not have to go forward at all.

When he had the jib set up he hoisted main and mizzen. The sails were new and made of dacron and beautifully fitted. *Senegal* lay over and began to drive. He had found a patent log coiled in one of the stem lockers and now he got it out and streamed it from the stem cleat. Eight knots and hardly trying. She was a dream ship all right.

He spent the morning putting her through her paces. Satisfied at last that he knew enough about her to take her to sea he sailed back in through the inlet on the rising tide and then motored back to the pier. He had decided to change his plans. Instead of waiting for morning he would cross the Stream at night.

As soon as he had made the decision he felt a sense of relief. Although he had done everything he could, in the short time allowed him, to make Gwen comfortable, he was still concerned about her. Apart from any physical danger it was probably the first time in her life that she had ever been so completely alone. The mind could play strange tricks. Alone in a house at night you were apt to imagine footsteps on a stair or the creak of an opening door. Who knew what a girl of Gwen's age might imagine coming up at her out of the sea. Inwardly he was still raging over her decision to stay with Dino but he could not let that affect his obligation to her.

He locked the hatch behind him and went ashore to a supermarket two blocks away and stocked up with enough groceries to last him for several weeks at sea. When he had stowed the various cans where they could not work loose even in a heavy sea he topped off his fuel and water tanks and took in his dock lines.

The yawl was ready for sea. He was going out again where he belonged. The world, or at least the three quarters of it that was water, lay before him. The wonderful feeling of excitement and anticipation that came over him when he cleared the land was with him again. But this time it was tinged with just a hint of sadness. He was leaving his own country, perhaps for years, and there was no one to say good-bye to. No pretty girls standing on the pier and throwing leis into the wa-

ter. No scream of whistles or shriek of horns. Just the gray stone jetties dropping away behind him. No sound but the creak of *Senegal's*
rigging and the murmur of her bow wave.

As he passed the jetty he saw a solitary fisherman sitting on a slab of
granite. He waved at the man, thinking that even if he was a stranger
he was at least someone to say good-bye to. The fisherman, apparently
a misanthropic soul, did a curious thing. Instead of waving back he
raised one arm with finger extended in an obscene gesture.

Robinson threw back his head and laughed. He was laughing partly
at the loony on the rock but mostly at himself. It seemed so fitting. He
had chosen to cut himself off from the world of conventional men and
now this world was not even saying Aloha to him. It was saying, Up
yours, Jack.

Starting from the center of her small domain which was marked by
the green tarp, Gwen walked fifty paces to the right and then a hundred to the left. That was as far as you could go in any direction. By
walking to the limits of the land and by observing the small sea creatures that lived along its edge, she had been able to overcome her initial feeling of claustrophobia. At first the reef had seemed utterly lifeless but now she saw that there were tiny pink and white crabs that
scuttled away into their holes at the sound of her steps. One little chap,
braver than the others, stayed close to his doorway but refused to go
below. He stood there, claw raised and stalk eyes glaring. The creature
made such a comical picture of indignation that she found herself smiling. She kicked a little sand in his direction and with a final glare of rage
he scuttled away.

Besides the crabs, something else had visited the island. On the lagoon
side, where the sand sloped down into the shallows, she found the
tracks of some huge creature. The prints of four great paws edged out
at forty-five degree angles and at least two feet apart. For a moment
she felt a chill of fear. What could it be—dragging its armored belly low
in the sand—that had crawled ashore here and might return again? A
montage of horror scenes from science fiction movies flashed across her
mind. Giant squids and unknown monsters of the deep. If it had come
once might it not come again?

She had taken several steps back from the water's edge before she suddenly realized what it was that had made the tracks—one of the great
sea turtles that she had sometimes seen floating lazily on the surface of
the Gulf Stream. More than likely the turtle, harmless enough despite

its size, had crawled up here on the sun-warmed sand to lay its eggs. The thought intrigued her and she decided to stay up late in the hope of seeing one of the creatures emerge from the sea.

Gus had told her a story about watching turtle hunters at work on a small island off the coast of Ecuador. At night, under a full moon, the beasts would lumber onto the sand to lay their eggs. The hunters waited until the eggs were laid, a matter of forty-five minutes or an hour, and then grabbed the turtles and flipped them over on their backs. It was not always easy to turn over an angry five-hundredpound turtle, but once it was on its back the great beast was helpless. At that point, said Robinson, the hunters dug up the eggs and at the same time something strange and disturbing began to happen. The mother turtles, upside down and helpless inside their armor, would see the eggs being dug up and they would begin to weep. Great, gelatinous tears shining silver in the moonlight dripped from their leathery brows.

"But that's absolutely heartbreaking," she had told him. "How could you stand it?"

"There wasn't much I could do about it. Turtles constitute the main source of meat in those islands. For me to try to stop them would be like walking up to some bird in a restaurant and snatching a seven-dollar sirloin from under his nose. Only more so, because at least the guy with the steak could order another."

"But my God, those tears. Didn't they feel anything when they saw the mother turtle weep?"

"Not a thing. In fact they seemed to think it was damned funny."

"I still think you should have stopped them."

"How?"

"Well you could have bought the turtles and their eggs from them."

"I'm not the New York Museum of Natural History, you know. I was more broke than the turtle hunters."

"Then you should have stopped them by force," she said angrily.

"Gwen, honey, there were roughly fifty of them to one of me and it was late at night on a lonely beach and they were all carrying machetes. In about two seconds I'd have been in the soup along with the turtles."

"Did they really cry or are you teasing me?"

"I swear it. Big fat tears as large around as the end of your thumb."

"I thought only man could weep."

"Turtles cry and hyenas laugh. Raccoons wash their hands before eating and wolves marry for life."

"And tell me, Doctor," she had said, "what do young girls do who are hopelessly in love with dirty old men?"

"Why they can do this... or that... or that..."

"I'm afraid I like all of them. Oh, I'm shameless."

"You remind me of an iguana."

"A what?"

"One of those big lizards."

"Well thank you for nothing. And you remind me of a..."

"Careful now. No, it's just the way you burrow in."

"Where did you ever burrow with iguanas? I thought they lived in the desert."

"There are marine iguanas too. They live in the Galapagos Islands. I swam in a little bay there with baby seals and penguins and iguanas, and the sea birds came down and rode on my shoulders."

"You're making all this up."

"Am I? Come with me and see for yourself."

She did not answer because she was suddenly remembering that Clare had actually paid to have her murdered. The shock of it kept coming back to her and setting up a tight hard knot in the region of her heart. It might have seemed a dream now except for the tangible evidence of this stick of sand and the limitless sea and sky.

Yet there had always been a streak of viciousness in Clare that had been hard to explain. She had walked softly enough around Gwen's father but she had probably been thinking of the inheritance even then.

There had been that summer long ago when Clare had come to visit them in the house on the lake. It had been a great twelve-room log cabin set on an island in the middle of a smoke-gray Maine lake. Just thinking about it now brought back the odors of fresh-cut logs and of sun-warmed pine needles on the forest floor and of wood smoke in the chill of evening. And at night there were northern lights flickering across the sky and the mournful calling of the loons. Someone, some boy from across the lake—she could no longer remember his name—had a saxophone and in the evening they would sit on the dock and he'd tootle to the loons and the birds would answer. He played very badly and the loons were the only audience he ever had.

Then Clare had arrived. It was typical that there had been no announcement beforehand. She just came. They had not heard from her in more than a year and they had thought she was still in Europe, but then they heard the mutter of an outboard and saw the boat and the woman in the bow and realized with a slight shock that it was Clare.

As always, she had looked ravishing. How she must have staggered those dour-faced Maine types in their wool shirts and rubber moccasins. Gwen had been only thirteen then and she had felt awkward and lumpy by comparison with her cousin. She had suffered a small case of hero worship and within a few hours caught herself unconsciously imitating Clare's hair style and the way she walked and even the affectation of her speech.

Then there had been the strange business of the boy with the saxophone. She remembered him now as a lanky towheaded boy with the stigmata of adolescence on his downy cheeks. It had seemed a daring thing for them all—there were three or four other teen-agers as well— to sneak ashore and to drive over to Greenport to that place where they had the band.

And of course it was all hush hush. Sneaking out was part of the fun. But she had told Clare. Why? Probably to impress her as a fellow woman of the world. And Clare had fallen in with the scheme at once and had said, "But, darling, it sounds like marvelous fun. You must go." And Clare had maneuvered and schemed and made a deliciously wicked plot out of something that had started out to be so simple. She had carried notes back and forth and had arranged for Gwen to slip out through her bedroom window to meet the rowboat coming in with muffled oars. In addition, she had even sent a bottle of Scotch along in a brown paper bag.

Despite all the preparations the party had not been a great success. The boys had been self-conscious and awkward. They had all had a go at Clare's whiskey but none of them had been able to stomach it and in the end they had thrown the almost full bottle away. When they had rowed her back across the lake it had been close to dawn and she had been tired and sleepy. Funny, though, how after all these years it should come back to her so clearly. The boys' voices, ragged voices on the edge of manhood, singing "On Moonlight Bay." And a fumbling kiss on the dew-wet dock. That was all there was to it. But he never came back again to play his sax for the loons because next morning Clare, who had been a co-conspirator throughout, had kicked the cat right out of the bag. She had done it casually enough but the end result had been the same as if she had taken an ad in the *Times*. It was just an offhand comment at the breakfast table about the circles under Gwen's eyes and she must have been dreaming because she could have sworn that sometime in the night she heard rowboats pulling up to the dock and on top of that somebody had swiped a bottle of Scotch from her room. By mistake, of course, but still it was gone.

Clare's treachery had borne fruit. Her father had laid it right on the line to her and she had denied nothing. She had never lied to her father and she would not start now. So the whole thing was magnified out of all proportion. Her father's disappointment in her was clearly evident. And equally evident was the hint of triumph in her cousin's brilliant blue eyes.

Afterward, crying on her bed, she had tried to understand. Why had Clare betrayed her? What could she have hoped to gain by it? The answer had eluded her then but now, now that she knew Clare was capable even of murder, it seemed clear enough. Clare had been attempting even then to ingratiate herself with Gwen's father and to discredit Gwen in his eyes.

And that night she had wept in her bed and vowed never again to trust Clare in anything. But the years had dulled her anger and the whole thing had been long since forgotten by the time Clare brought Dino to Spanish Cay.

She had never really understood Clare's connection with Dino. According to Dino he had met Clare in New York and she had expressed an appreciation of his work and had offered to introduce him to the people who might be useful to him. Clare always had somebody who could be useful. She collected and traded relationships the way stamp buffs traded stamps. I'll give you a lovely duchess for a marquis. How about a second-drawer movie star for a rather nouveau riche millionaire?

Anyway, from what Dino said, Clare was getting nothing out of it herself but the satisfaction of helping a young artist. But anybody who really knew Clare would find that a little hard to swallow. Gwen had been only half joking when she had asked Dino if he had been having an affair with her cousin and he had flashed his beautiful white teeth and said, "No, she is hardly my type. I have never enjoyed older women. In Europe, of course, a relationship between a middle-aged woman and a young man is not uncommon but I myself have never developed a taste for it. I suspect that I am really quite bourgeois and American in my outlook. It seems a shame to spoil your wicked schoolgirl fancies but I am afraid there has never been anything like that between Clare and myself."

She had taken him at his word then but now, with so much time to think it through, she was beginning to wonder if he had not been lying. She tried to visualize them in bed together or making love unashamedly on the beach but the image escaped her. Anyway, whatever their relationship had been, it was over now. Dino had told her that and she believed him.

She stood up and began walking along the beach. Yesterday the sand under her bare feet had seemed delightfully soft and powdery but today it had a harsh granular feel. And the air felt dank and cool. She could tell that the wind was rising too because surf was beginning to beat around the westerly point of the reef. She was suddenly lonely and the prospect of her second night on the reef was frightening. Gus had said that if things got too bad for her she should use the flare gun and now she was seriously considering it. Perhaps if she had seen a ship at that moment she might have fired one of the rockets, but there was no ship in sight. Only the white crested sea and the darkening sky. She was as much alone as if she had been fired to the moon. Only one other person in the world knew where she was at that moment, and suppose something happened to him?

The game, then, was not yet over. Clare still had a stack of chips on her side of the table and she might yet win.

Gwen shivered and walked back to her campsite and threw a fresh piece of wood on the fire. Gus had left a wire grill for her and she set it over the fire and filled her little aluminum pot with water from the jeep can and put it over the blaze. When the water was hot she threw in a few spoonfuls of instant coffee and watched the brown mixture bubble. The odor of the boiling coffee was reassuring. It spelled out familiar things instead of the dank windy night that was creeping up on her now and slowly devouring the sky.

CHAPTER TWELVE

Shortly before midnight the yawl, beating up against stiffening head seas, was in what is known to sailors as the Hump, midway in the Florida Straits. There the big purple seas of the Gulf Stream, driven north by a current circulating through hundreds of fathoms of water and traveling halfway around the world, can build up to brutal proportions. The stars, which had been sparkling brightly only an hour before, were now obscured by clouds, and looking back to the west Robinson could distinctly make out the darker shape of the squall line moving in on him.

He considered reefing the main but decided that there was not enough time to try to tuck in reefs in the dark before the squall hit and that he would do better to simply drop the main altogether and go on under jib and mizzen.

With the big sail down and securely lashed, the motion of the yacht became easier. Sheets of spray were no longer whipping against his face. *Senegal* now rode high and comparatively dry. The wind, which had been steadily freshening all evening, was now veering a little west of south and the yawl was on a broad reach. Even with the shortened sail she tore along at what seemed a terrific speed. A splatter of rain, colder than the ocean spray, slapped his cheek. In another five minutes the squall would be upon him.

He had already double-checked his hatches and lashed down any loose gear. He was not seriously concerned about the squall but it would certainly be better to take all precautions. As an afterthought he ducked below and made another quick check of all water inlet clamps. There would be no repetition of the sinking of *Charee*.

When he came back on deck he saw that the squall line was almost upon him. From his experience of northwesters in this part of the world he knew that the front of heavy winds and rain would not last much more than an hour. After that would come clear skies and strongly steady winds and a sharp drop in temperature. By the next day the Stream, building up steadily under the battering of the wind, would be wild. Great seas ten to twenty feet high would come crashing over the Hump.

As a concession to the rain and cold wind he had put on a suit of oilskins. The parka had a pouch pocket over the chest and while be kept one hand on the wheel he rummaged in the pocket for his pipe and matches. He filled the blackened briar and cupped his hands for the match. When he finally had the pipe drawing well he settled back on his seat and brought the yawl back on course.

As he had anticipated, the wind was followed almost immediately by hard driving sheets of rain. Robinson grinned. Despite his knowledge of the fearsome effects of storms at sea he could not help but enjoy it. There was an elemental challenge in a storm at sea that brought out the best or worst in a man and a ship. He turned the pipe upside down to protect the tobacco from the rain and clamped the stem tighter between his teeth. The driving rain now obscured everything and he could barely make out the dim red light of the compass binnacle, but he managed to hold her pretty much on course by the feel of the wind.

The mountainous following seas came hissing up behind him now like muted express trains but the yawl showed no desire to broach. She had been well and honestly built and he was proud of her. The great seas foamed under her counter and the wind bit off the tops of the waves and spewed them away. The little ship rushed over the cliffs and down the valleys. She was going a little too fast now, once or twice he had the uneasy feeling that he was about to lose control, and he decided to drop the mizzen. He had taken the precaution of fastening a lifeline around his waist and clipping it to a backstay, and now he unclipped it and moved it around to the other stay and fought the wet fabric down onto the boom and lashed it fast.

It had occurred to him that while he was at it he might take in the jib too and run under bare poles, but going forward in the dark and leaving the helm untended seemed a risky proposition and he decided against it. Instead, he played an old sailor's trick on the sea. He held the two ends of the heavy anchor line and let the body of it trail out astern in a great loop. That would work the same as a sea anchor and it would be easier to handle.

With the drag of the heavy line slowing her down the yawl was now under control. She rode the great seas lightly and showed virtually no tendency to broach. It had long been a theory of his, contrary to accepted practice, that in a major storm it was safer to run a small boat before the seas than it was to head up into them. The main thing was to keep her from going too fast and he had achieved that by trailing the anchor line astern. *Senegal* was behaving beautifully in her first test and he was more than pleased with her. He settled back in the cockpit with his eyes on the ruby red spot of light that marked the binnacle and let the ship ride forward into the heaving dark.

The knife edge of panic sliced through Gwen's sleep and brought her awake and trembling. Wind and rain were shaking her meager shelter and a spray of sand whipped her face. For a moment she could not remember where she was nor how she had gotten there. The earth beneath her vibrated to the hammer blows of the surf. The world was sliding out from under her. In another moment the reef would be overwhelmed and she would be adrift in the wild sea. She wanted to scream for Gus but she might as well have been on the polar ice for all the good it would do. She slid back down under the poncho and pulled the hood over her head. The sand still vibrated under her but at least this way when death came with the rising water, she would not see it.

The minutes dragged by. The wind keened like a lost soul under the tarp. The great seas pounded the western point where she and Gus had made love in the shallows. Suddenly she remembered the flare gun he had left with her. She found it tucked away in the box of food and, holding the poncho tightly around her, she knelt on the wet sand. Had something red flickered in the dark or had she imagined it? Surely that was the running light of a ship. She raised the gun and pressed the trigger and watched the small orange-colored moon split the dark. It was extinguished all too soon by the wind and rain. She reloaded it and fired again. The light hung briefly suspended and was gone. Had they seen it? She strained for another view of the ship's light but that was gone now too. Perhaps she had only imagined it. If there had been a ship out there they would have a man on watch and he must surely have seen the flare. Anyway, whatever had been there was gone now.

Like a frightened child with the covers drawn over its head, she huddled under the poncho. To ward off the growing sense of panic, she tried to think of something comforting. A childhood memory came back to her. Madeline, her French nurse. A vaporous, weedy woman who lived on herb teas and was always looking for a remedy for a sickness of the head or the sickness of the sea or the sickness of the automobile. It was someone—Clare perhaps—who once said that all Madeline really needed was twenty minutes in bed with a husky French peasant. Gwen had not understood it at the time but now she understood it all too well. If Gus were here, if his arms were around her, the reef could go under for all she would care.

The thought was vaguely comforting. She began to feel a little better. There was a rhythm to the sea that was like the pounding of a train pulling out of a station. Madeline used to say the train sang:

> Frère Jacques,
> Frère Jacques,
> Dormez-vous?
> Dormez-vous?

It was true. All slow-speed piston engines sang that song. Anyway there was some comfort in remembering it. Her heart was no longer trying to jump out of her breast. She was even able to manage a little wry amusement at her own expense. Gwen Leacock—world traveler, darling of international society and old hand on the Via Veneto—now a target for assassins and marooned in the middle of the ocean, singing her old nursery song, "Frère Jacques." What a twist. If Madeline could see her now, the poor old soul would faint dead away.

Now that the first surge of panic had been driven back she was able to remind herself that the reef had withstood far greater storms than this. If there had been any real danger Gus would never have left her there. And tomorrow he would be with her. All she had to do was to get through this one last night.

She dozed off. The earth no longer shook. The storm passed and the moon shone clear from a sky that looked as frosty as ice. This time when she sat up she did see the running lights of a ship. No doubt about it. All lit up like a blooming Christmas tree. And, of course, it couldn't have been there when she had really needed it. Well now they could go to the devil. There would be no more screaming for help or firing flares like some panicky virgin. The night had passed and she had survived and she was a real woman now, waiting for her man. In the end the reef had been stronger than the storm and she herself had been stronger than the damned reef.

Robinson saw the sun rise on a smoky, windswept sea. Very far off he could barely make out the spidery trace of a ship's mast but the vessel itself was hull down below the horizon. Apart from that there was no sign of life. Steadying himself with his back against the mizzen mast he was able to catch a morning sun sight and work out his position. With the wind behind him all night he had made excellent time so far as distance was concerned, but the storm had set him almost twenty-five miles south of his course. He corrected his position on the chart and put the yawl on her new course. She was balanced nicely under mizzen and jib and he was able to leave the wheel long enough to go below and put on a pot of coffee.

While he was below he examined his face in the mirror. He was tired from the long night at the wheel and his face looked drawn but there was nothing wrong with him that a shave and a few hours rest would not cure. His skin felt raw from the spray that had been whipping against his face all night and he decided not to shave until later in the day.

The wind seemed to ease slightly as the sun rose and he hauled up the main. He kept the boom sheeted home until the sail was secured but then, when he was no longer in danger of a jibe, he let the boom swing out so that *Senegal* was now running before the wind with all the sail she could carry. The yawl was almost flying. Several times she planed right off the tops of the big crests. *Charee*, at her best, had never been capable of such a turn of speed. *Senegal* was all the boat any man could want. Why, then, couldn't he just relax and enjoy the trip? Why did he have this nagging sense of uneasiness, even of loss? For years he had traveled light without any excess emotional baggage. But now, because of Gwen, there was an anchor holding him to the shore. Well, cut the bloody line, he told himself angrily, and drop the damned hook. Despite everything that happened on that reef the cold-blooded bitch never hesitated for a second in choosing Dino. It must run in the family. To hell with her. The world is full of tail. The last thing a rover needs is a wife.

Something moved in his field of vision. A stick that seemed to jut briefly above the horizon and then as quickly disappear. When it came again he almost missed it but there it was, rising and falling with the big crests. It was curiously canted and looked almost like a spar buoy, but what the devil would a marker be doing out here?

He drew the binoculars out of their case and focused on whatever it was he had seen. The 7x50 lenses brought it up sharply. It was briefly white against the blue sea and then plunged down into the trough and was gone. When it rose again he was ready for it and this time he was able to see that it was a small boat that had been dismasted. What had looked like a spar buoy was the mast broken off halfway. He was still too far off to see if there was anyone on board. With a sigh he changed course and headed for the fleck of white.

As he approached he saw that it was a small lapstreak sloop not more than sixteen feet long. The gunwales were almost down to the water and it appeared to be sinking. An arm waved at him and then another. He dropped the sails and started the auxiliary engine and maneuvered closer under power.

Senegal reared up onto the top of a crest while the little boat was in the trough. There were two women in the boat and a young boy. The boy shouted something at him in Spanish. One of the women appeared to be sick, or dead. She was lying in the bilge and greasy water rolled over her with each heave of the boat. They had made an attempt to cover her with the remnants of the sail but it did no good. The other woman was gray-haired and dressed in black. She sat huddled on the stern thwart, shoulders hunched, face expressionless. Only the boy appeared to have any real life in him. He continued to wave and shout as Robinson maneuvered the yawl closer.

The yawl rose above the little boat once more and this time Robinson saw that the woman under the sail was not dead but obviously sick. Her head rolled weakly and she opened her eyes. The water sloshed over her. The gray-haired woman bent down and patted the sick woman's ankle in a gesture of comfort.

Robinson considered the situation. He obviously had to take these people off the sinking sloop, but how? If he tried to come alongside in these towering seas he might complete the destruction of the sloop and perhaps even drive a hole through Senegal's planking. On the other hand, he could not ask them to swim for it. The boy might make it but it was clearly out of the question for the two women. Another great sea heaved the little boat skyward and slopped water over the side. She might go at any moment.

He remembered now that *Senegal* carried an inflatable life raft in a locker under the forward vee bunks. He made a hand signal to the boy to hold on and ducked below and got out the yellow rubber bundle that was the raft. Maneuvering very carefully he worked up to windward of the sloop and yanked the lanyard that inflated the raft automatically and dropped the big yellow rubber doughnut over the side.

He had fastened a line to the raft's bow and now he let it pay out and drift down on the sloop. The first time he tried it it missed. He was about to come around for another pass when he saw that the boy had slipped over the side and was swimming strongly for the raft. Robinson nodded approvingly and made a gesture with clasped hands above his head. The boy seized the raft and began towing it back to the sloop.

When he was alongside he shouted something at the gray-haired woman but she continued to sit on the thwart staring at him helplessly. Again he said something to her and this time she seemed to understand. She left her seat and maneuvered past the woman in the bilge and got her under the arms and began to drag her over the side and half into the rubber boat. As she did so the covering sail slipped away and Robinson saw that the sick woman was comparatively young and in an advanced state of pregnancy. Her great swollen belly was distended by her awkward position and she cried out in pain. The old woman gave another heave and the pregnant woman tumbled face down into the life raft. But the weight on the sloop's gunwale was too much. Another sea seized the little craft and tipped it onto its beam ends. The old woman was thrown headfirst over the side. She waved once in a despairing gesture and went under. The last thing Robinson saw of her was her face, still calm, utterly resigned.

Robinson acted as smoothly as a well-oiled machine. He tossed a coil of line over the stern, knotted it to the cleat with two fast half-hitches and flung himself away from the boat in a long flat dive. He came up twenty feet from *Senegal's* counter, saw a glimmer of black cloth, and in five powerful strokes had his hands on her before she went under again.

When he surfaced with her he was already pushing out with both legs to drive himself back to the yawl. Even though he had acted so quickly to save her he had known it would be risky. What had worried him then, and worried him even more now, was getting back to the boat. The yawl was broadside to the wind and drifting fast. If he missed her she would be gone forever. And he was missing her. Although the old woman did not fight him, her weight was enough to slow him down. He heaved forward onto a wave crest and saw that *Senegal* was now a good forty yards away. For a moment he was tempted to abandon the old woman. She was half dead anyway and what good would it do her if they both died out here? Alone, he might still make it. For a moment the temptation was so strong that he actually released his hold. Who would ever know? He could say she had slipped away from him.

And what about Gwen? She had the flares and someone would find her. Or would they? The flares might go bad. The reef might be awash. Her drinking water might have been spilled and lost. She might be dying of thirst now.

The ugly image racked his brain. He gulped raw sea water and spewed it out, burning his throat and nostrils. His strength was drifting away and he had to fight harder to keep the old woman's head above water. Let her go. Alone he might still make it back to the yawl. He owed it to Gwen. The old woman was a stranger and half dead anyway. Let her go and save Gwen.

But even as he thought it, he knew that no matter how logical it seemed he could never willingly let the old woman go. There was still a chance and he had to take it or die with her. He tightened his grip and struggled forward.

The boy, who had been in the water beside the raft, now clambered aboard. He bent over the pregnant woman and said something to her and then seized the rope that tied the raft to the yawl and began to pull the raft forward. When he was close under *Senegal's* counter he gripped the transom in both hands and pulled himself aboard. He dropped down into the cockpit and in a quick motion cast off the line that secured the raft. The yellow doughnut bearing the pregnant woman drifted loose and, under the force of the wind, was quickly swept away.

Robinson had been watching all this with a sort of despairing astonishment. Then he saw what the boy was up to; he was trying to start the yawl's engine. Smoke bubbled under her counter and Robinson could see water coming out of the exhaust. The boy was at the wheel and bringing the *Senegal* around in a big circle. It was clear now why he had cut the raft loose. He had realized that it would be hopeless for him to try to get the woman aboard the yawl unaided and that in maneuvering the boat he might crush the raft. He had, therefore, in seemingly abandoning the raft displayed remarkably quick thinking.

Nor did the boy make the amateur boatman's mistake of charging straight down on Robinson. Instead he kept the yawl to windward and let it drift slowly down on the man in the water. Robinson saw the counter over him and with a sigh of thanksgiving grabbed the trailing line. He held onto the line with one hand and the old woman with the other and looked up at the boy's grinning face.

"Get your hands under her shoulders," he said to the boy.

The boy nodded and reached down and got his hands under the old woman's armpits.

"Now," Robinson gasped, and with the last of his strength pushed the old woman up while the boy pulled. For a moment she teetered there on the edge but then the boy pulled her over into the cockpit. Robinson hung onto the rope, drawing breath into his lungs and waiting for the strength to come back to his arms. When he thought he could make it he gripped the rope and pulled himself up. His own weight was killing him but he managed to hook an arm over the transom. He hung there while the boy pulled at him and then he was up and over. For a moment he was too exhausted to do anything but give the boy an encouraging pat on the jaw but then he managed to stand up and reach forward to take the wheel. He swung the yawl around looking for the yellow raft. It was now almost a quarter of a mile away, bobbing up and down on the crests and then dipping into the hollows. He ran down toward it.

CHAPTER THIRTEEN

By the time they had gotten the pregnant girl into the big bunk in the main cabin, the old woman had recovered enough to lend a hand. Robinson left her there with the girl and went back to the wheel. The boy followed him.

"What's your name?" Robinson asked.

"Hector Rafael Emilio Oliva Torres Hernandez Robaina," the boy answered, flashing the big grin in his brown face.

"That's quite a mouthful. What was the first name again?"

"Hector."

"All right, Hector. I'm Gus Robinson. What are you, Cuban refugees?"

"Yes." The boy's accent was strong but he appeared to understand English quite well.

"And who are the others?"

"One is my grandmother. The other is my sister."

"How far did you think you'd get in that floating matchbox?"

The boy shrugged and said, "We would like to have taken a bigger boat, señor, but it was the only one I could steal."

"Well you were damned lucky. Another ten minutes and you'd have been gone."

"A man on the sea must always have luck, Capitán."

"Where did you learn about boats? By the way, that was quick thinking on your part. You saved my life."

"You risked yours to save ours. It will not be forgotten."

"How did you know about the motor and handling a boat of this size?"

"My father has built many boats in Havana and ever since I was a little boy he has taught me many things. Do you know the Havana Yacht Club, Capitán Gus?"

"I've been there."

"Then maybe you knew my father—Lorenzo Robaina."

"I knew him," Robinson said. "He was a marine architect."

"A good one," the boy said proudly.

"A very good one," Robinson agreed. "Where is he? Why didn't he come with you?"

The boy had been very manly up to that point but now his lip trembled and tears formed in his eyes. "He is dead. They shot him."

"I'm sorry, Hector. He was a fine seaman. I remember meeting him once when he sailed on the Havana-St. Petersburg race. You must be quite a seaman yourself to have survived the storm in that little boat. Where were you trying to get to?"

"Key West."

"But you're way off course. You're nearly a hundred miles to the north."

The boy shrugged. "What could we do. It was one hell of a big wind. We had to run before it."

"And your sister? When is her baby due?"

"Right now," Hector said smiling. "I thought maybe it would come last night in the boat. That would have been bad."

"I'll say. And it will be damn near as bad if it comes on this one. I've handled a lot of things at sea but never a baby. We've got to get her ashore."

"Where will you take us?"

"I've been thinking about it. The nearest place would be Spanish Cay, which is where I'm headed for anyway. The trouble is I know there are no hospital facilities there. I guess I could take you to Nassau but that will be one hell of a long jog out of the way. Do you think you can keep her on the wind while I go below to talk to your sister?"

"I will sail her beautifully, Capitán."

"You do that. By the way, what's your sister's name?"

"Maria."

"A lot shorter than yours, eh?"

"It is important that a man should have a big name. It is necessary for his dignity."

Robinson turned the wheel over to the boy and watched him for a few minutes until he was confident that he could handle the yawl. Hector had difficulty seeing over the cabin top but his short, sturdy body looked fiercely proud and confident. Robinson nodded approvingly and went below.

The girl was stretched out in the big bunk with a blanket pulled up to her chin. Her face was pale and she looked very ill but he could see where under better circumstances she would be an extraordinarily pretty girl. There was something about her, perhaps it was only the dark hair and eyes or the pointed chin and heart-shaped face, that reminded him of Gwen. The girl looked a little frightened when she saw him coming down the ladder and he remembered the way Gwen had looked when he had first told her that he had been hired to murder her.

"Do you speak English, Maria?" he asked.

"A little," she answered softly.

"How do you feel?"

"I am hokay."

"Well I'd hardly say you're okay but we're going to try to get you ashore to a doctor as soon as possible. In the meantime you've got to be brave and hang on." He made two fists and shook them in the air to demonstrate his point. The girl nodded. She tried to smile but the shadow of pain darkened her eyes. She was holding her body rigid under the blanket. The old woman said something to her in Spanish and the girl shook her head.

"How about something warm to drink?" Robinson said. "Some tea? Or better yet, how about soup?"

"If it is not too much trouble."

"It's no trouble."

He lit the stove and opened two cans of soup and poured them into a pot. When the soup was hot he poured it into four cups and passed one up to the boy at the wheel, gave the others to the two women and kept one for himself.

"*Gracias*," the old woman said.

"*De nada*," Robinson answered.

For the first time she gave him a tentative smile, but almost immediately her features turned back into a mask of frozen sorrow.

The soup was hot and the warmth brought returning strength to all of them. The old woman held the girl's head up and poured a little of the soup between her lips. Robinson got out a loaf of bread and cut thick slices from it and handed it around.

When they had finished eating, Robinson said to the girl, "How soon do you think the baby will come?"

"I am trying to make him wait but he is very impatient."

"Are you in pain?"

"A little." Even as she said it a spasm caught her and her face was contorted.

"I have some aspirin. Would that help?"

She shook her head. Her lips were blue against her pale skin. "I do not think aspirin will be of much help with a baby."

"Your first child?"

"Yes."

"And your husband?"

"Dead." She said it without any visible display of emotion. It was either too soon for her to feel the real pain or else she was learning to live with it. There was something about her face then that was rather like the old woman's—a frozen, stoic dignity.

"I'm sorry."

"Where are you taking us?" she asked.

"That's what I wanted to discuss with you. Nassau is about eighty miles from here. There are plenty of doctors there and they will take good care of you. With luck we can be there by tonight."

She was about to say something but then she stopped.

"What is it?" Robinson asked.

"Nothing."

"There was something you wanted to say."

"No, it was nothing."

"Don't you want to go to Nassau?"

"It does not matter," she said. "We are very grateful." Another spasm of pain caught her and she turned her face away. The old woman bent over her, murmuring softly. Robinson left them and went back on deck.

"All right," he said to the boy. "I'll take over."

They sailed for a while in silence before Robinson said to the boy, "Tell me how it happened."

"How what happened, Capitán?"

"How you left Cuba. And what happened before you left. Or don't you want to talk about it?"

"I can talk," the boy said. "And you have a right to know." He looked out at the seas rushing by and hesitated for a moment before he went on. "You say you knew my father. That must have been before the revolution."

"Long before. I have not been to Cuba since. I often wondered what happened to him."

"He was a soldier of the revolution. He fought in the hills with the Barbudos. He hated the dictator Batista. When the revolution was won my father marched into Havana with the others. That was two years ago and I was only eleven then but I remember it very well. All the noise and excitement. It was the best day of our lives. And there was my father in his uniform and with a pistol and a great black beard. I remember how he smelled. He smelled of sweat and dirt from the mountains. He smelled good. And he looked big enough to reach the sky. It was like the day when we would launch one of his boats, only better.

"Then the war was over and my father shaved off his beard and went back to building boats. Only there were no boats to build. They said the boats my father built were for rich men and there would not be any more rich men in Cuba. So my father said all right he would build boats for fishermen, but they did not want that either. They said if the fishermen had boats they would run away. My father said he had fought in the mountains for freedom and what kind of freedom was it if a man could not run away when he wanted to.

"So then they came and took him away and put him into the prison. They let us come there once to see him. There were big yellow stone walls and where my father was the walls were always wet and it was very dark and the bearded ones were everywhere. My father had shaved off his beard a long time before because he was not with them any more and he did not want to look like them. He was very thin and his face was pale and he looked like an old man. He did not look like himself any more. If you remember my father you will know he always had a joke and a laugh."

"I remember," Robinson said.

"But when we went to see him in the fortress there were no jokes left in him. He took me aside and held me between his knees and he said, 'Hector, you are the man now. You must look out for the others. This is a bad place now and I do not think it will ever be much good again and when the time comes that it is too bad then it will be up to you to get a boat some place and take the women away. Take them to Key West. I have friends there and they will know what to do with you.'

"A week later Maria's husband Emilio came with some other men in the night and they fought with the guards and got my father out of the prison and ran away with him to the mountains. The bearded ones ran after my father in the mountains but they could not catch him. We heard that my father and Emilio had guns and that they had killed many of the bearded ones.

"Then the Barbudos came to our house and they took Maria and my grandmother and myself to the prison and they sent word to my father that if he did not come down from the mountains they would shoot us. They said that if my father and Emilio came down they would let us go and that my father and Emilio would be put back in the prison and that nothing bad would happen to them. I think my father did not believe them but he said he would come down anyway and he did come down and when the Barbudos had my father and Emilio in the street and away from the mountains they shot them. After that they let us go.

"Then I remembered what my father had told me and I knew it was time to find the boat. I knew where there was a little sloop lying in the mud and because it was no good any more the bushes had grown up around it and no one remembered it had been there. But I thought it could be fixed because my father had showed me how to fix boats and I stole some wood for the new planks and I fitted them and caulked them as he had shown me.

"When the boat was ready my grandmother sewed the sails and late at night when it was dark I took the boat down the river to a secret place and picked up Maria and my grandmother. Maria was already very big with the baby and I knew it was a bad time to go but Maria said that she did not care, she would rather die than to have her baby born in that country with those people. She wanted her baby to be born in Key West and to be an American. That was what Emilio and my father had wanted more than anything and she said she had to do that for them.

"So I took them in the boat and we got away but even though we were very quiet someone saw us and they shot at us from the wall and then they sent a patrol boat after us but because we were only a little boat under sail and very quiet they could not find us and so we got away. For two days we sailed very well and I thought that even though it was only a little boat and the caulking had worked loose and we had to bail all the time we would still make it. But then the storm came along and broke the mast and we were finished. And that was how it was when you found us."

"Then that's the reason why Maria doesn't want to go to Nassau? Because she promised Emilio the baby would be born in the United States?"

The boy nodded. "But of course, Mister Capitán Robinson, we cannot ask you to go out of your way."

"I'm sorry it means so much to her," Robinson said. "I would like to do it if I could but it's impossible now."

The boy nodded. Robinson sat at the wheel with his eye on the compass. The seas were beginning to moderate and *Senegal* was heeled over and making knots in an easterly heading. Robinson opened his chart case and plotted a course to Nassau. With the yawl moving as she was now at close to ten knots he could make Nassau in roughly twelve hours and unload his passengers and be back at the reef to pick up Gwen at dawn. It would mean the devil of a lot of sailing plus the strain of worrying about the pregnant girl but it could be managed. On the other hand, going back to Key West would mean losing an entire day. It would also mean another crossing of the Stream, and this time with a passenger who might go into labor at any moment. It was out of the question.

But the thought continued to nag at him. They wanted the child to be born in the United States. That was all they had left now and it was tremendously important to them. He had not known Lorenzo Robaina too well but he knew the boats he had designed and they were sound boats and he had respect for, and a certain kinship with, Robaina as a fellow seaman. There was really nothing the dead man could ask of him now but somehow he was asking it. Or perhaps it was only in the boy's eyes and in the girl's white face. Or was it in his own mind? Was there a feeling that he had come by *Senegal* in a way that was not quite honest and that there was still an obligation to be discharged?

Don't be a sucker, he told himself. Don't build this thing up into some sort of half-assed morality play. You've already done enough. You saved three lives, four counting the baby, and that's plenty. So let the kid be born somewhere else. What does it matter?

But it did matter. It had mattered to Lorenzo Robaina and it mattered enough to these people now to have risked a crossing in what was really no more than a leaky rowboat.

And Gwen is still sweating it out on that sandbar. An extra twenty-four hours to her now will be like twenty-four years. You can't treat her like a lump of stone chucked over the side on the premise that you just might come back for it at your convenience. If you play it that way you'll be playing Clare's game after all. She may be picked up and raped or murdered. Come off it now, rapists and murderers don't go sailing around the Bahamas. Don't they? You slept with her yourself and may have damned near murdered her at that. She'll be all right. She's safer there then she would be in New York's Central Park. Anyway she can take care of herself. She and her precious Dino. The damned pimp will have to wait another day for his reward. He'll have his hands on her soon enough as it is.

Although he was hardly aware of it, it was probably that last sour note of jealousy that brought about the decision. It was more powerful than any nobility of purpose he felt regarding the refugees. Why should he rush back to throw her into Dino's arms? Perhaps with an extra twenty-four hours in which to think it over she would realize how impossible it was.

He had a good excuse but a poor motive. He felt a little ashamed of himself as he put the wheel hard over and steadied the yawl on a southwesterly heading.

"Hector, go below and tell your sister to hang on with everything she's got. With a little luck that kid will be born in the States after all."

Hector grinned and darted below. Robinson could hear the babble of excited voices. He took in a little on the main sheet to urge the yawl to an even faster speed. She was flying now, a bone in her teeth and the wake streaming clear.

By mid-afternoon they were halfway across. The seas were still running big but the wind was hard on the beam and the yawl was responding with everything she had. As her bow sliced through the seas, clouds of spray flickered in the shining air. Much of the time the lee rail was covered by foam. Her sails were taut as a drumhead and the rigging sang under the strain. There was tremendous exhilaration in handling a boat that was driving forward with such power and now and then Robinson would find himself and the boy grinning at each other out of sheer enjoyment. It was one of the best days of sailing he had ever experienced. It was almost as if the yawl knew that she was in a race for life and that each minute lost might be the fatal one.

When *Senegal* was well established on her new heading he turned the wheel over to the boy and went below to fix lunch. It was a harrowing experience for him. The girl was in a great deal of pain. She lay moaning on the bunk while the old woman wiped her face and tried to comfort her. Child birth was a new experience for Robinson and he was unprepared for the violence connected with it. He took a bottle of aspirin tablets out of his medicine kit and offered it to the old woman to give to the girl but the grandmother shook her head. Unable to understand her Spanish, Robinson told the boy to stick his head below long enough to translate.

Hector listened to his grandmother and then grinned at Robinson and said, "She says you know much about boats but nothing about babies. God has willed that a woman must suffer before bearing a child. It has always been thus and always will be and the women and the children survive. The suffering is God's will and it is good for her. She says also," Hector went on, "that it is something a brave man cannot stand and that if it bothers you too much you should go away and let her cook the lunch. She says you know no more about cooking than about childbearing."

"It's fine with me," Robinson said. "Tell her she is captain of the cabin and that I will stay up above where I belong."

The old woman nodded with satisfaction and took over the galley.

All through the day the yawl plunged on. Once, even above the rushing of the seas, he heard the girl scream. The sound sent a chill down his spine. He cursed himself for having been fool enough to let himself be talked into this maniacal expedition. He should have followed his first hunch and taken her to Nassau. What if she died on board the boat before he could get her ashore? The only reassuring thing was Hector's apparent indifference to what was happening below. When Robinson questioned him he said that he had seen many babies born and that the women always screamed and that his sister was a strong, healthy girl and that he himself would rather have a baby than a toothache.

At dusk they were still forty miles from land. The wind had freshened again but the yawl was carrying every stitch of sail she could bear. She drove steadily westward over seas the color of purple ink toward the last red glow in the sky. The girl's pains were coming with increasing force and regularity. The old woman called for towels and a big pot of hot water. Robinson went below just long enough to show her where they were. Maria's face was as pale as the sheets and her brow was beaded with sweat. Robinson fled.

The Rebecca Shoals light was clear against the night sky now and to the northwest he could see a dull glow cast by the lights of Key West. The yawl drove forward with tremendous power. Robinson could only hope that everything would hold. Twenty minutes later he could distinctly make out the lights of the naval air station on Boca Chica Key.

They were coming into the lee of the keys now and into somewhat calmer water. The yawl still had the wind in her sails and was still moving forward with marvelous speed but the seas had moderated. In the comparative silence that came with smoother water he was aware of a sudden rush of noise and excitement from the cabin. The girl's cries tore him apart. He knew now that they would not make it after all. He could hear the old woman praying. Even the boy, who had been so ebullient throughout the trip, now looked gaunt and worried. Robinson tried to force himself to concentrate on the tricky channel that led into Garrison Bight but he could not close his ears to the dreadful sounds from below. He remembered the Hemingway short story about the Indian who had cut his throat while listening to his wife in labor in the bunk below. He could understand it now. He thought that in another minute he himself would have to leap over the side.

He slowly became aware that for the past ten minutes there had been comparative silence. Then he heard the thin squeak of a baby's first cry. He and the boy stared at each other wordlessly. The old woman thrust her head out of the hatch and for the first time her lined face was creased in a smile. She said something to the boy and then her head disappeared.

"What does she say?" Robinson asked.

"She tells me that Lorenzo Robaina lives again."

"And your sister?"

The boy made a negligent gesture and said, "I told you she was strong and healthy."

Robinson said nothing. He felt too exhausted to speak.

After a while the boy said, "It is too bad we did not make it."

Robinson clapped him on the shoulder and said, "Hector, you're a hell of a seaman but you still have a little to learn about navigation. We did make it. We were inside the three-mile limit when he was born. Lorenzo Robaina's grandson is as much an American as if he had been born in the middle of Kansas. And by the way, how does it feel to be an uncle?"

"Uncle?" The boy's eyes widened in wonder. "Me?"

"Of course. Uncle Hector."

"Holy sheet," the boy said in grave tones. Then he turned and looked to the southeast where his homeland lay, and spat over the side.

CHAPTER FOURTEEN

The immigration people were very efficient. They were accustomed to handling Cuban refugees. Maria and her grandmother and the baby were taken off to the hospital. Hector had fallen asleep in the cockpit and Robinson did not have the heart to wake him. When the customs officials in their khaki uniforms had completed their investigation he made his way forward and slumped down on one of the vee bunks. He was asleep almost before his head had touched the pillow.

He awoke to the first light of dawn and pulled himself stiffly off the bunk. The odor of fresh coffee came from the galley. He looked aft into the main cabin and saw that Hector had set the table for two and had coffee and bacon and eggs going. Maria's soiled bedding and towels had been neatly rolled into a ball and the bunk was freshly made. The floor had been swept and the dishes that had been used the day before had been washed and stowed in their racks.

Robinson pulled his clothes off, and climbed through the hatch onto the forward deck and turned on the hose from the dock and let the water pour over him. The fresh water felt icy in the pre-dawn coolness. When he had finished washing himself he pulled on a pair of clean khaki trousers and ran a razor over the stubble on his jaws.

When he came into the main cabin the boy held out a mug of steaming coffee to him and said, "Good morning, Capitán Gus."

"Hello, Hector. When did you do all this?"

"While you slept, sir."

"Good boy."

"Do you like your eggs this way, sir?"

"Any way."

They ate in silence. While Gus finished his second cup of coffee the boy did the dishes. The cabin was immaculate. The boy gestured at the pile of linens and said, "As soon as the sun comes up to dry them I will wash these things for you."

Robinson shook his head. "Thanks anyway, but there won't be time for that."

The boy's grin faded. "No time?"

"I'm getting under way in ten minutes."

"You are moving to another berth perhaps?" the boy asked hopefully.

"No, I'm putting out to sea."

"So soon?"

"Yes. I must."

The boy swallowed hard and looked serious. Robinson could see the way his heart jumped in his naked brown chest "Take me with you, Capitán."

"I'm sorry but I can't, Hector. I'm going a very long way."

"It does not matter where you go, sir. Go to the moon if you like. This is a big boat. You will be glad to have help. I can cook and clean and handle the wheel. Also I can paint very well. My father taught me everything. You will see, Capitán Gus. You will not be sorry if you take me."

The words came out in a rush. The boy's eyes were like those of a spaniel Robinson had once owned. The only thing the dog had ever asked of him was to be with him. When he had gone ashore and left it on the boat it had pleaded with him with its great liquid eyes. The dog had been washed overboard in a wicked storm off the Azores. That had been two years ago but its eyes continued to haunt him.

"It wouldn't work, Hector," Robinson said gently. "You have to stay here and go to school."

"School? What do you learn of the sea in a school? On a boat one learns. With a man like you or a man like my father one learns. With no one else."

"That isn't true. And there are other things besides the sea."

"What other things?"

How could he answer? He had made his own choice a long time ago and how could he explain now to the boy that it had not always been the best choice? "What about Maria and your grandmother?" he said, hedging.

"They are here now in the States. They have friends who will take care of them. And besides, they have the baby to play with."

"Didn't your father tell you to take care of them?"

"Yes."

"Then that is what you must do."

The boy saw that it was hopeless. His face took on a resigned look. His eyes were wet and he chewed his lip. "All right, Capitán. If you say so."

"For myself I would like to take you, Hector. But for your father I say no. For your father I say you must stay here."

The boy looked at him with the spaniel's eyes.

"Besides," Robinson went on, "there are many boats here and later on you will have plenty of time for sailing."

The boy looked around at the moored boats and said, "There are boats here, sir, but no Capitáns like you."

Robinson suddenly felt lonely. He stood up abruptly and said, "I'm sorry, Hector, but I can't take you. You must stay here and go to school and study to be a naval architect. That is what your father would have wanted and that is what you must do."

The boy did not answer.

"One day we'll meet again, Hector."

"Yes, sir," the boy said, his disbelief written clear in his eyes.

Robinson went below to start the engine. The boy's shirt was on the bunk. On a sudden impulse he took out the rest of the money Clare had given him and thrust it into the boy's shirt pocket and buttoned the flap. He was glad to get rid of it. He came back on deck and tossed the shirt to the boy. As he edged away from the pier the boy gave him a rigid salute. He was still holding it as the yawl turned seaward.

Robinson did not look back. He had learned a long time ago that for a man who sails alone it is unwise to look back.

An hour before dark he saw the fringe of pines that stood up from the sandy skull of Spanish Cay. He altered his course to the southeast and headed for the reef. Twenty minutes later, through the binoculars he was able to make out the hump of sand and the rickety framework that held the tarp. As he closed the reef he saw that her things were still there, stacked neatly under the tarp, but that there was no sign of life.

She must, he decided, have been picked up by a ship and taken back to Spanish Cay. There was a sour taste of loss in his mouth but he told himself that it was just as well. That way he didn't have to see her again and go through another painful scene. Still, it would have been nice if they had been able to say good-bye in a civilized manner. Civilized, hell.

What you really wanted was another roll on that blanket. Anyway it's over now and someday you can send her a postcard from Funafuti. Mrs. Dino di Buonaventura, care of The Stork Club, El Morocco or the Tour d' Argent. Weather lovely, wish you were here. Christ, how he would wish she were there.

Something stirred on the far side of the sand spit. A wisp of black followed by a flash of gold. He moved the binoculars quickly. The top of her head and her bare shoulder. He felt himself grinning wolfishly. She had been swimming on the far side of the reef and now, as she emerged, he could see that she was naked. Her beautiful, honey-colored body shone in the dying rays of the sun like wet gold. The tilt of her breasts and the gently curved pubic mound knocked the breath out of his throat.

At that moment she must have noticed the yawl for the first time. Although he was too far off to hear it he could see by her face that she had let out a startled yelp. She dropped back into the water like a shot rabbit.

It was several minutes before her head was again raised above the level of the ridge. By this time he was close enough so that when he stood up in the cockpit and waved at her he needed no binoculars to see the smile of delight on her face. She made a wild dash for the shelter of the tarp and drew the blanket over herself and waved back at him.

He let the main and mizzen drop and ghosted in with just the jib, pulling to within fifty yards of the beach. At that point he was in the lee of the reef and over good-holding ground in four or five fathoms of water. He put the tiller hard over and brought her up into the wind and as she hung there, jib flapping, he dropped the smaller of the two patent anchors from the foredeck and saw the flukes dig into the sand. He gave the anchor rope plenty of scope and let the yawl ride well back on the line before he took a turn on the post. He had been too busy with the anchor to keep an eye on Gwen and now as he looked back at the ridge he was a little disappointed to see that she had already gotten into her shirt and dungarees.

He took the lashings off the Fiberglass dinghy that was secured to the cabin top and heaved the little boat over the side. The oars had been lashed underneath and, carrying them in one hand, he stepped carefully down into the nervous dink.

As the keel touched the shelving sand that formed the reef Gwen rushed forward to hold the bow for him. Together they dragged the little boat up on the beach and then she threw her arms around him and said, "My God, I've never been so glad to see anybody in my whole life. I had just about given you up for lost. You said you'd be here yesterday."

"I know. I'm sorry about that. I was almost here and then I had to turn back." He told her how he had picked up the Cubans and had taken them back to Key West.

"And she really had a baby on board your boat?"

"Cross my heart. And I can tell you I never want to go through anything like that again."

"But I think it's marvelous," Gwen said. "And I'm very proud of you. Doesn't that make you the godfather or something?"

"I suppose it might have if I'd been willing to wait around for it but I was in a hurry to get back here to take you off your desert island. Here, let me look at you. How was the storm?"

"Did you get it too?"

"And how. Was it kind of rugged for you, Gwen?"

"A little."

"Come on now, don't kid old Captain Gus. I'll bet it scared the pants off you."

"You're right. That's why I was in the raw when you came sneaking up on me."

"I don't call it sneaking exactly. It's just that sailboats don't make much noise."

"Why didn't you blow a horn or a whistle or something?"

"And spoil the view? Don't be silly."

"You're a terrible man."

"There's nothing new about that. You've known it right along. Anyway, you seem to have thrived on your isolation. You're as brown as a fig newton and twice as pretty. And unless those binoculars are out of whack you've even gained a little weight."

"Wretch." Suddenly she dropped the bantering tone and asked softly, "Are you still angry at me, Gus?"

"Why should I be angry?"

"You were pretty mad when you left here. You wouldn't even say good-bye to me. It was hardly the gentlemanly thing to do, marooning a gal on a desert island and then going off without so much as a good-bye kiss. I'm sure that Captain Kidd and Blackbeard always kissed their victims good-bye before making them walk the plank."

"If they were pretty enough to kiss, there were no planks for them to walk."

"So that's it. I'm not pretty enough. Well this is a fine time to tell me."

She was standing very close to him and he was almost painfully aware of her. In another moment his awareness would be obvious. He wanted desperately to reach out and take hold of her and he had even taken a step toward her before he remembered Dino. She was still bent on marrying Dino or she would have said something about it. Then to hell with her. Much as he wanted her he would not expose himself to the same hurt again. He looked directly at her unbuttoned shirt and at the honey-colored softness of her half revealed breasts and said coldly, "Button your shirt."

A touch of red tinged her cheekbones. She looked down at herself and said, "I'm sorry." Her slender brown fingers fumbled at the buttons and she added, "Did you have to use quite that tone of voice?"

"Yes."

She turned away from him to look across the water and said, "That's a very beautiful boat. What do you call her?"

"*Senegal.*"

"Now you've got everything you wanted, haven't you?"

"Just about."

"Oh you really are impossible, Gus. I've been sitting here day and night counting the minutes until I saw you again and now you're behaving like such a clod." There were tears in her eyes.

"I've never been noted for fancy manners. I leave that to your gigolo friends."

She turned away from him and stamped angrily off across the beach and sat down under the tarp with her face averted. After a while Robinson walked after her and said, "Well? Are you coming or do you want to stay here?"

Without looking at him she answered coldly, "I couldn't care less."

"Why didn't you tell me that before I sailed such a bloody long way to get here?"

"And why didn't you tell me that you were going to behave like such an absolute... bastard? Anyway, you might just remember that this whole thing was your idea. I'm here by your invitation. I can assure you it was hardly my notion of a weekend at the Ritz."

"All right. It was my idea and you cooperated beautifully and I appreciate it very much and now I've come back to get you as I said I would, so will you please, for the love of heaven, get your butt into the bloody boat?"

Tears were making little rivulets on her cheeks. She brushed them angrily away and said, "I'll thank you not to yell at me, Mr. Robinson. I'm not your wife."

"That's a break for both of us."

"What do you want of me? All you ever really wanted was your damned boat and your freedom. Well now you've got them both so why don't you leave me alone?"

"Because I've got to get you out of here and so I'm inviting you politely to step into the goddamned bloody dink!"

"Well I'm not going. I wouldn't go across the street with you."

"I'm not in the mood for games," he said bending down and picking her up in his arms. She kicked and twisted and tried to sink her teeth in his shoulder.

"Go ahead. Bite. It's what I would have expected from a bitch like you," he said.

She stopped struggling and lay quiet in his arms. He carried her down and dumped her in the stern of the dink. Then he went back and dismantled the tarp and picked up the rest of the gear and carried it all down to the boat. He had to make two trips.

When he came back the second time she said softly, "Gus."

"What?"

"Come here."

He did not answer and she said, "Please."

He waded through the shallow water to the stern of the boat and she reached up and put her arms around his neck and her lips against his.

"Are we really in such a terrible hurry? Can't we stay a little longer?"

"For what? Batting practice?"

"Now what does that mean?"

"I don't like being a warm-up pitcher for brother Dino."

She turned her face away and said nothing more. He got into the dink and shipped the oars and rowed back to the yawl. When they came alongside the yacht he tried to help her aboard but she pushed his hand away and immediately went below and lay down on the bunk with her face to the bulkhead.

Robinson hauled the dink aboard and lashed it down. Then he started the engine and worked the yawl slowly forward on a shortened anchor line until he had broken the hook loose from the bottom. He stowed the anchor in its chocks and hoisted the sails and put *Senegal* on a course for Spanish Cay.

When they touched the pier Gwen came on deck for the first time. She stepped ashore even before he had the lines secured and said curtly, "Good-bye, Gus," and walked away.

When she was out of sight behind the old frame hotel he finished securing the boat and then went ashore to buy liquor and ice. He felt a hundred years old. In a few hours he would be at sea in the boat he had always wanted, but suddenly there was damned little joy in the prospect.

CHAPTER FIFTEEN

A cat exploded under her feet and went squalling down the alley behind the straw market. Gwen leaped sideways. Her nerves felt tight as bowstrings. She wanted desperately to run away but she controlled the impulse. She had to have it out with Clare. More powerful than her fear was the desire to see Clare's face when she knew the truth.

She passed through the darkened village and continued on toward Clare's house. The road, outlined by moonlight, had the dead, cold look of bone. The huge banyan tree at the crossroads cast shadows that looked like hanged men. Somewhere a dog howled. Gwen put her hand over her breast and felt the pounding of her heart. Not since the night of the great storm when she had been alone on the sandspit had she felt so vulnerable.

Did she really need this brief victory? She hesitated in the patch of black shadow cast by the banyan but then went on. It had to be done this way, and now. It would be the last time she and Clare would ever see each other.

She went on along the road and then stood hesitating outside the house. The place was dark. Her palms were moist and she was breathing as hard as if she had run all the way. Why was she so petrified? Clare's sting had been drawn and all she could do now was to buzz harmlessly.

There was gravel on the drive. Her feet made a crunching sound like walking on dry snow. The night was clear and the stars raged overhead in icy splendor. She screwed up her courage and moved toward the door.

At that moment a light flashed on in the bedroom. It startled her. She backed away and stood waiting. When nothing further happened she tiptoed forward.

The bedroom window was half obscured by the terrace wing and she crept around the concrete structure and took up a position just outside the window. Even there, however, it was impossible to see through the heavy drapes. But she could hear a voice, a man's voice. She moved closer until her face was almost pressed against the glass.

Suddenly, like a stroke of lightning, the curtains were drawn apart and the face of her cousin appeared at the window.

The confrontation shocked them both. Gwen felt as though her heart had stopped. Clare screamed.

In the brief moment before Gwen turned away the scene in the room was photographed indelibly on her brain. Clare in a nightgown, her hair rumpled and some sort of grease on her face. She was smoking a cigarette and her eyes were narrowed from the smoke. She looked older than Gwen had ever seen her and the nightgown revealed bulges of excess flesh.

At the sight of Gwen Clare's eyes blazed with such an expression of fury that they seemed to glow with an inner light of their own. And when she screamed her face was contorted with rage. In that ghastly instant of revelation she appeared to have aged ten years at one stroke.

But the real shock was not Clare; it was Dino naked on the bed and jerked upright by Clare's scream. As he looked past Clare into Gwen's eyes an expression of sadness, of hopeless self-knowledge—something like that of a two-dollar bettor who has played a long shot and torn up his ticket only to find that a photo finish has called his horse the winner—flickered across his face. Then he leaped out of bed and snatched up a robe and ran toward the door.

Gwen ran wildly down the path toward the beach. She heard voices, half muffled by the wind, calling after her, but he did not stop. She ran without knowing why she was running. All she knew was that she had to get away from both of them. Her heart seemed to be bursting. When she heard Dino's voice coming closer she threw herself off the path and rolled down the side of one of the dunes and lay hidden while he rushed by.

She lay still with her face pillowed on her arm and her body racked by sobs. She was torn by a sense of loss. Loss of what? she asked herself. Loss of Dino? No, she never really had cared about Dino or she could not have given herself to Gus. It was more the loss of innocence and youth. She had seen, blazing out at her through the window, the consummate face of evil and, like the sailors who looked on the face of Medusa, she felt turned to stone.

She could hear Dino still calling after her down on the beach. She got up and ran back the other way to the road. One of her sneakers came off in the sand. She ran on without it.

A few minutes later a car came blazing down the road, lights bouncing. When it was almost upon her she flattened herself on the sand. As the car went by she thought she recognized Dino at the wheel. When it was gone she ran on. At first she had only fled blindly, running in any direction to get away from Clare and Dino. But now she knew where she was running.

The car was coming back. Because the land was so flat she could see it coming a long way off and she had plenty of time to find a hiding place. The car moved slowly; he was searching carefully. She lay flat behind a low bush. She heard him calling out to her, "Gwen. Where are you, Gwen?" She lay face down until it was gone and then she got up and limped along through the soft sand by the side of the road.

Now that her need to reach Gus was crystallized she realized that she might be too late. More than likely he had taken the yawl straight out to sea again. If she missed him now she might never find him again. Something sharp pierced her bare foot and she cried out. She bent down and pulled a long thorn from her instep and saw blood run black in the moonlight.

A full hour had gone by before she reached the pier. She was gasping for breath and soaked with perspiration. All the while she had been telling herself that the yawl would still be there but now, as she came around the corner of the hotel, her heart sank. *Senegal's* tall mast was gone. Only the stubby fishing cruisers squatted in the nest.

Too tired to cry any more and overwhelmed by hopelessness she let herself sink down on the pier's damp wooden slats. The small voice said, "Are you all right, lady?"

She looked up and saw a boy of nine or ten. His round, dark face offered her a tentative smile. His ragged trousers were held at the waist by rope. He shuffled his bare feet uneasily as he stared down at her.

She felt pathetically glad to have someone to talk to. She said, "Hello. What are you doing out at this time of night? Shouldn't you be in bed?"

"I brung ice for the boat, lady."

"What boat?"

"The sailboat."

"The big sailboat with one man aboard?"

The boy nodded.

She sat up abruptly. "Where is he?"

"He's gone."

"When? When did he go?"

The boy shrugged. "Before you come, lady."

"Did you see him go? Do you know which way he went?"

The child pointed toward the velvet darkness of the sea and said, "He went out there."

CHAPTER SIXTEEN

In the first light of dawn *Senegal* drifted on a windless sea. Robinson had set his course for the island of New Providence but in the past three hours he had not made good more than five miles. The sails hung slack and the air was lifeless. Spanish Cay was still dimly visible on the horizon.

He went below to fix his breakfast and then lay down on the bunk. It might be an hour or two before the wind came up and in the meantime he might as well sleep. He closed his eyes but sleep eluded him. The image of Gwen in Dino's arms, that had tortured him all night, continued to plague him. Jealousy gnawed at his guts. He felt as if he were being eaten alive. How long would the pain last? He supposed if you got drunk and stayed drunk long enough it might help.

The boat, the sea, all the things he had savored for so many years, had turned to ashes in his hands. Without her they were meaningless. He had built a trap for Clare and ended up in it himself.

The damnable part of it was that if he had not been such a stubborn bastard he might have found a way to have both Gwen and the sea. He could, for instance, have worked something out with Caldwell that would have enabled him to work on the auxiliaries without confining himself to shore. When consultations were necessary he could have flown in for them but apart from that there would have been no reason to stay in Miami.

He could have taken Gwen to the Mediterranean or down to the Aegean and the isles of Greece. They could have made the best of both worlds. All it had needed was a gesture on his part, and he had been too goddamned bullheaded to make it.

Dino's hands were on her now. His lips on hers. Head thrown back, eyes closed, nipples erect under his touch. Christ!

The distant hum of a motor brought him up on one elbow. He had thought at first that it was a light plane but now he recognized it as the unmistakable high-pitched whine of an outboard. What bloody lunatic would be this far at sea in an outboard?

He picked the binoculars out of their rack and went out on deck. The sky was red and there was a fierce glare off the water. He adjusted the glasses and brought the little skiff into focus. A dark-haired girl sat on the stern thwart and was waving furiously. Now, even above the whine of the motor, he could hear her calling. His heart seemed to flip over in his chest.

The skiff came alongside and she switched off the motor. He reached down and swooped her up on deck and held her tight against him.

When he finally let her go he said, "You're absolutely nuts."

"Didn't you know?"

"There's only one lousy can of gas in that skiff. Suppose you hadn't found me? How would you have gotten back?"

"I didn't stop to think about it. There was no time."

"What do we do with the skiff? Do we take it back?"

She shook her bead vehemently. "I never want to see Spanish Cay again. Can't we just take it along to wherever the next port is and then send them a check for it?"

"Of course. Stop trembling."

"I can't. It may take me years."

"We've got years," he said.

THE END

A NIGHT OUT
Basil Heatter

There was the hot blue sea and the scrubbed white coral and the fort. There was sun-blasted brick spattered with bird droppings and an overgrown parade ground and the long Civil War cannon that had rusted away without ever having been fired in anger. The gun emplacements stared out at the sea like empty eye sockets and the warm rain blew through it all and the sun nibbled the mortar away from the bricks.

Few people can remember now just why or how they had come to build it in a place that was bone dry and where it was necessary to bring the water in kegs from the mainland two hundred miles away but in Key West they will tell you how the bricks were brought down from Boston and were six months on the way and of how the men who went out to build the fort were a motley crew and of the various ways in which so many of them died.

On the charts they call it the Dry Tortugas but the men who sweated there called it something else. The story goes that for every brick laid a life was lost. That would be an awful lot of lives but they might be about half right at that.

In the end it was abandoned entirely because of the yellow fever, but the bricks still stand.

CHAPTER ONE

I got to stop sleeping in the street, Cruze told himself. It's cold now. It's getting on to be winter and even here in Key West it's damn cold. And the nights are long. I bet you if I opened my eyes I'd find out the sun isn't up yet. In the summer it comes up early and you can feel the heat on the stones but the way it is now you can't hardly tell the difference.

Maybe you think I can't open my eyes if I want to but I'll tell you right now you're wrong, buddy. I can open my eyes any time I want to. I got perfect control over my eyes. But why the hell should I? Just to please you? What have you ever done for me? I'll keep them shut. You can go to hell, buddy.

He hunched up tighter in the doorway and hugged himself but there was no warmth in his arms. He was all bone anyway. The whiskey had eaten the flesh off him.

He dozed a little and then somebody was kicking him and without opening his eyes he said, "Yes, sir. Just resting. Moving on now."

"Wake up," Flake said.

Cruze opened his eyes. The sun hurt and he closed them. When he opened them again Flake was still standing there.

"Get up, rummy," Flake said.

Cruze sighed and pulled himself together. He got up in sections, unfolding his stiff-legged length like one of those collapsible toys.

"What do you want, Flake?"

"I'll buy you a cup of joe."

"Well, I don't know," Cruze started to say, but Flake took him by the collar and dragged him off down the street. Cruze was a head taller than Flake but Flake could have carried him easily under one arm.

They went down the street to the Cuban place in back of the turtle pens where the ten drunks sat on the bench like chickens on a roost. They were sitting there soaking in the sun and holding each other up. They had been there all night or maybe forever. Flake could not remember when they had not been there. He put his wide-shouldered bulk through the sagging doorway and dragged Cruze after him. He ordered coffee for two and eggs and sausage for himself. The rummy made an effort to drink his coffee. He held the cup in both hands but it was no use. He shook uncontrollably.

"Give him a beer," Flake said to the girl.

"What kind?"

"Any kind."

The girl brought a bottle. Cruze picked it up in both hands and let the cold beer pour down his throat. His skinny neck worked on the beer and his Adam's apple bobbed up and down. He drank the whole thing without stopping. When he finished he wiped his mouth with the back of a grimy hand and pleaded, "Lemme have another one, Flake."

Flake was eating. Without looking up he said, "No."

"Just one more."

"Damn it, I said no."

Cruze muttered to himself.

"You want some eggs?" Flake asked.

"No. If I can't have a beer I don't want nothing."

"Then that's what you'll get. Nothing."

They sat in silence while Flake finished his breakfast. After he cleaned the plate he bought two cigars for fifteen cents. He put one in his mouth and lit it and blew a cloud of smoke into Cruze's face. The rummy wrinkled his eyes and coughed.

"What did you do that for?"

"To wake you up."

"I was awake."

"You want your coffee now?"

"Yes."

The girl brought another cup of coffee and this time Cruze was able to drink it.

"What did you want to see me about, Flake?"

"I'm going out this morning and I need a man."

"You already got a crew."

"I lost Benninger last night."

"How?"

"Knife fight."

"He was a nice guy."

"Yeah."

"You know I can't work. I got the shakes too bad."

"Shakes or no shakes, you can still make a diesel run."

Cruze shook his head. "I think I'll stay ashore."

Flake turned and with a short jolting motion hit him hard on the side of the face with his open hand. The hand was like a piece of wood and it made a flat thumping sound on the rummy's head.

Cruze fell off the stool and lay on the floor. There were tears in his eyes. His mouth worked. "What did you do that for?"

"Get up."

"We don' wan' no fight in here," the Cuban girl said. "I gonna call the cops."

"This isn't a fight," Flake said.

He picked Cruze up and guided him out into the sunlight.

"Here's a dollar," Flake said. "Get whatever you need and meet me at the docks in half an hour. If you're not there I'll come and get you. You know what that means."

"Okay, Flake."

"You better be there."

"I'll be there."

Flake left the rummy and walked two blocks west and came out on Duval Street. Although the sun had been up for only a half hour they were already playing the piano in Sloppy Joe's and half a dozen sailors were drinking at the bar. The place smelled of whiskey and stale smoke and sweat.

"Shut up a minute," Flake told the piano player. "I got to make a phone call."

He called the police station and talked to the duty sergeant and asked about Benninger.

"We just got the report from the hospital," the sergeant said. "He's dead."

Flake didn't say anything.

"Who're his people?" the sergeant asked.

"I don't know. He didn't say."

"Where was he from?"

"He didn't say."

"You didn't ask him?"

"Look," Flake said. "All I know is he was a good man. He worked hard. He didn't give me any trouble. He's dead."

"Okay. Okay," the sergeant said.

Flake hung up. As he turned to the door the bartender, a thin tubercular man with sideburns and a mustache said, "Hi, Flake."

"What do you say, Snow?"

"How's it goin'?"

"All right. How you doin'?"

"I'm livin'."

"Well, that's something," Flake said.

CHAPTER TWO

The *Jezebel* had been stuck in port for three days now with a busted winch and Flake was getting edgy. To begin with, that business of running into Molly was bad luck. He hadn't figured on that at all. It had been his impression that she was somewhere in New York. When you've busted up with your girl and haven't seen her in a year you don't expect to run into her in the corner saloon. When you do, it gives you quite a jolt.

And then too there was Benninger. He had been a good engineer. He had been on the *Jezebel* for three months, which was a long time for any shrimper to work steady. During that time he had not given more than the normal amount of trouble and he had kept the worn-out engine running nicely. A diesel is a bitch under any circumstances and good engineers are always in demand and Flake had counted himself lucky with Benninger. Then the poor damn dumb Swede had to go and get himself knifed over a lousy tart and they had picked him up in an alley with six inches of steel in his gut.

Engineers were scarce and it might take a week or more to replace

him and with the shrimp running so good right now Flake did not want
to give up that week. He had brought in more shrimp than any other
skipper this year and it galled him to think of losing the record. He
wanted to get out and get to work again. But it wasn't just the shrimp.
It was Molly too. He hated to admit it but he was scared of running
into Molly. The only sure way of avoiding her was to get back to sea.

He stopped at the marine hardware store across the street from the
aquarium and bought three orange-colored floats for the nets and a
square of copper mesh for the intake strainer. The boy who waited on
him was new. He had to tell him the name of the boat twice. "Owner,
Mangio. Captain, Flake."

"Anything else you need, Captain? How about charts?"

"I got my charts,"

"For the whole area?"

"For all the way to Mexico."

"You're not going to Mexico, are you?"

"No," Flake said. "I'm sure as hell not."

Just talking about it gave him the itch. He could remember the leg
irons and the rats and the rotting stones in the rotting cell. In bad
weather he could still feel the irons. He had been thirty-two days in jail
in Campeche for fishing Mexican territorial waters. That was before
they had discovered the Tortugas beds, when the shrimpers were starv-
ing, when they had to run to Mexico to try to make a living. The gun-
boat had caught him six miles out of Campeche. They had let the crew
go but they had put him in irons and hauled him off to jail. In the end
it had cost him a thousand dollars and the flesh off his ankles. He did-
n't fish Mexican waters any more.

He took the bundle the boy gave him and put it under his arm. He
bought a carton of cigarettes in the drugstore and a fifth of Irish
whiskey at Joe's. He went up the stairs to Mangio's office above the Chinese place.

He sat there waiting for Mangio, smelling the Chinese cooking and
listening to the distant rumble of the bullhorns on the destroyers in the
Navy yard. Through the window he saw a girl come out of Freddie's.
She was a blonde girl and she was a little drunk, teetering unsteadily
on her high heels. She went off down the street and he watched her, liking the way her bottom moved under the tight blue skirt. He wondered
if she was the new girl at Mom's. Mom got a new girl about once a
month and for a while there was a big rush on her until every man in
town had been with her and then it began to taper off. After that she

was just another girl.

Mangio came in and said, "What do you know, Flake?"

"I'm ready to sail."

"You get another man?"

Flake nodded.

Mangio was short and plump and wore a pink silk shirt with pearl cufflinks. He had started as a busboy at the Casa Marina and now he owned a shrimp boat and an icehouse and a bar on Duval Street and a big new seafood place out near the Bight. He was doing all right, that Mangio. He had pale unhealthy-looking skin and even at this hour sweat ran down his neck. His hair was thick and black and he was very proud of it. An ivory comb stuck out of his shirt pocket.

"Too bad about the boy who died," he said.

"Yeah."

"He should of stayed away from that dark stuff. They cut you for nothing."

"That's right."

"Who you got to replace him?"

"Cruze."

"The rummy?"

"Yeah."

Mangio shook his head. "That's no good. Rummies bring trouble. He'll be loaded the whole trip."

"You show me another man and I'll take him."

"I don't like it."

"He knows engines as good as anybody."

"I don't like it."

"I'll handle it," Flake said flatly.

Mangio belched. He rubbed his hand over his paunch. "My stomach is killing me."

"You ought to quit eating that Chinese food."

"You think it's bad?"

"Anything you get too much of is bad."

Mangio grinned and squinted at the saliva-wet end of his cigar. "Except one thing."

"Even that."

Mangio closed his eyes and hugged himself. "You see the new girl at Mom's? Listen—"

"Save it," Flake said. "I haven't got the time. I want to shove off before noon."

Mangio shook his head. "Not today."

"Why not today?"

"I got a job for you."

"What kind of a job?"

"A special job."

"My job is catching shrimp. The longer you keep me tied up here the less shrimp I catch."

"Settle down," Mangio said. "Have a cigar."

Flake didn't want a cigar but he took it. He didn't want any part of Mangio but he took him. It was good business. They worked on shares and they both made plenty. One more good season and he would have his own boat and then he could spit on this greaseball.

"I want you to go to Havana," Mangio said.

"What the hell would I go to Havana for? There's no shrimp in Havana."

"That's right. But there's plenty of other things."

"Such as?"

"Whiskey."

Flake stood up and ground out the cigar in the ashtray on the desk. "No," he said.

Mangio smiled. "Don't get excited."

"I'm not excited," Flake said evenly. "All I said was 'no.'"

"Take it easy. Let me tell you how it works."

"I don't give a damn how it works. I'm not interested."

"You can make a thousand dollars."

"A thousand dollars for a year in the can is pretty thin pay," Flake said, remembering Campeche and the leg irons and the rats running across his face in the dark. "I've had all the jail time I want."

"Will you let me talk for five minutes?"

"Sure, you can talk. But it won't do you a damn bit of good."

"Take it easy. Sit down."

Flake sat down.

Mangio reached into the desk drawer and got out a small yellow box of Bisodol tablets. He put two in his mouth and began to chew on them reflectively. "This is the way it works," he said. "You fish a couple of days and then you get engine trouble. Maybe a clogged strainer or a busted fuel line or something. When you're close to Havana you get your engine started just long enough to bring you into port. It's all nice and open. Everybody sees you. Maybe you even sell your shrimp before they spoil just to make it look good. Then you start out again. Only you have more engine trouble. That's one lousy engine, hah? Anyway, this time your trouble is at night. So you go into Matanzas about fifty miles down the coast. It's a small town and everybody's asleep. A truck will bring the goods and load it into a small boat and bring it out to where you're anchored. When you got the load on board you get the hell out of there. If anybody asks any questions you just had more engine trouble, is all."

"And how do you figure to get it ashore here?"

"You come in at night up around Content Key. A fishing boat meets you there and takes it off. They keep it for me in a shack on the keys and only bring in a case or two at a time, as I need it. If nobody sees a big load nobody gets suspicious. What do you think?"

"It might work but it's not for me. Get yourself another boy."

"Don't be a damn fool. We're making plenty of money, ain't we? This way we make a lot more in a hurry. What's the matter, Flake? Don't you like money?"

"Yeah, I like money. But I don't like jails. And I'm taking all the risk."

"That's not so," Mangio said. "If anything goes wrong I lose my boat."

It was true. If they got caught Mangio stood to lose the *Jezebel*. And thinking of the *Jezebel* brought a swift image to Flake of his own boat, his own business, and no more slimy Mangio. One deal like this and he could swing it. The temptation was very strong.

"I still don't like it," Flake said.

Mangio leaned back in his chair, picking his teeth with his fingernail, knowing he had won.

"A thousand dollars, Flake. You got to catch a hell of a lot of shrimp to make a thousand dollars."

"Who handles the deal over there?" Flake asked.

"Cutter."

That startled Flake. Cutter was a deckhand on the *Jezebel*. Flake had never thought of him in terms of any responsibility.

"Why Cutter?"

"He's a Cuban. He has friends over there."

"I won't take any orders from Cutter," Flake said.

"Of course not. You're the captain. But he'll go ashore and make the contact."

"Okay," Flake said. "But I want my dough now."

Mangio smiled and said, "Sure." He felt good. Not only because of what the *Jezebel* would be bringing in but because the conversation with

Flake had proved once again that the world was full of whores. It was the rule he lived by—that every man or woman had a price. After that it was just a question of knowing who would do what and for how much.

Mangio worshiped at twin altars, women and money. As far as he was concerned the two were synonymous. In his early years as a busboy at the hotel he had seen the rich, bejeweled women coming and going, their bare flesh powdered and painted, their bathing suits revealing breasts and thighs. He had lusted for them hopelessly, and it had become clear to him then that only through money could he hope to enjoy such women. He had worked faithfully toward that goal.

He had made love to a rich woman once at the hotel but she was old and her breath was stale and when she wiped the powder from her neck you could see the wrinkles of age. The others, the beautiful ones, young and fresh as peaches, were not for him. They were for the rich men, the men who drove big cars and had an iced bucket of champagne sitting beside them at the table.

They were whores, these rich women. Whores for diamonds and furs and automobiles. He could remember as clearly as though it had happened yesterday that time in the late afternoon when he had been ordered to bring a pitcher of ice up to one of the rooms. He had knocked on the door and had received no answer, so he tried the knob and found it open and stepped into the room.

At first he had thought the suite was empty but then he looked through the open door of the bedroom and saw someone there. It was a naked woman with long red hair and she was sitting up on the bed with her back turned to him and her shoulders and hips were incredibly beautiful. As he stared at her and his eyes became adjusted to the gloom he saw the man. At that moment she turned her head and looked at him. She gave a little impatient gesture of her shoulders and closed her eyes and Mangio put down the tray and backed out of the room and fled down the hall.

"Well?" Flake said. "Do I get the dough or don't I?"

"Sure. Tomorrow."

"Why tomorrow?"

"Because you don't sail until tomorrow."

"We could save a whole day. I'm ready now."

"But I'm not," Mangio said.

Flake's lips drew together in a thin line. "Okay," he said. "Then while I'm waiting I'd like to see the books."

"Books? What books?"

"Account books. I want to know how much dough I've got riding with you."

Mangio shook his head. He had quit smiling. "Nobody sees the books. Nobody but me and Uncle Sam."

"Then you look at the books and tell me. I haven't drawn any dough for six months. I've got six months' shares riding with you."

"What's the matter with waiting until you get back?"

"What's the matter with now?"

"You don't like your job, Flake? I can get another captain."

"And I can get another berth. Hunchy has been after me all season."

"You won't get another boat like the *Jezebel*."

"Don't give me that. All shrimp boats are the same. The hell with you and your boat." He threw down the package of floats. "Here. These belong to you. You know what you can do with them."

Mangio didn't say anything.

"And I still want to see those books."

"Go to hell," Mangio said.

Flake shot a thick arm across the desk and grabbed Mangio by his pink silk collar. Mangio wheezed. His face turned purple. He was trying to get something out of his hip pocket. Flake pinned his wrist and ground the bones together. Mangio tried to scream but there was no wind in him. The knife fell out of his hand. Flake released his grip and shoved Mangio back into his chair.

"The books," Flake said.

Mangio couldn't speak. He pointed to the filing cabinet and to the keys on his desk. Flake unlocked the cabinet and found the ledger he wanted. It was an accounting of the Jezebel's voyages and the boxes of shrimp she had brought in and the market price and the various shares. The money was divided into two shares—one for the boat and one for the skipper and his two men. In good times it would run as high as five hundred dollars a month per man. The crew had been paid in cash but Flake had let his credit ride. He took a slip of paper out of his pocket and compared it with the book.

"You perfumed bastard," he said. "You're eight hundred short."

Mangio started to say something but the look in Flake's eyes shut him up.

"I want a check for forty-eight hundred and I want it now," Flake said.

Mangio wrote out the check. Flake folded it carefully and put it in his ragged black wallet.

"Well?" Flake said. "What now?"

"We go on like before," Mangio said, rubbing his throat.

"We do, hey?"

"Yeah. Business is business."

"There's one thing different. From now on my share is an extra five per cent. And it doesn't come out of the crew. It comes out of you."

"There's no other captain gets that much. Why should I pay you more?"

"Because I bring in more shrimp."

"All right," Mangio said slowly. "But I want you to know one thing, Flake. Some day I'll cut your guts out for this. Remember."

"Sure," Flake said. "But until then I guess we understand each other."

He went out of the office without bothering to close the door.

CHAPTER THREE

1

"All right, look," she had said, leaning toward him over the small round table. "I love you. Doesn't that mean anything?"

"Nothing. Less than nothing."

"You can't do this to me, Johnny."

"Why not?"

"Because when someone loves you it imposes a responsibility on you."

"How much responsibility did it impose on you?"

"But that's all over. It was over long ago. It's dead."

"Not for me it isn't."

"And you're going to walk out of here now and leave me? Just like that?"

"Just like that."

"Don't do it Johnny. You'll be sorry."

"Sure I will. So long, Molly."

"One slip," she said desperately. "One lousy slip. Do I have to carry it all the rest of my life?"

"No," he said. "I do."

"And what about you? Are you so blameless? Didn't you ever make a mistake?"

"Plenty."

"Then can't you understand how it was with me?"

"No."

"I don't understand you. You were always hard but you were never cruel. Now you're a hard cruel man."

"I'm the way you made me. So long, Molly."

She sat staring down at her drink. Two large tears had formed in her eyes and now they ran slowly down her cheeks. Flake looked at her and at the tears and for a moment he wanted to comfort her. But then he remembered that she could always cry when she wanted to and that she had cried the time he found her with Morgan. At the memory of it he felt the old bitterness knot around his heart. He pushed back his chair and stood up and put a dollar on the bar for the drink he had not tasted and walked quickly out of the place.

He walked up Duval Street past Sloppy Joe's and the Cuban's. Someone called to him but he did not turn around. He walked until he came to the end of the street and then he sat down on the sand and looked out at the water. It was a black night with no stars and he could barely make out the dividing line between the sea and the sky.

He sat there for a long time looking at the red and green channel flashers and the sweep of the big Sand Key light. Far off he saw a cluster of lights that looked like a nightclub. But the lights were moving fast so he decided it must be the old passenger liner for Havana. He wondered idly why she was so close inshore. Then the lights swung away and slowly disappeared and he did not think about them any more. Instead he thought about Molly. It hurt him to think about her and he kept testing the hurt in his mind like a man pressing his tongue against a sick tooth.

The sea wind, warm and soft, felt fine on his face. All those bars were damned stuffy and it was good to be out here in the wind. I can think about her now, he told himself, testing the hurt again. I could even sit right there and drink with her and it wouldn't bother me. The worst of it is over now. I think even if some guy came up and made a pass at her it wouldn't bother me.

But still he didn't really believe it and he was glad he hadn't stayed to find out.

When he was stiff from sitting he got up and walked back to the *Jezebel* and opened a bottle of rye he had locked in his sea chest. He took two stiff drinks out of it and put the bottle back and locked the chest and got into his bunk and went to sleep.

2

Key West is a strange town. It is the southernmost city in the United States and for many years it was an important seaport. The ships from South America and from farther up the Gulf Coast used to put in there and it had a kind of high society that was half Cuban and half American. There was even an opera house and behind it the big homes of the wealthy shippers. But later the ships began to find better ports and the elaborate homes were turned into rooming houses and the opera became a second class restaurant.

But then things began to boom again when the Cubans came in with the cigar industry. For a while everybody was rich and happy again. However, it didn't last long. The Cubans had a fight with the City Fathers about taxes and one morning the City Fathers woke up and found that during the night the cigar factories had moved out. They had just loaded everything, the machines and tobacco and everything else, and gone to Tampa. So that was the end of that.

For a long while after that they stayed busted. It didn't seem to matter so much because the whole country was busted. The only industry the town still had was women. It was always a great town for women. No matter how bad things got there was always a market for it and there was never any shortage of imports because Key West is close to Havana and Havana specializes in the production of women.

And later on the sponge fishermen came and things began to pick up again. There were plenty of sponges and they fetched a good price. The houses began to boast new paint and there were a lot of boats around and there was even some talk of repairing the railroad that had been washed out by the hurricane of '35. But just as they were getting ready to do something about it the sponges got sick. They contracted some disease that no one really understood and which made the sponges useless. And anyway someone had invented a plastic sponge that was almost as good and never got sick and was a lot cheaper. So that was the end of the sponges.

The thing that saved them next was the same thing that saved so many people. The war. The Navy came in and decided to make a major base out of Key West and for that purpose they finished the road from the mainland and put in a fresh water pipe all the way from Miami.

Now they had good times again and if you were too lazy to do anything else you could always go to work for the Navy. And as if the tide of good fortune had finally begun to roll in their favor they got something else as well. Shrimp. Giant shrimp from the Tortugas beds and a thousand shrimp boats and ten thousand shrimp fishermen came to reap the harvest.

Shrimp boats are stubby. High in the bow and stern and with plenty of freeboard between. They are built that way to buck the short choppy seas that build up in the Gulf. Before leaving port their holds are filled with ice and then the big pink shrimp are thrown in with the ice and when they return the whole mixture is dumped out and separated.

The boats carry a crew of three or four men and sometimes a woman. Very often the woman belongs to everybody on the boat, but sometimes if the man is man enough, she belongs to one. On the *Jezebel*, owned by Vincent Mangio and skippered by Johnny Flake, there were no women. It was not any nonsense about women being bad luck at sea; women could be bad luck anywhere. It was just that they meant trouble. And during the season, when you were trying to get your shrimp in at the same time the northwesters were booming out of the Gulf, you had trouble enough without them.

CHAPTER FOUR

1

The forty-four-foot motor sailor *Vixen* rode to her anchor in the mouth of the government channel. Her sail covers were neatly furled and her teak decks newly scrubbed. Her white topsides shone in the morning sun. Her sheets and halyards were carefully flemished. Her windows, which had been streaked with salt after her voyage outside from Miami, had now been washed clear with fresh water. She was a credit to her owner and master, Allan Chambers III. But at the moment that gentleman was deriving neither pride nor joy from her. Instead he lay on his bunk staring blindly at the ceiling and occasionally beating his fist against the oaken bulkhead. The knuckles of his hand were already bruised and bloody but he did not notice it.

He was on the verge of tears. He wanted to throw back his head and howl like a dog. An almost intolerable sense of grief and loss overwhelmed him. The grief was for the obvious and unquestioned infidelity of his lady love, and the loss was the loss of his own manhood. The lady's unfaithfulness had so shredded the fabric of his ego that he felt he could never recover from it, never again be a whole man. The only thing that prevented him from completely unleashing this tide of grief was the knowledge that his sobbing would be audible through the ventilator to anyone on deck.

The cause of his anguish was a tall dark girl named Jessica Martineau. She had been tormenting him for over a year now. She was not Mrs. Chambers. Mrs. Chambers was at that moment attending a dog show in Westchester and feeling the flanks of an Irish terrier. Mrs. Chambers did not know where Mr. Chambers was and couldn't have cared less. For a long time now she had been more interested in dogs than men.

Chambers was a tall man who looked substantially the same as he had when he rowed stroke in the Princeton shell fifteen years ago. His shoulders were still very good although his legs were going a bit thin. He wore his hair cut close to the skull and what with the tan and the J. Press clothes you had to look twice to see that he was no longer a college boy.

In the past few years he had developed a passion for boats. This expensive hobby was made possible by fifty thousand shares of gilt-edged securities left to him and wisely invested by his father who had been a hard-working mining engineer in the goldfields of South America. Soon after Chambers' wife began to give so much of her time to showing dogs he became interested in yachts. He would go off on ocean races to Bermuda and Nassau and Cat Cay and he could talk with authority about roller reefing and genoas and Merriman hardware.

It was a good life and it kept him healthy and the last thing he ever had to think about was Allan Chambers. He might have gone along that way for years if he had not been struck by lightning in the form of a dark-haired girl named Jessica.

Jessica had been married twice. Her first husband had laboriously committed suicide by shooting himself in the liver with an incredible amount of Vat 69. The second, after receiving a particular letter from home, had volunteered for a patrol through a mine field and they had not even found the pieces.

All that should have been a warning to Chambers but it was not.

Jessica was a great girl. Everyone who met her went crazy about her. She was pretty and vital and intelligent and warm-hearted and loving and wide-bosomed. But she had one failing. Every so often she liked to spend a night out.

She and Chambers would be sitting at a bar and she would excuse herself and go to the ladies' room and out the back way and that would be the last he would see of her until the next day. He never knew where she went or whose bed she had been in.

It had happened in Paris and in New York and in Bar Harbor and in Southampton and in Palm Beach and now in Key West. Each time it happened they had a terrible fight about it and Chambers swore to kick her out and she promised that it would not happen again. But each time it did, and he did not.

That was why he had bought the boat. He had thought that at least on the boat she would not be able to pull any tricks. But somehow she did. She always managed to get ashore. One night when they were anchored well out in the bay she left him and took the dinghy and rowed half a mile to the city docks. He did not see her for two days. In his fury he pulled up the anchor and went fourteen miles out of the harbor before he turned back.

When she finally did return she was as chic and smiling and affectionate as ever and she refused him any explanation. Underneath, way down, there was iron in her. Chambers had always thought of himself as a strong man but she had taught him what a miserable weakling and coward he really was. She had taught it to him with all the finesse and murderous cruelty that the American female can bring to bear when she really wants to.

Now he got out of the bunk and wiped his face with a wet towel and went up to the chartroom. The charts were neatly rolled in an overhead rack. He pulled out the one he wanted and studied it carefully. It was a chart of the area between Key West and the Dry Tortugas.

He had never been to the Tortugas but he had heard about it. There was a huge abandoned fort there, Fort Jefferson, that they had made into a national park. It was entirely dry, with no water and no accommodations. And there was a lot of historical background. All that stuff about Confederate prisoners and the famous Dr. Mudd who had set John Wilkes Booth's broken leg and been imprisoned for his pains. But the best thing about it, from Chambers' point of view, was that it was completely deserted. Jessica would have a tough time finding a playmate there.

He took a bottle of scotch out of the mahogany side cabinet and fixed himself a drink. Then, holding the chart in one hand and the glass in the other, he returned to his bunk to wait for her. He was beginning to feel better already.

2

Jessica lay on the beach with the sun warm on her and her hair spread out around her on the towel. She felt marvelous. The sun was always so good for her. She hoped no one would speak to her. She just wanted to lie like this with her eyes closed and the sun burning through to her bones.

She was thinking about the boy she had met last night, the Naval aviator. What a nice boy. Fliers were sometimes difficult but this one was so nice. They were all nice. She loved them all. Allan was nice too. Moody sometimes and surprisingly childish with his jealousy but really very nice. She hoped he wouldn't start drinking again because of what had happened last night. He was always so proud of his condition and did those pushups and things on deck every morning and drinking could ruin all that.

It occurred to her that the boat might be gone when she got back. There was always that chance. He had tried it once before and some day he would get really angry enough to do it. But not now. He was still too fond of her. Anyway there was not much point in brooding about it. The big thing now was to close her eyes and to let the sun do all those delicious little things to her legs and thighs and breasts and to wonder again about the business of last night. Such a *strange* boy. At least she could say nobody had ever done that to her before. Such a nice boy.

But still it made you stop and think. She was getting close to thirty now and they all said thirty was a turning point in a woman's life. After thirty you began to lose your looks. She did not think that would happen to her but still it might and she really ought to make some provision for it. She really ought to marry Allan. He was still not divorced from his present wife, that dog fancier—imagine, dogs!—but she knew perfectly well that she, Jessica, could make him do it if she put pressure on him.

All she had to do was to exploit that jealousy of his and she could really make him do almost anything she wanted. That was a dreadful thing to say. It was really quite cruel. But he was so impossibly childish about it. All men were childish about it. The male ego was such a funny thing. Something to do with guarding the cave and my woman and all that. But Allan was more vulnerable in that respect than anyone she had ever met.

It was probably because he had led such an easy and sheltered life. His father had made the money and his wife had made the home and the only thing he, Allan, had ever really made was the Princeton crew. That he had done all by himself. Yessiree. As a result he had no real confidence in himself—although he did know about boats and he was surprisingly adequate in bed—so that when she went around sleeping with other people it just shattered him completely.

It was too bad because he was a nice boy and she hated hurting him. She had even tried to get him to meet other girls, thinking that would ease the pain for him, but it didn't seem to help. It was really too bad. It was too bad about the others too. She hadn't liked hurting them either. Chuck was the one she really felt bad about. Poor darling Chuck, getting blown up by a land mine. And all because of a silly letter. It was such a shame about that letter and yet it had seemed like such a good idea at the time. She had thought that he would want to know the truth and that he would be understanding and forgiving. How could she possibly have known that he would go dashing off into a field full of mines? It was incredible. Poor darling lovely Chuck.

But she had learned her lesson. Never tell anyone anything. People don't really want to hear the truth. All they want is a pack of lies. But she hated lying and she was a bad liar anyway. It was much simpler, much more honest, not to say anything at all.

She gently eased the vision of her dead second husband Chuck out of her mind and began to think again about last night. What fun. Anyone who said it wasn't fun was absolutely insane.

Oh my, but that sun felt fine.

Toward noon she stood up and gathered her things together and walked back along the beach. In front of the little concrete blockhouse that sold hot dogs and sun tan lotion, several sailors were playing volley ball. In a group apart from the sailors, several other young men lay close together and looked at the sailors and giggled. They were writers and actors and all very talented. They anointed each other with sun tan oil and looked at the sailors.

The sailors looked at Jessica. She was well worth looking at. She was tall and dark and she walked with the kind of stiff-backed stately quality that is usually developed by native women who carry things on their heads. Jessica had never carried anything on her head except a diamond tiara that her first husband had given her, but she walked that way anyway.

She was a big girl and well developed everywhere and her full wide breasts pushed hard against the thin madras of her bathing suit. She swayed slightly when she walked and with her long hair hanging down her back she had a kind of lush quality that made the sailors pause in their game and whistle in unison. She ignored them, keeping her eyes on the strip of sand and the water. They watched her until she had disappeared behind the building, and then, amid considerable banter, they went back to their game. The writers and actors went back to rubbing each other's backs.

Jessica pulled her cotton skirt and blouse on over the bathing suit and walked slowly down the road to the pier. She walked barefoot, carrying her shoes in one hand and her towel in the other. People turned around to look at her as she went by. She did not mind being looked at. She had gotten accustomed to it in her first job, the showgirl one. She had come east from California and had gotten a job in the Latin Quarter in New York. The job required a good figure and a minimum of talent. All she had to do was wear a handful of imitation jewels over her belly and breasts and stand there in the spotlight looking lovely and powdered and unconcerned.

Through this job she had met Max Friedkin. Max was a Viennese photographer who had done extraordinarily well in the New York fashion world. He had a very real talent for enhancing the beauty of his already beautiful models. He was a small pleasant little man with pink cheeks and yellow hair. He lived in a charming house on Sutton Place and kept a staff of excellent servants and gave elaborate dinner parties. And in spite of everything he was terribly lonely.

Twenty minutes after he met Jessica he fell wildly in love with her. Two days later she moved out of her furnished room and into Max's house. A week later he proposed to her. They were married on Jessica's birthday. She was twenty-one. Max was forty-nine.

At first they were very happy. Then they were not so happy. Within two years Max drank himself to death.

Her second husband, Charles Rawlings, III, came from a fine old Southern textile family. He met Jessica at a cocktail party and suggested that they go off to Mont Tremblant on a skiing weekend. They never came back. They were married in Canada and went to Macon, Georgia, to live on the family estate. They were very happy. Then Chuck began to bring some of his fellow officers from the National Guard home for weekends. After that they were not so happy.

The first time he discovered that she had been unfaithful to him they had a frightful row. He threatened to kill the man and then Jessica and then himself. She promised to be good, and finally, amid tears and ardent lovemaking, he forgave her. They were very happy again until he went overseas a few weeks later. Before he left he made her promise always to tell the truth.

When he got the letter in which she told him the truth he was with the U. S. Seventh Army near Mannheim. He immediately volunteered for a patrol and walked straight into a mine field. The mines had been clearly marked *Achtung! Minen!* and there was no question about his seeing them.

Jessica went into mourning for him. She wore black for a month and for six months she was more faithful to the dead Chuck than she had been to the living.

After that she met Allan Chambers.

CHAPTER FIVE

1

The big ground swells came surging under the open-work piers of the Gulf docks and banged the *Jezebel* up against the pilings. Flake had rigged spring lines on her but it didn't do too much good. The big swells that piled up in the deep-water channel packed too much wallop. It was, he decided, one hell of a place to put the gas docks. They could just as easily have put them around in the bight or over opposite the Navy yard, but no, they had to put them right here in the open where it was rough even on a calm day and sheer bloody hell when the northwesters blew. It was typical of the way they did things in this town. A dirty, lazy, sprawling, mismanaged town. A man decides to build gas docks, so he just socks his timbers down somewhere near the water line and starts building. After he's got them built he realizes he's stuck right out in the channel facing northwest and the storms will beat him to death. But by that time he's got it finished and the big silver tanks are set up and what can the poor bastard do?

But still, in a way, it was a good town too. It was a town without any civic pride and therefore people left you alone. You could live any way you pleased. Anything went in a town like this. If you didn't want to shave for a week nobody would look at you crosseyed and if you wanted to walk barefoot in the rain it was your own damn business. And if you wanted to live with a tramp or a goat that was your business too.

The only trouble was, a town like that would naturally attract a lot of crums. You take all these queers who were coming in with their little theatre groups and art galleries and Cape Cod clothing stores and taking over the bars and laying around on the beaches in nothing but a jockstrap. It was enough to turn your stomach.

Or the other crums, the loonies and hard boys. The only thing they could do with them was dump them back over the line into Dade County. It was the easiest way to get rid of them. No use calling the authorities in Sweet-potato, Alabama, or Hogwallow, Georgia, and saying, "We got Crazy Joe here escaped from your pen." They would laugh at you and tell you to keep him. No danger of them spending a couple of hundred bucks to extradite the bastard. They were happy enough to get rid of him.

So what a smart sheriff did here was to put old Crazy Joe in a car with a deputy and tell the deputy to take him up to about ten miles south of Miami and let him out on the road and then call up the law in Miami and say, "There's a man out here on the Dixie Highway exposing himself." And when they asked what the caller's name was, the deputy gave them a phony moniker and ran like hell. Only after a while the Dade County boys got wise to it and they would begin dumping Joe back over the line and the sheriff was right back where he started from.

Flake shrugged mentally and told himself, oh, well, what the hell, it wasn't his problem. He got up off his bunk and stepped outside. The sun was low and the little sand cays seemed to float in the late afternoon haze. A destroyer, looking as big as a block of apartment houses in the funny light, was making up the channel. She was coming fast with a bone in her teeth and Flake thought about the wake she would kick up and the tossing they would take and he stood there cussing inside himself, using all the foul language he could think of. It almost seemed as though they could hear him too, because all of a sudden they slowed down and crept the rest of the way in, leaving hardly any more wake than a row-boat.

He strolled back aft to where the three men of his crew sprawled on the fantail. Bush, the big Negro, was playing *St. Louis Blues* on the harmonica, and he played it soft and sweet. He was a good man, Bush, one of the few Negroes who got along well in a white crew. He never said much but there was an air about him that let you know he wouldn't take too much crap from anybody.

Cruze was sprawled out on deck with his head on a pile of tar-blackened rope. He looked sick and pale in the fading light of the sun. Cutter was sitting on the stem bits carving a nude woman out of a soft block of pine with a big pearl-handled knife. He was clever with the knife. The woman's face was shapeless but her body was all there.

Cutter was a medium-sized, wiry man with light hair and cold flat eyes. He was wearing grease-blackened dungarees held up on his narrow hips by a wide leather belt, and shapeless shoes with no laces. His bare ankles were blackened with dirt and even in the open air a sour unwashed smell hung about him. He wore no shirt and his hairless chest and arms were covered with obscene tattoos.

Cutter's mother had been a Cuban whore and his father an English sailor on weekend liberty from his ship. How and why the whore had conceived after all the precautions she had taken to prevent it was a mystery no one could solve. And afterward she had tried a dozen tricks to abort but none of them worked. Young Cutter had been just as stubborn and tenacious of life then as he turned out to be later on.

For a while, during her pregnancy, she was very much in demand. It was something new and different. Later she took three weeks off to have the child and then went back to work. But every time an English ship came in she went down to the harbor to meet it, thinking the boy's father might be on board and she would tell him about his son. After two years she forgot all about him and no longer met any of the ships. The only thing she remembered about him was his name. She had named the boy after his father, James Cutter.

By the time he was five Cutter was a photographer's assistant. He carried equipment for a small baldheaded man with thick-lensed glasses who came to make pornographic pictures of his mother. For his pains he received a few coins. No one seemed to regard it as an unusual arrangement. The boy had to earn his keep.

When he was nine his mother had been strangled by a drunken Danish wiper off a Scandinavian ship, and young Cutter ran away. For a while he lived on the docks, sleeping in the sheds with the great gray rats, rolling drunks, diving for pennies in the murky water of Havana harbor.

The divers around Havana are a tough lot. They have to be to survive the racing currents and sewage-polluted waters. Cutter was one of the toughest. By the time he was twelve he had a job as deckhand on a banana boat working between Havana and the Gulf Coast. There he learned to use his fists and then a knife. The knife was better. If a man acquired a reputation as an artist with the knife nobody bothered him. Cutter had the reputation. He had killed his first man when he was sixteen. He had done it by knifing him in the back on a dark night at sea and then slipping the body overboard for the sharks. Everybody on the ship knew what had happened but no one could prove anything.

But Cutter had other skills with the knife as well. He was a masterful wood carver. The steel seemed to come alive in his hands and in turn to transmit life to the wood. In another time and another place he might have developed into a very real artist. As it was he remained a killer.

Flake stood on the fantail for a few minutes listening to Bush's music and watching the sun drop in a florid burst of color into the Gulf. The destroyer had gone on past them and tied up in the Navy yard and he could faintly hear its bullhorn issuing orders.

While he stood there a small disheveled craft came wobbling in astern and made fast to the pier. It was about thirty feet long and slab-sided and had a jerrybuilt cabin with a stovepipe sticking out at a rakish angle. A short fat man with a red face and gray hair was at the helm. He brought the boat in too fast and the tide caught him and threw the boat up against the pilings. There was a loud crash and a batch of splinters flew into the air. At the same moment a female voice from below called out in strident tones, "What the hell do you think you're doing?"

"Nothing, dear," said the man at the wheel, throwing a two-inch hawser onto the dock.

The hatch opened and a small gray-haired woman appeared. She wore an apron and a cotton dress and held a frying pan in one hand. She looked as tough and gamy as a fighting cock.

"Sink the lousy tub," she said loudly. "See if I care. Sink the sonofabitch and then we can go home where we belong." She cast a final contemptuous look at the man at the wheel and then vanished below.

The man looked up at Flake and grinned. "My wife," he said.

"Congratulations," Flake said.

"She's not so bad. She just gets excited easy, is all. My name is Murphy. I had a hardware business in Jacksonville. I sold out to my son-in-law and bought this boat. The bastard who sold me this boat was a potato farmer. I don't think he ever saw the water in his life. He built this boat in a potato patch. Looks it, too, doesn't it? Looks like a damned floating outhouse."

"Sort of," Flake admitted.

"How about a drink? I got plenty of booze on board. If the sonofabitch sinks under me I'll die drunk and happy."

"Some other time," Flake said. "I was just going ashore."

"Okay," Murphy said. "Any time. Any time."

Flake went back to the small sink in the galley of the wheelhouse and shaved. After that he put on a clean shirt and fresh khaki trousers. By the time he came topside again the Murphys were sitting in the cockpit of their ridiculous cruiser and eating dinner. Mrs. Murphy had spread a clean white cloth over a bridge table and set a bottle of booze in the middle of the cloth. Now Mrs. Murphy was tossing off half a glass. Every time a swell built up under the pier their boat pounded against the bulkhead and more paint and splinters were scraped off. The Murphys didn't seem to care. Mrs. Murphy reached up and pinched her husband's cheek. Mr. Murphy saw Flake and waved the bottle at him. Flake waved back. He envied them. They looked very happy together.

He stepped ashore and walked across the grease-stained cinders to the entrance of the Lobster House and went inside. He had a quick drink at the bar and then went out the back way, crossing the catwalk of the turtle pens where the big stupid turtles were waiting to be made into soup. He came out near the narrow mouth of the Bight. Several fast deep-sea fishing boats were tied up there and Flake regarded them with a critical eye.

These boats were not like the Miami charter boats. In Miami they went in for size and radio telephones and three motors and outriggers eighty feet high. The Miami boats had leather cushions and venetian blinds and electric heads. These boats were smaller and less fancy. They were fishing boats, not yachts.

Flake walked down to the dock, looking at the row of boats. Only one of them really caught his eye—a custom-built Hubert Johnson hull with a lovely sheer to her bow. She looked like the *Mistress*. Very much like the *Mistress*.

And thinking about the *Mistress*, he began to think again about Stuart. And of course about Molly.

2

Stuart is a small lovely town on the east coast of Florida. It is built on the banks of the St. Lucie River, a fine deep-water river that runs for miles through the back country and on down to the sea. There are tarpon in the river and giant snook and largemouth bass. A good fisherman, trolling with small spoons or working a fly against the current, can find contentment there at almost any season of the year.

Stuart is a sports fishing town. Its stores boast wonderful arrays of tackle. Its hotels are accustomed to fishermen who rise at dawn and want their lunch prepared for a day on the river. And almost anyone in town can tell you when and where the various species of game fish will be running.

Flake had grown up there. He had loved the small town and the small school and the fact that he knew almost everyone by name. The town bustled during the winter season and then dozed away the long hot summer days. For a boy like Flake, who could never get enough of the river and the back country, it was great.

His best friend was a man named Cash Myers. Cash lived in a shack far up on the east branch. He eked out a precarious living renting skiffs to fishermen, but money never seemed to worry Cash. In fact, nothing worried Cash. His tough hide defied weather and insects, and his soul was at peace. He wanted nothing better than the river. No other place or way of life would have suited him more. He had his dogs and the fishing and his wife.

Bess, Cash's wife, was an exceptional woman. She was slender and gray-haired and had deeply tanned skin. Her mouth was a slash of crimson and her eyes were the deep purple blue of the Gulf Stream. She wore tight blue jeans and combed her hair straight back from her wide forehead and knew as much about the innards of an outboard motor as did old Cash himself.

Bess was not a local girl. She had been born in Boston and married a New York advertising man and lived in Westchester in a sixty-thousand-dollar house with two servants. It was a nice house. Her husband was a nice man. It was a nice way of life. Bess hated it.

One day she left the house and never went back. She got into her car and drove south until she reached the winding river and the sun-struck palmetto country. There she turned off on the first dirt road she came to. At the end of the road she found a shack and inside the shack she found a hard bare-chested man with happy eyes. His name was Cash Myers.

Bess and Cash never had any children of their own but the kids in town were crazy about Cash. And of all his admirers none was more faithful than Johnny Flake.

They met in a strange way. Johnny was drifting down the east branch in an open skiff, hunting wood duck with his .22 rifle. He had been on the west branch many times but this was the first opportunity he had ever had to hunt the narrow shining waters of the east branch.

At a bend in the river he heard thrashing in the underbrush and saw a great green shape slide off the mud bank into the water. His heart jumped and then he recognized the shape for what it was, a huge alligator. The gator lay half submerged in the water, only his eyes and snout showing. The eyes seemed to glow with evil intensity in the dark shadow of the mangrove roots. The great tail swirled once and a surge of water rippled out toward the boat. Cautiously, moving very slowly, Johnny reached behind him for the rifle. He raised it slowly to his shoulder, sighting down the barrel toward the heavy-lidded eyes. He would have a chance for only one shot and he would have to make it a good one. He wondered if he would be the first boy who had ever killed a full-grown alligator with a .22.

At that moment, as he was about to press the trigger, he heard a voice behind him. It was a big heavy voice and it seemed to be coming right over his shoulder. The voice said, "Son, if you shoot that gator I'll just naturally come out there and bash your head in."

Johnny lowered the rifle and looked toward the far bank. He saw a skiff tied to the mangrove roots. A man was standing in the skiff. He had a fishing rod in his hand. He was a big man who wore no shirt. Ropes of muscle coiled on his shoulders. A mat of wooly hair covered his chest.

"I suppose he's your gator," Johnny said sarcastically, feeling the disappointment of having come so close to getting off his shot.

"Matter of fact, he is," the man said. "Or at least he's a good friend of mine. Ain't nobody can own a gator but you can get right friendly with them. Now that there gator has been living on that bank for seven years, summer and winter. I call him Homer. Once had an uncle named Homer and he looked just like that there gator. Here, Homer. Come and get it, you ornery ole bastard. Come on, Homer."

The man whistled and the monster began to swim easily, silently across the river to him. Johnny watched in fascination as the alligator approached the skiff and opened its huge jaws.

"Hungriest, laziest, most no-good creature God ever made," the man said, tossing a handful of fish entrails into the cavernous maw.

The alligator's jaws clamped shut and the evil, greenish gray head disappeared under the water.

"I like to keep him around," the man said. "Eats up the moccasins. Ain't been hardly a snake on this part of the river since Homer took up residence there."

He cast off the skiff and shoved out in the direction of Johnny's boat. The gunwales bumped together and the man extended his hand. "I'm Cash Myers," he said.

"Johnny Flake."

"Didn't mean to speak to you so rough, but you was just about to pull that trigger."

"I guess so," Johnny admitted.

"Don't you know it's against the law to shoot gators?"

"No."

"Well it is, and I happen to be the game warden around here."

Johnny looked down at the man's jeans. The small silver shield of a game warden was pinned to one of the belt loops.

"I better run you in," the man said.

"But I didn't pull the trigger."

"Intention to commit a crime is as good as the crime itself. You come along with me."

Sullen, a little frightened, Johnny accompanied Cash to the shack. As they stepped ashore Cash said, "How old are you?"

"Sixteen."

"You've got a pair of shoulders on you for sixteen. They'll put you to work building roads up at the state prison."

At the expression on Johnny's face Cash suddenly grinned and clapped him on the back. "Hell, son, can't you take a joke?"

"When I know it's a joke, I can."

"Scared you, did I?"

"Sort of."

Cash whistled and a big hound raced around the corner of the shack. Behind him came a tall woman in blue jeans and a khaki shirt. She had a tanned face and wore a yellow ribbon in her hair. The boy liked her immediately.

"This is my old woman," Cash said. "Bess, this is Johnny."

"Hello, Johnny. How about something cold to drink? I've got some lemonade in the icebox."

Cash made a face. "Lemonade," he said in tones of disgust. "A boy with shoulders on him like this ought to drink whiskey."

Bess smiled. "You're a dirty old man," she said. "And you won't be feeding whiskey to any minors around here."

Cash put his arm around her shoulders. "She makes the best damn lemonade in the state," he said.

And it was too. She served it in tall glasses, cold enough to make your teeth ache. They sat there in the shade of the cypress trees drinking the lemonade and listening to the river chuckling under the dock. Cash talked steadily. He was vastly entertaining. He talked politics and women and religion and the weather and fishing. He knew something about almost everything. Johnny got the idea that Bess probably knew a good deal more about some things but she made no attempt to interrupt the flow of her husband's homespun wisdom.

"Been living on this river all my life," Cash said. "Wouldn't live in Palm Beach or Miami if you give me the town. Bunch of damned overdressed overstuffed old goats who wouldn't know how to skin a rabbit or change a sparkplug in an automobile. Call themselves men because they wear pants. Purple pants. Yellow pants..."

The voice droned on. The hound, Duke, came over and put his head in Johnny's lap. He looked up at the boy with wise brown eyes and waited for his ears to be scratched. Behind the shack, in the wire pen that protected the chickens from foxes and weasels, a rooster crowed loudly. The river made liquid music around the dock. Bess looked at the river and at the puffs of cloud that hung in the pine tops on the far shore. She reached out and put her fingertips lightly on Cash's hairy brown forearm. Something big and dark splashed in the river, Homer. A big heron, startlingly white against the brush, stepped delicately down to the river's edge and stood there staring at the water. Cash was telling a long story about hunting possums as a boy in Georgia. It was a good story.

They were, Johnny decided, the happiest and most wonderful people he had ever known.

CHAPTER SIX

1

Chambers, sweating out his anguish on board the yacht *Vixen*, waited for his lady love until noon and then made up his mind to look for her. He had no idea of where he would look but he knew from experience that any activity would be better than sitting alone with his grief.

He climbed down into the dink and pulled for shore. The wind and tide were against him but he made good progress, putting his shoulders and back into it and making a smooth easy motion of rowing that shot the light boat over the surface.

And for a little while, if he closed his eyes, he could imagine that he was back in the Princeton shell and that the sweat running down his back was a boy's sweat and that around him were his good friends and crew mates and that all you had to do in life was to pull and pull until you thought your heart might burst, except that you knew it would not. And in that happy time you had the confidence of youth and strength and you had never been defeated in anything because no real test had ever been made of you.

All right now, he told himself, stop it. It's daylight and you got through the night and somehow, if she's not back, you'll get through tonight also and all the ones after that. You won't kill yourself and some day, please God, it will be over. Some day the fever will stop and the sickness will be gone and you'll wake up and look at her and know her for the rotten treacherous bitch she is. And she'll put her hand on you and nothing will happen and she'll put her lips on you and you'll turn away.

But until then you're helpless and you've got to live through it and go on walking and talking and eating and drinking like anyone else. And you can stand it, or most of it, except that time when you wake up in the night. That's the time when you're really alone in the middle of a polar waste and the ice is cracking all around you. Somebody, I guess it was Fitzgerald, another poor Princeton bastard, wrote: "In the real dark night of the soul it is always three o'clock in the morning."

Fitzgerald was tied up with one, Allan thought. She must have given it to him right in the same place I'm getting it now. I remember reading about it. There was that time on the Riviera with that French aviator and God knows how many after that. And it busted him up altogether so that he was lost in darkness and died without ever really coming out of it. Or if he did come out of it, it was too late.

He brought the dink in neatly in back of the icehouse, careful not to let it rub against the tar-blackened pilings, and pulled himself up onto the pier. A girl was sitting there with her feet dangling over the edge and she said to Chambers, "Have you got a match?"

"Certainly."

He flicked his lighter and extended the flame. She bent her head and put her hand on his and sucked in the smoke.

"Thanks," she said.

"Not at all."

"Some tub," she said, looking out toward the *Vixen*. "Yours?"

"Yes."

"Tough."

He managed a small smile. He was pleased that she had talked to him. At that point he would have been pleased if anyone talked to him.

"Cigarette?" she asked, extending the pack.

"Thanks."

"What's it like on a boat like that?"

"What is what like?"

"Just living. Just waking up in the morning and eating and sleeping and all of that. Tell me about it."

"Would you like to see her?" Chambers asked. He said it fast, without giving it any thought.

She gave him a long look and there was a peculiar expression of contempt on the young—not so young—face.

"It's all right," he said. "I won't give you any trouble. You don't have to worry."

"I wasn't worried."

"Then shall we go?"

"Why not?"

He got back into the dink and helped her down and rowed out toward the yacht. She sat in the stern with her feet tucked up under her and the blue skirt drawn tight over her knees. Her hands were blue-veined and cold-looking.

"What's your name?" Chambers asked.

"Molly."

"Molly what?"

"Smith."

"That's a good name."

"Isn't it? And you?"

"Allan. Allan Smith."

She scrambled up from the pitching dink to the deck and with a quick charming gesture reached down and pulled off her shoes and went barefoot along the deck.

"It's enormous," she said.

"Comfortable."

"A seagoing hotel. From out there she didn't look nearly this big."

He showed her over the boat and then seated her in one of the varnished wicker chairs and mixed a drink for her.

"Where are you from, Molly?"

"I don't know. Here and there. Everywhere."

"Where are you going?"

"I'm not sure. Just drifting, I guess."

"How did you wind up here?"

"This is the end of the line. This is where all the drifters come. You can't go any further."

She might have been a whore but he did not think so. She did not have the toughness of a whore. Maybe she was close to it or on the way but she had not got there yet. Anyway he didn't much care. He had no interest in her that way. He only knew that he was pathetically glad to have someone to talk to and she had a sort of I-don't-give-a-damn quality about her that appealed to him. It was not until much later that he realized she was quite drunk.

"Would you like to take a trip?" he asked.

"All right."

"You haven't asked where."

"What's the difference?"

"You really don't care?"

"I did yesterday but I don't now."

"How soon can you be ready?"

"I'm ready now."

"No baggage?"

"It doesn't matter."

"You're a remarkable girl, Molly."

"Oh sure."

"We'll leave this afternoon. I'm just waiting for a friend."

"I thought you might be."

"And by the way, my name isn't Smith."

"I never supposed it was," she said.

He gave her some lunch and then suggested that she go below for a nap.

He thought he had it all figured out.

"Darling," Jessica would say, "there's a girl asleep in my cabin."

"Is there?"

"Who is she?"

"Her name is Molly," he would say, turning away, feeling very pleased with himself.

But in the end he weakened and could not go through with it. Jessica might get really angry and leave him for good. He woke Molly and told her it was all off and rowed her back to the shore.

"I'm terribly sorry," he said.

"That's all right. It doesn't really matter."

"You understand, don't you?"

"Sure I do. But you know something?"

"What?"

"You should have gone through with it anyway."

She went off down the pier and he rowed back to the yacht. She was absolutely right. He had not had the guts to do even this one small thing, and having failed at it, he was really sunk.

2

Molly walked slowly back into town. She decided to have a drink. With a drink you could get through almost anything. She had a nice edge on already and she did not want to lose it.

It was too bad, she reflected, about the chap on the boat. He was certainly in a bad way. The girl, whoever she was, must be a frightful bitch. They were all frightful bitches. The world was a frightful bitch.

She would have a drink and then go back to the hotel and get her things together and go somewhere. Anywhere. As she had explained to Chambers, she was a drifter. It made no difference where she went. The only thing she was sure of was that she would not stay here in the same town with Flake.

There must be a late bus—midnight or something like that. She would take it and go back to Miami. Or maybe even farther. Maybe even to Stuart. Why Stuart? There was nothing but hurt in Stuart. Stuart would remind her of Bess and Cash and the *Mistress*. And most of all it would remind her of Flake.

3

The first time she had ever seen him was when she climbed down off the bus in Stuart. The big shiny vehicle had roared off in a cloud of dust, leaving her standing there blinking in the sudden glare. She had carried her bag across the road to a patch of shade provided by the concrete portico of a gasoline station. A dark young man in sweat-stained khakis was sitting there at the wheel of a jeep.

"Excuse me," she said. "Can you tell me where I can find a cab?"

"There's generally one at the train station but it's a tough walk in the heat of the day."

She followed his glance along the length of sun-struck asphalt that shimmered in the brightness.

"Or I guess you could call them from here and they'd come down to get you," he went on.

She nodded. "That might be better."

"Where are you going? Maybe I can help."

"I'm going up to Cash Myer's place. I understand it's some distance out of town."

The dark-haired young man sat up straighter and regarded her with renewed interest. "You must be Molly."

"I am," she said, astonished by this recognition, "but how did you know?"

"Cash is an old buddy of mine. I was up there yesterday and they were talking about you. Bess said she was expecting her kid sister in one of these days. Didn't seem to know just when."

"I thought I'd surprise her."

"You'll do that, all right. They'll be tickled to see you. Forget about the cab. I'll drive you out there myself."

"That's very kind of you. Were you going out there anyway?"

"I practically live there. Come on, hop in."

He opened the dusty olive-green door for her and threw her bag into the back.

"My name is Flake," he said, extending a heavy suntanned hand.

"I'm glad to know you."

"My God," he said, "I wouldn't miss this for the world. Old Bess will light up like a Christmas tree."

A colored boy came out of the office and handed Flake some money. "Here's your change, Major."

"All right, Harry. And don't forget that oil for the boat."

"No, sir."

"You'll get it down there this afternoon?"

"Yes, sir."

"Good boy."

The jeep motor ground into life and they bumped out onto the road and headed north across the bridge.

"This is the St. Lucie," Flake said, pointing to the murky foam-flecked water. "Quite a river."

"Yes," she said.

"Cash lives about five miles up the highway here and then a couple of miles in."

"He called you Major. Are you a major?"

"Used to be. The war hasn't been over long enough for them to forget it. Won't be long before he'll be calling me Johnny again."

"You said you've known Cash a long time."

"Ever since I was a kid."

"Of course." She raised her hand and tapped her forehead with her fingers. "Johnny Flake. Bess told me about you."

"There's a real woman, that Bess."

"And Cash. What's he like?"

"Nobody can describe Cash. You'll have to see him for yourself."

"Is it always this warm?"

"Sure," he said. "And getting hotter. You'll get accustomed to it. Anyway, up where Cash is there's a breeze off the river."

They crossed the bridge and went on past the big red seafood place called the Lighthouse. They rounded the bend of the river and saw the charter boats tied up below at the dock, and the pennants standing out stiff in the breeze, and the white boats rocking to the chop that came across the river, and the pelicans sailing by in a slow majestic line.

"That's my boat down there," Flake said, pointing.

She tried to follow the direction of his finger but her gaze was lost in a forest of masts and outriggers. Then they passed on by and there was the flat road stretching out ahead and the scrubby green countryside on either hand.

"How long will you stay?" he asked.

"I don't know. I quit my job."

"What kind of job did you have?"

"Copy writer in a New York advertising agency."

"Sounds good."

"It was all right."

"Why did you quit?"

"Fed up, running away, New Yorkitis. That sort of thing."

"Can you go back?"

"Oh, I suppose so. Bess's former husband is my boss. He's a nice guy. I guess he'd take me back if I really wanted it. Right now I couldn't care less."

"Sounds like an unhappy love affair," he said, grinning at her.

"No," she answered, suddenly serious. "I just needed time to think."

"Well, you came to the right place for that. There isn't much else to do around here. Except fish. Do you fish?"

"I'm afraid not."

"We'll teach you."

"We?"

"Me and Cash. There's nothing Cash likes better than teaching people to fish. When he can take some poor guy who's holding down an honest job and turn him into a fishing bum, he's like a priest with a new convert."

"I think I'm going to like Cash."

"He's rough but you'll like him, all right."

He swung the jeep off the main road onto a sandy track that wound through the pine forest. They passed a small farmhouse with a few skinny cows grazing in the scrubby pasture and then plunged deeper into the woods. The road was mostly loose sand at this point but the jeep plowed merrily through. Ahead there was a shimmer of dark water and then a long low white cottage. Two young beagles ran after the jeep, barking hysterically. A tall bare-chested man who was splitting logs put down his axe and stared at them for a moment before walking slowly toward the car.

"Up to this point I never approved Johnny's taste in women," Cash said. "But he sure hit the jackpot this time."

"Hello, you old goat," Flake said, "Meet Molly."

"Our Molly?"

"Absolutely."

"Well. Well, well, well."

"Is that all you can say?"

Molly opened the door and stepped out and gave him her hand, "Hello Cash."

"Welcome to the river, Molly."

"Where's Bess?" Flake asked.

"I'll call her. Ho, Bess."

A figure moved behind one of the windows and the door burst open and Bess ran toward them. She threw her arms around Molly and squeezed her tight. Then she pushed her away to arms' length and asked angrily, "What kind of a girl are you, not to let us know?"

"Just wanted to surprise you."

"Well, you did that, all right. And where did you run into this bum?" She indicated Flake.

"Picked him up at the station," Molly said airily.

"Flake's rapid cab service for wayward girls," Flake said.

"How about a drink?" Cash said.

Flake grinned. "Well, how about it?"

"You're staying for dinner, Johnny," Bess said.

"Can't, honey," Flake said. "Got a charter this afternoon. Fellow thinks he can catch a sailfish."

"But you'll be back later, won't you?"

"Sure will," Flake said, looking at Molly. "I'll be back, all right."

4

Flake went off to his fishing and Cash resumed work on the wood-pile. The two women could hear him banging lustily away out back.

"You look wonderful," Molly said. "Better than I ever remember."

"It's a nice life here, sweetie."

"And you've got quite a guy there."

"Do you really like him?"

"I think he's great. All man. But not aggressive about it. I'm beginning to understand a lot of things now that always puzzled me before."

"I doubt if you really do understand yet but maybe some day you will."

Molly had been carefully skirting around the subject of Bess's former husband, but now Bess brought it up herself.

"How's Bart?" she asked.

"He's all right. Working hard."

"He always did. Has he got a girl?"

"I don't think so. Or at least I've never seen him with one."

"I'm sorry about that."

"He sent you a message."

"Oh?"

"He wants you to let him know if you ever need anything."

"That's sweet. Typical of Bart."

"He's really a very nice guy."

"And I'm a bitch?"

"Of course not."

"But sometimes you think so. Or did for a while, anyway."

"Maybe just at first, but not any more."

"It was just that I'd had it, sweetie. He's a nice guy and it was a nice life and we had nice friends but it wasn't living. The years were going by and one melted into another and none of them meant anything. Do you know what the worst feeling in the world is?"

"No."

"To wake up every morning and say to yourself, 'Oh my God, another day.'"

"How long had that been going on?"

"Years. But here it's different. Here I wake up and I'm glad it's morning. I have a million things to do."

"And a man you want to do them with."

"Exactly."

"I'm glad, Bess. I used to worry about you. I won't any more."

"And what about you, sweetie? Why did you come?"

"I'm not sure. I guess I just wanted to get away."

"In your letter you said you need time to think."

"That's quite true."

"About what?"

"So many things. About you, for one."

"And for another?"

"Frank."

"Is he the one you were with so much last summer?"

"Yes."

"He sounds nice."

"He is nice. Maybe too nice."

"And you're not sure yet how you feel about him?"

"I thought perhaps if I went away for a while it might clarify things for me."

"Did you tell him why you were going?"

"No."

"Then I suggest you forget the whole thing for a while. Put it all out of your mind. Relax and have fun. Stay with us as long as you like. A month, a year, ten years. You're home now and you're not to worry about anything. What do you say?"

"I say that you may just possibly be the nicest person in the world."

"Yes," Bess said, putting her arm around Molly's waist and squeezing. "I might be just that."

CHAPTER SEVEN

1

Flake came back in the evening and took her fishing. They went down the river in Cash's little aluminum outboard and crossed the wide shallow expanse of Tarpon Bay. The sun was low, almost touching the scrub pines. A plume of smoke hung straight in the luminous air to the west.

The mosquitoes, which had begun to annoy them on the river bank, vanished out here in the open water. A flock of pelicans glided by in ghostly silence, maintaining a perfect line of flight without flapping their wings.

Flake pointed to a jut of land on the far shore. "See that point over there?"

"Yes."

"Some day I'll build a house there."

"Do you own the land?"

"Yes," he said happily. "I bought it last year."

"It's beautiful."

"You can see the sun rise and set and there are no two days when the colors of the sky and water are ever the same. It's high land and it catches the breeze and even a hurricane won't push the river up that high. And there's snook and tarpon and bass and redfish laying all around that lagoon. What do you think?"

"I think it's one of the loveliest places I've ever seen. I can't imagine what you're waiting for."

He shut off the motor and picked up one of the light casting rods.

"It wouldn't be any fun alone," he said.

"No girl?"

"Not one to keep. Just the little ones you throw back."

"Maybe you're not using the right bait."

"Or maybe they're just not biting. Anyway, there's no hurry."

Behind them, where the bay dwindled to the mouth of the river, a large fish jumped. The splash left a series of ripples spreading across the still water. Molly caught her breath and stared round-eyed at the disturbance.

"What was that?"

"Tarpon."

"But he was enormous."

"Thirty, forty pounds."

"Isn't that big?"

"Big enough."

"Well, what are we waiting for?"

"We're not after tarpon. They're too rough for a beginner. We'll try to locate a couple of snook."

"Are you sure that's a fish?"

"Absolutely."

"Sounds like something they play in a pool hall."

"Now pay attention."

"Yes, sir."

"I've let out enough line for you. We'll troll back and forth around the edge of the mangroves. When you get a strike be sure to set the hook. Keep your rod tip up and the line taut. Got it?"

"Bring on your snook," Molly said.

They fished until after dark, standing on a sandbar at a point where the river divided, working the plugs in the shallow water, fighting heavy fish in the darkness. After a while the moon rose and the night took on a soft luminosity and the air became alive with the chatter of birds and animals. Something called at them in rasping tones out of the dark and Molly asked what it was and Flake said, "Wildcat."

2

When he took her back to the cabin he kissed her. It was not much of a kiss. She had been kissed better many times before. But his mouth tasted clean and his hands on her were strong and hard and she liked kissing him. She liked too the fact that he didn't try to push it further.

"Good night, Molly."

"Good night."

"I like you."

"I'm glad, I like you too."

"See you tomorrow."

"You know where I'll be."

"I've got a charter in the morning but I'll be here after that."

"Fine."

"I think you'll make one hell of a fisherman."

"Really?"

"Greatest natural talent for casting I've ever seen."

"You're kidding."

"Yes."

"But I *did* catch a snook. Isn't that something?"

"I'll say it's something."

"If Cash will lend me a rod I'll practice tomorrow."

"Wait for me and I'll practice with you."

"Wonderful."

"It's hard to realize I just met you for the first time this afternoon."

"I know what you mean."

"I guess it sometimes just happens that way."

"I guess sometimes it does."

"Good night then."

"Good night, Johnny."

He kissed her again and this time he did not seem at all awkward. She put her arms around his neck and returned the kiss. It was the first time she had kissed anyone since Frank.

He got into the jeep and waved to her and went off down the sandy road through the woods. She watched the red lights vanish among the pine trees and then she was alone with the moonlight and the river. The light breeze off the river felt surprisingly cool.

Somewhere out in the black ribbon of water a big fish jumped. The solid smacking sound of him made her heart jump. You rascal, she thought. Jump while you can. Your jumping days are numbered. Izaak Molly Walton is here to fix your wagon for you.

Something big moved on padded feet through the brush and she remembered Flake saying there were wildcats here. For a moment she tingled with fright but then she saw it was only the dog. He came up to her and put his warm brown muzzle in her hand.

"Hello, lover," she said. "Been off sowing a wild oat or two?"

He nuzzled her hand again and suddenly a tide of warm affection for the dog and the river and the fish ran through her. She sank to her knees and put her arms around the dog's neck and hugged his head to her cheek.

"I love you," she whispered to him. "I'm absolutely mad about you. Let's elope together. We can live on champagne and dog biscuits. Can't you just picture a kennel for two in a grotto in Capri?"

"No," said Bess's voice behind her. "I can't. And I'll thank you to stop seducing my dog."

"Didn't think you'd hear."

"Oh, I heard, all right. Don't imagine for a minute that you can get any hanky panky past me. What's the matter? Can't sleep?"

"I'll sleep, all right. It's just that it's too beautiful to leave."

"I know," Bess said. "I always get a little catch in the throat when I come out here at night this way. I've been seeing it for years now but I still feel it. When did Johnny leave?"

"A few minutes ago."

"He's a nice boy."

"Yes."

"He likes you."

"I like him too."

"Don't hurt him, Molly."

"Why would I hurt him? Do you really think I'm such a *femme fatale?*"

"Of course not. But he's been cooped up in this small town for a long time now. You're a rather more exotic piece than most he's apt to come in contact with."

"Really, Bess, He's a big boy now. Been off to the wars. Major Flake, and all that."

"I know, but still I have a strange feeling about him. Maybe it's because I've known him since he was a kid. He can twist iron bars with those hands of his but still I think of him as a boy. I don't think anything has ever really gotten to him emotionally and I'm not sure what will happen when it does."

Molly put her arms around her sister's shoulders and hugged her. "Look, honey," she said. "He's a nice boy and we went fishing and I kissed him good night, and that's that. I've got troubles enough already without taking on the major."

"I know, sweetie. Want to tell me about it?"

"With your good man pining for you in the house? I don't want to start off on the wrong foot with him."

"He's been snoring like a moose for the past hour."

"I wondered what that was. Thought for a while it was the mating call of an alligator."

"It's just nature boy after a hard day's work. But I adore him, snores and all."

"I know you do. And I'm so darn glad for you."

"Maybe we'd better turn in," Bess said. "We get up with the dawn around here."

Molly suddenly began to feel tired. The excitement of her arrival, which had been carrying her through the day, finally had faded away. The prospect of bed was suddenly the most attractive thing in the world.

Bess led her to the cabin they had set aside for her and kissed her good night.

"Sleep tight," Bess said.

"I'm half there already."

She knew she ought to wash her face but she couldn't quite make it. Instead she shucked out of her clothes and climbed naked in between the cool sheets.

The bed felt marvelous. "Bed," she murmured drowsily, "I love you."

An owl called in the pine woods. Something scampered through the brush, and the chickens set up a sudden clamor in their pen. Perhaps, she thought, I ought to do something about it. But even as the thought formed she fell deliciously, finally, irrevocably asleep.

3

Thinking back on it afterward, she could never remember where the time had gone. She had no responsibilities but still the days flew by. But the best times of all were on the river, either alone or with Flake. She had developed a real passion for fishing and she could never seem to get enough of it.

In the middle of May, on the morning of her twenty-fourth birthday, she boated an eighteen-pound tarpon. It was the first really large fish she had caught and the battle left her trembling with excitement and exhaustion. Her wrists ached and there was a gash on one hand where the flying reel handles had struck.

Flake bandaged her hand and then kissed her soundly.

"Happy birthday, chum," he said.

"It's the best birthday present I've ever had. If I was any happier I'd bust. It really *is* something, isn't it? I mean catching a fish like that on a casting rod?"

He assured her that it really was something and kissed her again.

"How about some breakfast?" he asked.

"Wonderful."

"We'll go over to the island."

Actually the island was a spit of land with a private sandy beach but it was cut off completely from the surrounding area by a dense and impenetrable wall of mangroves, making it in effect an island. They had picnicked there many times and had come to regard it as their own private domain.

Flake built a fire, then expertly filleted two small sea trout they had caught shortly after dawn. Molly sat on the sand, hugging her knees, watching him, liking the quiet assured way he went about things. In a few minutes the strips of fish were smoking in the pan and Flake had unearthed a battered coffee pot which he hung on a forked green stick over the edge of the blaze.

After eating they lay back on the sand, soaking up the warmth of the early morning sun, listening to the whisper of the river a few yards away. Flake put his arm under her head and she lay back on it, looking up at the sky, watching a long gull wheeling in eccentric circles against the blue.

Molly sighed with contentment. "What more could anybody want?" she asked.

"I don't know. How about a six-piece orchestra and a Cadillac convertible?"

"Not interested."

"Ticket on the Irish sweepstakes and a week at the Waldorf with all expenses paid?"

"Uh-uh."

"Silver blue mink and a five-year Hollywood contract."

"Do they have tarpon in Hollywood?"

"Never heard of any."

"Then you know what you can do with it."

"Yes," he said, "I guess I do."

He leaned over and kissed her again. He kept his mouth on hers until her lips grew soft and warm under his and her mouth opened and he felt the tip of her tongue. Her fingers were tightening on his back, the nails biting through his shirt. With his free hand he had opened the buttons of her shirt and then he moved his face down to her breast. Her breathing quickened and she held his head pressed tightly against her bosom.

Once she whispered, "Someone will see us."

Then there was only the whirling blue sky that seemed to be spinning dizzily and the chuckle of the river and the whisper of the wind in the treetops and the warm pressure of his muscular body close to hers.

CHAPTER EIGHT

Flake had been steering the *Jezebel* by the Morro light but now with the dawn coming up he didn't need it any more. The sky turned pink and clear and the buildings of Havana rose tall and white and cool out of the sea. And with the dawn there came a slight breeze from the southeast and the shrimp boat began to roll easily in the chop.

"What are we waitin' for?" Cutter asked.

"I want to make sure they can see us," Flake answered.

"They can see us, all right. They can see us for half an hour now."

"That's right."

"Then why don't we go in?"

"When I'm ready. When I'm good and ready."

He was ready now but he wouldn't give Cutter the satisfaction of thinking he had influenced him in any way. To hell with Cutter. The bastard stank. The whole expedition stank. Why had he let Mangio talk him into it? For a thousand dollars. A thousand dollars was a lot of money. Not in jail it wasn't.

"Hey, Cruze," he called. "Come up here."

The rummy came shambling forward. He looked a little better. His face had gotten sunburned in the past two days and his hands didn't shake so much any more. A bloody little miracle, Flake thought. A ship with a hole in the bottom floating like new.

But when Cruze got close you could smell the booze on him. That was the answer then. With whiskey in him he was fine.

"You got that strainer fixed the way I want it?" Flake asked.

"Yes, sir. There ain't no engineer in all of Cuba could figure out that strainer. I done a good job. I'm a good engineer."

"I know," Flake said. "That's why I brought you."

"I can fix 'em or foul 'em up," Cruze said. "Any way you want it."

"All right," Flake said. "That's fine."

"There won't be nobody able to fix that engine now but me."

"Shut up."

"It's the truth. I tell you—"

"All right. Shut up."

Cruze gave him a funny look and then shambled off, some of the confidence gone from his step. Flake didn't like to talk to him that way but what else could you do? When Cruze had a couple of shots in him he was apt to run off at the mouth. All rummies were that way. It was one of the hazards of using Cruze for this job.

He let her lie out there for another hour. Half a dozen fishing smacks came beating up against the westerly breeze. The water was blue and purple, flecked with golden patches of weed. Beyond it the city looked cool and pleasant. Flake knew it was not really cool and pleasant but across the water it looked that way. Anyway, there would be cold beer and plenty of women. Would there be time for women? Why not? They would have to do a real job on fixing that strainer to make it look convincing,

It was ten o'clock before he brought her in. They came in with the tide making behind them and a surf beginning to foam against the big yellow sea wall. They went past the P & O docks and the yacht club and straight in to the Customs pier. The Customs officer, a thin man wearing glasses and a mustache and a khaki uniform that looked as if he had slept in it, came aboard and Flake gave him the crew list and the ship's log.

"How long will you be there?" the Customs officer asked.

"I don't know. We got to fix that strainer."

"What about your cargo?"

"I'll have to get rid of it. It'll spoil if I keep it."

"All right," the Customs officer said. "I got a brother-in-law in the fish business. I'll call him."

That was the nice thing about Cuba. Everybody had a brother-in-law in business. Any business you wanted.

Flake sold the shrimp at a loss. He bargained for a while to make it look good but eventually he sold it for less than the going price. That was all right. It put the Customs officer in a position where he would not want to talk too much about their visit.

When they got the shrimp off they cleaned the ice out of the holds and hosed the ship down. In the afternoon Cruze worked on the strainer and Cutter went ashore to set up his contacts.

It was nearly six when Cutter came back.

"Okay?" Flake asked.

Cutter nodded. "We get to Puerto Matanzas around midnight tomorrow night. There'll be a fishing boat waiting outside the breakwater for us."

"All right. You'd better stay on board now. The less time you spend ashore the better. Cruze, you stay here and work on those engines. Make it look good."

"Listen, Flake—"

"Yeah," Flake said. "I'll bring it back with me. You want to go ashore, Bush?"

"Sure," Bush said. "I like Havana. A man can have a lot of fun here."

"Don't have too much fun. We'll be shoving off before dawn. I want you back here by one o'clock. Remember that. Don't get loaded and forget it."

"Not me," Bush said. "I don't drink."

"All right then. Let's go."

They went up the street in the early evening. The city was just beginning to cool off. It was a big wide street with an island in the middle and benches on both sides. The benches were white with bird droppings.

The wall was comparatively clean. They sat on the wall and watched the people going by. The street was crowded. In Havana in the evening everybody likes to stroll. The men wore white shirts and black shoes. The women wore tight skirts and looked like whores. Some of them were whores but even the ones who were not managed to look as if they might be.

While they were sitting there a police car came up. A short fat man in civilian clothing got out, followed by two policemen. For a moment Flake had a nasty feeling. Maybe Cutter had pulled some kind of a double-cross on him. Cutter hated his guts. It would be just like Cutter to put the finger on him.

But the fat man went by on the run with the cops right behind him and Flake breathed easier. They went up to one of the bums sitting on the wall and the fat man pointed his finger at the bum and began screaming in Spanish. Then the cops grabbed hold of the bum and began to beat him across the face with the flat of their palms.

The bum was small and skinny and he stood there not fighting back, not saying anything, his head lolling and shaking every time they hit him.

"What's it all about?" Bush asked.

"I don't know," Flake said. "I don't savvy too much of the lingo. Seems like he stole something from the fat boy and they're working him over to get him to talk."

"Why don't they take him down to the station house? What's the good of hitting him here?"

"I don't know," Flake said.

"Maybe we'd better get out of here."

"Yeah," Flake said. "That's not a bad idea."

They walked away, looking casual, and went into a bar a couple of blocks down.

"They're tough," Bush said. "Those cops are plenty tough."

"Two of them with a guy half their size."

"That's what I mean," Bush said.

The waiter came over to their table and they ordered Hatuey beer. The beer was cold and very good.

"Why can't they make good beer in the States?" Bush asked.

"I don't know," Flake said.

"They charge enough for it."

"It all goes into advertising."

"That don't make the beer any better."

"No."

"Maybe they don't use enough hops. Or maybe it's the water."

"Maybe."

"You feel funny sitting here with me?" Bush asked.

"No," Flake said. "Why should I?"

He did feel funny sitting there drinking beer with a Negro but he didn't intend to say so. Bush was all right. Bush was a good man. What the hell difference did his color make? But it did make a difference.

"You think this deal is all right?" Bush asked.

"You mean about the boat? About coming to Cuba?"

"Yeah."

"Sure I think it's all right. If I didn't think so I wouldn't be doing it."

"Don't get sore," Bush said. "I was just asking."

"You ask too many questions."

"I know," Bush said, standing up.

"Forget it. I guess I'm a little jumpy."

"That's all right," Bush said, smiling at him. "I wanted to take a walk around town anyway."

"Okay," Flake said.

"See you on the boat."

"One o'clock. Don't forget."

"Sure," Bush said.

Bush was all right, Flake thought. They were all all right. It was just that he felt so jumpy. Something about this thing smelled. He ought to get back on the boat and go shrimp fishing and take his cargo back to Key West and tell Mangio to go screw himself. But he knew he would not. He was in the thing now and he would go through with it.

He ordered another beer and when he was halfway through it three whores came in and sat down at the table next to him. One of them was blonde and young, and the second was dark and not so young, and the third was Chinese and the oldest of the three.

A Chino, Flake thought. Funny, seeing a Chino whore in Havana. I wonder how she got here. She ought to go over big in Havana.

The three girls kept looking at him and giggling among themselves and when he looked back at them the Chinese put her tongue out at him. Then she made a curious little gesture. She closed her fist and rapped it smartly twice on the table. That's a funny one, Flake thought. Bang bang.

He shook his head but the Chinese stuck her tongue out at him again. He paid his bill and went outside, walking slowly down the street toward the Malacon and the sea wall. Finding a small restaurant there, he went in and sat at a table under a striped canvas awning facing the sea and ate lobster and drank a couple more beers.

With darkness, a cool sea breeze came in and rattled the canvas awning and it was very pleasant sitting there eating lobster and feeling the moist night wind off the sea.

They kept the food in a wooden refrigerator with a glass front. The glass was coated with moisture so you couldn't easily see inside, but under it, half lost in the shadows, there was something gray and dead. Flake squinted at it carefully. It was a dead rat.

He called the waiter over. "What kind of a stinking place is this? You've got a dead rat over there."

"What?" said the waiter.

"Rat. *Postizo. Muerto postizo.*"

"Impossible."

"Not impossible. Look." He pointed to the counter and the waiter looked. At first he saw nothing but finally he made out the rat and called the boss. They stood there gesturing at it and talking fast and after a while the waiter got a broom and swept the rat across the floor and through the doorway into the street. The dead rat lay in the street looking big and fat and shapeless. The waiter turned and smiled brightly at Flake. "Okay?"

"No," Flake said. "Not okay."

He put his money down on the table and got up and went outside. He walked up the Malacon half a dozen blocks and sat on the sea wall, smoking a cigarette. A car went by slowly with two *policia* in it. They looked at Flake but kept moving.

He heard the tap of heels long before he saw her. The tap of heels along the Malacon in the cool of the evening is one of the nicest things about Havana. The girls wear high French heels and they walk along the Malacon at all hours of the night and the tap of their heels combines with the sighing of the wind to make a kind of exciting rhythmic music.

This one was alone and walking fast and when she came abreast of him in the street light he saw that she was tall and blonde and full bosomed and astonishingly beautiful. When she saw him she stopped and lit a cigarette and then sat down close to him on the sea wall. "Hello," Flake said.

"Hello," she said in English.

"You're a pretty good walker. I was watching you."

"Yes," she said. "I'm a great walker."

"You want to walk with me and have a drink?"

She shrugged. "Why not?"

"Where is there a place?"

"Nearby," she said. "That way."

She was a little unsteady on her feet. He saw now that she was slightly drunk.

"You sure you want a drink?" he asked.

"No," she said. "Let's go to a hotel."

"Where?"

What kind of professional is it that doesn't know a hotel?

"What's your name?" he asked.

She shrugged. "What does it matter? Come on. Hurry up. Let's find a hotel."

Flake hailed a cab and they got in. The girl said something to the driver, who nodded and drove them down a series of winding streets to a small shabby hotel. Flake paid the driver and they went into the hotel. The night clerk showed them a room, a small room with a balcony on the street. There was a bathroom with a bidet but no door. The clerk did not ask them to register.

In the strong light of the naked electric bulb he saw that she was even more beautiful than he had thought. She wore a tight black silk dress cut low to the crease between her full breasts and her skin was milky white. She had little on under the dress.

Her mouth was wide and generous. Her eyes were not a whore's eyes. She sat down beside him on the bed.

"Have you got a cigarette?" she asked.

He gave her the pack.

Her fingers were long and beautifully kept. He wondered what he had gotten into. This girl was not a whore.

"You have to give me money," she said.

"How much?"

She looked worried. "I don't know. How much do you usually give?"

"I don't usually go with putas," he said flatly.

"Why did you go with me?"

"I don't know."

"Don't you like putas?"

"No."

"Do you hate them?"

"Sometimes."

"Do you hate me?"

"No."

"I'm a puta. Why don't you hate me?"

"We're talking too much."

"Yes. Give me money."

He took his wallet out of his pocket and handed it to her. She opened the wallet and extracted the first bill she touched. She did not look at it. It was a dollar. She handed him back the wallet and stuffed the dollar into her purse.

"You see?" she said. "You see what a good puta I am?"

"Yes," Flake said.

With an abrupt movement she crossed her arms and pulled the dress up over her head. She wore small black panties and nothing else. Her skin was astonishingly white. It was a remarkable body. She glanced challengingly at him and said, "Am I a good puta?"

"Fine," he said. "Fine."

Her face was suddenly burning pink, as though she had a fever.

He reached for the light switch and she said, "No, leave it on."

CHAPTER NINE

When he left her he went back to the boat and sat there on the stern with the lights of Havana around him and the sounds of the night—cars going along the Malacon, the creak of the rub rail against tar-blackened pilings and the chuckle of the odorous waters of Havana Bay under the counter.

He felt eased of tension and desire but curiously incomplete. It had always been incomplete with anyone since Molly. That was the sad truth of the matter. Always, when he was with another woman, he was trying to wipe out the memory of Molly. And yet it always came back to him more sharply than ever. Like that time on the *Mistress*...

2

The *Mistress* swung to her anchor in the broad lagoon formed by the passage of the river to the sea. The moon set a path of silver straight to the reef and the curling crests of the breakers beyond. The booming rumble of the surf made a hollow thudding on the night air. The sea buoy, flashing redly in the darkness, bobbed drunkenly on the outgoing tide. But inside the lagoon the water was very still and the cruiser lay motionless.

Molly lay with her head on Flake's chest. They were in the starboard bunk. The port above them was open and a cool breeze came through and with it the shaft of moonlight. Molly was listening to all the boat sounds she had come to know and love so well—the gentle slap of water against the hull, the faint rubbing of the anchor rope against its chock, the creak of the outriggers when she oiled, and an indefinable skittering of sound among the timbers that might have been the scampering of tiny feet.

"Asleep?" she whispered.

Flake made a grunting sound deep in his chest but said nothing. She ran her fingertips lightly down his ribs.

Suddenly she rolled away and he gripped her arm and said, "Where do you think you're going?"

"It's hot. I think I'll take a swim."

"Later."

"Now."

"Later."

She wriggled out of his grip, and he had a fleeting glimpse of delicately curved white hips darting through the hatchway. Then there was only her mocking laughter floating down to him from the deck and a sudden splash as she went over the side.

With a sigh he swung his legs off the bunk and went up after her. When he came out on deck he could see her swimming strongly a dozen yards off the bow. Bent over to keep her from seeing him, he scampered along the deck to the stern and let himself noiselessly down into the water.

The water was warm and very black. He moved hand over hand along the side of the boat until he could see her. She was resting on the anchor rope with her back to him. He moved carefully along until he was just behind her. Then he made a sudden lunge and had his hands on her. She shrieked in fear and tried to fight him off and then collapsed against him.

"Don't *ever* do that," she said brokenly.

"Sorry. I didn't realize you'd take it so hard."

"I thought an octopus had me."

"There are no octopi around here."

"I don't care. That's what I thought."

"All right now?"

"Yes."

"Not mad at me?"

"No."

They were still clinging to the anchor rope, their bodies caressed by the soft warm water. The path of moonlight ran away from them straight down to the sea. He put his hand on her breast and could feel her heart thudding.

"You poor kid," he said. "I really did frighten you."

"It's all right now."

He began to caress her gently and her hips pressed against him, warm and full.

"You're mad," she whispered.

She swung around to face him. He clung to the anchor rope with one hand and supported her with the other; the moonlight made a shining backdrop behind her. Her lips tasted of the sea and salt.

"You're mad," she whispered again.

Then her mouth was buried against his neck and her teeth were digging into his shoulder but he felt no pain at all.

3

When they came back on board they were cold from the water and they drank a great deal of brandy straight from the bottle. After the brandy they were ravenously hungry and Molly prepared bacon and eggs and coffee on the two-burner alcohol stove.

Flake switched on the radio and brought in a dance band. It was very cozy, sitting there in the neat little cabin, eating their meal, listening to the music. Molly had put on one of Flake's gray flannel shirts and a pair of faded blue dungarees. She was barefoot and she sat cross-legged on the bunk with her feet tucked under her.

"How do you feel?" Flake asked.

"Marvelous."

"You know you're a damn good cook."

"Thank you, kind sir."

"That's what this boat needs, a damn good cook."

"That shouldn't be hard to find."

"The cook would have to have special qualifications."

"For instance."

"Oh, I don't know. Hanging onto anchor ropes and that sort of thing."

She made a little face at him. "I imagine that takes a special talent."

"Sure does."

"Do you suppose Cash knows about us?" she asked abruptly.

Flake shrugged. "Maybe. Does it matter?"

"Well, yes, I think it does."

"What about Bess?"

"What about her?"

"Does she know?"

Molly smiled. "Sisters can usually tell a lot just by looking at each other."

"You mean that sparkle in your eyes and the rosy glow in your cheeks? That could come just from the healthy outdoor life you've been leading."

"Oh, shut up."

"To get back to the subject of cooks and cooking."

"Yes?"

"What about it?"

"You mean you're offering me the job?"

"Yes," he said, suddenly serious. "I am."

Molly got up and walked away and stood looking out of the hatchway. "I'd have to think about it."

"What's there to think about? If you like the boat and the skipper why not take the job?"

"I love the boat and I can just barely tolerate the skipper but there's still a lot to think about."

"You know I'm asking you to marry me, don't you?" he said.

"Yes," she said. "I know."

She turned and walked back to him and put her small cool palm against his cheek and said, "Let me think about it, skipper."

"All right," he said, trying to sound gay, although a leaden sense of disappointment filled him. "Take all the time you want. Take ten minutes or an hour or even until tomorrow. Tell me tomorrow."

"No," she said, not looking at him. "Not tomorrow. I won't be seeing you tomorrow."

"Why not?"

"Have you got another cigarette?"

"Sure."

He took out a cigarette and lit it and handed it across to her.

"What's on your mind?" he asked.

"There's something I've got to tell you and it isn't easy."

"Shoot. I'm a big boy now."

"All right then. I won't be seeing you tomorrow or the day after that. Not for about a week."

"I still don't get it."

"I have a friend coming down from New York and I promised him that while he was here I wouldn't see anyone else."

"What do you mean, a friend?"

She sighed. "A man I've known for a long time. A very dear friend."

"What's his name?"

"What difference does it make?"

"It makes a difference." His voice was cold and his lips were compressed into a thin line.

"His name is Frank."

"Frank what?"

Molly resented Flake's tone of voice and the third degree quality of his questions but she was anxious to avoid a flareup if possible.

"Frank Mason."

"And what about him?"

"What do you mean, what about him?"

"Have you been having an affair with him?"

"Johnny, darling, stop it."

"Answer me."

"I won't answer you."

"Then I guess that's answer enough."

She was getting angry now. "What right have you to judge me? The relationship between Frank and me goes back a long time before I met you. And what about you? Surely I'm not the first girl you ever went to bed with. There were others."

"Yes," he grated. "Plenty."

He stood up in cold fury. He went forward and pulled the anchor out of the sandy bottom and started the engines and headed the boat back up the river. When they reached the dock he bustled her into the jeep and drove in angry silence over the twisting road to the camp. Once they skidded on the loose sand and Molly thought for a moment they would go off the road but Flake held grimly on and slammed the jeep through the soft spot and back into the open again.

At the camp she got out and said, "Do you want to leave it this way?"

"Just tell me one more thing," he said, glaring at her.

"Yes?"

"Are you going to sleep with this guy when he gets here?"

"Oh, stop it!"

"Answer me."

"I don't know," she said, turning coldly away. "I haven't made up my mind."

CHAPTER TEN

1

They came out fast on the morning tide, leaving behind the boulevards and parks and tall buildings and the steep weathered walls of the fortress of Cabanas, and they were past the rocky headland of the Morro and out into the clean purple water of the Gulf Stream.

Flake took her far out into the Stream until the Morro had dropped away behind them and then he throttled her down and let her lie that way. A couple of fishing smacks with dark-skinned men in them went by to the westward but after that nothing moved on the placid sea.

Cruze came up from the engine room wiping his face with an oily rag. He looked good this morning. He had been working on the bottle Flake had brought back for him.

"We're having engine trouble again," Flake said. "You're one lousy engineer."

Cruze smirked and winked. "I sure am."

"You finish off that bottle?"

"No, sir."

"How much you got left?"

"Half. More than half."

"Bring it up here to me."

"Hell, Flake, I can handle it."

"We got a big job tonight. I don't want anything to go wrong."

"You can count on me."

"Sure," Flake said. "Like a busted leg I can count on you."

With a resigned air of suffering Cruze brought the bottle to him and Flake put it away. It was not half full. It was less than a quarter full.

"All right," he told Cruze. "Go sleep it off. We got all day with nothing to do anyway."

They drifted out there through the long morning and Flake had time to think about a lot of things. He was still thinking about Molly and about the girl in Havana last night.

She was a beautiful girl and maybe she was crazy. Or maybe she was getting even with some guy. That was more likely. Maybe she'd had a scrap with some guy and maybe he'd called her a whore and she had said okay, if I'm a whore I'll go and be one. Or maybe she had caught him in the hay with another broad and was getting her own back this way. Or it could be any one of a hundred things. Who could begin to understand the female mind? Anyway, it had not been too satisfactory. It was never really satisfactory with a whore. You never really found what you were looking for. And what the hell *are* you looking for? You get your money's worth, don't you? You got your dollar's worth last night, didn't you?

"Hey, Cutter," he called. "I want to talk to you."

Cutter came up to the bridge. His pale skin, which never tanned, looked unclean in the daylight. Flake noticed for the first time that Cutter had almost no eyelashes. It gave his eyes a lidless, snakelike quality.

"How do you feel about tonight?" Flake asked him.

"What do you mean, how do I feel?"

"Just that. You feel everything is okay?"

"Sure," Cutter said. "How else would I feel?"

"Who is the guy we're meeting?"

"He's a Cuban."

"I know he's a Cuban. What's his name?"

"Diaz."

"He'll be on the boat?"

"No," Cutter said. "He'll be with the truck."

"You mean they're not loading the stuff till after we get there?"

"That's right."

"What's the idea?"

"They won't move it until we show up."

"What's the matter? Don't they trust us?"

"They trust us, all right. They just want to make sure we show up."

"I don't like it."

"Well, that's the way it is."

"Some day you and me are gonna go round and round for good," Flake said.

"Yeah," Cutter agreed unemotionally, accepting it as fact.

2

They drifted through the long afternoon and toward nightfall Flake put the *Jezebel* on a course for Matanzas. The headland went down in a flaming sunset and darkness settled over the sea. It was a black night with plenty of stars but no moon. Flake was just as happy about the moon.

The swells were long and rolling but there was no chop and the *Jezebel* held easily to her course and there was not much to do. Flake had time to think now—too damn much time to think—and time to remember again all the bitter, still painful business about Molly and Mason...

3

Three days after Mason's arrival in Stuart the whole thing came to a head. Mason and Molly had been out on the river, fishing, and now, late in the afternoon, they came back to the camp with a string of fish. Bess was on the dock to greet them. Molly proudly held up the fish and said, "Not bad for a beginner, hey?"

Mason, a tall slender man whose fair skin had gone lobster red in the bright sun, wiped his forehead and said, "If all else fails she can always make a living as a guide. She knows every hole in this river."

"She should," Bess said. "She had a good teacher."

"Yes," Mason said. "She's been telling me."

I wonder how much she really told him, Bess thought. This past couple of days must have been damned awkward for Molly. And yet there's nothing in the situation that she didn't bring about herself. Mason looks like a regular forgive and forget boy. I never could stand that sort of man. Don't trust 'em. Too damn sweet.

They moored the boat and went back up to the house. Molly was demonstrating her newly acquired mastery of the delicate art of filleting when they heard the dogs barking and Flake's jeep grind up the road.

Flake drove the jeep up to the side of the house and sat there at the wheel. He hadn't shaved and dark patches of sweat stained his khaki shirt. When it spoke it was obvious that he was quite drunk.

"Hi," he said thickly.

Bess looked up smiling. "Howdy, stranger."

"Hello, Johnny," Molly said in a small strained voice.

Flake didn't answer. He climbed out from behind the steering wheel and walked over to inspect the fish. "Not bad," he said, turning one of the larger fish over with his foot. "You catch 'em?" he asked Mason.

"I'm afraid not," Mason said. "She caught most of them. I was lucky on a couple but Molly's the real fisherman. I lost most of mine."

"Modest," Flake said. "Nice and modest."

"I'm afraid I haven't had the pleasure," Mason said.

"Pleasure," Flake asked thickly. "What pleasure?"

"My name is Mason," Frank said, putting out his hand.

Flake ignored the hand. "I know," he said. "Frank Mason of New York City. Come a-courtin' of our little Moll."

Mason withdrew his hand. "You must be Flake."

"Smart," Flake said. "Smart and modest. A very high class type."

"Let's all go in and have a drink," Bess said.

Flake ignored her. "Your nose is red," he said to Mason.

"I know. Too much sun."

"And your ears are red too. Damned big ears and damned red."

Mason had stopped smiling. He stood his ground but he had gone a little pale beneath his sunburn.

"Yessir," Flake said thoughtfully, his dark eyes narrowed with drunken wisdom. "You ought to do something about them ears. Got to take better care of 'em. I aim to fix your ears for you. Gonna beat them off your damned head."

"Johnny," Bess said warningly.

Molly had not moved or spoken. She stood as if frozen, watching the two men.

With a sudden casual loose-jointed movement that was beautiful in its simplicity, Flake's left shoulder dropped and his right fist swung forward. The punch caught Mason flatfooted. He toppled backwards and lay sprawled with his face among the pine needles.

Bess shouted something at Flake but Molly uttered no sound. The whole scene, hideous as it was, seemed to lack reality for her. It was all curiously disjointed and out of timing, like one of those slow-motion films that pause with a high diver in mid-air. In the same dreamy way she saw Mason get up swinging erratically at Flake and heard Flake say disgustedly, "Why didn't you stay there, you silly bastard?" And then she saw Flake hit him again and this time Mason went down and did not get up again.

Flake was looking at them all and shaking his head. He said, "Ah, the hell with it," and then he got back in the jeep and ground off down the road.

Only after he was gone did the scene come into focus again for Molly. As the noise of the jeep died away she darted across to Mason and bent down beside him and took his head in her arms while Bess stood staring down at them.

4

Flake staged the biggest, longest, toughest bender anyone in that town had ever seen. He had canceled all his charters and the *Mistress* lay forlorn and empty at her dock. Sometimes he would come back to the boat to sleep it off for a few hours but for the rest he simply slept where ever he lay.

He was a quiet drunk. He made no noise and he did not look for trouble. He sat off in a corner of whatever bar he was in and drank quietly by himself. No one bothered him. The thick murderous rage in his face turned people away. He looked like a man about to explode. No one, taking in the width of his shoulders and the size of his hands, wanted to provide the spark that might touch it off.

He drank everything. He started with scotch but then he went to beer and bourbon and finally to gin. He would sit in a place until closing time and finally the bartender would approach him and say very politely, "About time to close up now, pal." Flake would glare at him in a way that made the man back nervously away and then Flake would rise and go lurching out of the door and off down the dark street.

Once he went to West Palm Beach and spent the night in a hotel room with a small blonde girl who looked something like Molly. When they got to the hotel he saw that she was really nothing like Molly, after all, but he took her anyway in a cold brutal fashion that still left him unsatisfied. The girl was too frightened to ask for money but in the morning, while she lay with the sheet drawn up to her chin watching him, he pulled ten dollars out of his pocket and put the money on top of the bureau and walked out without saying good-bye.

But none of it helped. Neither the drinking nor the whoring nor the fight he got into with three flyboys from the air base. It was a good fight and he half killed two of them before the third nearly ripped his right ear off with a looping overhand punch. Then the MP's came in the front and Flake went out the back. He ran through the scrubby palmetto growths and into a dark hollow and lay there gasping with senseless laughter.

But the vision of Mason as he had last seen him, prostrate and quivering in the pine needles, and Molly's face frozen in disbelief, remained with him. Try as he might he could not shake it off, and finally it was too much for him. He got back into the jeep and started up the sandy road to Cash's place for the last time. Even then he was not sure just what he had in mind, but thinking about it later he knew that if he had gotten his hands on Mason he would have killed him.

He came up the road in the hot afternoon with the pine scrub shimmering in a sea of heat waves. He was driving hard, brutalizing the jeep in the sandy ruts, slamming through the soft spots. The dogs came out to greet him and after them came Cash, naked to the waist, the sweat running off his lean shoulders.

"Hell, son," Cash said. "We just about give up on you. Told Bess you done joined the Navy or the Foreign Legion or some damn fool thing like that. Anyway, I'm glad you're here. I'm puttin' me a fiberglass bottom on one of those skiffs and I could use a hand."

"Where's Molly?" Flake asked, climbing out of the jeep. Cash spat in the dust and looked out across the river. "I reckon she's around somewhere," he said casually.

"Where?"

"You don't look too good, son. You're as whiskery as an old goat and twice as ornery. Come on in and wash up and have a drink."

"No. Where's Molly?"

Flake's eyes were bloodshot, his heavy jaw marked by a two-day growth of beard. He rocked unsteadily back and forth on his feet.

"Hell," Cash said. "I guess you don't need a drink, at that. You got a breath on you would knock over a bull alligator."

"Damn it," Flake roared, "where's Molly?"

"You better clear out of here, Johnny. Clear out and cool off. Come back when you ain't so loaded."

"The lousy two-timing bitch is in that shack," Flake said thickly. "In there with that sonofabitch from New York. Rolling in the hay with him like the whore she is. I'll kill the both of them."

Cash moved in quickly behind him and grabbed his arm in a hammer lock and said, "No you won't, son. You won't kill anybody. What Molly does is her own business."

"Let me go," Flake muttered, the rage bubbling like phlegm in his throat.

"Just take it easy," Cash said.

Flake twisted sideways in a whiplash motion, throwing off the arm-lock. At the same moment, blind with rage and jealousy, he knotted his fist and hit Cash hard on the side of the jaw. The older man went down and then got up quickly and stepped inside Flake's guard and hit him solidly in the belly. Flake grunted and feinted with his left and hit Cash a thundering blow over the heart with his right. Cash turned very pale and wavered for a moment like a tall pine receiving the last blow of the woodsman's blinking, and then fell forward on his face. Flake stood there blinking, his fists held before him like clubs, letting the slow awful knowledge that he had hurt Cash flicker through his drunken mind.

He was only dimly aware of Bess running out of the house and then of Molly darting out of the cabin and rushing forward to bend over Cash.

But what really struck home to him then were Molly's words—the words that still echoed through his brain on bad nights. If he let himself remember he could still see it all very clearly. Her contorted, tear-ravaged face and her mouth saying, "You fool. You fool. Frank left here two days ago. I sent him back up north."

5

Cash lingered on for a week before he died and during that time he never really recovered consciousness. The stroke had paralyzed his entire left side and his face was contorted into a speechless mask.

The doctor's words, absolving Flake of any real blame, were small comfort. "He had been suffering from heart trouble for a long time," he told Bess. "He came to me several times for treatment. Didn't he ever tell you?"

Bess shook her head without speaking. In the past week she seemed to have aged ten years. A broad streak of gray had suddenly appeared in her black hair. Her eyes were dry and her skin had a parched withered look as though she had been wandering in a desert.

"That's surprising," the doctor said. "Very few men would carry a load like that without telling someone."

"Cash always carried his own loads," Bess said.

"Of course the fight precipitated matters, but he might have suffered the stroke at almost any time without it. It's always hard to say in these matters. It might have happened when he was chopping wood or rowing a boat or even just sitting quietly reading a paper. On the other hand..."

For Flake, the words "On the other hand" seemed to reverberate through the still room like a sentence of execution. He could not bear to look at Bess. He wanted to go to her and put his arms around her but he knew how hopeless it was.

The doctor's voice had faded away. A leaden silence hung over the cool dark room. Flake watched a small black spider crawling up the wall. The spider hesitated for a moment before a crack in the wall and then disappeared into it.

Flake stood up and without looking at either Molly or Bess walked to the door and let himself out of the office. He closed the door quietly behind him. Within twenty-four hours he had sold the *Mistress*, packed his gear, and left town.

More than a week of numbed silence passed before the two women knew he had gone.

CHAPTER ELEVEN

1

The *Jezebel* picked up the sea buoy at Matanzas at eleven and lay to off it. The lights of the town twinkled against the black hills. The wind had freshened and a fair sea was running. It would make loading difficult.

Just before midnight they saw the launch swing out from the town. It nuzzled alongside and banged heavily against the *Jezebel's* stern.

"Put some fenders over," Flake told Bush.

Bush got out two of the spare tires they used for fenders and hung them over the port quarter. The launch lay in their lee then, not banging so heavily.

There were two men in the launch, one at the wheel and the other sitting in the stern. The one in the stern was Diaz. Flake couldn't see much of him in the darkness but he looked small and slender. He stood on the gunwale of the launch and talked to Cutter. After a few minutes the launch cast off and pulled away.

It was nearly one o'clock before they came back again with the first load. Flake felt uneasy. He didn't like hanging around out here like this. It wasn't healthy. Too exposed. Too close to town. Too many people.

Too damned many people.

"I thought you said Diaz would be on the truck," he told Cutter.

"Changed his mind."

"I don't like people who change their minds. Not on job like this."

"It ain't my fault," Cutter said. "I don't tell him what to do."

"Well, you better start telling him what to do. Tell him to speed it up. I don't want to hang around here a night."

Cutter said something to Diaz and the Cuban shrugged and said, "*Esta bien.*"

"Come on, come on," Flake said.

They were loading the stuff fast now, handing up the hams of liquor to Cutter and Bush who took them forward and stowed them in the hold under a pile of old nets. I was nearly three by the time they finished. It was not much of a load. Not as much as Flake had expected.

"Is that all?" he asked, looking at the eastern sky.

"It's finished," Cutter said.

"It's not much."

"That's all."

"All right, to hell with it." It was Mangio's worry, not his.

Diaz clambered up from the launch and stood on the *Jezebel's* deck.

"What does he want?" Flake asked Cutter.

"He's coming with us."

"The hell he is."

"He got to come with us."

"What for?"

"For the money."

"Mangio told me you had the money with you."

"No," Cutter said. "Not really."

What was Mangio up to? What kind of a fancy deal was he pulling?

"We can't take him," Flake said flatly. "He's not on the crew list."

"He don't have to be," Cutter said. "We'll put him ashore with the booze."

"To hell with that. I'm not smuggling any aliens. It's too big a rap. Tell him to get off the boat."

Cutter said something to Diaz and the Cuban reached into his pocket and pulled out a small flat automatic pistol. It was not much of a pistol. Flake looked at him and, at the pistol, trying to figure how many shots Diaz could squeeze off before he got his hands on him. Once he got his hands on Diaz the pistol would not be much use to him.

It was obvious that Diaz knew what was going through Flake's mind. He took two steps back, still holding the pistol pointed at Flake's middle. Cutter stepped back with him. Bush was standing very carefully off to one side.

So that's the way it is, Flake thought All right. Good. I'll fix the sono-fabitch when we get out to sea. I'll fix him good. He'll have a long swim back to Cuba.

He turned his back on them and went up into the wheelhouse. He rang the engine room and kicked her ahead and the *Jezebel* turned and headed for the open sea, leaving the launch bobbing behind them in the darkness. The man in the launch watched them for a few minutes and then began to row swiftly for the shore.

2

The only real problem you have, Allan Chambers, owner and master of the yacht *Vixen*, told himself, is this. If you can get through enough time you can make it all right. It's always worse just at first and then after a while it begins to ease off. The big thing is killing the time without killing yourself. Maybe she'll be back tonight. I have a very strong hunch, he told himself without really believing it, that she definitely will be back tonight and that we can sail tomorrow.

He rowed ashore and left the dink at the pier and walked up past the turtle pens in the direction of town. It's this filthy place, he told himself. At least if there was a regular yacht anchorage here and civilized people to talk to it wouldn't be so bad. There would be cocktail parties and the coming and going between the boats and all that pleasant sort of ship-to-shore life. But then he remembered that he had come here to get away from that sort of thing. There were too many temptations for Jessica in that sort of place. Too many attractive men, too much drinking, too much promiscuity. Here, he told himself bitterly, remembering that he had not seen her now in almost thirty-six hours, there were no temptations.

He went up a narrow alley and saw a group of men buying tickets at a gate, and passing through the gate into a tent. Not knowing what it was and not much caring, knowing only that it was some kind of local show and that it might pass the time, he followed them in.

Tiered benches that ran in circles like a sort of miniature bleachers at a country baseball game, had been set up inside the tent. In the center was a small ring with a low barrier and a dirt floor. The benches were filled with Cubans and a sprinkling of tourists in the inevitable hula shirts and with the inevitable cameras slung over their inevitable shoulders. In the narrow passageway behind the seats other Cubans were walking around with small brightly colored roosters under their arms, and Chambers realized then that he was about to see a cockfight.

He had never seen a cockfight before and he felt a stirring of interest. The handlers used thread and wax to fasten the steel spurs to the roosters' legs. The birds, which had not seemed particularly impressive up to that point, looked vicious after they had the spurs on. All the time the handlers were preparing the birds, they kept talking to them in Spanish.

An old man, blind in one eye, was making book. He had a face so lined and narrow that it looked like a dried prune. As the bets came to him he kept calling them out in a high singsong voice.

Chambers could not understand what the bookmaker was saying but he raised his hand and bet five dollars on the red bird. He had no reason to bet on the red except that it was smaller and looked as though it would lose and it was always more interesting to bet on the underdog. Except that in this case, he told himself, with a feeling of weary amusement, the underdog was the undercock. And there was a parallel in that somewhere. He too was the under... Stop it now. Stop it fast. Don't let it get started, Don't let it build up. Concentrate on these bloody chickens. It was proved long ago by eminent Chinese philosophers that one rooster can lick another. Yes, but which one?

The handler of the red seemed to be whispering instructions to his fighter. I wonder if the referee tells them to break clean and to go to a neutral corner in case of a knockdown, Chambers thought.

The handlers held the birds close to each other and made stabbing motions with them to stimulate them to fighting pitch. Then they were released from opposite sides of the ring and flew at each other across the dirt floor. They met in mid-air, slashing at each other with the spurs and seemed to hang suspended for a moment amid a cloud of feathers. Then they fell heavily to the floor of the pit, the red one underneath. The strategy of the black was clear. He was going for the head, trying for an outright kill. In the meantime, the red was sinking his spurs into the breast of his larger opponent.

They fought until time was called and then the handlers reclaimed them and began working over them with swift professional care. The red was in bad shape. His head and beak were completely covered with blood and one eye was gone. The eye, a spot of jelly against the red feathers, hung down by a thread. The handler wiped it away and wiped out the empty socket and then did something Chambers would not have believed possible. He took the bloody mangled rooster's head between his lips and began to breathe heavily into the chicken's nostrils in an effort to restore him. Chambers felt his stomach knot into a ball and turn over.

Again the birds came out and again they fought with hopeless savage gallantry. From the standpoint of sheer blind courage it was impressive. From every other standpoint it was disgusting.

The red was weakening badly. In almost all the exchanges he was underneath. The black bore him to the ground by sheer weight and strength and pecked him heavily about the head. He was working on the remaining eye. The red was completely blind now, fighting by instinct alone. But still fighting. And Chambers saw that each time the birds fell to the ground the red had his spurs upright and was working them hard over the black's chest.

The black was losing blood and beginning to weaken. Both birds were very tired now. Neither of them had the strength to get up in the air. They pecked slowly, stupidly at each other. The black staggered and sank until his breast was in the dust. The blind red kept feeling for him, still working with beak and spurs. Finally the steel reached a vital spot. The black collapsed and fell over heavily on his side. The red was still staggering around trying to find his enemy when the handler took him away. A feeble crow of victory came from the mangled head before he was carried out.

The bookmaker with the harrowed face looked around for Chambers in order to pay him his winnings at odds of three to one but Chambers was outside, too sick at his stomach to care about money.

3

After the cockfight he went to Harry's for a drink. He needed a drink pretty badly after what he had seen. What a bloody cruel atrocious spectacle, he kept telling himself. He did not tell himself that the roosters enjoyed it, which probably was true, or that it satisfied a natural instinct, which certainly was true, or even that it was a nobler death for a chicken than having its neck wrung and being dumped into a pot.

There were not too many people in Harry's. It was comparatively early. Two men were sitting at the bar drinking vermouth and soda. They wore charcoal gray flannel slacks and yellow espadrilles. They were sitting a little too close together and their voices were loud. They kept looking around the room to make sure everyone could hear them. "That's rich," one of them kept saying. "That's very rich."

Chambers sat at the far end of the bar and ordered a double scotch and fought the impulse to look at his watch. In a battle against time it is always a tactical error to look at your watch. When you look at your watch you are appalled to discover how slowly the hours are going by. And when that happens time has gained another victory over you. The big thing is to put off looking at your watch as long as possible.

But then, on the other hand, he told himself, it may be later than you think. And in that case you will definitely be ahead. One little peek? Absolutely not. Finish the drink first and then look. Discipline. Control. Finish this drink first and then have another one after that. He swallowed the drink fast and ordered another one. While waiting for it he looked at his watch. It was not as late as he had hoped.

A round-faced young man with a mustache came in. He was a very famous playwright. Chambers recognized him from his pictures. The playwright ordered a drink in a voice that was too loud and too British. Chambers knew for a fact that he had been born and bred on a farm in Georgia. He was a very sensitive playwright. All his plays were the same. They were always about lonely, half-mad women living in decaying mansions in the South.

With the playwright was a vicar. He was a very old vicar. He wore a white linen suit and a round collar. Having a vicar with him in a bar was a great coup for the playwright. By tomorrow it would be all over town. The two men at the end of the bar were talking about it already. "Rich," one young man in yellow espadrilles said to the other. "It's really rich."

Chambers began to feel better. The liquor was beginning to take hold. He had not looked at his watch for ten minutes. He could not be certain it had been ten minutes without looking at his watch but he felt sure it must be at least that much. Control, he kept telling himself. Iron control.

It was almost eight o'clock when Jessica came in. She was alone. She did not see Chambers at the bar. She crossed the room and sat down at one of the tables. Chambers looked at his watch again. The action was automatic by that time. He had looked at his watch exactly thirty-four times in the past two hours. His heart lunged inside him when he saw Jessica.

Holding his drink, he got up from the bar and crossed over to her and said stiffly, "Good evening, Jessica."

He was shaking all over. His knees were knocking and his hands were shaking and his lips were trembling.

Jessica stood up and kissed his cheek and said warmly, "Hello, darling."

She said it as though everything was fine. As though nothing at all had happened.

Control, Chambers warned himself.

"Let's go home," he said thickly.

"Of course, darling," Jessica said, smiling brightly at him. "Just let me finish my drink."

4

It was almost noon before the *Vixen* got under way for the Tortugas. Chambers did not much like the looks of the weather but still he was determined to get Jessica out of Key West. A heavy bank of clouds was building up to the northwest and the air was too clear and bright. If they were in for a northwester the short steep seas building up over the shallow waters of the Tortugas would be murderous, but he decided that no matter how bad it might he at sea, it would not be as bad as another session of waiting ashore for Jessica.

This morning they were very happy. They were always happiest after a period of Jessica's transgressions. The reconciliation was delicious. And in some way that neither of them could understand her unfaithfulness acted as an aphrodisiac for them both. It aroused Chambers to new heights. They went at each other in a sort of fury, in a feverish attempt to dominate and consume.

In the morning, emptied of all passion, they stood happily on the *Vixen's* slanting deck and watched the Key West shoreline slip by.

A solid southeast eighteen-knot wind was blowing and Chambers had the *Vixen* close hauled under jib and reefed main. With the leeward scuppers awash and spray glistening on the teak decks, she went charging off dawn the main channel. Chambers worked her as close to the banks as he dared and then brought her about in a flurry of canvas and shot off again on a broad reach.

It was skilful sailing. He handled the boat with a reckless abandon that was entirely uncharacteristic of his behavior ashore. Ashore he was undermined by insecurity and competition but here he was masterfully at ease. Jessica came and stood beside him, her long legs brown and boyish in the bright sun, her hair loose on the wind. With one hand on the wheel and the other around Jessica's waist, Chambers held the boat on her new course. Once again, as he had so many times in the past, he told himself that from now on everything would be just great.

CHAPTER TWELVE

Flake had decided to do a little fishing on the way up from Cuba. He would have to bring in half a load anyway, just to make the thing look legitimate in case anybody got too curious.

The net was heavy now. He kept his hand on the cable and he could feel her pull.

"Take her up," he told Cutter.

The winch groaned as the cable began to rise. The ship heeled to starboard under the weight.

"Put some oil on those winch bearings," Flake told Cruze.

The rummy started forward with the oil can. He walked stiffly, as though his joints hurt. Suddenly Flake let go of the wheel and darted through the doorway and jerked Cruze away from the winch.

"Watch your hands, man. That thing will chew you up like hamburger."

The rummy began to shake. Tears formed in his eyes and ran down his furrowed cheeks. "Give me one, Flake."

"All right. One."

"One's all I need. Honest. Let me have one and I'll be a good man. You know I'm a good man. If I wasn't you wouldn't have taken me."

"Stow it," Flake said.

He went back and got the bottle of whiskey and handed it to Cruze. After the rummy had a good long pull at it Flake forced his hands loose and took the bottle away from him.

Cruze grinned and wiped the back of his hand across his mouth. "You're a good man, Flake."

"Get back to work."

The first haul was a good one. The nets came up slow, alive and heavy. The shrimp were thicker than a man's finger and of a fine pearly color. There would be maybe fifty or sixty boxes of them, and at fifty-four dollars a box that amounted to a lot of shrimp and a lot of money. This would be a good trip, after all, Flake decided. He would make it both ways. On the shrimp and on the booze.

They dragged again and while the nets were down Flake went back to the wheelhouse. There was a cold stillness in the air that he did not like. The air was too quiet and it had a touch of north in it. It was usually still at this hour, just before dawn, but there was something strange about it this morning.

He tapped the barometer and was surprised to see how the needle had dropped. He switched on the receiving set but could not pick up a clear signal. The air crackled with static. That means a northwester coming, he thought. Here we are hauling them in and we get a lousy northwester. Now it will blow for maybe three or four days and fishing will be out of the question and we'll be stuck with half a load and no ice. Damn!

He stepped out on deck and said, "Speed it up. There's a blow coming."

Cutter didn't answer.

"You hear me?"

"Yeah."

"Then answer me."

"Okay."

"Where's your amigo?"

"What amigo?"

"The one with the popgun."

Cutter shrugged. "Asleep."

"Maybe I ought to toss him over the side."

"Maybe he don't toss so easy."

"He'll toss," Flake said.

He returned to the wheelhouse and flicked on the radio phone and let it warm up for a few minutes. Then he called the marine operator in Key West and asked for a weather report.

"Marine operator to *Jezebel*," the voice said. "A cold front is moving across the Gulf and will strike us sometime tonight. Winds will veer to the northwest and increase in velocity."

"What velocity?"

"Gusts of twenty to thirty- knots."

"Great."

"What did you say, *Jezebel*?"

"Nothing. Thank you."

Twenty to thirty. That meant forty to fifty down here. It always blew harder down here. There would be nothing for it but to run in behind the Tortugas and no one knew how long that would be or how much of their haul would go bad.

He looked out and saw that Cutter had abandoned his station at the winch. That cold-eyed Cuban sonofabitch. He would have to do something about Cutter and his Señor Diaz. He would have to do something about them real soon now.

But he did not want to make a decision. Any decision would mean trouble. It was better to let things slide. Let Mangio worry about it. Except that if anything went wrong—and in a deal like this there were always fifty ways it could go wrong—it would be Flake's neck that would feel the axe and not Mangio's. Mangio could always pick up another boat but new necks were hard to come by these days. This Diaz was not on any crew list and if the law found him on board the *Jezebel* it would mean real bad trouble.

They were dragging again for another haul and Flake was fiddling with the radio trying to get a later report when Bush put his head through the doorway and said, "You better do something about that old Cutter."

"What about him?"

"He's about to kill Cruze."

Flake went out fast, thinking: This is definitely not my night. Some other night maybe but not this one. This night I should be in a room in La Concha Hotel in a big bed with the curtains open and the moon coming in and a bottle of whiskey and a soft loving girl and to hell with shrimp and booze and northwesters and Mangio and all of it.

Cruze was curled up on the deck, holding his arms over his head to protect his face, and Cutter was kicking him hard in the ribs. Flake took Cutter by the collar and spun him around and hit him solidly in the throat. His fist made a meaty sound against the man's throat and Cutter fell to his knees, his mouth working for air like a stranded fish.

Flake picked Cruze up and propped him against the winch and went back for the bottle. He poured whiskey down the rummy's throat and waited until the sick bewildered eyes opened and stared at him blankly. Cutter was still on his hands and knees, shaking his head like a dog with the heaves, trying to work the wind into his clogged throat. Flake capsized a bucket over the side and pulled it up dripping and sloshed water over Cutter's head.

Cutter glared up at him and Flake said, "Get up, you pig."

"Why you hit me?" Cutter managed to grate out.

"You're some boy. Beating up on a rummy. Some boy."

"I'll fix you," Cutter said, managing to pack new viciousness into the old threat.

"Sure you will. But not when I'm looking at you."

He took the rummy into the wheelhouse and stretched him out on one of the bunks. Cruze's long limbs rattled and shook like palmetto fronds in the wind.

"Sorry, Flake. Sorry I made trouble for you."

"Nothing I can't handle. Forget it. What was it all about?"

"I guess I got in his way. He cussed me and then he hit me."

"You want another shot?"

Cruze shook his head. "Not now."

"Good man."

"I guess I'm no damn good, Flake. I'm a lousy old rummy, is all. I guess I make trouble every place. I'd be better off dead."

"I told you to forget it. Cutter's been asking for it ever since we left Key West. I was bound to tangle with him sometime."

"But what about the other one?"

"Diaz?"

"Yeah."

"I don't know. I haven't figured that one out yet."

CHAPTER THIRTEEN

1

The real trouble came an hour before dawn. It was blowing hard by that time. The ship was climbing steep crests and black water was plunging over her bow. Sheets of rain boiled out of the west and spattered the wheelhouse windows. The wind howled through the rigging. The short rough seas on the edge of the Stream pounded up against the current. The *Jezebel* twisted and tossed, creaking under the shock of the seas.

In fair weather the Gulf Stream can be one of the pleasantest places imaginable. The purple-blue depths roll with lazy placidity under the broiling tropical sun. But when a northwester lashes the Stream it goes mad. The four-knot current fights the wind with a fury unmatched almost anywhere else on earth. Even the big fellows, the ten-thousand-ton tankers and southbound liners, try to avoid the Stream under those conditions. For a small boat it is plain bloody hell.

Flake reached for his yellow oilskins that usually hung from a hook in the wheelhouse and found them gone. He reached over with his foot to where Bush was sleeping, curled up on the wheelhouse deck, and nudged him in the ribs. Bush awoke and sat up quickly and said, "You want me, Cap'n?"

"Yeah. Take the wheel for a few minutes. I'm going below for my foul weather gear. Keep her headed into the wind."

"Anything you want?"

Bush grinned sleepily. "A double bed, a six-piece orchestra and a yaller girl from New Orleans."

"Coming up," Flake said.

The wind and rain lashed at him as he went through the doorway. He skidded a few steps on the slippery deck and caught hold of the engine room hatch. He hung on with both hands while she took a big one over the bow, and then fought his way down before the water swirled around him.

By the light of a sickly yellow bulb in the engine room he saw Cruze sitting with his back against the bulkhead. At first glance he appeared to be asleep, but then Flake saw that his eyes were open and that he was simply sitting there staring into space. He held a small neat machinist's wrench in his thin grease-stained hands and his fingers made a slow caressing motion on the steel.

"You all right?" Flake asked.

Cruze didn't answer.

"You okay?" Flake repeated.

Cruze nodded slackly, his eyes still focused on something invisible.

"It's a regular bitch up there." Flake said. "You're lucky to be down here."

"That's right," Cruze muttered, not really believing it, knowing that in foul weather the engine room was as bad or worse than any other place on a small ship, and not caring. He just sat there with his back to the bulkhead and his eyes locked on some invisible, impossible shape or dream of the past.

"Take it easy," Flake said, and went forward for his oilskins. He found them hanging amidships and climbed into the damp heavy salt-smelling rubber jacket and the knee-length black boots with the white rubber soles. Remembering the pint of bourbon locked in his sea chest, he thought about getting it out for a short one to fight off the damp, but then decided against it. There was still plenty of the night ahead of him and a long tough day after that and the whiskey might make him sleepy or, even worse, careless.

Coffee would be the thing. He would break Cutter out of his bunk and tell him to put on a pot of joe. And the boy with the popgun, Diaz. He would put that sportsman to work too. He would put him up on deck some place. Let him get his dainty little pointed shoes wet. And in the course of passing Diaz on deck he would grab him by the neck and take that damn fool gun away from him and drop it over the side.

As he stood there buttoning his jacket and thinking about the two Cubans, he saw a flash of light up in the forepeak. And, for just a moment, over the drone of the engine and battering of the storm, he heard the whisper of voices. What are they up to now, he thought. What nasty little eggs are they hatching up there in the forepeak? This whole thing had smelled from start to finish and the stench was getting worse by the hour. Damn Mangio anyway for ever getting him into it. Better to chuck the bloody whiskey over the side and forget about it and go back clean. And chuck Cutter and Diaz over too if they want to play rough. Except that putting everybody over the side in this sea was murder. And he hadn't come to that yet. Or at least not since Cash. Cash, he thought bitterly, the last man he had murdered.

He moved very quietly and slowly toward the forepeak, the rubber boots soundless on the floorboards. The swift blink of white against the darkness came again, and this time he knew it for what it was. A flashlight. They were playing games with flashlights in the forepeak at four o'clock in the morning. Regular milkmen, the two of them. The ship lurched violently under the impact of a heavy wave and Flake had to lean against the bulkhead for a moment to keep from being thrown sideways. The flashlight in the forepeak wavered back and forth and then resumed its steady glow to the accompaniment of considerable muttering and cursing in Spanish.

The two men, Diaz and Cutter, were kneeling among the mass of ropes, anchor chains, nets and buoys that cluttered the dark forward hold. They were examining something in the small circle of light cast by the electric torch. Their shadows, enormous and weird, flickered back and forth in the dark narrow place. The banging of the waves, up here in the forward part of the ship, was like the thudding of giant hammers against the hull.

Flake edged slowly forward, watching his footing on the slimy floorboards, until he could see what they were doing. Spread out before them on a large piece of heavy brown wrapping paper was a collection of small leadfoil envelopes. While Cutter held the light Diaz poured a fine white powder from a single larger envelope into the smaller ones. As he filled each envelope he carefully closed and sealed the ends.

Well, Flake thought. Well, well, well. Whiskey, the man said. Whiskey my ass. Heroin. Nice pure lovely white heroin. Easily transportable, easily salable, and worth probably a hundred thousand bucks or so.

What a sucker he had been to believe that Mangio would risk the *Jezebel* for a few thousand dollars' worth of booze. This was why Diaz had come aboard with the load and had brought a gun with him. And this was why Cutter kept getting so tough. They were playing for big stakes. A three-way split for Mangio, Diaz and Cutter. And Flake? What about dear old Flake? Flake was the fall guy, the patsy, the one who would take the rap if anything went wrong.

For a moment he was torn between anger and greed.

The thought went through his mind that by the simple procedure of knocking a couple of heads together he could inherit this stuff himself. The fortune in those little envelopes of white powder could buy up half the shrimp boats in Key West. Or a string of Cadillac convertibles. Or a fleet of the finest charter boats on the south coast. Or forty-nine over-developed Hollywood blondes. Or any number of wonderful things.

Powerful medicine resided in the little silver envelopes.

The stuff of dreams. And you could buy other things with it as well... Like maybe ten or twenty years in a federal pen for bringing it into the country. And prostitution. And thievery. And murder. And the hollow eyes and rickety arms and lingering death of the hopeless addict.

No, Flake decided as he stood there with the ship banging and thundering all around him and the gear slapping against the wall. There was only one thing to do with a cargo like heroin. Over the side with it fast. Get rid of it. Feed the fish with the bloody stuff.

At that moment the ship slipped into the trough of the seas and rolled heavily on her side like a wounded animal. Flake felt it coming and braced himself against the bulkhead. Cutter, the seaman, said something to Diaz who spread a protective arm over his fortune in silver envelopes. The *Jezebel* groaned under the strain as she staggered with the weight of the sea and then lurched back upright. The flashlight swung in a wide arc and for an instant the light caught Flake full in the face. The glare dazzled him briefly but even as he blinked against it he knew that they had seen him. Trust Cutter for that. With his ratlike quickness, damn little got by him. Flake had to move and move fast.

He moved in the only way he could. He lowered his head and charged forward into the forepeak, hoping to make it before Diaz got to his gun. But the hatchway was narrow and the light blinded his eyes and in the time it took him to scramble through they were ready and waiting for him.

Diaz had backed against the far bulkhead, snarling like an angry cat, the silver of blue steel clenched in his fist. But Cutter had not moved from his perch on the mass of tangled rigging. As Flake, heavy and awkward in his oilskins and boots, came charging through the hatchway Cutter hit him square on the forehead with the big flashlight.

He saw the light coming at him, looking as big as an aircraft beacon and then there was a brighter light that exploded inside his skull and then there was no light at all. He did not know that he was on his hands and knees shaking his head like a wounded bull or that the glass in the light had shattered over him or that the blood was running down his forehead or that Cutter was deliberately getting ready to club him again.

"Sonofabitch got a hard head," Cutter grated as he swung the battered light downward.

2

They dragged him out through the engine room hatchway, the heels of the rubber boots leaving a trail behind him on the slimy deck. Cruze, still lost in a melancholy vaporous world of his own, still sitting with his back to the bulkhead, saw them go and was roused briefly by the contact.

"Hey," he said, blinking at them in the yellow light. "What you fellows doin'? What's wrong with Flake?"

The Cubans whispered together for a moment and then Cutter let Flake's shoulders fall slackly to the deck. He went over and took Cruze by the neck and shook him until he rattled, the way a thin reed slats in the wind.

Cruze choked and sputtered but made no move to defend himself.

"You rummy bastard," Cutter said. "You see nothing. Nothing at all. Savvy?"

He released Cruze's tortured windpipe long enough for a feeble, "Sure, sure," to wheeze through.

Cutter pulled the knife out of his back pocket and opened it and held the blade against Cruze's throat. A thin trickle of blood appeared along the edge of the steel and ran slowly down onto Cruze's sweat-stained shirt.

"Hey," Cruze whispered without moving. "Hey, now."

"You been asleep," Cutter said. "You been asleep all the time. If you wake up I cut your goddamn neck like a chicken."

"Sure," Cruze said, sitting very still, his whole body rigid with fear of the knife. "Sure, Cutter."

Diaz said something in Spanish and Cutter answered him in English. "A lousy rummy," he said. "Nobody believes a lousy rummy anyway."

Cutter closed the knife and put it away. Then he and Diaz picked Flake up by the shoulders and dragged him through the hatchway and up onto the rain-swept deck. Cruze did not watch them. He had his eyes closed. Only after they were gone did he open his eyes cautiously and let one thin-fingered hand steal up to the long shallow cut on his neck.

The rain and wind slapped fiercely at them on the open deck. Forward, in the dimly lit charthouse, they could see Bush's back and shoulders as he stood at the wheel. The great black seas came foaming up under the counter and the Jezebel's square stern rose and fell in dizzying swoops. They waited to see if Bush might turn around and spot them, but the helmsman concentrated on his work, peering forward into the breaking seas, keeping the *Jezebel's* bow up into the wind.

Moving cautiously, on the slippery deck, they dragged the heavy inert mass of Flake's oilskin-clad body to the rail and hoisted it half over. Exhausted by the effort, they let it balance precariously for a moment, and then, before they could give it the final push, the sea completed their work for them. A great breaking crest roared along the side of the hull and snatched at the body and took it out of their hands and carried it off into the darkness.

CHAPTER FOURTEEN

1

The first Flake knew of anything, he was dreaming, and in his dream they were back in the big clumsy Liberator and coming in low across the channel with the port outboard engine afire and a trail of gas streaming out of the flak-torn tank. They had been over Bremerhaven and the Jerries had clobbered them with flak and the wounded plane was laboring along now over the gray wind-swept Channel with the coast of England maybe ten or twenty or a million miles ahead.

They were losing the air fast now, with the big plane clumping along on two engines and the water creeping closer every minute. He turned to say something to his navigator Buck Grundy before he remembered that Grundy was dead with his jugular severed by shrapnel and his eyes rolled up into his head and his mouth grinning slackly and a pool of blood under his seat.

And now the water was coming up very fast, looking as hard and cold as a field of cement, and she was settling down toward it like a tired gun-shot goose, and he knew that he could not hold her any longer. So at the last moment he let go of the wheel and leaned forward with his head in his arms and let her go and sat there, waiting to take it.

And out of the darkness and oil and jangle and the cold scissoring him down the middle he was fighting his way through the smashed plexi-glass and up to the surface and kicking off the boots and trying to get out of the oilskin jacket and knowing that it was not a dream after all and he was really in the water and his head hurt and something had happened to him but he could not remember what.

2

Cutter took his time about going up to the wheelhouse, but when he got there he pushed Bush aside and put the helm hard over and said bluntly, "Man overboard."

"What?" Bush asked incredulously. "What man?"

"Flake."

"The captain?"

"That's right."

"How?" Bush asked, shaking his head in disbelief. "How could the captain be washed overboard?"

"He was back aft coming through the engine room hatch when a big sea caught him and took him right away."

"It don't sound like Flake. It sounds mighty strange."

Cutter turned his head and looked directly at him. Bush lowered his eyes.

"We'll keep swinging in circles. Maybe we'll find him," Cutter said, knowing they would not find Flake and that if they did spot the body in the water he would run it down instead of trying to pick it up.

He flicked on the big searchlight that protruded from the charthouse roof and the yellow beam made a faltering path of light through the rain and dark. There was nothing out there. No quick gleam of the yellow oilskins against the black water. The hardheaded sonofabitch went straight to the bottom, Cutter thought with some satisfaction. Like a stone. He liked the idea. He felt good about it. He was a man who always liked to pay his debts.

3

Flake had gotten rid of his oilskins and was swimming easily, not trying to get anywhere, just staying afloat. The big seas heaved him up and dropped him down and when he rose again he saw that a gray watery dawn was chewing away at the blackness.

He knew he would drown after a while but still he kept swimming. His head hurt and he put his hand up to it and brought it away bloody and thought how much easier it would be to quit and let it go at that. But there was a stubborn core in him that kept his arms and legs moving slowly regardless of any decisions from the brain.

He had been in the water before and he knew that if a man nursed his strength he could stay afloat for a surprisingly long time. He knew also that in the end it would not make any difference but still he wanted to stretch it out as long as possible. He was not afraid of dying but he wanted very much to live. More than anything else he wanted to get his hands on Cutter. That need alone would sustain him. That and the desire for his own boat.

He did not want to work any more for Mangio or anyone else. With his cut from this trip and with what was already in the little green box he could have done it. He had been working toward it for a long time and now that he was finally ready they had taken it away from him. It was like one of those crooked crap games where you're going good and you let everything ride and it looks like you've got it made and then on the last pass they switch the dice on you and it's all over.

Where was the sense in it? Where was the sense in the war and the fighting and Molly and Cash and all that if it ended this way? One lousy boner and they had finished him. He should have known better than to fool around with Cutter. He should have tackled Cutter and Diaz the minute they set foot on deck, but he had waited and they had got to him first and now he was through.

He rose again on a crest and this time he saw something white a long way off, looking as far off as the moon, but there. At first he could not believe it because it was such an incredible piece of luck, and then when he did believe it he thought what a lousy trick it was to show him a ship now when it was too far off or too late or maybe going to swing the wrong way, with him struggling to reach it and not being able to and dying struggling.

But even while he thought about not being able to reach it he started toward it and it seemed bigger and he was able to judge its course. He knew that they would not see him in these big seas unless they were right on top of him and so he swam straight out toward them, not saving anything any more, using it all up, knowing that if they missed him there would not be another along after that, and the rest did not matter.

CHAPTER FIFTEEN

1

Just before noon, Chambers picked up Loggerhead Key. He had been moving slowly because of the heavy weather, trying to ease the *Vixen* as much as possible. The man they had fished out of the water was wrapped in blankets and was asleep down below. Jessica had been there with him most of the morning. She was very good about that sort of thing. She had taken charge of the half-drowned man and had undressed him and bandaged his head and put him to bed. Now she was sitting beside him, waiting for him to wake up, wanting to reassure him when he opened his eyes.

Isn't she marvelous, Chambers thought. Why did she have to turn out such a bitch? Why did all that warmth and tenderness have to turn into a crazy nymphomania that ruined everybody it touched?

He could see the fort now. He dug the Zeiss glasses out of their brown leather case and studied the shape of the island carefully. It was a bad day for a landfall. The water would be milky and he would not be able to see any variations in depth and he would have to be right on top of the markers before he picked them up.

He eased his throttle and studied his chart again, and this time when he looked up he saw a boat ahead of him. A shrimper putting in to the fort to get out of the weather. That was nice, Chambers thought. Very handy indeed. The shrimpers must know these waters from way back. All he had to do now was to follow the boat down the channel. Except that as he watched it he realized that it was not going anywhere. It was fast on the reef and pounding hard and beginning to break up. Well, Chambers thought, at least I got one thing out of it anyway. I know where *not* to go.

While he was edging in slowly toward the wreck Jessica came up through the hatchway, and with her was the fellow they had taken out

of the water. He was a short dark man with heavy arms and tremendous hands. He had close-cropped hair and a dark intent face. He might
have been thirty-five or so but probably he would look younger when
rested.

Chambers glanced at Jessica. She shrugged and said, "I couldn't keep
him down there. He insisted on getting up."

"She told me you were heading for the Tortugas," the man said.
"Maybe I can help."

"Do you know this channel?"

"Yeah," Flake said. "I've been through here maybe a hundred times.
There's nothing much to it in good weather but in a blow like this it's
tricky because sometimes a northwester will shift the bar. But if you
hold her as she goes you'll be about right."

"I think one of the markers is gone. According to the chart there
should be a nun out there but I don't find it."

"Let me see your glasses."

Chambers handed him the glasses and Flake studied the entrance carefully. Suddenly his face changed and Chambers knew that he was looking at the ship on the reef.

"That wreck probably marks the edge of the channel," Chambers
said. "How long has she been there?"

"Not long. Maybe a couple of hours."

"How can you be so sure?"

"Because she's my ship."

"What about the marker?"

"Gone."

"What do we do now?"

"I can take you in without it."

Chambers looked at the sea and the sky and then back at Flake. He
did not particularly fancy the idea of turning his boat over to a man
he had never seen before, but his only alternative was to put back to
sea again and return to Key West, and that would mean a long tough
beat to windward. Then, too, there was no way of knowing how long
they might be holed up in Key West and he had already been through
enough with Jessica there. Anyway, this dark tough-looking stranger
had a direct competent air about him that Chambers liked.

"All right," he said.

"I'll go up on the bow. Take her in at half speed and follow my hand
signals."

When they came abeam of the wreck Flake gave him a slow-down signal and then walked back from the bow to the wheel.

"I have to go aboard her," Flake said, pointing to the *Jezebel*.

"How do you expect to do that?"

"Swim."

"Look, mister. You came within about a minute and a half of drowning last night. Do you want to finish the job?"

"I'll make it," Flake said firmly. "If you want to wait for me I'll be back in ten minutes. If you don't wait I'll go anyway."

"I think we have a very determined man on our hands," Jessica said.

"What about it?" Flake growled.

"You don't leave me much choice," Chambers said.

"You're in good water here. You've got a hundred feet on either side. Just hold her into the wind and I'll make it as fast as I can."

Chambers shrugged. "I guess you know what you're doing but even if you don't I can't stop you. Suit yourself."

Flake mounted the rail and went over the side without hesitation. He was under water a long time and then they saw the dark cropped head looking as dark and shiny as a seal's head, moving steadily. He was swimming breast stroke, not wasting his strength on anything showier.

"Quite a man," Jessica said.

Chambers gave her a severe look. Is it starting already, he wondered. "Yes," he said.

They saw Flake seize a line trailing over the stern and go up it quickly hand over hand. Five minutes later he let himself down and started back toward them. Chambers had put down a swimming ladder for him and Flake hung on for a moment, gathering strength before pulling himself up.

His back muscles stood out in sharp relief under the wet shirt and his face showed lines of strain. His eyes were red-rimmed from salt. Jessica handed him a towel.

"Did you find what you were after?" Chambers asked,

Flake shook his head.

"What do we do now?"

"This is Hospital Key. That's Bush Key dead ahead and then Garden Key where the fort is. There are markers between Bush and Garden and that's where the channel lies. Keep her as she goes."

The wind was on their quarter now, pushing them toward the massive domination of the fort. The fort occupied almost the entire key. It was a huge six-sided pile with a tower in the middle. Sheets of spray were beating up against the great brick walls. Another line squall sent hard-driving rain slashing at the yacht.

"When you get in the lee you'll find a pier," Flake said; "You can pull right up to it. There's plenty of water."

Chambers was dividing his attention between the channel and the big following seas that came boiling up astern, letting the yacht fall off every now and then to avoid the danger of being pooped. Flake watched him with approval. He was not sure yet what kind of man Chambers was but if nothing else he was a seaman.

2

When the *Jezebel* struck the reef she hit hard and Cutter knew right off that she was through. The coral had taken the bottom out of her. You could tell by the way she settled into it, the kind of easy relaxed way she gave herself to the coral, that it was all over with her. By the time Bush came bounding up from the engine room Cutter and Diaz were already sliding the raft over the side.

"What did we hit?" Bush shouted.

"What the hell do you think?" Cutter answered. "The bloody reef."

"Man, man?" Couldn't you see the channel?"

"Save the talk. Give us a hand with the raft."

"You leaving her?"

"Damn right we're leaving. She'll break up fast in these seas."

"What about Cruze?"

"The hell with him."

"You can't leave him here."

"What's the difference to a lousy rummy? He's better off dead."

"You got to take him."

It was not so much the way Bush said it that decided Cutter, as the realization that with two men missing he would have to answer too many questions. It would be nice to get rid of Cruze right now but it would make things damned awkward later on.

"All right," Cutter growled. "Get him out here."

Diaz, wet with spray, was shaking all over with a steady trembling that made his teeth chatter. His tight-fitting Cuban suit was beginning to shrink on his skinny frame and his pointed yellow shoes looked thoroughly incongruous on the slippery deck.

"What the hell's the matter with *you?*" Cutter asked.

Diaz managed a sickly grin. His thick black hair was plastered across his forehead and his eyes had a queer glazed look. "I don't swim," he answered.

"Too bad," Cutter said coldly. "You got the stuff?"

"Sure," Diaz answered, patting his breast pocket. "You can bet I don't leave that behind. How about you?"

"I got mine."

Bush came out through the hatch, dragging Cruze behind him. The rummy staggered on rubber legs.

"What happened?" Cruze asked, blinking in the sudden daylight.

"She's on the coral," Bush answered. "We got to get off her."

"Where's Flake?"

"Overboard."

Cruze started to say something but Bush took him firmly by the shoulder and said, "Come on now."

"Listen," Cruze said, shaking his head. "I don't understand. What's going on?"

"Never you mind. Come along now."

"But where's Flake?"

"Never you mind."

Bush got an oilskin jacket out of the wheelhouse and put it over Cruze's shoulders and buttoned it around him. The rummy had a breath on him that was enough to knock over a mule. Bush was not a drinker himself and the stale smell of the whiskey sickened him. He felt sorry for Cruze and at the same time a little angry with him.

"You come on now," Bush said.

Cruze allowed himself to be led to the side and pushed down into the raft. Cutter and Diaz were there already, cursing at him to hurry. Bush stowed Cruze where he would not fall out and then pushed them away from the side. There were two paddles in the raft. Bush took one and Cutter the other and they set out through the sharp-breaking seas for the fort.

The wind and the waves took them and beat them back. The white-flecked crests spattered over them. Cruze was shivering, his jaws rattling, like some sort of spring-wound doll. Then they were in the lee and out of the worst of it and making it to the beach. They grounded in the shallows and Bush took the rummy by the shoulders and dragged him up on the shore.

"Is there anybody on this island?" Bush asked Cutter.

"No."

"Then what do we do for food and water?"

"I don't know," Cutter said.

"If you wasn't in such a hurry to get off the boat we could of took something with us. And if you wasn't in such a hurry to get away from where Flake went over we might of found him."

"What do you mean by that?"

"You're a smart man. You figure it out."

Cutter stood up. Bush watched him carefully. Cutter reached inside his denim jacket and took out a short, snub-nosed Colt .38. Bush's face changed. It did not reflect fear so much as intense caution.

"For a lousy nigger you talk too goddamn much," Cutter said.

"Yes, sir," Bush said.

"I don't want no more talk."

"Yes, sir."

"Don't forget it."

"I'll remember."

Diaz stood off to one side watching them both. He made no move to interfere. He took a purple silk handkerchief out of his pocket and wiped his face with it. The salt water had reduced the handkerchief to a sodden rag.

I got to get rid of the nigger, Cutter thought. He talks too much. He smells something about Flake. If he puts his mind to it he'll begin to talk about it. I can get rid of him and say he drowned trying to swim ashore. For that matter I could say they all drowned. Who would know any different? The way it's blowing it will be a couple of days yet before the Coast Guard comes after us and that will give me time to figure it out.

Bush was looking over Cutter's shoulder. Suddenly his bright teeth shone in a broad grin. "There's a ship coming," he said.

Cutter spun around and saw a white motor-sailer working its way toward the pier. A heavy-backed, dark-headed man was standing on the bow. Even at a distance of five hundred feet it was unmistakably Flake.

For the first time in his life Cutter knew the meaning of real fear. He felt as he had when Flake hit him in the throat: he could not breathe. A cloud of rain swept down over the yacht and obscured it for a moment. It seemed to shimmer in front of him as in some sort of dismal nightmare.

Without a word Cutter turned and ran for the shelter of the walls. Diaz was only a few yards behind him.

CHAPTER SIXTEEN

1

Bush was waiting on the beach, his black face split in an ecstatic grin. As Flake stepped ashore he pounded him happily on the back.

"Man, we sure thought you were dead," Bush said.

"Me, too," Flake answered.

"How in the world did you make it?"

"I still don't know. Just one of those things."

"Where did they pick you up?"

"Not too far from where our pals dumped me."

"So they *did* dump you?"

"They sure did."

"That's what I figured."

"Where are they now?"

Bush gestured toward the frowning walls.

"I thought I saw them light out while we were coming down the channel," Flake said. "I'll take care of them later. They can hide but they can't go anywhere."

Bush shook his head. "Better not mess with them. That Cutter is one mean man."

"Yeah," Flake said, rubbing his wound on his forehead. "We'll see how mean the sonofabitch is with his back to a wall. Where's Cruze?"

Bush pointed down the beach toward what seemed to be a pile of rags lying on the sand.

"What's the matter with him?"

"He don't feel too good."

"Let's take a look."

Cruze was lying face down on the sand. His clothes were soaked and his hair was encrusted with salt and sand. Flake put his hand on his shoulder and the rummy turned over and stared at him, blankly at first and then with a swift flash of fear across his pallid features.

"My God, Flake, is that you?"

"It sure ain't Santa Claus." Flake tried to smile although his head hurt and he was still bone weary from being in the water.

"Cutter said you went over the side."

"I know. I did."

"How did you get back?"

Flake pointed toward the yacht lying at the pier.

Cruze shook his head in wonder. "I always said you were lucky."

"That's right. Come on."

"Where we going?"

"Down to the pier."

When Cruze tried to stand his legs went rubbery and limp under him. Flake put an arm around him and half carried him down to the beach. Cruze's skinny frame was shaking all over and even through the wet clothes he felt burning hot.

"What's the matter with you?" Flake asked.

"Nothin', Flake."

"Don't con me. You're sick."

"No, sir. I just need a little shot to fix me up. They got anything on board that boat?"

"I don't know."

"Could we maybe ask?"

"I'll ask."

"You're a fine fella, Flake."

"Sure I am. Just peachy dandy."

Suddenly Cruze collapsed on the sand. A fit of coughing sacked him. "Let me rest a minute," he wheezed.

Flake sat down beside him, glad of the opportunity. His head was a brute now, pounding like a bloody drum, "You know somethin', Flake?"

"What?"

"I saw it."

"Saw what?"

"I was in the engine room when Cutter and that other fella took you out."

"That's nice."

"That was when they dumped you, wasn't it?"

"It sure was."

"I should of done somethin'."

Flake shrugged. "What could you do?"

"Well, listen now. I can still fight. Maybe you don't know it but I can. I may be kind of skinny but there's lots of skinny guys fight like wildcats. Just gimme a chance and you'll see."

"All right," Flake said, wishing Cruze would shut up and that his head would stop hurting.

Suddenly Cruze began to weep. Large tears formed in his red-rimmed eyes and slid down his raddled cheeks. Flake turned his head away. It was terribly embarrassing to see Cruze cry that way.

"I'm no good," Craze said. "No damn good at all. I couldn't fight no-body. I saw them two fellas take you out and I knew they was gonna kill you and I didn't do nothin' about it. I just laid there and pretended like I was asleep."

"It's all right," Flake said, pulling Cruze erect. "It doesn't make any difference now. Come on."

"I'll make it up to you. You'll see."

"Sure you will," Flake said, setting out again for the pier and the yacht that seemed an incredibly long way off.

The exhaustion had passed from his muscles into his bones now. Even the fragile weight of poor sick dilapidated Cruze was too much for him. He was sorry now that he had told Bush to stand by the pier and not come with him when he went to fetch Cruze. For some reason that he could not remember, it had seemed like a good idea to talk to Cruze alone. Now it no longer seemed like a good idea. Nothing was a good idea any more, except to rest.

The wind beat at him with blurred fists and the sand stung his face. He was dimly aware of Cruze gasping hoarsely and of the surf beat-ing against the shore. The pounding of the waves made a rhythm with that of his own heart. He tried to time his steps to the crashing of the surf. It would be better when he got in under the lee of the wall.

Except that the wall was not so great either. Behind the wall Cutter and Diaz were probably watching him right now, with maybe a gun or a knife lined up on his back. Well, to hell with them. He was too damn tired to worry about them. Let them come at him if they wanted. Sooner or later he would have to do something about them, but right now—no. Right now all he wanted was to lie down.

Then the ship was there and Bush and even Chambers, and they were lifting Cruze out of his arms. He stumbled toward the boat and his eyes closed even before he got there.

2

Jessica was wonderful about the shipwrecked men. Jessica was always wonderful about shipwrecked men, Chambers thought bitterly. Her heart went out to every lonesome bum cast up on every beach in the world. She had insisted on bedding poor sick Cruze down in the empty crew's quarters and now she was changing the dressing on Flake's head.

She was wearing khaki shorts that showed off the magnificent sweep of her long brown legs and a white silk shirt opened low to expose the high full rise of her breasts. She had Flake's head bent toward her while she replaced the dressing and Chambers could see Flake looking at her breasts.

Chambers felt edgy. He didn't like the way she was looking at Flake. He knew all about that look. The feeling of jubilation that had come with being at sea in the storm was beginning to fade, slowly being replaced by the misery he had known in Key West. This Tortugas trip, which had looked so promising at first, might develop into a real disaster. A woman like Jessica, surrounded by men on an abandoned island, could be dynamite. But then, how the hell could he have anticipated that they would pick one man out of the water and two more off a reef? For that matter, how could you ever anticipate anything about Jessica? Except anguish. You could always be sure of that.

The sight of her fingers brushing Flake's dark head had become intensely annoying to Chambers. He stood up abruptly and said, "I'm going for a walk."

Jessica didn't look up.

"I'll be back in a few minutes."

"All right, dear," she said.

Chambers jumped onto the pier and walked off down the beach. He was trying hard to keep a grip on himself. It's nothing, he kept telling himself. Nothing at all. It's what she would do for any man who was hurt. Would you want her to do less? You're damn right. A hell of a lot less.

Jessica leaned back and, gave the bandage a final pat. "There," she said. "You're beautiful. How does it feel?"

"Fine."

"You can do something in return if you like."

"What's that?"

"Show me around the island."

"There's not much to see. Nothing but ruins."

"But they're marvelous. It's a fantastic place. Come and walk with me."

"What about your husband?"

"What about him?"

"He might not like it."

"There's certainly nothing wrong in our taking a little walk together."

"He might think it was plenty wrong."

"Well, I'll tell you a little secret. He's not my husband."

I didn't need a blueprint to figure that one out, Flake thought. Not with your shirt open and everything showing down to your belly button. "Whatever he is, he's still the guy who pulled me out of the water."

"Oh, don't be silly. All I wanted was to take a walk."

"Where I come from a girl doesn't go walking with a man unless she's got a pretty good reason."

"Aren't you the stuffy one? Where *do* you come from?"

"Key West."

"Such a strange town."

"Maybe so. I don't pay any attention to it."

"What *do* you pay attention to?"

"Shrimp."

Oh my, she thought. This one is a dilly. You've known all kinds but this is a really strange one. Awfully attractive, though. Sort of brooding and difficult and awfully tough looking but probably very nice underneath. How sweet he was with that ghastly drunk on the beach. And the colored man. He was terribly nice to that colored man.

"Don't be such a difficult little man," she said. "Come and walk with me."

"Look. There are two good reasons why it's not such a hot idea to go promenading around this island. One is your boy friend—Spencer Huntingly Van Tilsbury the Third, or whatever his name is. The other reason is two guys who are inside the fort. They'd like nothing better than a clear shot at me."

"Now you're being dramatic."

"What the hell do you think I was doing in that water with a lump on my head? Trying to swim the English Channel?"

"Are you trying to tell me someone actually threw you overboard?"

"No," he said bitterly. "I slipped and fell trying to tie my shoelace."

"Well, why are they after you?"

"Because I raped their sisters."

"Did you really?"

"Sure."

"But that's marvelous. How was it?"

"Just fair."

"All right," she said. "But just tell me one thing. Why do we have to stay here and fool around with your murderous friends? Why can't we just sail out and leave them?"

"It's your boat. You can go anytime you want to—except for a forty-mile-an-hour blow that would knock you flat as soon as you got out of the lee of the island. And for another thing, the channel marker is gone."

"But you know the way. You could take us."

"Not me. I'm staying."

"You're determined to fight with those men?"

"That's right."

"Have you got a gun?"

"No."

"You're impossible."

"Yes."

"If we called the Coast Guard they'd come and take them, wouldn't they?"

"This has nothing to do with the Coast Guard. It's my own affair."

"Are you really so tough or just stupid?"

"Both."

3

The long watch of the night before had exhausted Chambers and now he could feel the weariness creeping through his bones. He returned despondently to the yacht and went directly to his cabin and took a long drink of the scotch and lay down on his bunk. In spite of himself he was asleep in a few minutes.

In the late afternoon he awoke to find Jessica and Flake sitting on the fantail with a bucket of ice and a bottle of whiskey between them.

"Hello, darling," she said brightly. "Have a good nap? Mr. Flake was bashful about staying for a drink but I insisted."

"Of course," Chambers said stiffly. "Perfectly welcome."

"And then too I wanted to change the dressing. Doesn't he look beautiful with a turban around his head?"

"I don't know if that's exactly the word."

"Of course it is. All sort of glowering and dark and beautiful. Do you always scowl, Mr. Flake, or do you do it just because you know it's so attractive?"

What a bitch, Flake thought. If she was mine I'd boot her into the bay like a shot. Why does he take it from her? Oh she's a hot-looking piece all right but there's plenty of others just as hot or hotter. She's got the knife in him right up to the hilt and she's twisting it. Poor bastard. I better stay clear. After all, he did pick me out of the drink. I guess I owe him that. But that's all. Let him put up his own No Trespassing sign. I'll keep out of their way but if she chases after me, it's up to him to do something about it. If he doesn't want to do anything about it then to hell with him. To hell with both of them.

He stood up. "I better go and see how Bush is making out."

"But you'll be back for dinner, won't you?" she said.

"Bush has been fishing with a handline in the lagoon. He's got him a mess of grunts. I'll eat with him on the beach."

"Yes," Chambers said. "That might be better."

"Sure," Flake agreed. "Better all around."

Flake was barely over the side before Chambers turned her and said, "You can't wait, can you?"

"For what, darling?"

"You know what."

"You're not going to start that again, are you, sweetheart?"

"I'm not starting anything. I'm trying to finish something."

She gave him a loving smile. "You will, sweetie, you will. But in the meantime we're here to have some fun, so let's relax and be gay."

"It's all so simple for you, isn't it?"

"Not really. But what good does it do to stew about things?"

"I would like just once to understand what goes on in that head of yours."

"So would I," she said.

CHAPTER SEVENTEEN

1

Toward sundown the wind increased, and with it came a series of heavy rainsqualls. The rains were of short duration but hard driving and uncomfortable. Flake and Bush huddled behind the dripping walls. They kept a fire going but the rain-wet wood gave off more smoke than heat. The peculiar tropic cold that is somehow colder than northern cold bit at them out of the bricks. Flake considered moving farther back into the shelter of the fort but decided against it. Cutter and Diaz were somewhere back there and with nightfall they would be prowling the fort like a pair of hungry cats. He much preferred meeting them on his own terms, when he was ready for them, instead of letting them come upon him unaware while he slept by a fire. Of course, he was operating on the broad assumption that they would remain inside the fort; he believed they would until hunger and thirst drove them out.

Unable to rest, he walked down to the beach and began to collect another load of driftwood. In the last glimmer of day he could see the *Jezebel* on the reef. She looked almost intact but he knew she was completely gone underneath. In a few days the pounding would shake her apart and there would be nothing left of her but some rusting machinery and a few bits of wood on the beach.

It saddened him. She was not his boat and he certainly didn't give a damn what happened to Mangio's property but he had been her skipper and no skipper likes to lose his ship. He knew her all too well—her quirks and vagaries and virtues. In a way, he reflected, the relationship between a captain and his ship is like that of marriage. A ship develops personality—some are sweet and gentle, others tricky and uncertain—and a man learns to accept that personality and live with it and believe that he alone of all men is qualified to cope with it. And when the time comes to turn your ship over to another captain it's like watching a woman you have loved go off with another man.

The destruction of the ship was something more to add to the score against Cutter.

His head kept bullying him unmercifully. He thought of going to the yacht and asking for aspirin but decided against it. He did not want to become involved. This business between Chambers and his woman was unhealthy. She was a whore and he'd had enough of whores. Whores had a hard masculine quality that he found repulsive. Whether they peddled their wares along Duval Street or on board a yacht, they were still the same.

He gathered his wood and walked back to the wall and rejoined Bush by the smoky fire.

"How you figure Cruze is making out?" Bush asked.

"All right, I guess."

Bush shook his head. "I don't think so."

"What do you mean?"

"He's a sick man."

"He's been sick for years now. These rummies lead charmed lives."

"The charm is about over. I can smell death on him."

"Don't give me that."

"It's true though. You can smell death a long way off. That poor old Cruze is a dead man."

"I don't know," Flake said. "I don't pretend to understand those things. Maybe you're right. What do you smell on me?"

Bush sighed as he stirred the fire. His face was serious. "I don't know."

"Death?"

"I don't know. Not death." He grinned suddenly, his teeth flashing in the firelight. "Maybe money."

"That's not a bad smell."

"No, sir."

"What about Cutter? What do you smell on him?" Flake demanded.

"He just naturally stinks all the time." Bush grinned again, then said, "What you fixing to do about him?"

"I'll go and get him."

"When?"

"When I'm ready."

"He'll kill you if you give him half a chance."

"He already had his chance."

"Maybe he's looking for you right now."

"I doubt it. Too many witnesses here. If he killed me out here in the open he'd have to kill all the rest of you at the same time. That would be a big job even for Cutter."

"What about that Diaz?"

Flake shrugged. "I don't think he amounts to much. I'm not worried about him. It's Cutter."

Bush nodded. "That Cutter is a powerful hater."

"I'm a pretty good hater myself."

"You don't think you ought to do something about him now?"

"Let him sweat a while."

"What about you. Don't you sweat?"

"All the time."

Bush yawned. "It's going to be a long cold night."

"We've got enough wood to last us."

Bush lay down by the fire and fell asleep almost instantly. Flake moved a little farther away into the darkness. He hated to give up the warmth, but on the other hand, in spite of all his brave talk about Cutter, he did not want to be too close to the light. It was always possible that Cutter might get some bright ideas.

2

On board the yacht, Jessica was bathing. She lay in the warm scented water and looked at the length of her long sunburned body shimmering and faintly distorted. Her breasts bulged high out of the water. Idly she traced one finger down the soft valley between them.

She smiled to herself. She was pleased with her body. In spite of all the excesses it was still vitally alive, still ready to respond to touch or suggestion.

She slid lower in the water and closed her eyes, drifting into a languorous daydream for several minutes. Finally, she forced herself out of the tub and rubbed herself briskly with one of the thick yellow towels.

Afterward she put on a pair of bright blue silk pajamas and lay down on her bunk. She lay on her back with one hand thrown over her eyes to shield them from the light. She was not sleepy and that tingle of excitement kept running through her body.

She wondered if Allan would come in to her. She hoped he would. She felt clean and fresh after the bath and she wanted to have him lying there beside her with his mouth on her breast. She closed her eyes and dozed for a moment and had a brief dream in which she was standing on a moonlit terrace with a man who was bending over to kiss the inner part of her ear. At the touch of his lips and tongue her knees felt weak and she trembled all over.

She awoke with a start, trying to clutch the fading dream, trying to remember it. All she could remember was that the man was not Allan.

3

Chambers opened a fresh bottle of the Black Label. He enjoyed the feel of the tall slim smoky glass in his hands and there was an almost sensuous pleasure in peeling the foil away and uncorking the new bottle.

He poured himself a long drink, measuring it carefully with his eyes, then added a very small amount of soda and one ice cube. He hated to drown a drink. He had gotten that from his father. The colonel had sent his son to the very best prep schools in order to learn two things: how to get drunk decently like a gentleman and how to choose his clothes properly. Chambers had learned both lessons well and had never forgotten them.

Sometimes, at moments like this when he was lonely and despondent, he missed the old man. He had hated him with a passion when he was alive but now he rather missed him. The energetic, red-faced, ramrod-straight figure with his cocky walk and cold eyes. The well-brushed short crisp white hair and the faultlessly tailored tweed jackets smelling of tobacco and dogs. And the warm, hard, cruel hands that could pull down a skittish horse or a mischievous child with equal facility.

The colonel had asked only one thing of his son—that he look the part. Allan had done so. He always looked the part to perfection. But aside from that, the colonel had exercised a thinly disguised contempt for him. When Allan was still a child the old man had spotted a core of weakness in him that he found extremely distasteful. He had tried to toughen him with military school training and when that had failed he abandoned all pretense of intimacy with the boy. He was reasonably cordial toward him and unfailingly generous with money but there was never enough warmth in him to light a fire in the heart of a small boy.

He had died of a stroke in the apartment of a twenty-three-year-old girl while Allan was still at Princeton, and the family had hushed the whole thing up and tumbled him into his grave with as little ceremony as possible. Allan had felt no sorrow when the old man died and several years passed before he began to miss him.

Now, holding the glass of whiskey against the fading light and listening to the sound of water running in the tub, he thought ruefully how the old man would have hated a scene like this. The weakling son drinking in solitary anguish while the rampant bitch who was ruining him splashed in a scented tub a few feet away.

And now it seemed to Allan that the tub somehow symbolized what had happened to him. He had installed it in the *Vixen* at considerable expense. He knew of no other yacht her size that could boast a tub and an adequate water system. He had done all that for Jessica in an effort to make her happier and more comfortable. And what had it accomplished? Only that she used the tub before going ashore to meet another man.

What he should do, he told himself, was to get up and go in to her now. But at this moment he felt no desire. It had been replaced by hatred for her and dull loathing for himself. The desire would return, all right; he could count on that. But at the moment he preferred sitting here drinking the scotch and rolling the taste of his anguish over his tongue.

Slowly, thoughtfully, he reached for the bottle and poured himself another drink.

4

Flake couldn't sleep. He threw some more wood on the fire and sat for a while watching the eerie shadows the flames cast on the wall. The rain had stopped and the sky was clear but the wind was blowing harder than ever.

He was thinking of Cruze and what Bush had said about the smell of death. You could sneer at it all you wanted but there must be something to it at that. Not that you needed any special knowledge to see that Cruze was a sick man. He had been sick before they left Key West and he was sicker now.

The trouble was it was so hard to tell with a rummy. Cruze's guts were so pickled in alcohol that he had appeared almost indestructible. But Flake had to face the fact that Cruze would have been better off in Key West and that his own bullheadedness was responsible for Cruze being here now.

Just as he also had to face the fact that he had gotten in over his depth with Cutter and Mangio. He was a stubborn bullheaded sonofabitch, no doubt about it. But there was no backing out now. He had to finish with Cutter on his own terms, and when he was ready for him he would do it.

He stood up and walked down to the pier. The yacht seemed much bigger riding here in the darkness with the yellow light streaming out of her ports. A radio was blaring on board. The sound of it carried faintly to him above the bellowing wind. A nice little party going on, Flake thought. She's probably earning her keep right now.

But as he approached the *Vixen* he saw Chambers sitting alone in the wheelhouse. He had a bottle of scotch in front of him and he was wearing a pair of gray flannel beltless English slacks and a navy blue shirt and he was holding a half empty glass in his hand.

Flake stepped aboard and knocked on the window. Chambers looked at him, then got up and came over and opened the window.

"I wanted to see how my friend Cruze was doing," Flake said. "All right?"

Chambers nodded rather stiffly and said, "Of course."

"Can I go below?"

"He's up forward. It might be more convenient if you used the hatch in the bow."

"Sure," Flake said,

He walked forward along the port side and found the hatch and pulled it open and went down the ladder. He doesn't want me to see her, he thought. He's keeping her stashed away below and he figures as long as she doesn't see anyone she'll behave. The poor bastard doesn't know what a dead-end street he's on.

There were three bunks in the crew's quarters. Normally Chambers carried one deckhand who also served as a combination cook and steward, but for this one trip he had wanted to be alone with Jessica and so he had left the man behind in Key West. Like every other part of the ship this forward compartment was in beautiful condition. Bunks freshly made up, foul weather gear neatly stowed, bulkheads washed and painted.

Cruze was in the forward bunk on the starboard side. He appeared to be asleep, his breathing heavy and blurred, a hoarse rattle coming from his throat. But as Flake approached the bunk the sick man opened his eyes and said, "Hello, skipper."

"How're you doing?"

"Great. Ready to go six rounds with Marciano."

Cruze was gaunter than ever. What little flesh he'd had on his face to begin with had faded away. His cheek bones cast a deep shadow over a nose that appeared grotesquely long. His dank, grayish yellow hair was plastered to his forehead. Only his eyes, a faded luminous blue, still seemed vitally alive. The smell of his body, a mixture of sweat and soiled clothing and stale alcohol seeping out of his pores, filled the bunkroom.

Flake overcame a feeling of repugnance and bent down and put his hand on the sick man's brow. Cruze was burning up. His skin was so hot that it almost singed Flake's palm.

Cruze seemed to find some secret joke in Flake's action. He exposed his yellow teeth in a wolfish smile and his eyes sparkled with amusement.

"What do you say, Doc?" Cruze said.

"You'll be all right."

"Sure I will. For a long, long time."

"Now don't start talking that way."

"How should I talk, Flake?"

Flake shrugged helplessly. "I don't know."

"Sure you do. You're a smart guy. Tell me how I ought to talk. Should I tell funny stories? I once knew a funny story but it was a long time ago and I guess I forgot it."

"Shut up, Cruze," Flake said softly.

Cruze nodded and closed his eyes. "All right, Flake. I'll shut up. You could always make me shut up when you wanted it."

"I know."

"You're a nice guy, Flake. I like you."

"Sure."

"You'll see."

"All right. Fine."

"How about a little drink, Flake old boy?"

"No."

"Come on now," Cruze said in a teasing voice. "One for the road."

"What road?"

"Any damn road you please. How about it?"

"You're sick, you silly bastard. It's the worst thing in the world for you."

"Sure it is. But it's a little late to start worrying about it now."

There was no answer to this obvious truth. Flake said, "I'll see what I can do."

Cruze grinned the same wolfish smile. A spasm of coughing shook him and he turned his face against the pillow. When he managed to recover his breath he said, "You see. I told you you were a nice guy."

"Don't count on it," Flake said, climbing the ladder.

The cold air on deck felt good after the sickly odor Cruze had imparted to the forward compartment. Walking softly, Flake made his way aft. It would have been much simpler for him to go right through to the wheelhouse from the crew's quarters but he was playing it according to the ground rules laid down by Chambers. He kept his eyes scrupulously averted from any of the yellow ports that might have revealed the form of Jessica, and then he knocked again on the window as he had done the first time.

"Sorry to be such a pain in the tail," he said to Chambers, "but I have to ask one more favor."

"What is it?"

"Two things actually. First I want to use your ship-to-shore to call the Coast Guard and get a doctor out here to look after my engineer. After that I want to ask you if you can spare one drink for him. He needs it bad."

"If he's as sick as all that should he be drinking?"

"No, he shouldn't be drinking. He shouldn't have been drinking for the past twenty years but he has been. That's why he needs a drink now."

"All right," Chambers said. "I'll put in the call. What does he drink?"

"Anything."

"Scotch?"

"It's too good for him but he'll drink it."

"Take the bottle."

"Thanks."

"By the way, are you planning to go back with the Coast Guard plane when it gets here?" Chambers peered closely at Flake.

"I don't know. I hadn't thought about it. Why?"

"I just wondered."

"Either way I'll steer clear of you. You won't be bothered with me."

"You're not bothering me," Chambers said, averting his eyes.

"That's fine. I'm glad to know it."

"Here, take the bottle."

"No, he doesn't need the bottle. Just a shot."

"Go ahead. Take the bottle."

"Whatever you say."

"Are you married, Flake?"

"No."

"I didn't think so."

"How can you tell?"

"I don't know. You just don't look married."

"How do you look when you're married?"

"The way I look."

"I'll get the booze down to him. Thanks."

"Don't mention it."

They didn't say good night and they didn't shake hands. Flake took the bottle and went forward again. He felt a strong sense of irritation with Chambers. He could not understand a man who sat steeped in such obvious misery and yet did nothing about it. Either get rid of the woman or else beat her into line. A man who sat back and accepted such shenanigans must get some curious sense of satisfaction out of it. He must be very sick in the head. Flake did not have much patience with people who were sick in the head.

Cruze took the bottle and raised himself on one shaky elbow and poured the whiskey down his throat. Flake had to pull it away from him.

"Take it easy, you silly bastard," Flake said.

"That's better," Cruze said, wiping his lips. "That's much better. Lemme have one more, Flake."

"Keep the bottle."

"You mean it?"

"That's what the man said."

"He's a nice feller, ain't he?"

"Yeah."

"And his wife is real nice."

"Uh-huh. You all right now?"

"Sure, Flake. Sure."

"There'll be a Coast Guard doctor here tomorrow. They'll fly you back to Key West and fix you up."

Cruze giggled softly and took another pull at the bottle. "Will they, Flake?"

"Will they what?"

"Fix me up?"

"Sure they will."

"It'll take a hell of a lot more than the Coast Guard to fix old Cruze up."

"You know what I mean."

"Sure I do."

"Get some sleep."

"All right, Flake. And thanks for everything."

"Forget it."

He left Cruze lying in the bunk with his eyes closed and cradling the bottle in his arms. He was glad to be away from him. He felt responsible for the rummy but still he was glad to be away from him.

CHAPTER EIGHTEEN

1

The empty fort was mysterious enough by day but in the dry cool light of the full moon it was positively eerie. Great black patches of shadow trembled in the wind. The empty echoing courtyards were splashed with silver. Sea birds, escaping the fury of the wind, cowered like ghostly chickens in the lee of the casemates. The great dead bastions seemed to come alive with shadowy figures and the wind boomed through the empty rooms like the faint thudding of distant guns.

Flake was dead tired now but still he could not sleep. He kept thinking about Molly and Jessica and Chambers and himself, remembering his sense of irritation with Chambers who sat alone on his yacht drinking whiskey and mooning helplessly over a girl who lay in bed just a few feet away.

He had told himself that Chambers was sick in the head. The girl was sick in the head too. For that matter they were all sick in the head. And now, sitting here beside the fire with the shadowy walls looming over him and Cutter waiting for him somewhere inside, he began to wonder seriously about himself.

He had lived by a comparatively simple rule for the past few years. Money and the fist. They went together and between the two of them you could solve almost any problem. Or could you? They had not solved anything with Molly. They had been helpless to protect him from the shock and bewilderment of Molly's infidelity, and he could see now, looking back on it, that he had been no better off than Chambers. He had done his drinking in cathouses and bars instead of on a yacht but the net effect had been the same.

The wound left by Molly had never really healed but a scar had formed over it, an area of hard dead skin devoid of feeling but thick enough to protect him from being hurt again. And always, and best of all, there were the fists. He had used them to settle all his problems and he would use them again on Cutter and on Mangio.

As you used them on Cash? a small nagging voice seemed to ask.

Now don't start in on Cash. You know how it was with Cash. Sure I do. An accident. Do you believe in accidents? Why not? Maybe it was an accident with Molly. Accident hell, that was premeditated. It's always premeditated. Then a lot of people could say the fight with Cash was premeditated. Maybe poor Molly just got in too deep. I'll say she got in too deep. Everybody got in too deep. If you want to look at it that way you can excuse any tart. I guess you can even excuse Jessica.

And what about Cutter? Why are you so anxious to bust him? What if he got away? What if you let the Coast Guard take him? Then you wouldn't be proving anything. Well, what have you got to prove? That you're a better man than Cutter. Well, who are you proving it to? To Cutter? The hell with him. To yourself? You already know you're better. Then to whom? To Molly, you poor bastard. To Molly. And to Frank Mason and to Cash and to Bess and to all of them who were in on it and knew about it.

But who'll know? Nobody, you miserable sonofabitch. Not Mason, not Molly, not Cash, not Bess. Just you. And how long? How long what? How long do you have to go on proving it? Who knows? Maybe forever. Or maybe, now that you're beginning to understand something about it, not much longer. Maybe this is the last time, this one with Cutter. Do you need this one? Couldn't you let it slide? No, sir. This one you need. This one you've got to have. And after it's over? After it's over maybe you'll be dead, so why worry about it?

2

Jessica got up from her bunk and went over to the dressing table and sat there staring at herself in the mirror. The dressing table, like the bath, was an unusual luxury for a sailboat and it reflected Chambers' concern for her comfort. It was one of the things that should have made her happy but it only left her feeling more uncertain and inadequate.

She studied her face carefully in the bright light reflected from the mirror and she did not like what she saw. The light was harsh and she wore no make-up and she could see that her looks were beginning to go. Her skin was drying out. Under the golden tan little wrinkles were beginning to show around her mouth and eyes. There had been too much sun and wind. And too many parties. And too much smoking and drinking and everything else. She still had her figure but how much longer would it be before that began to show the coarseness of the years also?

How many good years did she have left? Three? Four? Five? Five at the outside. It was frightening. She supposed it must always be a frightening experience for every woman to come face to face with the sudden realization that her youth had passed, but it was particularly frightening for a woman like Jessica who had nothing else.

She still had Allan though. Or did she? She had never known him to be quite so despondent and withdrawn. Always in the past their differences had been resolved in bed. And she had expected him to come to her bed this evening. But he had not. He deliberately stayed away, sitting up there in the bloody wheelhouse drinking his bloody whiskey and listening to the bloody radio. It worried her. It was just possible that they were really coming to the end of their affair and the vista before her was empty and insecure. Always, in the past, she had faced the future with a sort of blind faith. If it wasn't one man it would be another. Men were easy to come by. It was astonishing how many lonely men there were drifting around the world looking for a woman like Jessica.

If Allan dropped her now she would find another. But it would not be quite so easy. And the one after that would be harder still. Would Allan really marry her if she insisted on it? There had been a time, of course, when he was dying to, but now she was not so sure. And she was not sure either that it would be an answer. Allan demanded complete fidelity. Complete possession. How could you possess a human being? Was unfaithfulness in the mind any less reprehensible than the act itself? Sooner or later Allan would grow jealous over a look, a glance, an innocent flirtation. Then would come all the accusations and recriminations, and after all, one might as well be hanged for a sheep as a lamb.

But she did love Allan, after her fashion. And she had been faithful to him too, in her way. If only he could understand that. If only he could understand how little any of these other men meant to her. All of them. The ones before Allan and during Allan and since Allan. The ones whose body odors she could recall at this instant and the ones whose names and faces were blank to her. The good ones and the bad ones. The one-night stands and the six-month stands. The innocent ones and the evil ones. The brutal ones and the weak ones. None of it really mattered. None of it diminished her value to Allan except in his own mind.

It just happened. She never looked for it. She didn't go out of her way to find it. It just happened. Like this man Flake. There was something between them already and something more might come of it (although she hoped not) but how could anyone have anticipated it? A man they had picked up out of the sea. A dark glowering delicious sort of man. Floating like driftwood in all that expanse of water. How could anyone have figured it? And why didn't Allan understand that it was not her fault?

She got up from the dressing table and switched off the light and paced restlessly back and forth in the cabin. Finally she returned to the dressing table and picked up a bottle of perfume and withdrew the stopper and touched the cool scented glass to her eyes and hair. Perfume always made her feel better. There was something indefinably reassuring and soothing about it. It was expensive and fragile and fleeting. Like love, she thought with a half smile to herself. Very much like love.

She took a belted raincoat out of the closet and slipped it on over the blue silk pajamas and opened the door to her cabin and went forward to the crew's quarters. She did not know exactly what she expected to find there or why she was going. She told herself there was a sick man there and it was her duty to look in on him. She had forgotten that she had heard Flake's voice there earlier in the evening and that he might still be there. It was only after she had entered the compartment and found Cruze lying there alone that she felt a vague sense of disappointment.

3

Cruze saw her come and go and it was a blow to him. He did not know exactly what he expected of her but her obvious repugnance had a shattering effect on him. She stood there in the doorway gazing at him while he looked up at her from under lowered lids, and then she wrinkled her nose in obvious distaste while a petulant shadow of disappointment flashed clearly across her face, and then she turned and left.

The incident was trivial enough but it had a shattering effect on Cruze. For it seemed to him that the distaste he had inspired in Jessica was typical of the reaction he, the outcast, the drunkard, produced on the entire world. He was the man apart, disheveled, useless and stinking. All his life he had been the outsider, the kid with his nose pressed to the bakery window. And none of his efforts had ever succeeded in changing it.

Only once had he ever felt that he really belonged, and that was for a brief period during the war. In those days, with Nazi submarines sinking ships in plain view of the pleasure palaces of Miami and Palm Beach, the merchant marine had been hard pressed to replace lost crews, and finally had taken to scraping the previously rejected scum that littered the docks of the country's ports.

Among those taken was Cruze. A younger Cruze, not quite so far gone, but in pretty bad shape even then. He had signed on for service on an ancient tramp destined to run to Panama and he could still remember the incredible pride of that moment when he first reported on board in clean clothing and with a fresh seabag over his shoulder.

He had told himself that he belonged once more to the living. The years of drunkenness and despair lay behind him. He was an active component of a functioning ship. Rusty she might be. Ancient and dilapidated, she surely was. But by God she was a real ship bound for foreign ports and he, Cruze, had shaken off the gin-soaked squalor of the back alleys and waterfront dives that had been his home for so many years.

And he could remember too the expression of distaste on the chief engineer's face as he had sized the new man up. The chief was a Swede, big, tough and cruel. A man like Cruze was mincemeat for him.

"Garbage," the chief said, regarding him with cold hate-filled eyes. "Garbage they send us these days. What are you good for?"

"I know engines," Cruze said, flinching from the glare of those pig eyes, wondering why a man he had never seen before should hate him so.

"You," the chief said decisively, "are good for nothing." He reached and took Cruze by the arm and twisted it until a shaft of pain shot through the rummy's shoulder. "Whiskey-soaked garbage. I catch you drunk on my watch I beat the hell out of you."

And so it began, the nightmare voyage that he had dreamed of as the high water mark of his career. They joined a convoy limping south under the inadequate escort of one destroyer and two PYC's, and the U-boats harried their flanks like wolves. The convoy was scattered and the limping ships fell behind. At night there would be a sudden glow on the horizon that meant a torpedo had struck home and in the morning another empty place in the ranks.

But bad as the submarines were, the bullying chief was worse. He never missed an opportunity to torture Cruze, and the rummy who had started the voyage with such high hopes began to go all to pieces. The contempt so clearly visible in the chief's eyes shook his unsteady soul to its foundations and the thud of the depth charges sent icy pangs of terror through him. He longed again for the anonymity of the waterfront and the undemanding companionship of the human wreckage he had drifted with for so long.

He was drinking steadily now and in a short while was completely useless. They tossed him ashore at the Dutch oil port of Aruba with orders to find his own way back and there he wallowed in good Dutch gin until the authorities poured him onto a north-bound ship.

It had been his big chance and he had muffed it. The fear, growing on him like a cancer, had been too much for him. He would hide for the rest of his life in the bottle until finally on a cold winter night he would freeze to death in an alley somewhere.

A man needs to grow a shell against the world the same way a soft-skinned and vulnerable turtle does. Cruze had never grown that shell. Every slight pierced him like an arrow. The only protection and comfort he found was in liquor. When he was drunk nothing hurt him too much.

And so at last he had come to Key West, and he had known instinctively that it was the end of the trail. He would die there. Not like a man but rather like a sick animal flung distastefully into a ditch by a society that had never been able to tolerate him.

He drained the bottle and got up from the bunk and stood there unsteadily, staring at his face in the small mirror. The face did not disappoint him. It was as gaunt and ugly as he remembered it. Two crazy blue eyes stared at him out of a wilderness of lank hair and faded whiskers.

He put up his hand and rendered himself a small salute and then giggled softly and said, "You look like hell, buddy. Need a shave. Need a haircut. Need a new face. Need a new life, buddy. You know where a man can get a new life? Hell no, you don't. Don't even know where to get a drink on this lousy bucket. Flake knows. Flake knows where to get everything. Flake is okay."

Again he giggled and put his hand up to his brow. The vague memory of something from the past flickered through his mind and, still rigidly saluting, he said stiffly, "We who are about to die—" but could not remember the rest of it. He stood there gaping with his mouth open and then grimaced uncertainly at the face in the mirror and said softly, "Nuts to you, Jack."

With that he turned and put his hands on the ladder and pulled himself up and opened the hatch and stuck his face out into the cold night air. The wind bit like a knife through his chest and he coughed endlessly, hanging there on the ladder, wheezing for air. Finally he managed to gain control of himself and he pulled his skinny body the rest of the way up on deck. He closed the hatch softly behind him and let himself down over the side onto the pier.

Out of the lee of the yacht, the wind and the cold snatched at him and he had the shocked illusion that he had turned instantly sober. He began to tremble all over. He reached into his shirt and took out the sheath knife he had secreted there and held it in his right hand and started off.

He could see-the pinpoint of light on the beach that was Flake's fire but he avoided it. Instead he headed for the darkness of the walls.

CHAPTER NINETEEN

1

Bush stirred in his sleep and then sat up. He looked at the fire and at Flake.

"You awake?" he asked the hunched figure.

"Yeah."

"I wonder where that Cutter is now?"

Flake shrugged.

"I hope he's freezing his ass off."

"Maybe he's got a fire going."

"Not him. He's too scared."

"What has he got to be scared off? He's got the gun."

"Yeah, but he don't know what you got," Bush said shrewdly.

"He can find out in a hurry any time he wants to."

"I wonder what he figures to do?"

"What *can* he do?"

"He could try to take the yacht."

"Where to?"

"I don't know. Cuba maybe, or the Bahamas. There's a lot of islands down there a man could tuck himself away in."

"You have to be able to navigate a lot better than Cutter to make it over the Banks to the islands. As for Cuba, the Stream would kill him, the way she's blowing now. He's already wrecked one ship. I doubt if he wants to try it again. He's just holed up in there, waiting."

"And what about that Diaz?"

"I don't think he amounts to much."

Bush nodded agreement. "I don't guess he does."

Flake got up and stretched and held his hands out to the fire. He was stiff and cold from sitting in one position.

"What do you figure to do when all this is over?" Bush asked. "You going shrimping again?"

Flake, thinking of Mangio and Cutter and the whole mess, shook his head. "I've had it."

"Then what do you aim to do?"

"I might go back to charter fishing again."

He had not really thought about it until he said it but now that it was out it seemed logical enough. Why not? Cash was dead and nothing he could ever do would bring him back to life. Why not go fishing if he wanted to? With the thought came an immediate feeling of relief and anticipation such as he had not known for a long time.

"Ah," said Bush, "that's the life."

"You bet."

"Those sports really pay."

"Sometimes. But it's not so much that. It's more the feeling of being your own boss. Out in the Stream all day in your own boat. It's clean."

"Where do you aim to do this fishing? Key West?"

"No. The hell with Key West. You know where the St. Lucie is?"

"Sure. A mighty pretty little stream."

"That's where I grew up."

"Sweet country."

"I might go back there."

"You could do a lot worse."

A silence settled between them, each man wrapped in his own thoughts.

Finally Bush reached out and picked up a long stick and stirred the embers with it. "You don't need a mate, do you?"

"I might."

"How do you feel about me?"

"I haven't even got the boat yet."

"I know," Bush said with gentle insistence. "But how do you feel about me."

"I guess I feel okay about you."

"About my being colored and all?"

"Oh, hell," Flake said, "what difference does that make?"

"You think you might take me on for a mate?"

"I might."

Bush smiled sleepily and stretched out by the fire. "It would be nice, wouldn't it?"

"Yeah," Flake said. "It would."

2

Chambers heard her leaving the ship but he made no move to stop her until it was too late. He caught a brief glimpse of her stepping down onto the pier with a coat slung over her shoulders and then she blended into the darkness. He sat motionless, every nerve in his body seemingly exposed. He heard every creak of the *Vixen's* hull, the ticking of the chronograph mounted on the bulkhead, the beating of his own heart.

This, he thought with a sense of mounting excitement, is really it. Now she has gone too far. Nothing has helped. Not all the warnings, quarrels, tears and reconciliations. But something has snapped now: some inner rubber band of emotion has been stretched too far.

Like a sick man who is overly conscious of the condition of his own body, he was intensely aware of the physical symptoms that always accompanied one of his emotional scenes with Jessica. An intolerable core of nausea had developed in his stomach and seemed to be pressing on his heart. His hands were clammy with nervous agitation. A bead of sweat started on his forehead and rolled slowly down his temple. He sat motionless in his chair and yet it seemed to him that he was somehow engaged in a violent struggle. A low moan of suffering passed between his clenched teeth.

Suddenly he got up from his chair and wrenched open the door and darted out on deck. But it was too late; she had vanished. The only thing visible in all that howling wind-swept darkness was the yellow pinpoint of Flake's fire. Moisture welled up in Chambers' eyes and the light of the fire became a flickering blur.

He felt as though he had somehow been thrown into a sewer and had come up filthy and evil-smelling. The sense of his own shame suffused his limbs and covered them like some kind of foul envelope. At the same time another part of him stood off remotely detached and observed his sickness with a clinical eye. He was even able to derive a curious satisfaction from the validity of his suffering.

And the worst part about it, the absolutely rotten part about it, he thought as he stood on the exposed deck in the wind, was that the desire for her which had been lacking all evening had begun to rise in him like a tide. Could it be that the only time he really wanted her was when she was involved with another man? The thought came as a shocking revelation to him and he stood appalled at his own weakness.

If that was the case he was truly a ruined man and there was no hope for him anywhere. Or at least not until the thing had run its course. Some day, somewhere, the physical passion would ebb to the point where he no longer cared what she did or whom she did it with, and he could only hope to hang on until that day.

Leaving her now would accomplish nothing. First of all, he could not go anywhere in the darkness and the storm, and secondly, he could never abide the loneliness and uncertainty without her. In the end he would only come creeping back, having sunk much lower into the bottomless pit of his own weakness.

Suddenly he pounded himself on the chest and bellowed aloud, "Be a man! For God's sake be a man!" His voice floated on the wind but the sound of his own roaring gave him a sense of courage and resolution. He would stop her. Always in the past he had been hamstrung by the fact that he had never known where she went or with whom. But this time there was only one place she could have gone. She must have bedded down by the fire with Flake.

Cursing aloud, Chambers leaped off the deck onto the pier and ran toward the flame.

3

Jessica was having a hard time of it. Shivering with cold and uncertainty, she walked back and forth on the sand. It was a frightening night. The wind howled in eerie cadence through the vast structure of the fort while heavy seas thundered on the beach. The moon came and went behind scuds of cloud, throwing grotesque shadows across the brick. Behind her were the reassuring lights of the yacht, and ahead, the uncertainty of Flake's fire. It was madness, she knew, to be out here alone walking the beach. Quite possibly the man Flake had called Cutter was dogging her footsteps right now. From his description he sounded like a hard character capable of anything, and she did not fancy having her throat cut under such circumstances.

But still she made no effort to return to the *Vixen*. She absolutely could not stand another session with Chambers. His recriminations and anger left her drained and emotionally exhausted.

It would be fun to go to the fire where Flake was sleeping. She was quite sure that there would be something tremendously exciting about Flake's strength and brutality on a wild stormy night such as this.

She remembered his dark head gleaming like a seal's as he came up out of the water, and the tight khaki shirt plastered to his muscular back. He had a hard unknown quantity with no perceptible chink in his armor. If he had any weaknesses they certainly didn't show. It seemed to her that making love with Flake would be infinitely reassuring. Rather like taming a wild animal. She was confident that she would bring him to heel in good time and that the victory would give her a sense of conquest and security.

Chambers made her nervous with his constant shifts in mood. She never knew what to expect from him. And then too, the knowledge that some day he would surely throw her out made life even more confusing. Poor Allan. He really did suffer terribly. And when he was in one of his jealous fits his hatred for her was alarming. She supposed it was entirely possible that some day he would kill her. She didn't think she would mind terribly. In fact, thinking about it now, it seemed to her that she had purposely steered him toward that end.

Although God knows she had never deliberately set out to hurt him. What he couldn't understand, what none of them could seem to understand, was that she never planned these things. And really she didn't see how anyone could say they were her fault. If Allan hadn't wanted to bury her down here in the Tortugas they would never have met this man Flake. And if Allan hadn't been so mean to her on the ship tonight she wouldn't be out here walking on the beach. And if she wasn't out here walking on the beach she wouldn't get cold and have to go to the fire for warmth. And if she went to the fire...

No, she told herself, absolutely no fire and no Flake. But what harm is there in getting warm. You know what harm there is. Oh, don't be silly. Flake wouldn't think anything special of it if she came up to the fire to keep warm. And what would Allan think of it? Well, Allan was probably thinking it anyway. She really couldn't help what Allan thought. He would accuse her of it anyway, whether it happened or not.

She continued to walk up and down for what seemed a very long time. It might have been an hour or minutes. She had lost all sense of the passage of time. Once something big, floating on monstrous wings, flickered by close to her head and she threw up her arm and cowered in fright. It was probably a bird, she told herself, but the thought of bats in those empty stone chambers terrified her.

And she was cold. She was terribly cold now. She simply *had* to go to that fire to keep warm. Flake could tell her if there were really any bats on the island. There was no harm in that, was there?

She was still debating the question when the shots came. They came sharp and crackling on the wind. She did not remember ever having heard a gun fired before but she knew immediately what it was. The sounds, evenly spaced, seemed to cut two clean little holes through the night.

She stood frozen in her tracks for a moment, and then, biting her lips in terror, she ran toward the yacht.

CHAPTER TWENTY

1

Chambers had approached the fire without caution. He came striding furiously across the sand. The bright moonlight full on his face revealed compressed lips and glittering eyes. He was not sure what he planned to do but all the pent-up fury and hurt were boiling up in him like so much steam. He wanted desperately once and for all to catch Jessica squarely in the act.

But when he came into the circle of yellow light he found it empty. He could see a depression in the sand where someone had lain but no sign of life. He stood there irresolutely for a moment, the waves of fury still welling up in him, searching the blackness of the walls. And then he saw the two men advancing toward him, Flake leading the way and Bush following behind.

"What's this?" Chambers asked rigidly. "The welcoming committee?"

"We saw you coming and we didn't know who you were," Flake said. "We wanted a look at you first."

"Where is she?"

Flake looked at him a long moment and then said levelly, "Damned if I know."

"Now look here—" Chambers began.

"No," Flake said. "*You* look. I don't know where she is and I don't care."

"She's been here."

"If she has I haven't seen her."

"You're lying, you sonofabitch."

Flake didn't answer.

"Answer me, damn you."

Bush had stepped outside the circle of light. This sort of thing going on between the two white men made him uneasy. He backed farther away.

"She's your woman, not mine," Flake said. "it's up to you to keep tabs on her. I wouldn't touch her with a rake."

All the pent-up fury, all the long months of suffering suddenly boiled up in Chambers. The anonymous, faceless men who had cuckolded him time and again solidified into this one who stood so tangibly and arrogantly before him. He had not been in a fist fight since his school days, but now, unexpectedly, without thinking about it at all, he launched himself forward and cracked Flake a stiff right-hand punch on the side of the jaw.

Flake saw the blow coming but made no move to defend himself. The whole thing had a curious aura of unreality for him, as if it were happening in a dream. And the strangest part about it was that he had dreamed it all before. In the split second before Chambers' fist hit him he remembered vividly the moment when he had sent Mason rolling in the dust outside Cash's camp and the even more intensely bitter moment when he had struck Cash over the heart and the big man had toppled like a falling pine. It was all etched on his memory in the acids of remorse and because of that ghastly picture he could stand here now and take Chambers' punch without moving.

Chambers stepped back with his arms up. He was frightened now. Hitting Flake had been like hitting a tree. His knuckles stung and his shoulders ached from the impact and Flake had not even flinched. Never in Chambers' life had he come into contact with such rocklike, apparently indestructible bone and muscle. He waited now in trepidation for Flake's fury to mount and for the battering ram to smite him. But to his bewilderment Flake did not budge. He stood there in the firelight with a small trickle of blood welling out of his cut lip, staring at Chambers with an expression that appeared to be astonishingly sympathetic.

At that moment they heard the two shots, spaced closely together, from somewhere inside the fort. Flake had his head cocked, listening like a bird dog.

"You better get the hell out of here," he said to Chambers.

Chambers thought of Jessica and panic clutched his heart. He turned and ran toward the yacht.

2

Cutter stared down at the corpse in the moonlight. He felt no remorse at having killed the wrong man but he did feel sudden fear at the consequences. It was all up with him now. He had killed a man in front of witnesses. He might have beaten the dope rap but murder was too much. There was only one hope for him now—to get off the island before the Coast Guard came. He would have to get back to Cuba. They would have a hard time finding him in Cuba. And from there he could get a ship to somewhere else. In spite of the storm and the reef that had already cost him the *Jezebel*, he would have to chance it. Without waiting to see if Diaz was behind him he turned and ran through the darkness for the yacht.

3

At the sound of the shots, Flake's indecision dropped away from him like a heavy load. There was nothing to wonder about any more, nothing to question. This was it now. He could huddle here by the fire like an old woman or he could do what he had to do. All right, you bastard, he told himself, what about it? Once and for all, do you have the guts or don't you?

The shots—hollow and thudding on the wind—might have come from almost any direction but obviously they had come from inside the fort. But the fort was mighty big and mighty dark. What with the booming of the wind and the pounding of his own heart, it was hard to take a bearing on the sound. Come on, he told himself. Come on now. You've got to start somewhere.

He began to run then, pelting across the sand with the wind in his face, racing toward the opening to the quadrangle and the blackness of the fort.

4

With frantic hasty fingers Chambers wrestled the Savage .30-30 out of the sheepskin-lined case. The rifle was in two pieces, barrel and stock separate. He had not used it for a long time now. Fumbling, cursing his own incompetence, he screwed it desperately together and got out a handful of the heavy, well-oiled bullets. He levered one into the chamber and held the others loose in his hand and dashed back up on deck.

Jessica was there, waiting for him.

"Are you all right?" he said quickly, not looking at her, his eyes searching the stretch of moonlit beach.

"Yes," she answered. "I'm fine."

"Fine," he raged. "Fine. I'll bet you're fine. Where the devil have you been?"

"Walking."

"A little stroll in the moonlight. A tender little waltz on the beach. You're a walker, all right. You bitch!"

"Hadn't you better turn on the searchlight?"

Sheepishly aware of his own forgetfulness, he flicked on the big searchlight and swept the white beam of light along the edge of the surf and the curving strip of beach. At first he saw nothing, and then, on the outer edge of the light, half obscured but flickering, something moved. He swept the light back that way and saw the man running toward the boat with the gun in his hand.

He was a thin man with lank hair and a naked chest and a face gone pasty white in the fierce light. He stopped running and stood there appalled for a moment in the glare. Then he raised the pistol and fired.

The gun made a little winking flash in his hand. Chambers heard the smash of the bullet and the sound of glass breaking in the wheelhouse, and then, seemingly a long time afterward, the sound of the shot.

What happened after that became a blur for Chambers. It seemed unreal, as if it were happening to someone else. Moving quickly, he threw himself belly down on the deck and thrust the barrel of the Savage over the gunwale and fired carefully at the running figure.

The rifle bullet kicked up a spurt of sand at Cutter's feet and stopped him dead in his tracks. The second shot followed almost immediately and struck even closer. The high-powered rifle bullets made a thin fierce sound in the air and a solid thump in the sand. Cutter turned and ran back the way he had come. The light followed him mercilessly. He felt naked and unutterably exposed, waiting at any moment for the clubbing impact of the bullet in his back.

Then he was out of it and in the darkness, with the shelter of the walls straight ahead. He fell behind a ragged clump of coral and lay there breathless, digging his belly into the sand. They had beaten him. Somehow he had never counted on the chance that man on the yacht might have a rifle. And that damned light. The rifle and the light had finished him. Venomously he raised himself on one arm and fired at the light but even as he did so he knew the range was too great. He couldn't match a pistol against a rifle. And he had only a couple of shots left now. If he had been able to get in closer he might have had a chance but this way it was hopeless. His bullet had gone winging off somewhere into the blackness and that damned light still burned. Almost immediately he saw the flash of the rifle again and heard the fierce, keening, heart-stopping sound of the bullet ricocheting off the coral.

With his belly to the ground, Cutter turned and wriggled away from the coral into the darkness of the fort.

Chambers felt quite calm now, and a marvelous singing elation surged in him. He felt wonderful. He only hoped the man on the beach would try it again. He scarcely heard Jessica's voice behind him saying, "Darling, you're marvelous."

CHAPTER TWENTY-ONE

1

Flake had kicked off his shoes and his naked feet made no sound on the stone paving of the quadrangle. He stood there for a moment, trying to see through the patches of shadow, wondering just where the shots had come from. The wind was deceptive and the stone walls carried an echo. Quite possibly Cutter was not in the fort at all. He might be down on the tip of the island where he would have clear ground in which to shoot.

He went over the wall and dropped down onto the sand and ran, crouching, across the moon-washed space. Out here the wind was stronger, buffeting against him, sending particles of sand stinging into his face and gritting through his teeth. Once something exploded in an angry flutter beside him and he leaped back with his hand up. Then he saw it was only a pelican rising up on black beating wings against the moon.

There was a patch of palmetto ahead and he got into them and crouched there, waiting, not seeing anything but expecting the thunder of the gun at any moment. Instead he heard nothing but the scrabble of the wind through the bushes.

A dank cold lump in his stomach kept him crouched there motionless when he should have been moving. Go ahead, he told himself. You started it and now you've got to finish it. Keep moving. Keep it simple. What could be simpler than a man with a gun? You're thinking too much. Keep moving. Come on, big man.

He jumped out of the palmetto and ran hard toward the heaped coral tip of the island. He found nothing there, but the activity had warmed him and part of the cold lump of fear that had been hanging like lead in his stomach had dissolved. Now, working back toward the fort, he was able to keep himself from crouching every time he passed through an open space.

Searching systematically, he began to explore one turret after another but it was not until he returned to the big stone quadrangle that he found Cruze. The rummy was lying on his back on the stone paving with the cruel moonlight bathing his dead face. In death he appeared incredibly thin, his limbs hardly sustaining his clothes. He looked like a pile of old rags tossed out into the yard.

One hand was splayed over his chest where Cutter's bullets had gone and the other still held the knife. A thin trail of blood, black on the pavement, showed where he had crawled a few feet before he died. In death his face had taken on a frozen dignity it had not possessed in life, and even the habitual odor of old whiskey had evaporated from his body and drifted away on the wind.

The smell of death, Bush had called it. But there was no smell. Only the sighing of the wind and the moonlight and the crumpled ragged body on the stones. Flake bent low over the body. He did not touch it. He crouched on his haunches, staring down at the dead face, thinking how pitiful and useless Cruze's gesture had been. The rummy had gotten up out of his sickbed and staggered out into the night with his knife in his hand in an effort to bring down Cutter. He had mastered the cowardice that had hunted him all his life and had gone seeking death in the empty fort in the high wind. He had done it for Flake. For Flake, a stranger who bad bullied him and dragged him out of the comparative security of Key West and launched him on this disastrous voyage. The gesture, the sacrifice, had been useless, and yet it had given him the final dignity he had never attained in life.

With the tip of one finger Flake closed the shining eyes that stared up blankly at the moon. All right, Flake thought. All right now. All right, friend Cutter.

2

It was not Cutter's night. He had made a lot of mistakes. The first mistake had been the killing of Cruze when the idiotic, half-dead rummy came shambling through the moonlight after him. The second had been in waiting too long for a try at the boat. The third was in getting panicky and firing a quick shot at Flake before he had the target properly lined up.

But that man potting at him with a rifle had unnerved him. He shied at every shadow now. And so when he saw the thick, heavy-shouldered outline of Flake moving across the quadrangle he had squeezed off a hasty shot at him.

The gun made an infernal racket in that stony, enclosed place. A barrage of echoes resounded hollowly along the ghostly corridors. And somewhere in the blackness the nesting seabirds, startled by the sound, went squawking into the sky.

Cutter had known, even before he pulled the trigger, that he was firing too soon and that he would miss. With panic clutching at his throat he waited now for some movement from the enemy. Nothing stirred. The only sound was the lash of the wind through the open gun ports and the distant pounding of the surf. A beam of light from the yacht flickered through a rift in the broken wall and lingered for a moment on Cutter's face.

With a muttered curse Cutter leaped out of his niche and dashed down the passageway into the blackness of the turrets. Something struck him a numbing blow across the thigh and he pitched forward onto the stones. Half dazed, he pulled himself up and ran his hands over the thing that had tripped him. It was one of the ancient rusting cannon, gaping empty-mouthed from the turret to the sea.

Cutter's face was bleeding from his fall on the stones and his leg felt half broken, but he pulled himself quickly erect when he heard steps behind him. For a shadowy second he had a glimpse of Flake outlined against the moonlight pouring through the doorway and he fired point blank at the dark shape. Blinded by the flash of the gun and deafened by its thunder in that narrow place, he ran limping across the floor toward the gun port and squeezed himself through the opening and dropped down onto the sand below.

He was on the windward side here and the surf came roaring up at him, the spray lashing his naked back, the wind buffeting his face. On both sides the narrow strip of sand curved in to the wall and the surf came beating up on top of it. He was on a tiny island of sand with his back to the wall and only surf ahead on either hand.

Cutter had never been afraid of the water and with the implacable Flake behind him now it seemed the lesser of two evils. Holding the pistol high overhead, he ran forward along the sand to where the wall suddenly loomed before him and the water clutched at his legs. He waited for a lull in the pounding of the surf and then dashed forward. The waves gripped at him with icy fingers and beat against the stones. Bruised and battered but still holding the pistol aloft, he forced his way through to the haven of dry sand beyond.

Gasping for breath, blood streaming from a dozen cuts on his chest and shoulders, the salt stinging his eyes, the moonlight building a world of crazy nightmare shapes around him, he ran forward around the corner of the buttress and found himself suddenly and unexpectedly back in the lee of the walls and with the quadrangle just ahead.

It was comparatively quiet there and he had time to steady himself and wipe the salt out of his eyes. But when he looked up again he saw Flake coming toward him.

Flake flung himself forward in a single furious motion, knowing the bullet was coming but not waiting for the blossom of flame or the brittle whisper of lead going by his head. He moved so fast that Cutter did not have time to squeeze the trigger again. Flake took him by the throat and bent him backward, with his thumbs going in right up to the joints, and the man flopped in his hands like a fish and he kicked the gun out of reach on the stones.

Cutter was trying to get a knee into his groin and Flake was squeezing him harder and bending him back. Cutter arched his wiry body and managed to free one long arm enough to punch Flake in the face. Flake made a growling rumble in his throat and took the arm and got it up behind Cutter's back and continued to bend it, feeling the bones grating and listening with a sense of vast satisfaction to Cutter howling and thinking not of Cutter but of the dead man lying on the paving. And then he felt the stiff point beyond which the arm would not go, and he heard a little snapping sound precisely like a dry twig breaking, and Cutter yelped and hung very quiet and limp in his hands. Flake let him drop.

Flake stood over him until he began to groan and then he kicked him hard in the ribs. "Get up, you sonofabitch," he said.

Cutter got up slowly and Flake chopped him meanly across the face with his fist. He wanted to kill Cutter with his hands but he wanted to do it slowly. He hit him on the nose with the edge of his palm and felt the cartilage break and the nose bend sideways and saw the blood burst out on Cutter's face.

Cutter tried to scream but Flake did not give him a chance. He held Cutter propped against the wall with one hand and chopped at him with the other until finally the bloodstained wreckage that had been Cutter slipped out of his grip and fell at his feet.

Cutter was still alive and still moaning and for a moment Flake thought of picking him up again and continuing to the end. But the anger had gone out of him now. He remembered the dead and the Coast Guard plane coming in the morning and the fact that they would hang Cutter neatly and efficiently in Key West and that Cutter's testimony was still necessary to convict Mangio of running dope.

And now too he became aware of his sweat-soaked shirt and the blood on his hands and the hoarse bull roaring coming from his own throat. He bent over and picked the senseless Cutter up by the collar and began to drag him across the quadrangle toward the beach. Cutter's broken arm flopped brutally on the stones but Flake paid no attention to it. When he passed Cruze's body he averted his eyes.

It wasn't until he was almost back to the fire that he remembered Diaz and wondered what had become of him.

CHAPTER TWENTY-TWO

1

At the sound of the plane motors Diaz began to tremble. He had been expecting the plane for a long time but now that it was finally here it frightened him badly. But still, he thought, whatever they did to him it would not be as bad as another night in the fort. All through the long wet cold hours he had huddled in a corner of the fort trying to make himself as small as possible. Hiding there, he had seen Cutter kill Cruze, and had trembled for his own life. With a murder charge against him, Cutter would not now hesitate to kill Diaz himself for the heroin he carried, and that knowledge had frightened the little Cuban badly.

He had slipped away in the dark and secreted himself like a chipmunk in a nest of stone. And there he had lain without budging all during the hideous fight between Flake and Cutter.

And with that long night a truth had dawned upon Diaz. He was not a man of violence. He was not a Hollywood gangster. The role of pirate in which he had cast himself when he boldly boarded the *Jezebel* was the wrong role for him. Cutter truly fit the role but not Diaz. Cutter had killed and fought while Diaz trembled in his hole in the rock. And now, with the bright sun already beginning to evaporate the pools of moisture from the quadrangle and a line of fleecy clouds skimming peacefully toward the empty horizon, he felt less of a hero than ever.

The big PBY circled slowly over the fort and settled to the water, plowing a shining furrow across the bay. It ran down the channel, turned in its own wake and taxied toward the pier. Diaz watched it come and then stood up, cramped and chilled, and walked slowly toward the edge of the water.

Heaving a wistful sigh, he reached inside his jacket and took out the aluminum-foil package of heroin and tossed it into the water. It sank swiftly to the bottom. A green and scarlet parrot fish came out of a hole in the coral and nosed around the package. Diaz pulled the pistol out of his belt and threw it at the parrot fish. The fish darted away. The pistol settled into the sand beside the shining package. Diaz watched it for a moment and then turned away and walked slowly down toward the pier with his hands in the air. The gesture, he thought, had been a little melodramatic and very expensive.

2

The plane's engines sent an iridescent spume of water into the clear air as it ran up toward the edge of the beach where Flake was waiting. When it was a few yards away the engines sputtered and died and the lieutenant, Huckins, stuck his long thin face out. He and Flake were good friends. They had known each other for a long time. Huckins tossed the bowline out with an easy motion of his thin arm and Flake caught it and ran it up on the sand. Huckins climbed out of the plane into the shallow water and waded ashore. He had a pistol clipped to a canvas belt strapped around his waist.

"Hello, Huck," Flake said.

"What's all the ruckus? We heard you got drowned. Knew it was too good to be true."

Flake told him about Cutter and Cruze. The lieutenant looked at Cutter and whistled soundlessly and said, "What ran over him?"

"We had an argument."

"Okay, there ain't much of him left but we'll take what there is."

They handcuffed Cutter's good arm to a galley stanchion and carried Cruze's body, wrapped in a tarp, back aft. After they finished they saw Diaz approaching along the beach. He had his hands in the air and his narrow pointed shoes were digging into the sand. His cheap suit had shrunk desperately and was hiked up around his skinny body.

"Who's this joker?" Huck asked.

"The silent partner," Flake said.

"Do we take him?"

"Sure."

Huckins dug another pair of handcuffs out of a kit bag and clamped them around Diaz's wrists. Diaz murmured something in Spanish and

Huckins asked, "What's he saying?"

"He doesn't want to be near Cutter."

"I don't blame him."

When they had the two prisoners secured, with Bush sitting between them, Huckins asked, "Who's on the yacht?"

"Guy named Chambers and his girl."

"They don't seem much interested, do they?"

"I guess not."

"I'll need a statement from them anyway."

"Can I use your radio while you're gone?"

"Sure. Jocko will help you. Give him a hand, Jocko," Huck said to the radioman.

Flake sent two messages. He advised the police in Key West to restrain Mangio from leaving town and then he had the Coast Guard base contact the Coral Reef Hotel to find out if a Miss Molly Smith was still registered there. When they answered in the affirmative he had them leave a two-word message for her. All it said was, Please Wait.

Huck came walking back to the plane and with him was Chambers. There was no sign of Jessica. Chambers looked pale and very tired.

"I wanted to say good-bye and tell you I'm sorry about last night," Chambers said stiffly.

"Forget it," Flake said.

"And I'm sorry too about your friend. I just heard about it."

Flake nodded.

Chambers stared at him for a long moment with a bemused air as if trying to think of something more to say, and then he gave it up and walked away. He was quite drunk. He lurched as he walked in the soft sand. Flake felt very sorry for him.

Huck let the nose of the plane swing slowly out with the wind and then started his engines. For a moment a cloud of sand and wind half obscured the fort.

Huck taxied her down the channel and turned into the wind. He gunned his engines and they could feel the water pounding under them as if they were running over a washboard. Then came the thrust of air and they were up. A flock of startled pelicans winged swiftly away on the port side, and far below they could see the *Vixen* sitting peacefully in that idyllic setting just as if nothing at all had happened. And beyond her, on the reef, they saw the shattered bones of the *Jezebel*.

After that the plane began banking and the wing obscured Flake's view. He sat and looked at the wall until Huck shouted something back to him.

"What did you say?" Flake asked, leaning forward.

"You'll have to answer some questions about what you were doing in Cuba," Huck bellowed.

"I know."

"It won't be much."

Huck turned back to concentrate on his flying and put the plane on a steady northeast course. Flake looked out through the port again and saw the fort far behind them now with the *Vixen* only a splinter of white against the beach, and off to starboard, the Stream running a deep purple, and ahead, swimming in a dun-colored haze, the mainland. It was surprising to realize how close Key West had been to them all the time.

He knew he should be thinking about Cruze who lay dead under a tarpaulin in the after compartment, but all he could think about was Molly.

Bush leaned over to him and shouted in his ear, "You still want to go fishing?"

"Yes," Flake said. "I sure do."

The words were lost in the roar of the engines but Bush was satisfied. The expression on Flake's face told him what he wanted to know.

THE END

Classic hardboiled fiction from the King of the Paperbacks...

Harry Whittington

A Night for Screaming / Any Woman He Wanted
$19.95 978-1-933586-08-3
"[*A Night for Screaming*] is pure Harry. The damned thing is almost on
fire, it reads so fast." — Ed Gorman, *Gormania*

To Find Cora / Like Mink Like Murder / Body and Passion
$23.95 978-1-933586-25-0
"Harry Whittington was the king of plot and pace, and he could write
anything well. He's 100 percent perfect entertainment."
— Joe R. Lansdale

Rapture Alley / Winter Girl / Strictly for the Boys
$23.95 978-1-933586-36-6
"Whittington was an innovator, often turning archetypical characters
and plots on their head, and finding wild new ways to tell stories from
unusual angles." — Cullen Gallagher, *Pulp Serenade*

A Haven for the Damned
$9.99 978-1-933586-75-5
"A wild, savage romp and pure Whittington: raw noir that has the feel
of a Jim Thompson novel crossed with a Russ Meyer film."
— Brian Greene, *The Life Sentence*. Black Gat #1.

"Harry Whittington delivers every time." — Bill Crider

STARK HOUSE

Stark House Press, 1315 H Street, Eureka, CA 95501
griffinskye3@sbcglobal.net / www.StarkHousePress.com
Available from your local bookstore, or order direct or via our website.

CPSIA information can be obtained
at www.ICGtesting.com
Printed in the USA
LVOW08s0308050817
543927LV00010B/524/P